Secrets for the Three Sisters

Annie Groves was originally created by the much-loved writer Penny Halsall, who died in 2011. The stories drew on her own family's history, picked up from listening to her grandmother's stories when she was a child.

This legacy has been continued by the author, Jenny Shaw, who lived in London's East End for many years. Fascinated by the history of the period, she has been a big fan of the wonderful novels by Annie Groves and feels privileged to have been asked to continue her stories.

Also by Annie Groves

The Pride Family series
Ellie Pride
Connie's Courage
Hettie of Hope Street

The WWII series
Goodnight Sweetheart
Some Sunny Day
The Grafton Girls
As Time Goes By

The Campion series
Across the Mersey
Daughters of Liverpool
The Heart of the Family
Where the Heart Is
When the Lights Go On Again

The Article Row series
London Belles
Home for Christmas
My Sweet Valentine
Only a Mother Knows
A Christmas Promise

The Empire Street series
Child of the Mersey
Christmas on the Mersey
The Mersey Daughter
Winter on the Mersey

The District Nurses series
The District Nurses of Victory Walk
Christmas for the District Nurses
Wartime for the District Nurses
A Gift for the District Nurses
The District Nurses Make a Wish

The Three Sisters series
The Three Sisters of Victory Walk

ANNIE
GROVES

Secrets for the
Three Sisters

HarperCollins *Publishers*

HarperCollins*Publishers* Ltd
1 London Bridge Street,
London SE1 9GF

www.harpercollins.co.uk

HarperCollins*Publishers*
Macken House, 39/40 Mayor Street Upper
Dublin 1, D01 C9W8

First published by HarperCollinsPublishers 2024
4

Copyright © Annie Groves 2024

Annie Groves asserts the moral right to
be identified as the author of this work

A catalogue record for this book is available from the British Library

ISBN: 978-0-00-840248-8 (PB)

This novel is entirely a work of fiction.
The names, characters and incidents portrayed in it are
the work of the author's imagination. Any resemblance to
actual persons, living or dead, events or localities is
entirely coincidental.

Set in Sabon LT Std by HarperCollins*Publishers* India

Printed and bound in the UK using 100% Renewable Electricity by
CPI Group (UK) Ltd

This book would not have happened without Kate, Teresa and Yvonne

CHAPTER ONE

Autumn 1940

'Doesn't she look lovely?'

Rose Harrison could hear the two women whispering at the back of the chilly church. They had crept in after the small group of immediate family and friends, not wanting to intrude on the special occasion. She guessed they were keen to share in the joy of a wedding and she couldn't blame them. After weeks of non-stop bombings, everyone had to cling on to whatever shreds of happiness they could find.

The trouble was, this wedding wasn't all it seemed.

From where Rose stood, in the second pew from the front, all looked well. Her cousin Faith and the groom, Martin, had their backs to the congregation as the vicar led them through their vows. Martin was in his naval uniform, which emphasised his height and broad shoulders. His close-cropped hair shone in the dim light. Faith wore a veil so long that you could hardly make out her elegant off-white dress beneath.

Rose's younger sister Daisy dug her in the ribs. 'Open your hymn book. You were miles away.'

Rose nodded with a wry smile as the organist struck up the opening bars of 'Love Divine, all loves excelling'.

1

She'd agreed to come along and show enthusiasm, as had all her family. As well as her sister, their parents and little brother Robbie were crammed into the pew, all in their Sunday best, even if it was a little threadbare after a year of war. In the first pew were her auntie Vera and two cousins, Faith's younger sisters. Uncle Arthur was on the end, having done his duty and given away the bride.

'. . . *All loves excelling . . .*' sang the congregation, and the two women at the back joined in with warbling voices. At the front, the vicar beamed at the young couple – so good-looking, so well matched.

The only problem was, Faith was heavily pregnant and Martin wasn't the father.

Rose and the rest of the family had been sworn to secrecy. As far as the vicar and the few other guests were concerned, Faith and Martin had got carried away on his previous leave back in the spring, with the result that they'd decided to get married as soon as he could get another few days at home. That was the official reason for the smallness of the gathering – it had had to be arranged at such short notice, and the groom would have to be back at base the day after tomorrow. There was no question of a honeymoon. Otherwise, Vera and Arthur would have spared no expense, showing off their beautiful eldest child to the great and the good of the local area of Dalston.

'. . . *Lost in wonder, love, and praise,*' they sang, and that marked the end of the service. There was nothing for it; Faith had to turn round and then everyone would be aware of the bump, if they'd somehow missed it before. Loyally, Vera and Arthur gathered closely to either side of the bride and their other daughters came in right behind, blocking the line of sight for any casual onlooker. Faith and Martin processed down the aisle arm in arm, Faith swishing the long veil around so that part of it hung down in front, concealing the bump still further in a stylish way. She smiled gamely, playing her part to perfection.

Blinking as she came out into the daylight, Rose looked around at the group. Faith's dress had been cleverly cut, she had to admit. Her cousin had always had a keen eye for fashion, and had managed to get hold of a decent cream fabric from somewhere. Rose and her sisters had always made do with what was available at Dalston's Ridley Road market, but Faith had favoured the West End. Perhaps they'd all clubbed together to make sure she looked as special as possible, despite the circumstances.

Faith turned her beaming gaze on Rose and raised her eyebrow a fraction. Rose didn't react. Her cousin was still playing an imagined game of assuming superiority, even now. They'd had a lifetime of it, something Rose could have done without. She supposed Faith wasn't going to change at this point. The A-line frock was a triumph, with delicate lace edging the three-quarter-length sleeves and the curve of the neck.

Daisy nudged her again. 'As long as all the photos are just head and shoulders she'll look gorgeous,' she muttered under her breath, and Rose couldn't help laughing.

'Stop it, they'll hear you.'

'Don't care,' said Daisy, sticking out her tongue, and tossing the chestnut hair that all the Harrison sisters had.

Rose bit back a chuckle. That was the thing about family gatherings: everyone immediately fell back into the roles they'd always had. Daisy had grown up so much over the past year – going from sulky factory worker to responsible member of staff at Manor House tube station, coping with all manner of crises – but here she was, acting like a naughty child again. She'd been the baby of the family until Robbie had come along years after the rest of them. It was a hard role to give up.

Auntie Vera's middle daughter, Hope, produced a handful of confetti and threw it over the bride and groom, which made them turn and laugh. The best man, evidently a naval colleague of Martin's, as nobody knew him, captured the moment on his camera. That would make a pretty picture, Rose thought. It was good that they'd have something nice to remember the day.

'Everyone in the next picture!' called the best man, gesturing to them all to line up.

Aunt Vera began organising everybody, as she always did. 'Robbie, you're youngest. We didn't have time to arrange bridesmaids and pages, but how about you come and stand in front of your cousin? Then everyone will see how smart you look.'

Robbie seemed about to protest so Rose swiftly stepped in. 'Go on, Robbie. Do what your auntie asks.' Robbie glared at her. Rose dropped her voice. 'It won't kill you. And it'll make Ma happy.' Robbie wrinkled his nose but gave in, dragging his feet in their polished school shoes. He was only eleven and his growth spurt was a long way off; years of bronchitis had left him thinner than many boys his age, so he looked even younger. He was exactly the right size to hide the bump without obscuring Faith's head and shoulders, just as Vera would have known.

Rose shuffled into place by her mother on one side, Daisy on the other, with their father just behind them, as he was by far the tallest. She felt a momentary pang that two siblings were missing: Peter, away with the army; and Clover, who was in the ATS and aimed massive searchlights every night over the south coast.

Still, Vera, Arthur and their two younger girls clustered in closely, and Martin's few family members huddled alongside him. 'Smile!' called the best man, and pressed the button. Everybody smiled, and the wedding party was captured for posterity.

Patty Harrison knew that her sister was putting a brave face on it, and had to admit she was doing so rather well. It didn't matter that, in other circumstances, Vera would have booked a function room at a quality hotel or one of the civic buildings for the wedding breakfast. Everybody knew that any big building might be a target for the bombers. It would have been awful to have gone to all that trouble and expense, only for the venue to be reduced to rubble in the run-up to the big day. No, far more sensible to invite the select few back to the family home and have a small celebration there.

That was certainly the argument that Vera had given the neighbourhood.

Vera's home was bigger than the terraced house on Victory Walk where the Harrisons lived, but it was not really so very different – even if Vera liked to think it was. 'It's an end of terrace, of course,' she always used to say, proud of the fact they heard neighbours' noise from only one side. 'Such an advantage when it comes to a garden.' Patty would have loved a proper garden, as she enjoyed nothing better than raising fruit and vegetables for her family to eat. Vera didn't make the most of what she had, and that was a shame.

Still, it meant there was room for them all to stand outside for more photos, although they didn't linger for long in the chilly late autumn breeze. There was a limit to how long you could hold a smile while longing for a cup of tea. All the while the wind whipped up dust from the most recent bombings. They'd all had narrow escapes. An unexploded anti-aircraft shell had landed one street over from Victory Walk, and Ridley Road had been hit twice in one week. But you just had to get on with things and not let the fear win.

Patty smiled obligingly as the best man persuaded them to line up for one last shot, and then dived into the warmth of the house. Most of the guests were heading for the front parlour, but Patty knew she'd be expected to lend a hand in the kitchen. For a start, she knew where everything was. Also, Vera would have had to cut corners, just as they all did, but her big sister wouldn't want anyone else to realise. If the sandwiches had been made partly with powdered egg, they would still be served on the best china, with tempting sprigs of parsley. That had come from Patty's garden; she'd kept a couple of pots going somehow, saving them for today.

Vera might be annoying, but Patty had no intention of letting her down.

Hope was already at the sink, swiftly drying a couple of small glasses. They glinted in the watery sunshine streaming through the window, which was criss-crossed with brown tape. She looked up and smiled at her aunt.

'Look, extra sherry glasses,' she said brightly, and Patty thought, not for the first time, that Faith had always revelled in being the beauty of the family, but Hope's expressions were far more genuine. 'Ma wants them kept in reserve as they don't match the others, but I bet they'll be useful all the same.'

'I'm surprised you've managed to find enough sherry,' Patty replied. She hung her good coat out of the way on the back door, and turned back the sleeves on her cardigan. She'd smartened it up with some new mother-of-pearl buttons, but it was showing signs of wear and tear, and she didn't want Vera's fussy friends noticing her frayed cuffs.

The sandwiches had been made in advance and had been covered with dampened tea towels to prevent the edges from curling. Patty gathered the towels and tucked them out of the way behind the draining board.

'I'll make a start, handing these around. People will be hungry after standing outside for so long.'

Hope nodded. 'I'm starving. I could hardly smile, my teeth were chattering by the end.' She popped the delicate little glasses on a tray, and Patty felt a rare pang of envy that such lovely things were only second-best in her sister's household.

'Everything all right, Auntie Patty?' Hope had instantly picked up on her brief change of mood. Patty was impressed; Faith would never have done that. Mind you, Faith was not known for thinking of anyone other than herself.

How short-sighted people were, favouring her eldest niece because she had the long blonde hair and traditional pretty face. Hope, who wore her own blonde hair cut into a tidy, practical bob, was so much more interesting when you got to know her.

'While there's nobody else here,' the young woman went on, 'I thought I'd just check about . . . well, you know, the elephant in the room.'

Patty raised her eyebrows, but didn't walk away.

'How Martin used to be sweet on Rose.' There, Hope had come out and said it, the topic that they were all carefully avoiding today. Well, one of the topics.

'Is Rose really happy about . . . about all this?'

Patty nodded emphatically. 'She is. You can ask her yourself – she doesn't mind at all.' No, Patty thought, her eldest was not bothered in the slightest. She'd always maintained that Martin was a good friend but nothing more. It had been him who had been so keen to change their relationship into something more romantic. The rest of the family had been certain Rose felt the same, but perhaps that was wishful thinking. In any case, Rose had recently met somebody new, and while it was early days yet, as far as she was concerned

Martin was a thing of the past.

'Good,' said Hope. 'I'd hate to think she was upset, thinking Faith had stolen her boyfriend.'

Patty shook her head. 'No, there's no chance of that. To tell the truth, we were all far keener on them becoming a couple than Rose ever was.'

Hope smiled again. 'I know. You see two people together and think they make a nice couple and then you've put two and two together to make five.'

'Exactly.' Patty felt Hope had pretty well hit the nail on the head. She made to turn for the kitchen door to bring the hungry guests their sandwiches, but Hope murmured something else under her breath.

'Sorry, didn't catch that.' Patty paused, platters carefully balanced on her forearm.

'I probably shouldn't say it but it's Martin I feel sorry for.' Hope's words came out in a rush. 'I'm sure he knows what he's in for but, blimey, he's going to have his work cut out from here on, isn't he?'

Patty gave a sympathetic smile. Hope was still young. She had that tendency to see matters in black and white, when in many cases they were anything but.

'Listen to me, Hope.' She set the platters down again. 'I know what it looks like, but it's not your job to worry for him, or for anyone else involved. He's a grown-up. He knows what your sister is like, better than most of us. They were walking out for ages, after all, before she went and fell for her married boss.'

Hope pursed her lips but nodded slowly.

'So we'll have to let them get on with life and stick together to make sure they know we're here if they need us. That's what families are for. No matter how different we are, we stick together when it comes to it.' With that, she picked up the platters once more and this time left the kitchen.

CHAPTER TWO

'Two with major burns, and one of those has a broken leg. Three with smoke inhalation, one with suspected broken ribs. The rest with minor injuries – no room to admit them. We're out of beds.' Katherine paused to draw breath and Rose glanced at her with understanding and sympathy, while making sure she had all the details noted down properly.

She admired Katherine, already a sister at Hackney Hospital even though she'd only just turned thirty. They'd worked together on the busy ward for several years now – and it had become ever busier as the Blitz had taken hold. Every morning brought a raft of new patients and it was getting harder to know where to put them all.

'All right, so Mr Stansfield can go home later today. He's got a sister coming to fetch him and take him to her place. His own is uninhabitable after last week.' Katherine pushed a strand of curly brown hair out of her eye and back into the cap she always wore on duty. 'Mr Peasgood can go into the convalescent ward. He'll go home when we can find someone to look after him a bit. He's still too fragile to manage with just district nurses visiting.' She sighed, not admitting how tired she was, although Rose could tell from the shadows under her eyes.

Before the war, Katherine wouldn't have been here. Faith wasn't the only young woman to be married in the chills of autumn. Katherine's wedding had been only a fortnight ago, and she'd been luckier than most: she and her new husband, himself an army doctor, had managed four whole nights away somewhere in Wales. In peacetime a married woman was expected to give up her career, no matter how highly trained she might be. Now, that convention was increasingly overlooked – just as well, as Katherine's skills were in great demand.

'Right, I'll make a start.' Rose had the advantage of having had a good night's sleep. That was the best thing about living in at the hospital. New nurses' quarters had been completed just before the war broke out and they had every sort of luxury, with proper indoor bathrooms and hot running water, and not having to share a room. It was more than Rose had been used to at Victory Walk.

'Oh, one more thing.' At Katherine's words, Rose spun round on her heel, the rubber sole squeaking on the newly cleaned floor. 'A new trainee is starting on this ward. Don't look like that – you'll be glad of an extra pair of hands once she knows the ropes.' Katherine managed to raise the energy to grin, and then she was off, clipboard under her arm.

Rose had persuaded Mr Peasgood to move to the less intense atmosphere of the convalescent ward and had instructed one of the more junior nurses to change his bed in readiness for the man with the burns and broken leg, once he was out of surgery.

'I know you'd never skimp on hygiene, but please be extra careful. The risk of infection with burns patients is always high, as you'll have learnt,' she said, glancing up to see a hesitant young woman in nursing uniform hovering by the edge of the bed.

'Er . . . Nurse Harrison? I was told to look for you.'

Rose nodded briefly to her colleague, who'd already begun to strip the bed, and then turned to give her full attention to the newcomer. 'Hello, yes, I'm Nurse Harrison. Rose,' she said. 'Are you our trainee?'

The young woman smiled shyly. 'Yes. Yes, I am. Er, they said I will be working here for a bit. Effie. Elfrida really, but they all call me Effie.'

'Well, then, pleased to meet you, Effie. And your other name? We should use that, at least when we're on duty.'

The young woman immediately blushed deep crimson, and looked at her feet. 'Oh, I'm sorry. Yes. I'm Effie Jenkins.'

Rose waited until the trainee had looked up once more and then gave her an encouraging grin. 'Pleased to meet you, Nurse Jenkins. Have you been in training very long?' She hoped Effie wasn't a complete novice. There was very little time to go over the basics, not when they had so many incoming patients.

'This is my second ward,' Effie replied with pride. 'I did the kiddies before. Ever so good, they were.'

Rose tried not to show her relief. Not an absolute beginner, then. 'Well, we get a bit of everything in here. Some are emergencies, just out of surgery – there are a lot of them and more due today. Then there are the older gentlemen who might otherwise have gone home, only their houses have been damaged in the blasts. You'll soon learn how to help those who have pneumonia and suchlike.' She checked for a reaction – would Effie back away in horror? But the new nurse seemed eager to learn. Rose registered that she appeared to be very young, although in fact she couldn't be so different in age from Daisy. She was also pretty, with very fair wavy hair, mostly hidden beneath her neat cap, and a true peaches-and-cream complexion. Rose ruefully wondered how long that would last in this stressful job.

'Come with me and I'll show you how we run the nurses' station on this ward,' Rose offered. 'Sister is strict, but that's for a reason. It's all very organised, even when it gets busy.' They wove round one of the cleaners, mopping up a spillage. 'Tell me about yourself, Effie. Are you from around here?'

Effie immediately grew animated. 'Oh, yes, not far at all. Limehouse. Do you know The Grapes pub? Near there.'

'I've heard of it,' Rose said as they approached the station, a desk bracketed by low cupboards, all covered in stacked files. She wasn't a great one for pubs, herself. Her brother Peter had most probably mentioned it. He had friends far and wide across East London, no doubt because, before joining the army, he'd played football on Hackney Marshes and insisted on slaking his thirst afterwards. 'And have you any brothers or sisters?'

Effie nodded. 'Two brothers, Nurse. I'm the youngest. Always lived with me ma and pa up till now.'

I'd have guessed that, Rose thought but didn't say.

'Yes, one's on the docks and the other went for the merchant navy.' She stopped abruptly. 'We're ever so worried about him.'

Rose was instantly reassuring. 'Of course, but he'll get the best training.' She didn't add that the brother on the docks was liable to be in the firing line as well, not to mention the nurses themselves, and everyone else who had to carry on working when the sirens sounded. 'Now then. Take a look at this. When a patient is first admitted, this is what you need to check . . .'

For some minutes they went through the procedures and Effie seemed to be taking it all in. That was about as much as Rose could hope for, at this stage.

'Right, then, I need you to get cracking preparing more beds for those burns patients I told you about. Then we'll have a brief refresher on the best treatment before they actually get here.'

Effie turned from the desk back to the rows of beds along the far side of the ward, and then beamed in recognition as a figure in a white coat passed the main doors leading to the corridor. 'Oh, there's that nice doctor.'

Rose was immediately on alert. 'Which one was that? There are quite a few.' She thought she'd seen who it was, but wanted to make sure.

'Well, I hardly know him. He held a door open for me earlier, and directed me here. He seemed a friendly old soul. Mr Prendergast, he said he was called.'

Rose's spirits fell. 'Ah, yes, he's a surgeon here.' She wouldn't have called him nice or friendly, although he could come across like that. He definitely wouldn't want to be called old.

'He said I was to come to him if I had any questions, isn't that kind?' Effie went on, happily unaware of Mr Prendergast's reputation.

Rose didn't want to cause alarm where there was no need. 'It certainly is, though he's a very busy man,' she said, at which Effie nodded gravely. 'Now, you make a start here at this end and call me if you can't find anything.'

As she made her way to the dressings cupboard, Rose decided to keep a close eye on this new nurse. Because if Prendergast had got her in his sights already, there could be big trouble.

For a moment she wished that she could share this potential problem with Philip, the young man she had met only a few months ago when he'd been a patient on this very ward. But she knew it was impossible. He'd had to go back to his airbase, and just because she was consumed with longing for him to return, that did not mean it would happen soon.

'Mr Rathbone! Mr Rathbone – can you hear me?'

Daisy could not quite believe that she was all but shouting at her boss. Until recently she never would have dared. He was so much more experienced in the ways of the underground station, with years of being a manager, and a well-liked and well-respected one too. Yet today he seemed to be in a world of his own. His face was drawn and grey, and she would swear his already receding hair was getting thinner.

Yes, they were all exhausted after many nights of bombing raids, but the job still had to be done. The tube wasn't going to stop running just because the office workers were tired.

He suddenly came to, sitting more upright behind his desk, his long fingers automatically straightening the sheets of paper in front of him.

'Miss Harrison. Daisy. Is all in order?'

Daisy took a step back. What she wanted to say was, 'Yes, but no thanks to you.' But she didn't. 'Yes, the platforms are all clear now,' she reported. 'The rubbish has all been removed and the last people have either gone to work or gone home.'

'Good, very good.' He patted his jacket pocket for his handkerchief and Daisy wanted to gasp. Her calm, competent, kind boss was nervous, and she didn't like it one bit. The world was all topsy-turvy.

To give him time to recover she looked away. The office, which faced the ticket hall, was lit by artificial light. The only daylight that penetrated this far down was from the many flights of stairs leading to ground level. Manor House was a modern station, completed not many years before war broke out, and Daisy knew she should be grateful that it had enough lamps and wasn't as damp as some of the horrors she'd heard about from fellow transport workers.

But many of the stations whose platforms were deep underground were facing the same problem. People wanted to use them as shelters in bombing raids. They were dry, they were safe, they were big – they seemed the obvious place. If you couldn't get to a public shelter, such as those opening up in church halls, then this was a good option.

Daisy knew she was lucky. Even though their Victory Walk back garden was more of a yard, somehow her father had fitted in an Anderson shelter, digging down into the ground and then curving a big metal roof over the top. Daisy and her sister Clover had helped to fit the roof, bending the sheets of metal as Bert hammered in the nails. It wasn't what anyone would call luxurious, but it did the trick. All the family could cram inside, including Robbie's pet rabbit, and there was room to sit, with cushions and rugs to ease the discomfort.

Not every family had the room for an Anderson shelter, or the skill to make one. Some people took their chances, staying home and squeezing under the stairs or beneath the kitchen table, but that was high risk. More and more were coming to the tube stations, desperate to get a place. They came clutching bundles of bedding, bags with food and flasks of tea, holding fast to their small children.

It wasn't meant to happen. Months ago, not long after Daisy had joined the office, there had been talk of the possibility, but that was all it had been. Now it was taking place right in front of them, although there was no official policy, and it upset Mr Rathbone no end. He had based his career on doing the right thing, sticking to the rules, keeping order. The only time he had been known to deviate from the straight and narrow had been when he decided to employ Daisy. He'd obviously guessed she was too young to apply, but had recognised how keen she was and how good she could be. She had always worked extra hard, to prove him right.

Now it sometimes felt as if she was the one in charge. Not of all the important stuff – the dealing with senior management, or budgets, or anything like that. But when it came to dealing with the crush of frightened people, or commuters wondering why they couldn't get down to the platforms to catch their usual train because of the press of bodies, it was up to her. She wasn't afraid to get out into the hall and mingle, to encourage those leaving to go one way and those arriving to go the other. To comfort a crying child while explaining to a confused parent how to take a different bus route if the main road was closed. On occasion, to help the station staff clear up downstairs.

There were other members of the Manor House work force, of course, although very few of her age. The younger men had been called up or gone into some kind of war work, as had the women of similar age. The men that were left were of Mr Rathbone's vintage, for the most part. They weren't overkeen on change either, and Daisy suspected that some had worked underground for so long that they'd lost all social skills. Somehow, the work of dealing with the distressed general public had fallen to her.

She had taken to arriving early if she was on the morning shift, even though the mornings were dark as the year headed towards the shortest day. She would let herself out of the house, or the Anderson shelter, trying not to wake her parents or Robbie. Sometimes she would make a cup of tea, but often she left without, worrying that the whistle of the kettle would disturb the last precious minutes of her parents' sleep. There would be tea at work. She'd cut herself a slab of bread to eat on the way.

Then she'd hit the ground running, doing whatever was necessary according to how bad the overnight onslaught had been. Sometimes the ARP wardens would be on hand, and once or twice the ambulance service, ready to patch up anyone who'd arrived injured. You never knew what you were going to find.

At some moments, that was a terrifying idea. Daisy often wondered what her younger self would have made of it all – the angry, bored girl who'd come to work here less than a year ago. Usually, though, she didn't have time to think about such things. She was rushed off her feet, dealing with all the practical problems that her boss suddenly seemed so ill-equipped to cope with.

She missed her former colleague, Sam. He had taken much trouble to show her the ropes, and she hadn't even appreciated it at the time. Now he'd gone above ground, to train as a bus driver. She'd been envious when she first heard, wanting to follow in his footsteps, until he'd pointed out the brutal truth that she was not only too young, but too short to reach the pedals.

Just as well, she thought now, as she cleared her throat. Somebody had to keep the Manor House show on the road.

'Mr Rathbone,' she said again, sensing that his attention was drifting. 'We need to make more space at the end of the southbound platform. The maintenance crews have been using it for their equipment, but it should all be stowed away more safely.'

He nodded, still slightly bemused. 'Ah, yes, indeed. That would be much better, good idea.'

'I'll see to it, then, shall I?' Daisy could tell what the answer would be.

'Yes, if you wouldn't mind.' He smiled, evidently relieved.

Daisy nodded, picked up her neat little jacket and headed for the down escalator. At least it was working today. The day crew wouldn't be happy, but they were more likely to take the instruction from her as she'd say it with a cheerful expression.

Her thoughts turned, as they did so often, to the person she was missing most. Not Sam, not her brother Peter or sister Clover, away with the armed services. It was Freddy who was always there in her mind and in her heart, Freddy who had held her tight on the first dreadful night of the Blitz, as they'd shivered in the shelter, not knowing what was happening in the skies above them. Freddy, who was now back with the navy, guarding the Western Approaches. She had no way of knowing when she would see him again. One thing she did know, though, was that he'd be proud of her for doing this job as best she could, helping in her own small way to keep the vital transport system going.

'Stay safe, Freddy,' she murmured, as she reached the bottom of the escalator.

Then she squared her shoulders and set off to find the maintenance crew.

CHAPTER THREE

'You don't mind me just dropping in like this, do you?'

'Of course not!' Patty exclaimed, holding the front door wide open so that her niece could step inside. 'We're always delighted to see you, you know that.'

Hope's anxious face brightened a little at the welcome and she made her way to the warm kitchen, the heart of the home. Something was bubbling away on the range, a bowl shape, wrapped in cotton and tied up with string. She sniffed in appreciation. 'Smells lovely!' she said.

'Thank you! I'm trying to get a bit ahead of myself for Christmas,' Patty explained. 'Daisy's been on an early shift so she's back home this afternoon, and was able to help me. A pity you weren't here half an hour ago. You could have helped to stir the Christmas pudding and wished for good luck. We've put a threepenny bit in, of course.'

Hope sat down at the big table in the middle of the room. 'Of course you have! I don't know if we're having one this year. I know my mother has made the cake – she had me searching all over the place to buy enough dried fruit – but she's not sure what will happen come Christmas itself, what with the new baby being due just beforehand.'

Patty nodded. 'Well, yes, that will be a big change for you all. Oh, here's Daisy now. Look, your cousin's here.'

Daisy burst into the room, having gone to change out of her work clothes and into something more comfortable, something that it wouldn't matter if it got stained while helping with the festive preparations. 'Mm, nutmeg and cinnamon – my mouth is watering!' she grinned. 'Hello, Hope, what brings you here?'

Hope shrugged and grinned back, but paused a moment, as if she wasn't sure she should say what she was thinking. Then she came out with it anyway. 'I'm fed up at home,' she confessed. 'It's not just all the busyness of Christmas coming. It's everything. Sorry, I sound like a spoilt child, but ever since Faith moved back in, it's all baby, baby, baby. She sits there like Lady Muck and expects us to run around after her.' She blew out her breath in exasperation.

Patty nodded in sympathy, knowing that if one of her own children had voiced such an idea she would have instantly told them, 'Don't speak about your cousin like that'. But she didn't want to reprimand her niece. After all, she knew only too well what Faith was like. She might be family but she was hard work, always had been.

'Must be awful,' said Daisy. 'I'd hate it.'

Hope sighed. 'I know we're lucky, compared to lots of other people. We don't have to share a room – of course Faith's got her old one back and it's the biggest, after our parents'. At least Martin had to go back to base immediately after the wedding so we aren't stuck with him too. And we can afford the extras. But it's enough to drive you stark staring mad.'

Patty busied herself over at the range. 'Why don't you have a nice cup of tea?' she offered. It might not solve the problem but it would allow Hope to let off steam.

She took three cups from the shelf and reached for the tea caddy, noting sadly that it was lighter these days. But she wouldn't serve reused leaves to a guest. Things would have to be really bad before she did that.

Hope fiddled with the cuff of her jumper. 'Perhaps there's one good thing that could come of it,' she mused.

Daisy looked up. 'Really? What's that, then?'

Her cousin closed her eyes a little as if thinking something through. 'It's just that, with all that's going on and non-stop fussing around Faith, my parents don't have much time to pay attention to anything else. So I might be able to do something I've been considering for ages.'

Patty carried the teapot across to the table and returned for the cups and milk. 'Oh? Did you have an idea?'

Hope nodded, more confident now. 'Ages ago, I wanted to do more than help out with the WVS. I mean, I know it's important and I do enjoy it, but loads of women volunteer for it nowadays. They've got families or part-time jobs, so they fit in a few hours here and there. I do nothing but sit at home all day really.'

Daisy raised her eyebrows. 'You must be bored silly.'

'Exactly.' Hope was delighted that here was someone who understood. 'And we all know that unmarried women will have to do something for the war effort soon. The government says so. So, months ago, I tried explaining this at home and they simply said I should be glad that my father worked hard to keep us all in comfort.'

'Well, he does, to be fair,' Patty said out of loyalty to Vera, even though her own children had had to start work as soon as they were old enough.

'That's all very well, but I don't want to sit back and knit, or whatever. I told them I wanted to join the ambulance service. I'd rather make a choice than have somebody tell me where to go. You'd have thought I'd said I wanted to fly to the moon. They were horrified.' Hope frowned at the memory. 'My mother said it wasn't ladylike to have to deal with blood and things like that.'

'Rubbish,' said Daisy. 'Good job Rose never heard that.'

Hope nodded again. 'I know. We'd be in a right pickle if we didn't have the nurses. Then my father said he didn't believe that women should be driving. Cars were bad enough, but they couldn't control a big vehicle like an ambulance.'

'That's just daft,' Daisy exclaimed. 'Who's going to do it if all the men have to go abroad and fight?' She put down her cup so emphatically that tea spilt over the side.

'It only made me more determined,' Hope said. 'And I know they can't stop me – I'm over twenty-one. Before, there never seemed to be the chance, but I bet that they won't even notice now. I'll go and sign up for it, that's what I'll do.'

Patty inhaled sharply. 'You're sure about this, Hope? You're not saying it just because you're cross with your parents or fed up with Faith? It's a serious decision, and your mother has a point: it won't be a walk in the park. Injured people, people in distress, and yes, blood everywhere – we hear about it first-hand from Rose. I realise you're no shrinking violet but it's not for everyone. You'd have to be tough.'

Hope sat back in the wooden chair and gave her aunt a big smile, her gaze determined. 'I know,' she said simply. 'That's why I want to do it.'

'Do you think she will do it, then?' Daisy asked her mother after Hope had left.

Patty nodded, without having to think about it. 'Yes, I'd say that once Hope gets an idea in her head she'll move heaven and earth to do it. Bit like someone else I know around here.'

Daisy made a face as she started on drying the dishes that were stacked on the draining board.

Patty began to hang up the clean utensils on their rack of hooks. 'I'm sure that Vera and Arthur will come round to it, given time. Like we said, we'll need ambulance drivers, be they men or women. Injured people won't care who's at the wheel as long as they can drive and get them to hospital as fast as possible.'

Daisy nodded, but was by no means as sure that her aunt and uncle would indeed agree. Some people were very set in their views and she knew only too well that lots of them did not like young women in responsible positions. She'd had her fair share of complaints at work, not because of what she did but because of who she was. She couldn't claim to be used to it, exactly, but it didn't surprise her any longer.

'Let me see the clock – can you move your head, you're right in front of it.' Patty craned her neck to check the old wooden clock, which hung on the wall near the inner door. Its loud ticking was so constant that it was easy to forget that it was there. 'Still a few minutes to go for the pudding.' She wiped her hands on her faded apron. 'I wonder who will be home to eat it. Not that we should get our hopes up, but wouldn't it be lovely if Peter and Clover could make it back in time?'

Daisy nodded but her expression was doubtful. 'Do you think they might? Really?'

Patty sighed and took a moment before answering. 'Well, it's always possible, isn't it? I'm sure they'll ask for leave, but then I suppose all their colleagues will too.'

'And Peter was home last Christmas. That'll make it more difficult, surely,' Daisy pointed out. 'Although it was embarkation leave – not that he could say so at the time.'

Patty pursed her lips at the painful reminder of what Peter had gone through in the past year. Being sent to fight in France, then getting evacuated from Dunkirk – all while those left at home had no idea if he was dead or alive. She'd never confessed to Daisy, or any of her children, just how afraid she had been for him.

'And Clover was here in September,' Daisy went on, unaware of what her mother was reliving. 'She timed it just right – first proper raid of the Blitz. Trust Clover – she always likes to be in the thick of it.'

Patty laughed ruefully. 'I don't imagine it was what she had planned. I was just glad we all fitted in the shelter. Even with extra guests.' She raised her eyebrows at her youngest daughter.

Daisy knew what she meant, of course. 'I don't suppose Freddy will have Christmas leave either,' she said sadly. She almost whispered it; she couldn't bear the disappointment that she was sure would await her. Fate had been cruel, allowing them that wonderful short time together and then parting them once more. Yet, it was better than nothing, and she knew she ought to be glad of the brief moments they'd had.

Patty put down the colander she'd been about to hang up and went over to her daughter, gently patting her shoulder. 'It would be lovely for you if he did, but you probably shouldn't expect it,' she said steadily. 'He'll be needed where he is. Those Atlantic convoys have to call on all the help they can get.'

Daisy swallowed hard. 'I know.' For a second she was tempted to give in to the tears that were suddenly forming in her eyes. Then she gave herself a shake. She wasn't a child any more. 'I'll send him a special present, and then I'll be sure he's thinking of me.'

Patty's face was warm as she nodded. 'I'm certain he will be.' Her heart turned over at the thought of the young man they'd met under such terrible circumstances, but who'd manage to impress them nonetheless. He genuinely did seem to care for Daisy. But heaven knew when the young couple would be reunited.

She checked the clock again. 'Right, that's long enough,' she declared. 'Grab that tea towel, Daisy. The pudding will be ready, so give me a hand, it's heavy.' Keeping busy would help, she thought, and luckily there was a mountain of work to do if they were to be ready for Christmas.

Rose was also thinking of who might be home for Christmas, as she gathered her notebook, pen and pencil together. She was going to her first meeting as the senior nursing representative for her ward. Usually this would fall to the ward sister, but Katherine had asked Rose to step in for once, as she herself had been caught up in a raid the night before and had sustained some injuries. 'Nothing major, as far as I can tell,' she'd said in her message, 'but we all know how vital it is to get these things checked as soon after the event as possible.'

Rose supposed she ought to be nervous but she'd been too busy to even think about what it might be like. Besides, any spare moments had been spent thinking of the letter that had arrived just as she was leaving the nurses' quarters. She'd had time only to scan it very quickly, but that was enough to make her heart beat faster. Philip had written to say he hoped to have a few days' leave in December. Of course, anything could happen before then, but at least this was the plan. He very much hoped that Rose would have some free time so that they could spend it together.

Rose privately vowed that no power on earth would stop her from seeing Philip if he was back in East London. Obviously, she would have to juggle her shifts at the hospital, but she'd volunteer for extra hours beforehand or swap with colleagues in order to see him. Whatever it took, she would do it.

When she rushed to the meeting room and pushed open the door she realised she was the last to arrive. Her spirits sank when she saw the closest empty chair was next to Mr Prendergast, the horrible surgeon. She cast her eyes around for an alternative but it would be hard, and too noticeable, to go right around the table to the opposite end. Anyway, Mrs Gleeson, the chairwoman, was starting to speak. 'Good, now we're all here, let's go through the minutes from last time . . .'

Mr Prendergast nodded at Rose, and took just a little too long to move his leg so that she could settle into her seat. She placed her notebook and pen on the table but kept her pencil on her lap with the sharp end aimed at his thigh. If he tried to move it closer to hers, he'd be in for a nasty surprise.

Rose didn't recognise some of the other attendees, but could see from a badge that one was the almoner, responsible for pastoral care of patients about to leave. The next person was a young woman who must be from the general administration, as she was making notes. Rose remembered one occasion when Katherine had arrived back from the meeting spitting with fury. 'They asked me if I would mind taking notes, as the clerk was indisposed! I said to them, I'm a medical professional, not a stand-in secretary. Never let them ride roughshod over you, Rose.'

Well, at least she'd been spared that. Subtly she shifted the angle of the pencil, and Mr Prendergast leant in the opposite direction with a swift tutting noise. Good, he wouldn't try that again.

Now they were going around the table to hear a verbal report from every ward. It would not be long before Rose would have to speak and suddenly the nerves were there, making her hands shake. She clasped them on her lap so that nobody would see. She didn't want the smug surgeon to notice or, indeed, anyone else. She tried to breathe more slowly, to calm down. She knew her subject; somehow she would have to convince the rest of the room of that. Then it struck her: she owed this to her patients. This was her chance to make suggestions that would improve their treatment. The idea gave her confidence, just in time.

'A-ha, Nurse Harrison. Welcome to the meeting.' Mrs Gleeson smiled, businesslike and friendly, in a slightly old-fashioned grey jacket and cream blouse, with pearls at her neck. Obviously not a practising nurse herself, then. 'How are things on your ward?'

Rose cleared her throat. This was it. 'We are coping well, but the main issue is the number of burns victims and the way they frequently arrive all at once . . .' As soon as she was underway, the nerves receded, and she spoke steadily but with conviction. She did not expect the chairwoman to be able to solve their dilemma with one wave of a magic wand, but at least she could state the problem and what Katherine felt should happen to help them manage it more efficiently.

'. . . So as soon as there is any space in the convalescent ward, we need to hear about it at once,' she concluded, keeping her gaze on the chairwoman.

'Thank you, Nurse Harrison.' The older woman made a few squiggles in her own notebook. 'We shall certainly consider it.' She tapped her pen. 'Now, Dr Fothergill, tell us about your morning clinic . . .'

Rose sat back in her chair, heartily relieved. She hadn't made a mess of it; they'd all paid attention to her report and request for help. She could not have done more. Guiltily, she allowed her mind to wander, as the newly set up minor-injuries clinic was no doubt important but unlikely to affect her own work.

For a moment she was far away from the hospital, which even in the meeting room smelt of disinfectant, the low winter light sloping through the high windows. She was by the bandstand in Victoria Park, walking with Philip in the warm sunshine. He was moving easily, no trace remaining of his broken bones after his plane crash. They were going to share a picnic . . .

'Then we shall reconvene on Thursday next week.' Rose abruptly came back to the meeting, as chairs were scraping on the tiled floor, everyone in a hurry to get back to the wards and theatres.

'Very interesting, Nurse Harrison.' She could hardly avoid the man now standing next to her, and so Rose painted a smile on her face.

'Thank you,' she said. 'Now if you'll excuse me . . .'

'Of course, of course.' He deliberately stayed still, not letting her pass. 'Just let me ask about your new trainee. Such a sweet young girl. I do hope she's performing well?'

Rose had to strain every nerve not to shudder in repulsion at the man's words. 'Yes, yes, she's learning fast. Now, if you wouldn't mind . . . ?'

Mr Prendergast smiled back, his lips thick and shiny. 'How very gratifying. I shall keep an eye on her progress.' Finally he stepped aside and Rose could make good her escape.

How typical that the surgeon should manage to deflate her happy mood. Her representing the ward, Philip possibly coming home – too much good news to last. Whatever might be happening at Christmas, in the meantime there was always Mr Prendergast to deal with.

CHAPTER FOUR

'Did you put her up to it? Or one of your girls?'

Patty had been stacking the shelves in the greengrocer's where she worked. As usual she was alone; since Clover had joined the ATS there had been no regular help, and the shop's owner was far too old to pitch in. Patty didn't mind most of the time. The delivery boys – and they were getting younger and younger, as the older ones had been called up – would carry the heavy sacks into the back room and so Patty could divide up the produce and avoid the really heavy lifting.

Today it was freezing cold and so she'd been grateful of the excuse to move around as much as possible, piling up the vegetables to hide the fact that there were gaps on the shelves, but in such a way to convince the shoppers that they would be tasty for family meals over the festive season. Everyone knew frost was good for parsnips.

She had been transferring a box of Brussels sprouts to the front of the shop when the door burst open and a furious Vera strode inside. It took a lot for Vera to venture out without checking her appearance very carefully, but today she'd buttoned her coat wrong and her scarf was all askew. Patty prepared for the onslaught.

'Don't tell me you didn't know. This has all the marks of Rose and Daisy on it. We'd never have suggested such a thing.' Vera paused to draw breath and Patty took the chance to try to calm her down.

'Come and have a seat at the counter,' she suggested, setting the remaining sprouts on the nearly empty bottom shelf.

Vera huffed. 'And I've told you before, you need to make more room by this door. People can't get through.'

Patty didn't reply. She could get through with no problem. Vera was noticeably stouter than her, always carried a chunky shopping bag, and she favoured expensive and well-lined coats; it was no wonder that she had difficulty where few others did.

'I'll put the kettle on,' she offered.

'You needn't trouble yourself,' Vera snapped, her hair falling into her eyes for once. 'I shan't be stopping. I simply want to know what you told Hope.'

'What about?' asked Patty, playing for time.

'You know very well. About this ridiculous idea she's come up with to join the ambulance service, of all things. It's beyond belief.'

Patty hitched up the sleeves of the cotton overall that she wore for work, wishing that her fingernails weren't full of earth from the root veg. Even when she was angry this was just the sort of detail that Vera would notice and bring up later.

'I think it sounds like a very good thing,' she said mildly. 'It's admirable that she wants to do something useful. Won't you be proud of her?'

Vera gave her sister a dark look. 'That's easy for you to say. It's not as if you have a position to maintain around here.'

Patty drew an audible breath – this was pushing it, even for Vera. 'So Bert's job as foreman at Sutherland's isn't worthy of respect? Or Rose as a senior nurse?' she asked, getting hot under the collar despite willing herself not to rise to the bait.

Vera could see she had overstepped the mark and hastily backed down. 'That's not what I meant. Of course they both do a grand job. Daisy too.' She sank down onto the wooden stool beside the counter. 'But working on the ambulances – it's not respectable. And, no offence, you know full well the circles Arthur moves in. It's vital that his family keeps to a certain standard. Whatever Hope does will reflect upon him.'

Patty struggled to see the problem. 'But surely the ambulance service is crying out for more volunteers? We had two drive along here as I was opening up. They can barely cope with all the injuries after the raids. They'll need young, able-bodied recruits, and yes, I know how keen Hope is. She'll be ideal for them.'

Vera shook her head. 'Have you considered what she'll actually have to do? What she might see? It's . . . it's not modest. Not for a young woman from a good home.'

Patty sighed. In truth she did sympathise a little. She'd been concerned when Rose had started nursing, not so much for the immodesty but more that the worst illnesses and injuries were bound to be upsetting. 'You'd be surprised what the girls can deal with,' she said. 'Give her some credit. Hope's tougher than you imagine.'

'What if she comes home covered in blood?' Vera burst out, voicing her fears. 'What if people see? Whatever will they think?'

Patty swallowed hard. This made no sense. Vera was perfectly happy for her beloved eldest daughter to have a child by her former boss and to pass it off as Martin's after the hasty wedding. Everything had been neatly tied up to look respectable, and to paper over the truth. So that was all fine. Yet Hope's desire to join a much-needed service was somehow wrong.

'I'm sure they aren't sent home in such a state,' she said, trying to remember anything that Rose had said that would lend weight to the argument. Inspiration struck. 'In fact, they wouldn't be allowed to. It would risk spreading infection. The ambulances are like the hospitals – they put hygiene above everything else. You'll have no worries on that score.'

Vera ran her fingers through her hair, realising it was unusually untidy. Her anger was slowly abating. 'I suppose that makes sense,' she said finally. 'All the same, when you think what she'll have to be touching . . . or seeing.'

Patty offered sympathy. 'Look, it was like when Rose started—'

'That's different, she's got a brother of the same age! She's used to young men!' Vera exclaimed, again forgetting her double standards.

'It's not really about that,' Patty went on. 'I'll pass on what she said to me after she'd done her first stint on the men's surgical ward. Once you've seen one male body, you've seen them all.'

'What!' Vera's hand flew to her mouth in horrified shock. 'What a terrible thing to say! It's . . . it's flagrant!'

'Not a bit.' Patty knew she had to make a good case or Hope's dreams could be left in tatters. 'It's about being professional. They'll have good training – lives will depend on that. They'll be taught to assess and then respond. I'm sure of it. Rose works alongside lots of ambulance staff, she'd know if there was anything wrong.' Patty didn't mention the dangers that all those staff members faced. Vera had enough to think about. 'Hope could be out there saving lives, Vera. Wouldn't that be wonderful?'

Vera looked baffled for a moment and Patty knew that her sister's world was being turned upside down. Well, of course that was true for them all; the war had changed everything, both at home and at work. But Vera had always valued a certain type of what she called 'respectability', and Hope performing such a role simply did not fit within it.

'I . . . I don't want her to have to put up with . . . with any funny business.' Vera gave Patty a direct look. 'You know what I mean. Men trying it on, that sort of thing.'

Patty sighed and nodded. It was every parent's worry – especially if you had girls, and she and Vera each had three. She'd struggled not to dwell on it as one by one they all went out into the world, beyond her protective arms. 'We can't keep them wrapped in cotton wool, Vera,' she said sadly. 'All we can do is bring them up right and then trust them to remember what we've taught them. And to be there if it goes wrong.'

Vera nodded back, biting her lip. 'Like when . . .' She couldn't say it, even now. Like when Faith, beautiful and spoilt, had fallen for the oldest line in the book: that her boss would leave his wife and support her and their child. Vera had wiped her mind of the uncomfortable facts of that case. 'Yes, yes, you have a point, Patty. I can see I shall have to think carefully about this.'

'You do that.' Patty hoped her sister meant it, for all of their sakes. 'Would it help if Hope talked to Rose? About the details of it all, I mean, the medical side? Then she'd know what she might be in for.'

Vera pushed herself up from the little stool and looked down at her coat. 'Good Lord, Patty, why didn't you say something? The buttons are all wrong.' Hastily she refastened them, scowling. 'Yes, yes, I'll ask Hope if she'd like that. That would help. I don't want her to be unprepared for . . . nasty things.'

Patty smiled, fairly sure that Hope would take whatever the job threw at her. She was the most practical of her nieces, and – she shouldn't think it but it was true – her favourite. 'She's a grown-up now,' she breathed. 'She might not seem it to you, but they all are, all our girls. If she's chosen to do this then we should be glad.'

Vera straightened her scarf and prepared to face the outside world once more. 'We'll see,' she said.

Patty nodded, knowing how her sister hated to admit to being wrong. This was as much as she could wish for at this stage.

'You let me know what she says. And here, have some sprouts. Fresh in this morning.'

Vera accepted the paper bag of bright green sprouts,

knowing this was Patty's way of ending a discussion. 'Thank you,' she murmured, before battling her way through the narrow doorway.

Another night of raids had brought a fresh round of admissions onto the ward. Rose barely had time to register how sore her feet were from not having had a moment to sit down, and so she was cheered up by the sound of laughter coming from the far end of the big room, down by the windows overlooking the courtyard.

She craned her neck to see who it was. She thought grimly that it wouldn't be another of the senior nurses – they all had too much on their plates. Sure enough it was one of the juniors, a fiery Welsh nurse called Coral Davies, and she was deep in conversation with the new trainee, Effie Jenkins.

Rose drew nearer, trying to hear what they were talking about that was making them giggle like schoolgirls. Some of the sisters would frown upon such behaviour, but Rose didn't see why the young women shouldn't enjoy themselves as long as they were doing the job as well. Heaven knew, they all deserved a few moments of relief from the grind of looking after more patients than the place was built for.

'Oh, I miss him something dreadful,' Coral was saying. 'I wish he was up here in London to make me laugh, I do. Never a dull moment with my Jonnie. But of course he can't get away. They need him down the mine. He says to me, I should be glad he hasn't got to go away to France or whatnot, to fight like

40

the others. But, to tell the truth, it's always a gamble going down the mine. Never know if you're going to come out alive.'

'Gosh.' The fun had gone from Effie's voice. 'You must be worried for him then.'

Coral shrugged, as she tugged free the used pillowcase from the bed next to the window and reached for the new one lying folded on the mattress. 'Doesn't do no good to worry,' she said staunchly. 'Won't help one way or the other. I just look forward to when I can see him again. Get one of his big hugs from his big strong arms.' She rolled her eyes.

Effie shuffled a little nervously as she noticed Rose approach down the gap between the two long rows of beds, and made to smooth out the bottom sheet.

'Got a fellow yourself, have you?' Coral asked, plumping the pillow with energy. 'Walking out with someone? Who's the lucky man?'

Effie blushed and gave a shy chuckle. 'No, no, nothing like that. My brothers say I'm far too young for such things.'

Coral tutted. 'You can't be that young, not now that you're working here. Anyway, none of their business. Go tell them to sling their hooks. I would.'

'Oh, no, I wouldn't want to do that,' Effie protested. 'They're only looking after me. They're good like that, always have been.'

Coral looked at her colleague. 'Older than you, are they?'

Effie nodded. 'One's in the merchant navy and one works on the docks down at Wapping.'

41

Rose remembered the girl saying as much before. Clearly they were important figures in her life.

'Always kept an eye out for me; they say that's what brothers are for,' she went on.

Rose bit back a chuckle. Peter had never said such a thing to her, but of course she was a couple of years older than him. And Robbie was still a child.

'Yes, they'd never let anything happen to me,' Effie said confidently. 'I wouldn't want to get on the wrong side of them. They used to get into all sorts of trouble when they were at school, with fights and all that, but they've calmed down now.'

Coral picked up the used bedding and rolled it into a bundle. 'Happens to the best of us. I used to be proper lively, but now Jonnie says I've gone all grown-up.' She flashed a gleeful grin at her colleague. 'Come on, we got to get all this stuff to the laundry before the new patients arrive.'

'Quite right,' said Rose as the two junior nurses passed her, as if that was the first piece of their conversation she'd overheard. 'Then when you get back we'll make sure there's enough burns ointment to hand. We don't want to have to keep running off to the stores in the middle of a treatment.'

As they made their way to the corridor, bundles in hand, Rose reflected that yet again Effie struck her as younger than her age, and more vulnerable than most of the trainees she'd had dealings with. Still, perhaps it was a case of being the youngest and coddled by her protective family. As long as she could strip a bed and remake it, that would have to do for now.

CHAPTER FIVE

Daisy was fed up and bone tired on top of that. There had been deafening raids for most of the night and all the family had been huddled in the shelter for hours. Her mother had done her best to keep them warm, handing round hot-water bottles and checking that they all had blankets, having prepared flasks of tea in advance. Daisy knew this was luxury compared to what many people endured. But she just could not get used to sleeping sitting up.

Then she'd had to do an extra-long shift at Manor House, once again arriving early to make sure the platforms were cleared of families who'd spent an anxious night there. Today there had been more than ever, and, if she was honest, the clammy heat and smell from all the bodies had turned her stomach. All the more reason to be thankful for her father's Anderson shelter, she told herself sternly. Be grateful for what you have.

Mr Rathbone had taken to keeping to his office, as if pretending nothing was happening one level further underground. As long as the normal train service could resume on time, he was prepared to overlook the entire matter.

It made twice as much work for Daisy, although in some ways she preferred him to stay out of the way and then she wouldn't have to watch him fussing. His keenness for detail was all very well under normal circumstances, but now, in the midst of the emergency, it was a hindrance rather than a help.

Daisy's mood had soured still further because she'd had a letter from Freddy. Normally this filled her with joy, but this one confirmed what she'd feared: he would not be home over the festive season. 'I really wish I was there with you,' he'd written, and she could have cried with the longing to see him, to be held by him. Now she knew it wasn't going to happen. Or not yet, she reminded herself. It wasn't for ever. She had to keep hoping he would stay safe in the meantime and make it home at some point in the new year.

The only bright moment in the day was when her old colleague, Sam, had popped by for a visit, in between his own shifts as a bus driver. 'I was on diversion on account of Green Lanes being hit last night,' he explained, smart in his new uniform, 'and being as what I know you can't run this place without me, I thought I'd drop in.'

Daisy knew he was winding her up, as ever, but she loved it all the same. He was so lively – she hadn't realised how much she'd relied on him to raise her spirits until he left. 'We're doing fine,' she'd replied at once, but Sam had raised his eyebrows.

'You sure?' he'd asked, nodding towards the glass in the office door, through which they could see the figure of Mr Rathbone, hunched over his desk.

'Of course.' Daisy didn't want Sam feeling sorry for her.

''Cos it don't look like it,' he pointed out. 'Finding

it hard, is he? I heard there were crowds coming down here, messing up his tidy station. He won't like it, I said to my old dear.'

Daisy met his gaze. 'Nothing of the sort. He's just catching up on paperwork. You know how it is.'

'Well, if you say so.' Sam had not appeared convinced. 'Bet you could do with a night out, Daze.' She pulled a face – hardly anyone called her that. 'Fancy a Christmas tipple with us down the pub? You can have your lemonade and I'll have something stronger what keeps out the cold.'

Daisy was on to the detail in a flash. 'Us? Do you mean you and Sylvia? You still walking out with her, are you?'

Sam blushed a bit but laughed it off. 'Course I am. Why wouldn't I? Keeps me on my toes, she does. And she'd love to see you, I know it. She still writes to your sister, but I bet she'd like to hear what you've heard from her too.'

Until the summer, Sylvia had worked with Clover in the ATS stores in central London, which is how Sam had met her in the first place.

'Of course I'll come,' Daisy said, heartened by the idea of a night when she could let down her hair for once. 'You let me know when you've got your shifts.'

'I'll try to arrange a raid-free evening as well, shall I?' he'd suggested, and she wished he could do just that.

Now Daisy got off the bus at the stop nearest Victory Walk and pulled on her woolly gloves. Darkness had fallen, as it wasn't long until the shortest day and daylight hours were few. Fewer still in the half-light of the station office. How lovely it would be to see the spring sunshine. She must hang on to that thought, believing that there would be a way out of the winter gloom.

The paving stones along the path to their house were growing slippery with frost and the leaves of the straggly plants by the front gates gleamed in the narrow beam of her shaded torch. White stripes criss-crossed the night sky from the anti-aircraft searchlights. Daisy wondered if Clover was on duty yet, aiming her own searchlight over the hills and fields of the south coast. If Daisy herself was cold, then Clover would be a darned sight colder.

The front of the house was hard to make out with all the blackout blinds in place, and Daisy groped for the familiar shape of the front door handle. Hastily she turned it and slipped inside, to minimise the chance of any light from inside becoming visible.

'Daisy! Is that you?' Rose's voice echoed down from the top floor.

Now Daisy remembered – it would have been her big sister's afternoon off.

'I know it's you! What have you done with my favourite lipstick?'

Daisy felt better after a warming dish of her mother's stew, which included pearl barley to make it more filling as everyone was saving their rations for Christmas. It was still tasty as could be and deeply satisfying, served with a big slice of bread with the treat of a scraping of butter. Daisy pushed back her chair and sighed happily.

Rose reached across for her plate, the brief row over the lipstick now forgotten. Daisy hadn't meant to take it, or rather, had meant to put it back, but somehow hadn't got round to it. Now Rose was keen to retrieve it, and of course this had nothing whatsoever to do with Philip coming home on leave any day now. Daisy gave a little grin. Her big sister wasn't immune to dressing up after all.

'You leave that washing-up to me,' their mother said firmly. 'You've been on your feet all day, Daisy, and Rose, you deserve a bit of time off for once. Sit back down, don't make me tell you twice. Bert, can you pass me those side plates? There, all done.' Patty went through to the back kitchen with her stack of crockery just as there came some frantic knocking on the front door.

Daisy sucked on her teeth. Who could this be? She didn't want to get out of her chair to find out. Here they were, happily gathered in the kitchen, with no siren sounding yet. Robbie was sitting in front of the fire, chewing the end of his pencil as he flicked through an exercise book, looking for his homework. It was as close to a peaceful evening as they'd had for ages, and she wanted to hang on to every moment.

But the knocking came again and she forced herself to her feet.

'Daisy!' her aunt Vera gasped as soon as the front door was open. 'Is your mother here? Is Rose?'

Daisy immediately noticed how anxious her aunt was, as she clutched her coat across her body. She must have rushed out without doing it up, and she had no hat or scarf. 'Come in, they're inside,' she said, gesturing towards the kitchen.

'There's not a moment to lose,' Vera cried, bursting through the doorway and hurrying along the hall. 'It's an emergency. Patty, are you . . . ? Oh, Rose, thank goodness. I was afraid you'd be on duty this evening.'

Rose looked up from the *Evening Standard*, which she had just started to read. 'Auntie Vera! Whatever is the matter?' she asked, as Patty came through from the sink, wiping the suds from her hands on a tea towel.

Vera grasped the back of one of the dining chairs, as if it would give her extra strength. 'It's the baby, it's coming already,' she panted, unused to running. Her face was red with effort. 'It's caught us all out. We thought it would be next week – we'd seen the doctor and everything – but it's coming now and he's away for a few days and now we're stuck.' She paused to catch her breath.

Patty nodded, unflustered. 'Well, that's what babies do. They arrive when they are ready,' she observed. 'As we all know. I've had five, you've had three, and I don't think any of them came when they were meant to.'

Vera shook her head. 'But this one, it can't be too early, it *has* to be next week.' She crumpled forward but then drew herself upright. 'If anyone adds up when Martin was home on leave in the spring . . . it can't be before next week. A Christmas baby, that's what we've been telling people.'

Patty looked heavenwards for a moment. 'Tell people what you like, Vera, the baby won't pay any mind to that.' She shook her head. 'And people won't add it up.

It's close enough, if that's what you're worried about. People forget. They won't care once you have a lovely healthy grandchild.'

'But we had it all arranged.' Vera was dejected, all her careful plans upended yet again. 'And now there's no doctor.'

Patty reached for her cardigan. 'I didn't have the doctor for any of mine,' she said, 'and you only had one for Joy. We managed perfectly well with Ma helping. How far along is she? When did the contractions start?'

Vera made a face. 'She didn't want to tell us. She knew the baby was meant to come next week, so she kept it quiet until she couldn't really hide it. It's been since yesterday.' She drew another deep breath. 'Rose, I don't suppose . . . I mean, I know you aren't a doctor or midwife, but . . .'

Rose pushed the paper towards her father and got to her feet. 'Of course. Like you say, I'm not a doctor or midwife, but I've been with mothers giving birth before. As long as you're clear, if there are any problems I'll have to call for expert help, never mind what week it is.'

Patty nodded in approval at her eldest coming to the rescue. 'I'll come too,' she said. 'After all, none of my five births were the same, so I know some of what can happen. Come on, then, Vera. Do up your coat properly. You don't want to catch your death out there. Here, have one of my scarves.' She took a bright green one from the hook on the back of the door. 'That's better. It won't help anyone if you get a chill. Right, Bert, Daisy, will you make sure Robbie finishes his homework? We'll see you later, I expect, but don't wait up.'

* * *

It was not far from Victory Walk to Aunt Vera's house, though the ever more slippery pavements made the short journey hazardous, ill-lit as it was, just the intermittent AA beams shining down on the familiar route. Rose wondered what lay ahead. First babies could be difficult, although she had no reason to suppose that this one would be. Faith was young and healthy, better nourished than most, and in a warm home. As long as the sirens didn't start, it might all go well.

Aunt Vera was clearly worried and that was only natural. She was just worrying about the wrong things, when really she was anxious for her daughter and grandchild. She'd soon calm down once she had the child in her arms, Rose was sure. She'd ask her mother to keep her busy, out of the way until she was less frantic.

'Here we are.' Vera rushed to the front door, grander than those on Victory Walk, with its elaborate knocker glinting in the dull light. 'She was upstairs in her room when I left . . . Coo-eee, we're back, and Rose is with us.'

They all stepped into the wide hallway and Patty hurriedly closed the door behind them, to keep in the warmth and ensure that no light seeped out.

Hope came rushing down the stairs towards them. 'Thank God you're here,' she said to her cousin, ignoring her mother and aunt. 'I don't know anything about babies, but it strikes me this isn't going right. She's not feeling well at all. Come and see.'

Vera's eyebrows shot up in alarm but Rose refused to

be panicked. 'Right, so I need you to make sure there's lots of very hot water available.'

'And towels?' Hope was prepared, at least.

'Yes, and towels. Maybe you and Aunt Vera could make us all some tea?' Rose hinted heavily to her cousin, who got her meaning, ushering Vera towards the kitchen. Rose, relieved, ran nimbly up the stairs, with their elegant mahogany banister shining and smelling of beeswax. Patty was but two steps behind her.

The sight before them as they came into Faith's bedroom was much more disordered.

The young woman lay on the bed, the sheets and blankets kicked aside and half on the floor. Her usually beautiful long blonde hair was dark with sweat, plastered to her forehead, which dripped with perspiration. 'Rose!' she cried. 'What's happening to me? Why does it hurt so much? Oh, I'm going to be sick.'

Hastily Patty dashed forward and grabbed an old enamel bowl that somebody had thoughtfully left by the bedside cabinet. She rubbed her niece's shoulders as she vomited into the bowl, moaning in distress as she did so.

'It's all right, it's all right,' she murmured, as Faith's shoulders shook. 'This is what it's like. You do get sick sometimes. Here, where's your hanky, let me wipe your mouth.'

All Faith could do was moan, so Patty reached for her own little square of cotton and used that.

Meanwhile Rose dragged aside most of the bedding so that it would not trip her up, and folded one sheet and blanket at the bottom of the bed.

51

'All finished?' she queried, as her cousin sank back onto her creased pillows. 'Let me put this thermometer under your tongue quickly – no, there's nothing unusual, I simply need to know you aren't running a high temperature. There, excellent. Now give me your wrist . . .' Swiftly she went through her usual routine, mentally noting the pulse rate, glad to discern there were no underlying problems.

It was just the business of childbirth, but maybe nobody had told Faith how hard it could be.

'What's wrong with me?' Faith's lower lip trembled.

'Nothing,' Patty said, stroking her hand. 'It's hard work, bringing a child into the world. Not called labour for nothing, you know,' she grinned, but Faith's eyes were brimming.

'But it hurts so much!' Her face contorted as the next contraction hit her.

'Yes, well, I'm afraid it often does,' Patty said sympathetically, continuing her calm stroking even as Faith arched her back and sobbed.

Rose took a little notebook out of her skirt pocket and noted the time. She waited for the contraction to ease before asking her question.

'How often do these pains happen? Is the gap between them getting shorter?'

Faith moaned again. 'I don't know! I don't know! Am I meant to count or something? Nobody said. Just make them go away, can't you?'

Rose shook her head gently, thinking that Faith was evidently unprepared for what was to follow. Pain was something other people had, not her.

She had had it easy so far: whatever she wanted handed to her on a plate. Even when her much-older boss had dumped her and refused to leave his wife, her parents had stepped in to make everything all right. But now, there was only one person who could give birth to this baby: Faith herself.

Rose hoped her cousin could find the reserves of strength necessary. There really wasn't much choice. Patty rose to stand with the smelly bowl, inclining her head to indicate that she was heading to the family's most useful luxury: an upstairs indoor bathroom. Not for them the chilly privy next to the back kitchen. Vera had insisted on all mod cons and Arthur had obliged and got the builders in. At the time Rose had been rather jealous, but now she was very glad. The facilities would make things much easier.

Faith lay panting, exhausted, her eyes half closed. Rose glanced at her watch. No new contraction yet.

They were in for a long night.

CHAPTER SIX

For several hours, Faith continued to moan through her contractions and the labour slowly progressed, every detail noted by Rose as she carefully watched her cousin. Hope's fears were unfounded; it was simply a case of both young women not knowing what happened at a birth. It was often bloody, and grisly, and painful. Once Hope had realised this, and that her sister wasn't in danger, she was a great help, fetching and carrying, doing much of the work that a nurse might do, while Rose supervised. It made Rose's job much easier now she knew that she could trust her young cousin not to panic. Vera had been kept busy boiling the kettle, bringing sandwiches and generally doing anything they could think of to keep her out of the way. Her anxiety only made Faith's fears worse.

Now Rose picked up a change in the room, Faith shifting in a different way on the damp sheets. Yes, the contractions were coming closer together. 'Not long now, Faith,' she said encouragingly. 'Listen to me. You'll feel the urge to push, but make sure you only do so when I tell you. Got that? Deep breaths now, deep breaths.'

That was the moment that the air-raid siren chose to go off.

Rose turned aside to hide the dismay on her face. Of all the crucial times. Still, they must cope somehow. They didn't stop treating people at the hospital during air raids; if possible, they moved the patients somewhere safer. She would have to improvise.

One option would be to stay where they were. The bedroom was large and, even with Faith in the throes of labour, a comfortable place. There were two small armchairs upholstered in peach velvet, now mostly hidden by cast-aside bedding, and a beautiful carved dressing table, groaning beneath the pile of towels instead of the vanity set, which had been hastily moved to the windowsill.

But they were high up in a tall house – not a safe place.

Being on the end of a terrace came with a larger outside space and Arthur had got people in to assemble an Anderson shelter. Rose remembered Aunt Vera boasting about it, how it would be so much more suitable than the one her father and sisters had put together in their own small yard. All the same, they would have to get Faith down the flights of stairs, through the back of the house and down to the shelter. It might be too much for her.

'Hope,' Rose said quietly, hoping the noise of the siren would hide her words from her labouring cousin, 'what room have you got under the stairs?'

Hope looked surprised and then understood. 'You mean, by the dining-room door?'

'Exactly.' Rose knew it wouldn't be perfect but it would be safer than where they were now, and easier for Faith to reach, even if it would be touch and go if she could walk down the stairs. 'Go now, there's not a moment to lose. Get something comfortable for her to lie on – cushions, anything. And take the towels. At least we'll be closer to the kettle for hot water.'

'Got it.' Hope grabbed the towels and left the room at a dash.

Patty came in, outwardly calm, although Rose could see she was worried by the way she tapped her fingers against her skirt pocket. 'What's the best plan, Rose? Can she be moved?'

Rose inhaled deeply. 'If we do it now, quickly, between contractions. Hope's preparing a place in the hall under the stairs. The contractions are getting even closer together, though.'

Patty's eyebrows shot up. She knew what that meant. The baby would arrive any minute now.

Faith caught what her aunt had said. 'I can't move!' she screamed, using all her energy to voice her pain. 'Not now! How can I possibly move?'

Rose nodded emphatically. 'You must, for your safety and your baby's. We'll help. Ma, take her left side, I'll take the right. Faith, you're going to have to stand, but we'll help you.'

Faith moaned but had no energy left to fight them off as they took hold of her and somehow moved her from the bed. Then it was a case of almost carrying her across the room, through the doorway and down the stairs as fast as they could safely go. Rose knew there would be blood on the stair carpet but there was no time to do anything about that now.

Hope was pushing large cushions snatched from the sofa and easy chairs against the wall under the stairs, as Vera came through from the kitchen. 'Hope! Whatever are you doing? Those are my best cushions, that three-piece suite was new . . .' She looked up and saw her eldest daughter, collapsing in the arms of her sister and niece. 'Oh my God, Faith . . .'

'More hot water, Vera, *now*,' Patty said at once. 'Boil as much as you can, before you have to turn the gas off during the raid.'

Vera dithered, in agony at seeing her child in such a condition.

'Come on, Ma, we'll be quicker if we do it together,' said Hope, taking her trembling mother by the arm. 'Tilley lamp's just there,' she added over her shoulder.

Rose and Patty didn't hesitate, lowering Faith onto the cushions. By now she was hardly aware of what was going on, and just as well, as Rose rushed to light the lamp and Patty fished out her torch from her pocket and tore off the shield from its lens. It was unsafe to leave mains gas on during a raid, and they could not deliver a baby in complete darkness.

In the dim light they crouched by Faith, who was panting and sweating more than ever. Rose could see how close the birth was now.

'Right, you're almost there,' she assured her cousin, keeping all traces of concern from her voice. 'Listen to me. Deep breath – and now push as hard as you can. Hold my hand,' she ordered, and Faith grasped it so tightly that she almost broke the flesh. 'That's it.'

'I can see the baby's head,' Patty announced, directing

the torch beam where it was most needed. 'Come on, Faith, you're doing so well. Your child's almost here.'

Faith choked back a sob and then groaned with the effort. She was beyond speech.

Patty knelt closer, her arms at the ready, glancing up at Rose to confirm they were of the same mind. One more push should do it.

The siren wailed on and somewhere in the background they could hear crashes and explosions, but all of their attention was focused on this shadowy space, this makeshift bedroom, listening for that most important noise of all, the baby's first cry.

Faith gave a sudden gasp and a shudder passed through her body, then Patty reached in and shouted for joy. 'It's here, you've done it, Faith. Congratulations, you've given birth to your baby.' She glanced down. 'A boy. You've got a little boy.'

Right on cue, the tiny creature let out a wail, so loud that it almost drowned out the sounds of destruction all around them.

Faith gasped, her face close to disbelief. 'I . . . I . . . is he all right?'

Rose took the squirming child and swiftly cleaned him with a towel and warm water, then looked at him carefully. 'He's perfect.' She wrapped him in yet another towel and passed him to his mother, who had managed to sit up a little, propped by the mismatched cushions. 'He's a little fighter, coming into the world in such a situation.' She laughed in relief. 'There you are, Faith. He's here and he's going to be absolutely fine.'

For a moment nobody spoke, taking in the timeless

miracle of new birth. The flame of the Tilley lamp flickered and they could see Faith's smile, a whole new sort of smile from her old smug sneer. This was a completely new side of her. Somehow she had given birth, despite the last-minute urgent scramble to a place of safety, the lack of a doctor, or even of proper light. She had managed it.

Hope came through from the kitchen with a fresh bowl of water. 'Here we are. We can't boil any more, the gas is off . . . oh.' She saw the bundle and stopped in her tracks.

Rose put her hand on Hope's shoulder. 'Come and meet your nephew. He's obviously going to be a force to be reckoned with. He was determined to arrive tonight, raid or no raid.'

Hope laughed in delight and squatted down. 'Hello, baby,' she breathed, turning back the edge of the towel. 'Look at his little face. He's beautiful.'

'He is.' Faith gently stroked his cheek, as Patty backed away to find Vera and let her know the good news.

'I might need your help again in a minute,' Rose said quietly to Hope, as Faith was absorbed in gazing at the baby. 'We'll have to deal with the afterbirth. Are you all right to do that?'

Hope hesitated. 'What's that?'

Rose, now exhausted herself, was tempted to snap, 'What does it sound like?' But she realised that Hope had no reason to know. So she explained as succinctly as she could and Hope nodded, not worried about what she was in for.

'Of course. You just tell me what to do.'

There, under the stairs, the final moments of the birthing process played out and Hope was unflinching at the sight of blood and bodily fluids, as indeed she had been throughout the long hours of her sister's labour. Between them Rose and Hope cleaned Faith up and made her comfortable, then Patty came to her side and showed her how to begin to feed her baby. Vera approached to meet her grandchild and shed a quick tear of relief before wiping it away.

Rose stepped back, convinced they had done as well as they could. No doctor had been needed and mother and baby were well. They would have to weigh and measure the child when daylight came, at least to satisfy her own professional standards, but all of that could wait.

She took a moment to go into the kitchen, where Hope now stood, barely visible in the shadows cast by a second Tilley lamp. 'Here.' Hope held out a flask. 'I made some tea while we could still boil the kettle. I reckoned we'd need it.'

Rose felt her shoulders release as she could finally let go of the tension of being the one in charge. 'Hope, you saved the day,' she laughed. 'You know what? After this, any ambulance crew would be lucky to have you. You kept calm, you did what was needed, and look, you've got a nephew.'

Hope poured tea into a pair of little enamel cups. 'You know what, Rose? I enjoyed it.' She gave a wide smile, tired beyond measure but also exhilarated. 'I was made for this. I can't wait to start.'

CHAPTER SEVEN

Daisy collapsed onto one of the wooden chairs around the kitchen table. 'Ouch! My feet!' she complained, edging out of her work shoes. 'I've hardly had a moment to rest, the station's been so busy. Everyone's been rushing out to get their last-minute Christmas shopping, even if there's not much in the shops to buy.'

Patty nodded sympathetically. She'd had a busy day herself, with customers trying to put together festive food for their families, despite the shortages. There was a great demand for carrots, as they could be used in place of sugar in some recipes, with a bit of ingenuity.

'I'm just seeing what we can do in advance of the big day itself,' she explained. 'Of course some things will have to wait until the last minute, but if we can get ahead of ourselves then it won't be such hard work on Christmas morning.'

Daisy shrugged out of her work jacket and folded it on the back of another chair. 'What would you like me to help with?'

Patty smiled. 'I haven't decided yet, but thank you for offering.' She thought that this was another change in her youngest daughter. For years she wouldn't have made the suggestion, relying on her big sisters to do the bulk of the work. 'Your aunt Vera came into the shop today. They've chosen the baby's name.'

Daisy sat up straighter. She'd heard all about the difficult circumstances of the birth, and in truth was quite glad she hadn't been called upon to help with it herself. 'What's it to be?'

Patty shut the notebook she'd been checking earlier, full of handwritten recipes that she'd compiled over the years of her marriage. 'He's going to be Arthur, like his granddad. Also, it turns out that Martin has an uncle with that name, so it's very fitting. They'll call him Artie, though, so there won't be any confusion.'

Daisy gave a wry grin. 'I like it. Artie. It's a good name.'

'I should think so,' Patty replied. 'A good British name. And nobody will ask how do you spell it or anything like that. A good solid name. Vera's over the moon, now he's actually here.'

'They could have chosen a Christmassy name,' Daisy suggested. 'Noel! Or Stephen for St Stephen. If he'd been a girl they could have had Carol. Or Holly.'

'Well, he isn't and they didn't.' Patty stood up. 'Here, put my recipe book back on the shelf so it won't get food on it while I prepare our tea. You can peel the potatoes. The peeler's by the sink.'

Daisy rose and did as her mother asked, knowing that this was the least that she could do to share the ongoing task of feeding the family. Furthermore, she knew the baby was not responsible for who his parents were, and it was up to the extended family to welcome him and love him. She would do her bit – no matter what she thought of her cousin Faith.

'Are you going to lend us a hand, Rose?' Katherine asked, from her dangerous position halfway up a ladder. She was holding a piece of spiky holly, red berries gleaming. 'Anyone who's off shift this evening is welcome to join in the decorating.'

'Better mind your hands!' Rose said, immediately pointing out the potential hazards of such an activity. She paused on her way back to her room in the nurses' quarters. Katherine had been hard at work making the hallway look festive, she could see. 'I'll have to let you down, I'm afraid. I have to go out this evening.' She kept the excitement out of her voice; she didn't want everyone to know who she was meeting, or at least not yet.

'Never mind, I'll ask some of the youngsters. They can probably stretch higher than me anyway.' Katherine fished a box of drawing pins from her skirt pocket, and carried on up the ladder.

Rose nodded and hurried to the sanctuary of her room, shutting the door and leaning her back against it, catching her breath. The moment had finally come. It was the day before Christmas Eve and at last Philip had his few days of leave from his air base. She glanced towards her desk, where his letter lay, confirming the dates and asking her to meet him outside the town hall tonight.

Rose shivered in anticipation. Her sensible self warned her not to get her hopes up; in truth she scarcely knew him, as much of the time they spent together had been when he was in a coma after his plane crash. He'd had late-onset concussion and nobody had been able to predict if he would survive or, even if he did, what sort of state he might be in. Rose had nursed him, and somehow realised even then that they had a deep connection.

It was like a miracle when he came back to life, able to move and without brain damage. Somehow he'd registered who she was: this constant presence who had watched over him. It hadn't been an illusion. Even though they'd been able to talk to one another for a matter of mere hours, that connection was definitely real.

But as soon as he was fit he had had to return to the airfield and they'd relied on letters ever since. Rose had kept each one, carefully straightening out the folds in the thin sheets of paper, pressing them between heavy books until they lay flat, and then collecting them in a box that had once held a stationery set. It was a pale grey with a matching ribbon across one corner, and she'd never been able to bring herself to throw it away. Now she had the perfect use for it.

Calm again, she began to lay out what she would wear. It was a chilly evening, but she had a new cardigan, knitted specially for the occasion. It was in a warm turquoise blue, with delicate pearl buttons at the neck and cuffs, and would set off her chestnut hair. Carefully she unclipped her nurse's cap and let her hair fall to her shoulders. It felt like a rare indulgence, not to wear it up in its practical bun.

If she'd been like her sister Clover, she'd have chosen

to wear trousers tonight. Clover had shocked some people when she'd come home on her last brief leave, choosing flannel slacks in place of a skirt. 'Like a boy!' Aunt Vera had exclaimed. 'Whatever does she think she's doing?'

Rose smiled at the memory. Clover had maintained they were warm and practical, and she could run for a bus if she needed to. They also had wonderful large pockets. Why didn't more women wear them?

All the same, Rose had not adopted the habit, and now took out her good wool skirt, a mix of indigo and cobalt, which would go well with the new cardigan. She might choose trousers in future, but she wanted to look her best for Philip – and, without false modesty, she had good legs. All that standing and walking miles along the hospital corridors every day did marvels for the calf muscles.

Swiftly she changed, hanging her uniform on the back of the door, shrugging into her big coat. She reached for a pretty patterned scarf, in more shades of blue, with a dash of crimson along the edges. To complete the picture she added her favourite lipstick, now reclaimed from Daisy. Not such a bright crimson as the scarf, but a good tone nevertheless.

She was ready. Willing her nerves to still, she stepped out into the hallway once more, her hands trembling a little now that the moment she had waited for was nearly here.

The town hall stood proudly set back from the busy road of Mare Street, though these days its walls were heavily sandbagged, and, like just about every other building nearby, its windows had been damaged in the night-time raids. Rose could remember it being built; it had been opened only a couple of years before the war began. The whole family had come to see it and thought it was all very modern. Now it had a big underground ARP control room. Rose had never been inside but some of the wardens she had met at the hospital had, and described how it had pumps and filters and even an escape hatch, to keep the whole system running no matter what was happening above ground.

Rose made herself remember all those details to calm her nerves. What if Philip had changed his mind and didn't come, or he was only here to tell her it had all been a mistake, or . . .

And then, there he was, his sturdy RAF coat wrapped around him, his face just as she'd pictured it since the day he'd had to leave, and now smiling at her so widely his cheeks must be aching.

All thoughts of caution fled from her mind and she ran the last few yards, as his arms opened to her and she rushed into his embrace. He hadn't forgotten, decided not to come or changed his mind. He was here to see her and nothing else mattered.

'You're here,' he breathed, his breath warm against the top of her head. 'I was afraid you'd change your mind at the last minute.'

She looked up at him and laughed: the sheer absurdity of it was impossible. 'Never,' she said. 'But I was worried that you thought that too.'

'Never,' he echoed, hugging her tighter, his broad shoulders meaning he could embrace her easily. 'Never, ever imagine such a terrible thing. I've waited for this ever since I left last time. There was not a chance on Earth that I'd miss seeing you.'

'Me too,' Rose admitted, gazing at him in the strobing beams of the AA lights. She held her arms around him, registering that his coat was so heavy she struggled to reach all the way. And he was so tall. 'Nothing else matters. You came home all right and now you're here.'

He nodded and then released his hold a little. 'You must be freezing. Look, I can see your breath in the cold air.'

'Yours too.'

'We should go somewhere warmer. I'm sorry, I didn't want to plan anything in case I was delayed. Another evening we might go for dinner somewhere. How about a pub? There's one around the corner, if it hasn't been blown up, that is.'

Rose nodded, realising just how cold she was, now he had reminded her of it. 'Let's go,' she said, releasing her hug but tucking her arm through his, as he offered it to her. 'I know the place you mean and it's still standing, despite the Luftwaffe's best efforts.'

Philip nodded. 'Let's hope they don't return tonight.'

Rose glanced up at him again. 'We might be lucky. There hasn't been a big raid for a couple of weeks, just the occasional unexploded bomb and the like. The sirens usually go off before now if they're going to. I reckon we can dare to order ourselves a drink.' She flashed him another smile.

'And you don't mind? Going to a pub, I mean?'

'No, not at all.' Rose gave a chuckle. How fast everything was changing. Before the war, many people felt it was not respectable for a woman to be seen in a pub, and frowned upon anyone who was. Now most people were inclined to cut everybody some slack; they were all living through such difficult times – why begrudge someone an hour or two of relaxation? She wouldn't choose to go to one herself, but now Philip had suggested it, things were different.

The street was busy with workers making their way home after an extended day shift or on their way to a night shift, shoppers who'd stayed out late to catch a last-minute Christmas bargain, and others meeting up with family or friends. Many were taking advantage of the absence of the air-raid sirens, wondering if the run of luck would hold. Rose paid them absolutely no attention. All her senses were fixed on this man walking next to her, who somehow seemed completely familiar, even if she'd only known him for such a short space of time. Holding on to his arm felt absolutely right, as if she belonged next to him and had done so for ever.

Her reverie was broken as they approached the pub, its blackout blinds drawn but with sounds of people enjoying themselves echoing out into the dimly lit side street.

Philip guided her to the big wooden door. 'I've been in here a couple of times, before I joined up. It was friendly, nothing special, but the beer was good. I don't suppose you're a beer drinker?'

Rose laughed again as he pushed open the door and held it for her as she slipped through, with him following at once to minimise the amount of time that any light could be seen from outside.

'Not really,' she acknowledged. She wasn't a big drinker of alcohol of any sorts. It brought to mind Auntie Vera and family's annual Christmas morning visit, when the sherry had to be brought out. As a result, none of the Harrison girls could stand the stuff.

Philip had the advantage of height and could look over the heads of the crowd of punters, searching for somewhere suitable. 'Over there,' he said, nodding towards a corner to one side of the busy bar area. 'There's a nice table that's just come free. Follow me!' and he took her hand, neatly weaving between those standing around and chatting, to the little table next to a sturdy wooden cupboard. There were two seats, one more of a stool, the other upholstered in faded but very clean patterned canvas, with brass studs around the seat. 'There you are. I won't be a moment – what shall I get you?'

Rose looked up at him, now able to see him better in the warm light of the bar. He had swept off his hat and she could see his hair was shorter, meeting the air-force regulations. There was no sign of the injury that had caused her so much worry. She felt her shoulders sink in relief, and realised she hadn't even registered she had been storing up so much concern.

'Just a lemonade,' she replied.

He nodded with another broad grin and disappeared into the crowd. People must have got here early, coming straight from work, keen to have a pint before any air-raid warnings went off. Now some had risked a second.

Rose took off her coat and knitted gloves, folding the gloves into her handbag. She couldn't see anybody that she knew. It was a little too far from the hospital for those just finishing work, and her friends from Dalston preferred to drink nearer to home, if they went out at all. Her brother Peter was the one who knew most of the local watering holes, but he'd laughed that Daisy was catching him up fast. Rose didn't blame her; her youngest sister deserved to enjoy her free time, when she wasn't too tired to even think about it. She hugged her secret to herself. She wasn't embarrassed to be meeting Philip, far from it, but it all felt so new and precious that she didn't want to share these first moments. She wanted to savour every wonderful second, not be distracted by small talk with anyone else.

Philip came back towards the little table, bearing a glass of lemonade and a smaller, heavier-looking one with an inch of amber liquid in it. 'Whisky,' he explained, noticing her glance. 'Warms the heart.' He grinned. 'Care to try it?'

Rose shook her head. 'No, you have it. I did try it once – my father and big brother like it. But it burned the back of my throat and then made me sneeze.' She lifted her glass. 'Cheers.'

'Cheers.' Philip met her gaze with his dark eyes and Rose felt her heart beat faster. She could look into those eyes all day. It was like coming home. She lost all sense of time. Minutes might have passed, and she didn't care.

'How have you been . . . ?'

'What have you done since . . . ?'

They rushed to speak over one another and then both stopped, smiling in recognition of wanting desperately to know how the other had fared in the last few agonisingly hard months and yet, somehow, knowing that there was no rush. They had all the time in the world. 'You first,' Rose grinned, suddenly overwhelmingly happy. This connection was solid and real. They could talk or sit in silence, and it would not matter. She hadn't imagined it. This man was part of her, no matter what. It was as if they had shared lifetimes together already – and, she fervently wished that, if fate was kind to them, they would share a future too. This was what she had longed for, all those nights when she had wondered if they would ever see each other again. Now he was here. He was really here.

CHAPTER EIGHT

When she was little, Hope had often thrust her fingers into her ears to avoid the voices of the rest of her family. That was what she felt like doing now. Of course that was impossible; it would make her look childish and unprofessional. But it was the very idea of her entering the world of work that was causing the trouble.

'It's one day to Christmas – how can they expect you to leave your home? Do they think it will decorate itself and the food turn up out of the blue?' Vera fumed, her face puce with frustration and poor temper. 'You know very well that it will be extra difficult this year, now that Artie's here. You'll have to send your apologies.' She swept the crumbs from the kitchen countertop with a furious wave of the dishcloth.

Hope took a deep breath and prayed her voice didn't betray her seething emotions. 'I can't do that,' she pointed out levelly. 'They don't know that there's a new baby in the house. They need me today and that's all there is to it.' She rose from where she'd been grabbing a swift piece of toast at the kitchen table, and tipped her unfinished tea into the sink.

The calmness of her tone and argument set Vera off even more. 'What nonsense. You'll have to explain to them, then. They must have hundreds of volunteers – they can jolly well spare you, my girl.'

Hope smiled grimly. 'You know they don't have enough. That's why they had all those posters up a few months ago,' she added smartly, and hurried from the room.

In truth, she was nervous anyway, without her mother carrying on. What if she wasn't good enough? She'd have to learn so many different things, all at once. She'd begged her father to let her try driving their car but he had flatly refused. So she would be starting from scratch in that area. Then there would be all the first aid. All right, so she was confident that she wouldn't faint at the sight of blood or go to pieces in a crisis, but what if she did the wrong thing? It was all very well helping deliver Faith's baby – Rose had been there – but on a bomb-ravaged site, there might be no helpful senior nurse to guide her.

Would she even be fit enough? She'd heard that women ambulance workers had to attend PT sessions, which sounded horribly like school, where that had been her least favourite lesson. And everyone knew you had to be strong enough to lift a patient into the top bunk of an ambulance. Would she manage it? If only she were taller.

Her mind was whirling with self-doubt as she approached the church hall where the first session of training was to be held. They'd said it would be little more than filling in forms and getting to know one another to begin with, which hadn't sounded too scary, but Hope was more shaken by her mother's comments than she cared to let on. Yet why should she give up her ambition in order to help out with Artie?

He was a sweet little baby, she couldn't deny it, but he belonged to her sister. Besides, their youngest sister, Joy, was still at home and available to step in. She, however, had had a lifetime of getting out of things, always indulged because of her youth. Not any more, Hope thought grimly. Joy could damn well step up. She was eighteen now, high time that she made herself useful. And it wouldn't do Faith any harm to look after the baby a bit more – he was hers, after all, for heaven's sake.

It was not long past daybreak, at this darkest time of the year, and the hall's blackout blinds were being rolled up out of the way as Hope drew near. Then she brightened. There was a face she knew – not well, but not a stranger. It was one of the district nurses from the other end of Victory Walk. Now she remembered, they often helped out with first-aid training. All her cousins swore that they were the salt of the earth and Hope felt a little tingle of anticipation. She mustn't worry. She was here to learn, and to enjoy it.

'Welcome,' said the district nurse as Hope pushed open the door. 'I'm Nurse Lake, but you can call me Alice. Hang on, I've seen you before. Are you related to Rose Harrison?'

'Yes, she's my cousin,' Hope said with a small smile, and just like that, the ice was broken. As she was directed to the registration table, she could feel her excitement growing. Looking around, other women of different ages were gathering, all with a similar look of slight nervousness but mostly eagerness and determination. Hope nodded silently. Yes, she'd found her place.

Just because it was 24 December it did not mean that the tube trains stopped running. Daisy dearly wanted to be back with her family, making the final preparations for tomorrow, but that prospect looked as if it was a long way off yet. Some people hoped that Hitler would take a few days off over Christmas but she was not convinced.

Still, there were far fewer people crowding the platforms today and so she commandeered the platform worker with whom she got on best, Larry.

'We're going to redo the white lines,' she told him. 'Mr Rathbone says we're to do half a platform at a time, let the paint dry and then do the other half.' He'd said no such thing, of course. It was all her idea. She'd noticed it had been a problem for a while; extra white lines had been painted some time ago, not only right at the platform edge to show where it ended, but some distance back from it. This marked the boundary between where shelterers could sleep and where commuters could wait for their trains.

Of course, with so many people using the tube station, the lines had soon become dull, and people found them hard to see. Then there were arguments, some claiming because they couldn't see the paint, they had every right to take up extra sleeping space. This did not go down well with anyone waiting to get to work in the morning, having to step over bodies under blankets.

'Must we?' moaned Larry. He was usually helpful

but he too had probably been looking forward to leaving early, putting presents under the tree for his family. Daisy knew he lived with his sister and her small children – she'd seen him coming in after his lunchbreak with parcels under his arm. He'd shown her the teddy bear he'd found for his nephew.

He gave a little cough. It was his bad lungs that had caused him to fail his medical – something he was not proud of but could do little about.

'We must,' Daisy said staunchly. 'Just think, there will be fewer squabbles to sort out when the lines are all bright again. Even when we're down to emergency lighting in a bad raid, there will be no question about who's to go where. Won't that make our lives easier?'

Larry pulled a face. 'Suppose so. Go on, then, give me that brush.' He held out his hand and Daisy passed him a paint pot and wide-bristled brush.

'You do northbound, I'll do southbound. Race you,' she grinned.

It wasn't quite how she'd imagined spending Christmas Eve, but it was too good a chance to miss. Mr Rathbone would be pleased, even if the work hadn't been sanctioned by a memo from the Board. In theory it was up to the local authority. But Manor House fell between two such authorities, Hackney and Haringey, and so it was twice as difficult to get a straight answer about anything. The Board were trying to get their act together, as things were happening almost too fast for the authorities to keep up, but Daisy couldn't wait for the official orders.

In the meantime, somebody could get hurt down

here, and then there would be a big hoo-hah about who was to blame – nobody was going to get hurt if she had anything to do with it.

'Finished!' she cried triumphantly when she had finished her bit, even though her shout was drowned out by a train pulling in. Hastily she indicated to the few passengers to avoid the wet paint. Then she set off to find Larry and see how far he'd got. She wiped a smear of white gloss on her hanky, careful not to get it on her face.

Larry was almost done on the first section and had put up a big sign to keep passengers well away. 'Time for a tea break?' he suggested, wiping his hands on a rag. 'That was a good idea of yours – sorry. Mr Rathbone's. Just about any other day it would have been too busy.'

'Exactly,' said Daisy. She knew their boss would be pleased, even if it hadn't been ordered from the top brass, but even more pleased that he hadn't had to cope with it himself.

Later on Christmas Eve, Rose was battling with more nerves of her own. Normally if she was free towards the end of the afternoon, she'd have made a beeline for Victory Walk, to be part of the last preparations for Christmas dinner and to share the excitement, especially with her little brother, Robbie. But time was precious, and Philip wouldn't be home for long. War meant that everything that would otherwise have taken weeks or months had to be concertinaed into days.

So here she was, setting off to meet his parents. It felt too fast, too soon. But they didn't have the luxury of weeks to explore and get to know one another's feelings. After their evening in the noisy pub, they were as certain as they could be that this was no illusion, no trick of the war exaggerating their closeness. She had felt almost overwhelmed by the powerful sense of attraction to him, of knowing they belonged together, come what may. The look in his eyes had told her that he felt the same. And so Philip had asked her to take the next step – to join him and his family for tea – as who knew when they would next have the chance?

She had taken almost as much care with her appearance today as she had for her rendezvous with him, brushing her hair out once more so that it lay along her shoulders, adding a smart maroon beret, and a different scarf. The wool skirt had been brought out again, this time teamed with a respectable navy jumper with a crocheted collar.

Rose had seen Philip's father from a distance, as Mr Sutherland was the boss of the factory where her own father was foreman. Rose hoped that this would not be a problem. She knew her father was well-regarded at the firm, and that he'd always spoken highly of his employer. All the same, there was a social divide between them: Philip came from the world of bosses and owners, and she didn't.

She squared her shoulders as she walked along the street of houses near Victoria Park, still terraced, but so much bigger and smarter than Victory Walk. Too bad, she thought. They'd have to take her as they found her. She could not and would not pretend to be something that she was not. She was a highly trained and experienced nurse, treating patients from all quarters of society; if that wasn't good enough for them, then tough luck. Besides, she reasoned, they were Philip's parents; look how he'd turned out. He must have got his kindness and strong character from them. She needn't worry. Yes, there was the social divide, but the war was changing everything. It shouldn't matter.

She smoothed her skirt as she checked the number on the gleaming front door, painted a staid deep grey. Then she made her way to the stone steps that led up to it, her heart hammering even though she willed it not to. Before she could raise her hand to the perfectly polished knocker, the door swung open and there stood Philip, looking much more relaxed than when he'd been waiting outside the town hall.

'Come in, come in, you must be freezing,' he said, giving her a brief but heartfelt hug.

'No, no, it's not fully dark yet, it's not as bad as yesterday,' she protested, allowing him to take her coat and beret. She straightened her pretty scarf so that it sat just right, and swallowed hard. She wanted his parents to like her; it was so important to Philip that they did.

'Through here. We're through here.' She could see there were a number of rooms leading off this grand hallway, with its polished dark wooden floor over which lay a rich runner. She could tell it was top quality by the sensation of walking on it to the door he'd indicated. Rows of little lamps glowed along the corridor as it extended towards the back of the house, like a grander version of the ones at the hospital.

Before going into the room, which she could see was also lit by warm lamps, Philip took her hand and squeezed it. 'It will be fine,' he said quietly, nodding encouragingly, and she could have hugged him again for being so understanding.

They stepped over the threshold into the sitting room.

'Mother, Father, this is Rose. Rose, meet my parents.'

Two people got up from the sumptuously upholstered wing-back chairs they had been sitting in, one to either side of a roaring fire in a marble fireplace.

The man looked exactly like an older version of Philip: tall, hair cut very short although noticeably greying at the temples, a wide smile.

'Rose, good to meet you. Philip's told us so much about you.' He held out his hand and Rose shook it, registering the straightforward firmness of his grip.

'Pleased to meet you,' she said, relieved that her voice sounded normal and did not squeak with nerves.

The woman came forward a little more slowly. She had hair the same colour as Philip's – deep nut brown – and very pale skin, her lips forming a smile that did not quite reach her eyes. 'Rose. How delightful. Yes, we've heard all about you.'

Rose shook the outstretched hand, which was rather cold. Was it her imagination or had Philip's mother paused slightly too long on the word 'all', almost drawling it out? No, it was just anxiety making her think that.

'Of course, you're Robert Harrison's girl,' Mr Sutherland went on, returning to his seat. 'Do sit down,

80

yes, that's right. Well, he's a splendid chap, can't say a word against him. Couldn't run the place without him. So it's no surprise that you're nursing. A fine job, fine job.'

'Thank you,' said Rose, somewhat overwhelmed. 'Yes, I love nursing. Always have, from the very first day.'

Mrs Sutherland inclined her head slightly. 'You're at Hackney Hospital, aren't you?'

Rose thought that an odd question. Obviously that was where she worked. Otherwise she would never have met Philip. Still, it felt rude to point this out. 'Yes, over at Homerton,' she said carefully.

'Yes, quite. Well, Philip received adequate care there, I cannot deny. Of course, we discussed moving him, having someone from Harley Street take a look, but we were told that to do that might have put him at further risk, so in the end we decided against it.' The woman turned towards the door. 'You'll take some tea?'

'Yes please.' Anything to give her something to do with her hands, Rose thought. 'And you made the right decision, without a doubt. Any unnecessary disturbance would not have been helpful.' She prided herself on the calm way she managed to say this, when she could have screamed at the implied slur on her colleagues.

Philip's mother waved at the doorway and Rose caught a movement at the corner of her eye. Somebody had been standing there, waiting for instructions. A far cry from Victory Walk, indeed.

Mr Sutherland clasped his hands and leant forward in his chair. 'Your parents will be very busy getting ready for Christmas tomorrow, I'm sure. Aren't there quite a few of you at home?'

Rose appreciated the way he was trying to make conversation and moving away from the issue of her hospital's competence. 'Not so many nowadays,' she explained. 'Two of us are away in the services. My sister Clover works on the searchlights at a base somewhere near the south coast, and Peter's stationed with the army up in East Anglia.'

Philip nodded in admiration. 'We have some girls who do that on our base. I don't know how they do it – manoeuvre those huge searchlights when they must be bitterly cold in the dead of night. Putting themselves right in the line of danger.'

'Clover loves it,' Rose said, but Mrs Sutherland chipped in.

'Of course our daughter, Charlotte, has just joined the WAAF. We know it will be difficult for her but you do get a better class of recruits there.'

Mr Sutherland cleared his throat in the manner of one who had heard all this many times before, but Philip waded in.

'You know that's not why she's done it, Mother. She knows she'll have to sign up for some sort of war work, and that was what appealed to her most. Give her half a chance and she'll want to be a pilot.'

Rose shifted awkwardly, realising she was caught in the middle of a long-running argument.

'I cannot imagine that the air force will let it come to that! The very idea!' Mrs Sutherland made a face that reminded Rose of when Robbie had decided to try the taste of beer, grabbing Peter's half-full bottle when he'd been home on leave. Disgust wasn't a strong enough word to describe it. 'No, she's bound to stay safe on the ground. Some suitable sort of administrative support, I dare say. And mixing with her own kind.'

'Now then, we'll worry about it if and when she mentions it again,' Mr Sutherland said in a placatory tone. He turned in his seat. 'Ah, here comes the tea,' he said in evident relief.

As soon as Mrs Sutherland was distracted by taking her cup and saucer of fine bone china, Rose turned to Philip to catch his eye. She needed some kind of clue to what was going on. She had walked into a situation not of her own making but it was causing her to feel very uncomfortable.

He gave her a sudden wink, which made everything seem better. He was no happier with his mother's behaviour than she was, but now was not the time to ask him more. She awkwardly took a cup offered by the maid, a middle-aged woman in a stiff white apron over a dark dress, as if she'd come from the previous era. It was very strange to be served in such a fashion. Rose declined the rare offer of proper lumps of sugar; there was no point in reviving a taste for it when she couldn't rely on getting it again.

Thankfully Mr Sutherland began to tell an anecdote about Philip when he was younger, and Rose could enjoy her tea without saying something else to provoke Mrs Sutherland. She nodded at the right moments but her heart was sinking. Despite her nerves she had been looking forward to meeting Philip's parents, but now she was counting the minutes until she could make her escape without being impolite. Surely they couldn't expect her to stay for long. They'd have Christmas preparations to make too – or perhaps the maid did it all. Maybe she should just try harder to see things from their point of view, make an effort to win them over somehow.

Philip joined in and pointed out where his father had misremembered, which Rose thought brought out how alike they were, down to similar gestures and the way they sat forward in a chair. She was glad; if he was going to resemble either parent, much better that it was his father. His mother had leant back, delicately sipping her own tea, her flinty grey eyes following everything, no doubt looking for the right moment to complain about something else.

Rose finished her tea and set the cup and saucer down on an elegant side table of golden wood. It was far more refined than anything in her own house; then again, with all of them crammed into a smaller space and Robbie still running around at top speed indoors and out, it wouldn't have survived long. Immediately the maid glided in and took the empty cup without making a sound.

Rose nodded to her to thank her, but she was gone in a flash.

'And will you be going back to the hospital this evening?' Mrs Sutherland asked, turning her gaze onto Rose once more. It could have been an innocent question but Rose had had experience of such things in the ward meetings. It was nothing of the kind; it was barbed, and intended as a dismissal. In the opinion of one of the hosts, she had overstayed her welcome.

Nevertheless, she took care to reply politely. 'No,' she said, 'I'll be staying with my parents, so that I can help out first thing in the morning. There's nothing like that moment when the turkey goes into the oven, and it has to be early enough to be cooked through by the time we all sit down to eat. So someone has to make sure all the vegetables are peeled and ready to roast alongside it.'

Mrs Sutherland gave that smile again, which could have been mistaken for warmth if you didn't watch her eyes. 'I'm sure you're right,' she replied. 'How commendable.'

The woman had never prepared a roast in her life, Rose would swear on it.

Philip picked up on the change of tone and turned directly to Rose. 'Then I'll walk you to your bus stop. It'll be dark by now. We all know there are more accidents in the blackout than get reported in the papers.'

Rose got to her feet. 'That's true enough. We see some of the results of that at the hospital.' She turned to her hosts, knowing she must remember her manners no matter what. 'Thank you so much for the tea. It's been a pleasure to meet you.'

Mr Sutherland came across and shook her hand again. 'No, thank you for coming. We're so pleased you could do so at such short notice. We hope to see you again soon.'

'Indeed,' said Mrs Sutherland, keeping to the bare minimum that might be acceptable.

Philip guided her to the door and into the hall, where the maid stood waiting with their coats. 'You go back to the warm kitchen, Bartlett. You'll be rushed off your feet soon enough – better make the most of any free time while you can.' The woman shot him a grateful look and disappeared down the long corridor.

He helped Rose back into her good coat, waiting while she settled her beret on her head. Then he took her arm and they stepped out into the cold night air, the stars visible above them as there were no streetlights. No air-raid siren yet, either.

Once they were on the pavement he let out a deep breath. 'Sorry about that,' he said. 'You mustn't take it personally. She's concerned for my sister.'

Rose looked up at him. 'I'll try not to. But . . . but, Philip. Some of that was aimed right at me, for being a nurse. Or at least, not being a Harley Street nurse.'

He shook his head. 'It's what she's like. Honestly, she'll find a way to get under anyone's skin. She's my mother and I love her, but I know she can be difficult. Say you'll put up with her? For me?'

Rose sighed and knew she could not resist agreeing to anything he asked of her. 'I'll try. We aren't responsible for our family, I know.' Her mind flew to Aunt Vera and the way she carried on, which pushed everyone to the limits of their tolerance.

'My father loved you, I could tell.' Philip was determined to make the best of a tricky situation.

'He was lovely. I can see why Pa enjoys working for him.' Rose slowed, holding back now, whereas before she had been walking along with her arm tucked into his. She could not bear to leave without knowing when she would see him again. 'Look, I know tomorrow is a day for family but I don't suppose you could slip away for an hour or so? Come and meet my lot. They're dying to see what you're like. Come after you've eaten, for a mince pie and a tot of Pa's whisky. After all, he won't have anyone else to share it with.'

He gazed at her in delight. 'Shall I? Are you sure they won't mind?'

Rose nodded confidently. 'Absolutely sure.'

'Well, in that case, I'd love to.' Then he bent his head to hers and kissed her, gently at first, and then more passionately, there in the street but with only the starlight illuminating them. Rose knew then that she would put up with anything to continue to see him.

CHAPTER NINE

'So, how did it go?' Daisy cornered Hope in the kitchen of Vera's house, where the aroma of roasting turkey and vegetables was making her mouth water. They were breaking with the family tradition – this Christmas morning the Harrisons had come over to Vera's rather than the other way round. Vera had declared that Faith needed help with Artie at all times and could not be left on her own with him for so long.

'Sure you don't want some sherry?' Hope teased.

'No, and you know I don't. What I do want to know is how you got on yesterday. Rose has stayed at home to keep an eye on the food and she's threatened me with horrible punishments if you don't tell me so that I can report back.' Daisy reached out and helped herself to a raw carrot.

Hope swept a short blonde wave of hair from her forehead. 'It was hard work as there was so much to sort out and make sense of, but it's going to be fun.' She grinned and her broad face lit up. 'We had to get the tedious forms out of the way to begin with and then we did some first aid. I know it was only the tip of the iceberg, but I'm certain I'm going to enjoy it. We just did the basics, what we might expect to find after a bomb has hit and how to assess the scene, what to prioritise. Not that I'll be deciding that for a while,' she added, reaching for a carrot herself. 'Rose would be proud of me – I put my hand up and got most of the answers right. Like, you don't just bundle in and move everybody. You could cause more harm than good that way.'

Daisy nodded. 'I've done a little bit, in case I have to help out at work.' She paused and sighed. 'I'm worried about it, really. All those people that come to shelter on the tube platforms, crammed in together. Even though it's winter, it gets terribly hot and humid down there. Rose says it's a health hazard. That's apart from the risks of accident.'

Hope raised her eyebrows. 'Maybe you should do a proper course. The Red Cross run them, or St John Ambulance. Or I could ask the district nurse who taught us yesterday.'

Daisy gave a small smile. 'Yes, perhaps I should. I'll see if work will pay or at least let me have a bit of extra time to do it. It'd set my mind at rest.' She paused as a wail came from the main living room in the front of the house.

'Artie,' said Hope unnecessarily. 'He's woken up again.'

'Come on, we should go through,' Daisy said, knowing that her cousin found the annual gathering as much of a chore as she did.

Faith was sitting in pride of place in the big front room, on the best chair, to one side of the bay window. She had a muslin napkin on her lap but the baby was being held by Patty, who rocked him expertly while patting his back. 'There, there. It's all strange when you first wake up, isn't it?' she murmured, with a big smile on her face. Daisy couldn't help smiling back. Her mother loved babies. Faith had handed him over to her aunt the moment Patty stepped through the door.

Uncle Arthur stood with his back to the fire, his chest puffed out in its tweed waistcoat. 'A toast,' he announced, raising his sherry glass. 'Good health to all.'

Bert dutifully raised his glass, and Robbie and Joy lifted their glasses of ginger cordial half-heartedly. Vera had a smaller sherry glass with a delicate twisted stem, which she lifted but did not drink from. 'Mustn't get carried away.' She made a face.

Fat chance of that, thought Daisy.

Faith simpered. 'Of course I can't touch a drop, as I'm feeding Artie. We don't want him getting a taste for sherry, or not yet anyway.' She grinned and looked around to check her audience was paying attention. 'Of course, not everybody gets the hang of feeding their baby, but the district nurses say I'm managing extremely well. One of the best they've seen, in fact.' Daisy gave her cousin a nod, but then turned back to Hope.

'When do you start learning to drive?' she asked, while the rest of the family was occupied with toasts and Artie. 'They'll want you to do that as soon as possible, won't they?'

Hope grinned happily. 'Oh, yes, it's very important. Driving, and maintenance too.'

'Your parents won't like that,' Daisy predicted.

'They won't,' Hope said cheerfully. 'Doesn't matter. It's what the ambulance service needs. If all's well, I start in a few days – perhaps before New Year! Imagine!' And her face told Daisy that this was the best Christmas present that her cousin had ever been given.

'Rose has got a boyfriend, a boyfriend, a boyfriend,' Robbie half sang, half shouted as the Harrisons let themselves back into their own house, having made good their escape after one too many sherries in Bert's case.

'Quiet, Robbie,' Patty said, but more with a view to stopping him from disturbing their neighbours' celebrations. She couldn't argue that it was gossip or untrue, not now that Rose had said they were to expect a visit from the young man himself. She wished she had more time to tidy up. He might be Rose's boyfriend but he was also the boss's son, and would no doubt expect things to be just so, rather than the pandemonium that usually accompanied a Harrison family Christmas.

'Daisy, you go and see how Rose is getting on,' she fretted. 'I'll just run a duster round the hallway and front room.'

Rose emerged from the kitchen doorway, steam billowing behind her. 'You'll do no such thing, Ma. I know what you're thinking. Philip will take us as he finds us. He won't be running a finger along the windowsills, looking for dust or smudges.'

Patty looked doubtful. 'But he's bound to expect . . .'

Rose shook her head, smiling. 'He doesn't expect anything special. He's coming to meet our family, not to inspect the place. Now come on through here and

91

check I've got everything right. The Brussels sprouts are all set to go.'

Robbie pulled a face and Daisy shoved him out of the way before anyone could see. 'Behave,' she muttered into his ear. 'Ma and Rose have gone to a lot of trouble to give you a lovely meal and, come to think of it, so have I. So don't complain, and try to look grateful.'

'But I hate sprouts,' Robbie moaned, glaring at his sister. Daisy shook her head, although she secretly agreed with him.

'Away upstairs and get your slippers on. Did you manage to spill cordial down your best shirt? I thought so. Better change that too while you're about it.'

Robbie dashed up to his bedroom, clearly glad to get away from the topic of vegetables he didn't like.

The turkey had been cooked to perfection and Bert had recovered from the sherries enough to carve it properly. The roast veg were delicious, and even the sprouts had all been eaten, although not very many by Robbie. Somehow Patty had managed to get hold of the ingredients to make a creamy golden custard to go with the plum pudding, which Rose knew was no mean feat. Now they were all gathered in the front room, their newly opened presents strewn over the floor. Patty gradually collected up the wrapping paper and refolded it, to be used again next year. Rose sighed in contentment. Auntie Vera might have a newer three-piece suite and fitted carpets, but this room was far cosier and more inviting.

Daisy had offered to start on the washing-up, which

usually took several goes, and Rose had been happy to let her. She herself was delighted with her new gloves, knitted in supposed secrecy by Patty, in a maroon the exact shade of her beret. She was wearing them now, making them into silly puppets to amuse Robbie. 'Look, if I pull the fingers up like this it looks like Snuffles and his long ears. Don't you think?'

Robbie huffed but they could all tell he was pleased that his pet rabbit hadn't been forgotten in all the hubbub, even though it was strictly banned from the front room after an unfortunate accident last time.

Rose cheerfully began to tickle him and Robbie laughed so hard that everyone in the room missed the sound of the knock at the door. So when Philip came into the warm room, having been let in by a suds-covered Daisy, it was to find Rose red in the face from laughing, with gloves half on, half off her hands, her little brother squirming on her lap.

'Oh.' She looked up and saw him standing there, half embarrassed that he should see her like this. But then he gave his widest smile. 'Hello,' he said, stepping forward, 'you must be Robbie,' just as Robbie fell off Rose's lap and landed in a heap on the floor, surrounded by the remaining scrunched-up wrapping paper and string.

Robbie looked up and nodded happily. 'You're the boyfriend,' he said wickedly.

'I'm Philip,' said Philip, 'and I'm very pleased to meet you.' They could tell he meant it, and Patty smiled in welcome and evident relief. This man didn't care about the chaos and mess after a Christmas dinner. He cared about Rose – anyone could see that – and judging from the expression on her eldest's face, she cared deeply about him too. That was what mattered, when it came down to it.

'Sit down, sit down. Robbie, get out of the way and let the poor man stretch out his legs. He'll have walked all this way and he'll want to take the weight off his feet. You take this chair, Philip, nice and near the fire. Will you have a cup of tea and a mince pie?' She rose, her hands automatically going to where her apron was usually tied about her waist, but today she was in her good skirt and blouse, for the occasion.

Bert stood up and held out his hand. 'Nonsense, he'll want a little something a bit stronger,' he predicted.

'Oh, Bert, do you think you should? You had all those sherries earlier,' Patty protested, but Bert simply grinned.

'I've eaten enough to soak up a barrel-load of sherry,' he pointed out, hitching up his shirtsleeves. 'A drop of Scotch is what's called for right now. You stay there, Philip, and I will fetch you a wee dram.'

Philip grinned happily. 'I'd be glad to,' he said, and Rose gazed at him. He was going to get on with her father, she could tell, and now that Patty had given in to the inevitable and stopped fussing, he would love her too.

Bert poured a generous glug of Scotch into two chunky glasses, only ever used for special occasions, and then insisted on filling a small pottery jug with cold water so that Philip could add a splash if he wanted to. 'That's what my old comrade Angus told me to do. We served together in the last war,' he added quietly, as he rarely mentioned it. 'When I was about your age, I'd say.'

Philip nodded. 'Thank you, Mr Harrison. My father was in that one too.'

'I know,' said Bert, and it made Rose realise that their two fathers had maybe talked about more than the smooth running of the factory. But that was for another day. She wouldn't think about sad things now.

Daisy came in, wiping her hands on a tea towel, a festive one with squiggles of green to represent holly leaves. 'We ought to play a game!' she said. 'How about Charades? Do you know how to play, Philip? I'd better warn you, don't give Robbie any film titles because he knows them all and he'll win if you let him.'

'I do know. We play it when we're waiting for the planes,' he said. 'So, young Robbie, you have a challenger in the room. Beware.' Robbie got to his feet and struck a strongman pose, while Philip turned quietly to Rose. 'We never play this at home, though. My mother won't have it. So I'm very pleased to get in some practice.'

Rose nodded happily. 'Robbie will still beat you,' she predicted.

Philip proved to be a tough competitor, however, and didn't mind making a fool of himself at all. His mime of Sherlock Holmes's famous deerstalker hat brought tears of laughter to Patty's eyes, and he could do a pretty good imitation of Charlie Chaplin as well.

'It's not fair!' Robbie protested. 'He's seen more films than I have.'

'Well, it's poor for your character to be allowed to win,' Rose told him severely. 'You'd hate it if you thought we just let you be the champion all the time, wouldn't you?'

Robbie wiped his nose on the back of his hand. 'Suppose so,' he agreed, as Patty automatically exclaimed, 'Hanky!'

After two rounds of Charades they decided it was a draw, and that the prize of first pick from the traditional box of jellied fruits should be shared between Philip and Robbie.

'Now how about Monopoly?' Daisy suggested, to Bert's delight, but Philip rose to his feet.

'I'd better go before you make a start,' he said apologetically. 'It can go on for hours, can't it? And I really should be getting back before too long.'

Rose got up as well, briefly and silently cursing Daisy for bringing out the tattered old box with the game inside, wanting this afternoon to go on for ever. Or evening, she realised, as she followed her guest into the hallway, which was now shadowy in the last vestiges of dusk coming through the window above the front door.

She was about to reach for his coat, when she felt his arms go around her waist. 'Wait a moment,' he murmured, drawing her back against his warm chest in its fine cotton shirt. 'Let's just wait a moment, like this.'

'All right.' Rose could feel the warmth coming from his mouth as he spoke. A bubble of excitement formed in her throat. Philip might have the grand house, much grander than Auntie Vera's, but he'd been happy here, sitting on the floor to act out Buster Keaton falling over, messing about with Robbie, drinking whisky with her father.

As if to confirm it, he whispered, 'I wish I didn't have to go. Your family really know how to celebrate Christmas.'

Rose turned in his arms to face him. 'We try,' she replied, suddenly shy. Not so much for herself, but somehow protective of her family, rubbing along without much money or room to spare.

'No, you do. We had expensive wine with our meal and lit the candelabra, all the fancy business my mother insists upon. But that's not the spirit of Christmas, is it? If anything, it takes away all the joy.' He swallowed hard. 'Your family know how to enjoy themselves, and I could tell that you'd all opened your presents together. It's like a proper celebration, of everything this time of year is meant to mean. Being with people who are special to you, treating them well, sharing food and drink. I miss that, sometimes.'

Rose didn't know what to say, so she said nothing, burrowing her hands into the warm pockets of his wool jacket. She gave a small sigh of contentment.

'I'm so glad you came,' she said eventually. 'I know it was all a bit last-minute, but I wanted you to meet my family. They are all very important to me.'

'I can tell.' For a moment they stood silently together.

Then a shout from within the living room brought them out of their shared dream and back to earth. 'Arguing over who has the top hat, I expect,' Rose said.

'I must go.' Philip buttoned his jacket against the winter's cold and pulled on his big airman's coat.

'Tomorrow's my last day of leave. Will you have any time to meet up, even if only for a short while? A walk in the park, something like that?'

Rose thought. 'I'm on late shift tomorrow. Lunchtime, maybe? But won't your parents mind?'

Philip smiled and she could just about make out the shape of his mouth in the dim light. 'Doesn't matter,' he said. 'The most important thing is to see you. Now I've found you I'm never, ever going to let you go.'

CHAPTER TEN

Hope could not remember having had a better day. She'd been bombarded with new things to learn, a session on what to do with broken bones being the first lesson. Then, after a hurried lunch break of the fishpaste sandwiches she'd thrown together that morning, it was on to the ambulances.

Her instructor was a man who must have been some years older than her own father, but far more friendly. His eyes twinkled as he grandly opened the passenger-side door to her. 'Welcome aboard,' he said. 'I'm James Allen, but you can call me Jimmy. No point in standing on ceremony. I drove these things in the last war, over in France and over here. If I could get them through then, I'm sure I can teach you to do what's needed here now.'

Hope held out her hand. 'Pleased to meet you, Jimmy.' She wondered if he had a title such as Captain, but if he didn't want to use it, then that was his business. 'I'm Hope. Hope Potter.'

Jimmy shook her hand in a firm grip. 'What we'll do is go for a little spin. Not a long one – we mustn't waste petrol – but I'll talk you through every stage of how this beast works, and then you can have a go.'

Hope had shivered in delight. At last, she'd be behind the wheel.

Jimmy commentated in his gravelly voice as he drove along. 'Sorry about the bumps, young Hope. We requested a nice smooth surface for your first lessons but Jerry had other ideas. Still, this'll be what you'll have to cope with day to day.'

Hope nodded, knowing all too well what the roads and pavements were like all over Hackney and beyond. She'd come close to twisting her ankle on a cracked kerb, and counted herself lucky it had been nothing worse.

'Now look at what I'm doing. This is changing gear, see. You have to do that for different speeds – do you ride a bicycle? Then you know what I mean. On this machine you must what we call double declutch. Sounds worse than it is. Now watch carefully.'

Hope stared at what he was doing, certain that she would never master the movement. But an hour later, she herself was behind the wheel and beginning to get the hang of the mysteries of double-declutching. 'We'll do it over and over again until you don't even have to think about it,' Jimmy told her. 'You'll have quite enough on your mind most of the time, you won't want to be trying to recall when to press the pedal and when to move the gearstick. Good, now pull over next to that garage and we'll try reversing.'

It took Hope a few goes to understand what she should do, but before long she was steering accurately backwards as well as forwards. Jimmy was delighted. 'You're a natural,' he proclaimed. 'Soon have you backing around corners and parking in narrow spaces. But that's enough for one day. Take us back to the depot, young lady. Let's see if you can remember the way.'

At least that was no problem, as Hope was driving around her home turf. She'd wondered if she would see anybody she knew, wanting to show off her new skills, but now it was getting dark. Never mind, there would be other chances for that. She dodged the final few potholes and pulled up outside the depot, where several of her fellow trainees had already parked. She noted privately that she was more accurate than most of them.

'Now we reap our rewards. They'll have tea all ready for us and maybe some biscuits too,' Jimmy said, rubbing his hands. 'Thirsty work, all this talking. And I dare say you are starving hungry, young Hope. Takes up a fair amount of energy, learning to drive.'

Hope nodded. 'Now you come to mention it, I am a bit peckish.' She followed him into the depot, hastily swinging the big door shut behind them, as it was lit with a mixture of new electric lighting and Tilley lamps. Sure enough, there were home-made flapjacks on offer, and she tucked in happily.

This was what she had signed up for. Here were other women, some around her age and some older, all ready to throw themselves into their training and drive in whatever conditions they were required to. Not one of them doubted that she could do it, and that she'd be as good as the men who'd had to leave to join one of the armed services. There was none of that confidence-sapping stay-out-of-danger attitude that Hope put up with at home. You couldn't accept the driving lessons and then refuse to go out when the bombs fell.

'And I've left my three nippers with my ma,' one of the

101

other women was saying, who was maybe in her early thirties. 'I'd best be getting back to them now. They like me to be there when it's bedtime. At least there hasn't been a big raid for weeks now, so with luck they'll get another decent night's sleep. I'll see you all next time.'

Hope knew that she ought to be getting back, but she was enjoying herself so much she was reluctant to return home. No doubt Artie would be crying, and everyone would be running around trying to stop him. She felt exhausted from lack of sleep, and she wasn't even the one feeding him. Still, his wails woke her several times a night. She could hear footsteps from her parents' room heading for Faith's, as her mother stepped in to help, but even her many years of experience couldn't always comfort the little boy. Vera tried to explain to them all that some babies were just like that, but Hope was running out of patience.

She'd refill her teacup one last time, and there was half a flapjack on its own on the plate – it would be rude to leave it.

Jimmy nodded sagely. 'You have it, young Hope. You deserve it for working so hard this afternoon.' She needed no second telling.

Then, just as she was tidying away her plate and cup in the corner of the big, chilly room that had been adapted into a makeshift kitchen area, the all-too-familiar noise began. The siren broke the hum of conversation, cutting through their chatter.

Hope looked around at the faces of these people that until a short while ago she had not known existed. She felt suspended in space. What should she do? Would they expect her to go home to the safety of the Anderson shelter or head for a closer public one? Jimmy's chin went up and he turned to her.

'Well, no time like the present to learn on the job,' he declared. 'Grab yourself one of those waterproof coats, young Hope. You'll all be getting them anyway so better claim yours now. Then you can come with me. I'll drive, and you can watch what it's really like.'

For a moment Hope was struck with disbelief. It was all too fast, and she felt far from ready. But at least now she knew her way around the ambulance, what it carried and where things were kept. There would be others who knew what to do. She would be a useful extra pair of hands.

She ran to find a coat.

The air-raid siren started to wail and the overhead lights on the ward began flickering. Rose groaned to herself. Just as the shifts were about to change, too. She had been looking forward to a quiet evening to herself, catching up on mending and perhaps finding an hour to read her book. She would not leave her patients, though, or at least not until an equally senior nurse turned up to relieve her.

It had been too much to hope that the raids had stopped altogether. It had simply been a lull, nothing more. Here we go again, she thought, checking all the patients' notes were up to date and ready to hand over, when the time came. Meanwhile they would all have to be on the alert and ready to evacuate the ward if things became more heated.

She also had to reassure her younger colleagues, one or two of whom she'd overheard swearing that the raids had finished for good and that Hitler was in retreat. She'd known then that they were being too optimistic, but hadn't wanted to spoil their moment of cheerfulness. Now she glanced around to see if they were still on duty.

Effie caught her glance and came hurrying over, her eyes wide. 'Oh, no, Nurse Harrison, it's starting all over again. I can hardly believe it.' Her voice cracked and she sounded as if she might cry.

'Now then, Nurse Jenkins. Chin up. Mustn't upset the patients,' Rose said, giving the young woman a meaningful look. It would do nobody any good if the staff started to go to pieces. 'You're meant to be going off shift, aren't you? Perhaps you should make for the basements until we get the all-clear. Or do you have somewhere else to go?'

The young nurse gulped, trying to stay calm and collected. After a moment, she nodded. 'Me auntie lives close by, just off Chatsworth Road. Sometimes I've gone to hers if there was a raid and not enough time to go home. She goes to her church hall. They're nice to me there, seeing as they know me, like.'

Rose nodded. That seemed like a reasonable idea. After all, room in the hospital basements would be at a premium if the raid was a bad one.

'Well, best you get going,' she said. Effie didn't move. 'What's wrong, Nurse Jenkins? Would you rather stay here after all?'

Effie's face was stricken. 'No, no, it's not that . . .

it's silly, really. I got my hopes up that it was nearly over and now it's happening all over again. It's daft; we got used to it night after night. I'll be all right in a minute,' she added, screwing her hands together to stop them from shaking.

Rose understood what she meant. It was having your hopes dashed that hurt. When they'd been in the throes of the nightly raids, all autumn long, there'd been no room for such ideas.

'Are any of your colleagues going that way? Is Coral coming off duty, perhaps?' She knew the two young nurses often worked the same shifts, although the Welsh girl had been moved to a different ward to cover staff shortages.

'Coral did an early one; she'll be safe already,' Effie said sadly. 'I ain't that close to any of the others, not really.'

Rose had failed to notice the ward door to the corridor swinging open, but now she turned as footsteps approached, barely audible above the siren.

'Good afternoon, Nurse Harrison, or rather, good evening. Such a nuisance, isn't it?' It was the creepy surgeon, Mr Prendergast. He was very skilled at appearing out of nowhere, Rose had to give him that.

'And Nurse Jenkins. My dear, whatever is the matter?'

Effie's attempts at self-control had faded and now she was trembling all over. 'I'm just a bit worried about the raid. You know, after we haven't had one for a bit,' she admitted quietly, gazing at the floor.

Rose felt she had to get both of them on their way.

105

'Yes, Nurse Jenkins has just decided to go to a local shelter where she has family,' she said firmly.

Mr Prendergast nodded in a wise fashion. 'That seems extremely sensible. Which one is that?'

Effie swallowed hard and managed to reply, 'Just off Chatsworth Road. It's up this end, it's not far at all. The church hall.'

Mr Prendergast beamed. 'My dear young lady, as it happens I am heading that way myself. Why don't I escort you? Then you needn't worry about getting there safely. You hear such stories about the blackout, but this way you'd be in good hands.'

Rose cringed and was tempted to tell Effie to go to the basements after all, as she would not trust the surgeon as far as she could throw him. But the girl should go to her aunt, if that's what she had done before. Besides, what could he do in a five-minute walk to a church hall? She was allowing her own views to bias the situation.

'Well, then, that's the ideal solution,' she said heartily, revealing none of her inner misgivings. 'Off you go, Effie. Mr Prendergast will look after you.'

He beamed again. 'Of course. I'll take very good care of you.'

Effie smiled in relief. 'Ooh, would you, Mr Prendergast? I'd be ever so grateful.'

Hope had rarely been caught out in the middle of a raid. She'd nearly always been within running distance of the family shelter in the garden. Even if she'd been out to the cinema or with former colleagues from the WVS, she'd found her way to a public shelter, or a friend's house. The closest she'd been to danger had probably been the night Artie was born, before they decided to move under the stairs.

Now she was racing through the streets, as Jimmy sped towards the first destination the ARP had passed to them.

When he had been teaching her earlier in the day he'd been steady, and encouraged her to be cautious. Now he was the total opposite, dodging potholes, swerving around newly toppled chunks of buildings. 'Whoops, mind that bit of chimney,' he said cheerily, as Hope held on tightly to her seat and wondered where her calm tutor had gone.

She could just about see where they were going, because as well as the ever-present strobing AA searchlights, the ambulance had cowled headlights. They didn't light up the buildings ahead but at least she could make out the road directly in front of them. Now and again it was also lit up by falling embers or burning timbers tumbling from roofs. The sky was growing more and more orange as fires took hold.

Hope could smell the smoke, and it caught in her throat. She risked moving one hand to check that she still had her gas mask slung across her, then hastily grabbed hold of the seat again as Jimmy took a corner without slowing down.

'Are we nearly there?' she croaked.

'Not far. It's by the Downs,' Jimmy replied, changing gear yet again and bumping over a fallen gatepost. 'High-explosive damage, they think.'

Hope nodded but he couldn't see, as he was concentrating hard on avoiding being hit with debris. She threw up one hand on instinct as a slate seemed to be heading straight for the windscreen, but he swerved at the last minute and the slate shattered on the ground just past the side panel. Hope breathed out, struggling to take it all in.

'There. That'll be it. Get that waterproof coat on, young Hope.' Jimmy swung the vehicle in tight to the kerb, right behind what looked like a badly dented van and a bicycle trapped under its front wheels. To one side a house was blazing, its top floor alight but a family running out of the front door.

'It's not raining,' Hope protested, snatching up the coat anyway.

'No, but the fire-fighters will be here soon and then it'll be water, water everywhere,' Jimmy explained, jumping from the cab. 'Follow me, and don't touch anything unless I tell you.'

Hope had no time to object or ask more questions as she was off at a run, belying his age. The smoke was thick and the air hot, even though it was a December evening. Her eyes streamed as she followed Jimmy, his outline hard to make out the closer he got to the fire. Just discernible in front of the house was a tall figure, wearing the distinctive helmet of an ARP warden. Jimmy came to a halt beside him and the two men began exchanging hurried words.

Jimmy turned as she caught them up. 'Hope, this is Stan Banham. One of the best,' he grinned. 'So you're in luck. Mr Banham has organised everything in order of priority. Quick test. What do you think that will be?'

Hope didn't have time to dither. 'Crashed van and crushed bicycle – what about the driver and the cyclist?' she said, wiping her eyes as they stung with soot.

Jimmy nodded. 'Not bad.' He pulled her out of the way of another lump of burning debris. 'Here, we'll stand closer to this wall, it'll shelter us. As it happens the driver is more shaken than anything else, and ARP have escorted the cyclist to a first-aid post to treat what looks like a broken wrist. Next?'

'That family. I saw children among them. They'd been inside the burning house. Burns, smoke inhalation, any other injuries – they need checking.'

'Excellent.' Jimmy nodded and then beckoned her to follow. 'Hard to tell from the way they were running down their front path but one of the kiddies seemed to be limping. Might have had to jump down the stairs or out of a bunk bed, we don't know. They're just across there, so over we go.'

Huddled in the lee of another tall garden wall stood the family, clearly in shock, and the youngest children crying as they hugged their mother's knees. An older child, a boy, stood transfixed, staring at the remains of his home. A teddy bear dangled from his hand.

'Look at that poor child,' Hope breathed, and Jimmy took a moment to turn to her.

'Yes, indeed. It's very sad all round,' he said. 'But it won't do them any good for you to be anything other than cheerful and professional. Sympathy is fine but they need practical help right now. Got that?'

'Of course,' Hope said, hoping she sounded convincing. The smell, the heat, the state of the family were threatening to overwhelm her – especially after the intense training day she'd had.

Jimmy had reached the family and was already crouching to the level of the youngest children, talking to them calmly, as their mother protectively leant over them. There was a man there too and, closer up, Hope could see he wore army trousers but was in just his vest on top. 'Me first leave for months,' he was saying in a shaky voice to Mr Banham, the ARP warden. 'Now we ain't got nowhere to go.'

The warden inclined his head in understanding. 'But are all the children here? There's nobody still inside?'

The man shook his head slowly. 'No. We're all here. We could go to my wife's sister's, I suppose.'

The woman looked up at him. 'Gracie don't have enough space,' she said shortly. 'Her back bedroom got damaged before Christmas – the roof come in. It'll have to be your cousin's.'

The man looked aghast, but the warden stepped in. 'Time enough to decide all that. Does anyone need medical treatment? How's your foot, young man?' He made eye contact with Jimmy, who cleared his throat.

'I think we might have a sprained ankle here, Stan. This fellow here said he hurt it running down the stairs to get away from his bedroom when it caught fire.'

The little boy, no more than five, began to cry. 'I know I shouldn't run on the stairs but I was frightened,' he sobbed.

'No, you did the right thing,' Hope reassured him. 'You had to get out as fast as you could. That was the most important thing.'

The boy flashed her a grateful look.

'So why don't you come with Miss Potter and me in our ambulance, and we'll take you to the doctors to make sure you haven't broken it or hurt anything else?' Jimmy suggested. 'Your ma can come too. Don't worry, you won't get separated from the others. Mr Banham here keeps a careful note of where everyone goes. So if your daddy and brother and sister go to a shelter, we'll know which one, and you and your ma can join them later. All right?'

The boy sobbed again but more quietly. 'All right.'

Jimmy edged closer to Hope. 'And then we can make sure the mother is checked for smoke inhalation. I heard her trying to speak, she don't sound right.' He raised his voice. 'Young man, will you be needing a stretcher or shall I carry you? It won't be as bumpy if I do that.'

The boy nodded, and allowed himself to be lifted into the ambulanceman's arms.

'Hope, you bring his mother over, and settle her in the back. You know where the blankets are.'

The woman, still in shock, allowed herself to be led across to the ambulance, as her boy was carried in front, brightly lit now by the blaze as it gained in intensity. Mr Banham followed them, passing Hope a piece of lined notepaper as they reached the vehicle's back doors. 'Here's the address of where the father and kiddies will go,' he murmured. 'Give it to her when she's a bit more with it. Well done – have you

111

had many call-outs? Jimmy said you were training with him.'

Hope nodded. 'He's teaching me to drive. Actually,' she admitted, 'this is my first evening.'

Mr Banham grinned, his face glowing in the brightness of the blaze. 'Right. Well done – I wouldn't have guessed. Now, best be on your way.'

He strode back to the blaze, where the neighbouring houses were being checked and evacuated where necessary. Hope showed the mother where to sit and made sure the boy was safely settled, with his ankle raised a little and wedged safely between two cushions to stop it getting knocked on the journey to the hospital.

'In you get,' Jimmy said, and they were off, almost before Hope could slam the door shut. She took a deep breath as the ambulance plunged into the chaos of the street. She'd done it – she'd attended her first call-out, and had been useful. Mr Banham, the respected warden, had praised her. She had the strong impression that he didn't do so unless it was deserved, and that she might not get a better compliment for a long, long time.

CHAPTER ELEVEN

Daisy was determined to celebrate New Year, raids or no raids. She began the evening by writing to Freddy, not a long letter but a short note to tell him that she was thinking of him on this last night of 1940 and that she wished him all the luck in the world for 1941. How she wished they could be together to see in the changing of the year, but it was not to be. This note would have to do, and so she signed it and finished with a row of kisses. Although they were a poor substitute for the real thing.

She shivered in her cold bedroom. Of course, she could have written her letter downstairs in the warmth of the kitchen but she didn't want Robbie reading her private words over her shoulder, which was exactly what he'd want to do. Her letters to Freddy were too personal to share. She bit her lip. Sometimes she was afraid she'd forgotten what he looked like, what it felt like to be held in his strong arms, that wonderful distinctive smell that was unique to him. It had been so long.

'Daisy, are you coming down?' Her mother's shout echoed up the stairs, and galvanised her into action. She stuck down the envelope and then changed into her most festive blouse, pocketing her newest lipstick. She was going to the pub to meet Sam and

Sylvia, and some of their friends. If she couldn't be with Freddy, she could at least be out on the town with people who would want to put the past couple of nights behind them, and enjoy themselves.

'Be there in a minute!' she called back. Then she checked she had enough money for a few drinks and the bus. Shoving her comb into her bag, she took a last glance in the little mirror on top of the chest of drawers she had shared with Clover, and then belted downstairs.

'Thought you'd fallen asleep up there,' teased Patty. 'I know you're off out, but your father and I thought we'd all raise a glass together before you go, to mark the new year. We probably won't be up by the time you get back.'

'Unless there's another raid,' Robbie chipped in, unnecessarily.

Daisy glared at him. 'Don't even think it. I've had it up to here with raids again.'

Bert came in from the back kitchen, nodding sagely. 'Let's look on the bright side. No sirens yet, and maybe Jerry feels he's done enough damage in the past couple of days.' He looked down at the kitchen table, where the day's newspaper was open. A chilling photograph showed the firestorm that had engulfed the City of London the very night that the bomb had fallen on Hackney Downs. Terrible damage had been caused to offices, warehouses and churches, with many brave fire-fighters being killed. Yet there was St Paul's, surrounded by flames but still standing.

Daisy followed his gaze. 'Mr Churchill said the cathedral had to be saved at all cost,' Bert remarked, his eyes scanning the article. 'They had a big team of fire watchers.' His voice held steady but for a moment Daisy thought she could detect the underlying emotion in it, the horror at the destruction, the pride and relief that St Paul's had survived against the odds.

Robbie perked up. 'Like at your factory?'

'Even bigger, I expect.' Bert ruffled Robbie's hair, his voice fully steady again. 'Right, your ma is keen for us to raise a toast. I'll fetch the glasses. A cordial for you all, and I'll have a tot of Scotch.'

Daisy wanted to get going, knowing that the others would be waiting, but she also wanted to share this moment with her family. They were in their warm kitchen, not crammed into the Anderson shelter in the garden, as they had been over the past couple of evenings, and for that she was immensely grateful. They'd had a leisurely meal of her mother's tasty stew, sitting properly around the table, not with plates balanced on their knees out in the cold. Such little things – but now she knew they could be taken away with one wail of the siren, she was immensely grateful for them. So many others were not as lucky.

'Here you are.' Bert handed round the drinks. 'Won't keep you long, Daisy, I can see you are raring to go. But I just wanted to say, cheers to you all, and to those of our family who aren't here at the moment. We've come this far. We'll stick together for the next year too.'

'Cheers,' echoed Patty, Daisy and Robbie, solemn for once, and if Daisy wasn't mistaken there was an unshed tear in her mother's eye.

For a moment she thought she might give way to a

swift tear herself. Then she drained her glass and set it down. 'See you next year,' she said with a determined twinkle.

The main bar of the pub was noisy with revellers. Daisy knew why Sam had chosen it – it was the place where he'd first met Sylvia, now well established as his girlfriend. He felt the place brought him luck, and, heaven knew, they could all do with some of that after the hell of the recent raids.

She cast her eyes around the crowded room, cursing her lack of height. Sam had always loved to tease her about that. The smoky atmosphere didn't help, but at least it was from cigarettes and not burning buildings.

Then she heard a familiar voice. 'Daisy! Over here!'

Sam and Sylvia had managed to snaffle a table over on the far side of the room and had saved her a little stool with an upholstered velvet seat. Sylvia had hooked one foot through its crossbar so nobody could take it for themselves. Daisy grinned – that was the sort of friend she appreciated. 'Can I get you some drinks before I sit down?' she offered, and turned back towards the bar when they eagerly accepted.

Daisy smiled to herself. To think that this time last year she'd been so keen to practise looking eighteen and buying drinks. Well, she didn't have to worry now. Not only had that important birthday come and gone but she felt she'd aged far more than a year in the past twelve months. Balancing the three glasses, she carefully made her way to her friends, neatly avoiding over-friendly punters who'd evidently started their celebrations early.

For two pins they would have been giving her unwanted hugs and kisses.

'Oooh, that one was a bit keen, wasn't he?' Sylvia grinned, accepting her glass of lemonade. 'Here's your pint, Sam, and better make it last. Don't want you coming over all funny.' She raised her eyebrows in mock-warning.

'As if I would,' said Sam cheerfully, taking a gulp. He was out of his driver's uniform now, in shirtsleeves and with his tie loosened. 'Well, Harrison, how did you get on this week? Bit of a shocker, wasn't it?'

Daisy pulled a face, and then decided Sam was the one person in the world who would understand. 'It's been hell,' she said bluntly. 'We had one bit of respite directly before Christmas when Larry and me did a spot of touching up of the painted lines, and after that, total bedlam, thank goodness it was quick-drying paint! The platforms have been overrun with people wanting to shelter. We've got nothing set up for them, no facilities, no water, there's no privacy or anything. The smell, it's just terrible. Then of course the regular cleaners don't want to clear up all that extra mess. Mr Rathbone doesn't want anything to do with it all – he's getting worse, if anything. So it's all down to me. I'm tired of it, I am. Tired.' She set her glass down and suddenly felt like crying.

Sam immediately patted her on the shoulder. 'Oh, I can just imagine,' he said, and the very words made Daisy instantly feel a little better. He could, that was the thing. None of her family knew Mr Rathbone and how much she usually relied on him; none of her family had been down on the platforms during or after a raid. Sam, though, knew what she was up against.

'It's not fair,' she said, realising that she sounded like Robbie.

Sam cocked his head. 'None of it's fair,' he pointed out.

'I know, I know. But I don't know what to do.' Daisy sighed and then pulled herself together. 'Sorry, I've had my moan. But this week, what with all that, then sitting up half the night in our own shelter, so doing it all on hardly any sleep – well, it's been no fun, I can tell you.'

Sam nodded sympathetically. 'It makes it worse, no sleep,' he agreed. 'But I tell you what, we've been on all sorts of diversions the last couple of days. No routes are the same 'cos of all the collapsed buildings. I've been all round the houses, I can tell you. So I've been going past tube stations what I normally wouldn't. One or two have got WVS ladies helping out. Couldn't you have that? Don't mind what old Rathbone says, just get on and sort it out. Then you'd have a way of getting hot drinks to them as wants it, and they have all sorts to help, and they can't half keep order, the WVS lot.'

Daisy brightened up. 'That's an idea.'

Sylvia sat up straighter. 'Even better, my sister's coming along this evening and she's started volunteering with them. You'd want a group local to Manor House, wouldn't you? Well, she's with the Tottenham ladies. She might know someone to ask – or at least, someone who knows someone.' She pushed up the sleeves of her pretty baby-blue cardigan as if getting ready to organise.

Daisy grinned broadly. If Sylvia and her sister were on the case, she didn't feel so alone. As if on cue, a woman's voice called, 'Cooo-eee' and there was Muriel, waving from the bar. There too was her new young man, home on leave, in his naval uniform. Daisy's mind turned once again to Freddy, who always looked so smart in his. He definitely would expect her to cope with this latest problem. So she better had.

'That's a clever idea,' she said. 'I'll speak to her in a minute. That way, we can get it sorted out and then concentrate on seeing the new year in with style.'

Sylvia smiled in return as Sam lifted his pint and added, 'I'll drink to that!'

Rose was running late, which she hated. It was not her fault; she had had no warning that she would have to go to the latest meeting, but Katherine had called in sick at the last minute. With some of the other staff, Rose would have suspected a case of overdoing it during the New Year celebrations, but in this case it was all but impossible. Food poisoning, Katherine had said. That was another problem: owing to the raids and shortages, some people cut corners with food hygiene. Rose felt for her colleague, who had tried to celebrate by going out for a rare meal in a restaurant, only to be laid low.

So here she was, trying to piece together what she might need, grabbing whatever files she thought might be relevant, all at a dash. There was no time to chat to the other nurses on the ward to ask how their festivities had gone, those who'd been lucky enough to have time off over the last few days. There was Effie, who she hadn't seen since the night of the raid, talking to her friend Coral at the far end of the ward. Rose made a mental note to check all was well with the young nurse after the meeting had ended. The trainee looked rather withdrawn and anxious, but that was not unusual. Coral seemed to be trying to reassure her. Well, whatever it was about would have to wait.

Rose was determined not to be last to arrive, and all but ran to the meeting room. She had no intention of being forced to sit next to Prendergast again. Her plan worked and she was able to slip into a seat between two women she knew, one a sister and one a senior midwife, both sensible professionals. Rose nodded to them and sank happily into her chair, her mind easier now she was among friendly colleagues. They murmured small talk as the rest of the people came in.

Exactly on time, Mrs Gleeson, the chairwoman, called the meeting to order and business began. Nobody wanted it to overrun as there was so much to do. Rose was impressed when the reports were kept brief and to the point, which would also mean she wouldn't be expected to speak for long either.

Her turn came, and she spoke about what she thought Katherine would have done: what had worked on the ward, what had not, and what they would need in order to improve. Rose then shut her file to show she had finished, and sat back, relieved to have got through it without fluffing her words.

However, she was not done yet. Although the chairwoman nodded and seemed prepared to move on, Mr Prendergast raised a hand. 'If I may . . . ?'

Mrs Gleeson looked a little surprised but acknowledged the surgeon. 'Please, Mr Prendergast, go ahead. Briefly, if you will.'

Rose felt an uneasy twist of suspicion.

'Nurse Harrison is of course competent enough, but is the least experienced attendee at our meeting,' he said smoothly. 'I have to question the relevance of her report. I do not believe it is fully accurate. We cannot commit to more resources for her ward unless the figures are true.'

Rose knew she was blushing furiously but had to defend herself. 'I can assure you—'

'Now, no need to get het up, Nurse Harrison. Mistakes are easily made,' he purred, his eyes narrowing.

'There have been no mistakes,' Rose said. 'The figures are from our ward sister.'

The chairwoman cleared her throat. 'Whom we all know to be scrupulous in all areas. Very well, I shall note that there was a query, but there is no need for the figures to be confirmed.'

'At this stage,' Mr Prendergast added.

The chairwoman glared at him. 'At this stage. Right, enough on this topic. Next, paediatric surgery . . .'

Rose felt unpleasantly hot all over. How dare he? Everyone knew that she was standing in and wouldn't have had time to compile her own figures. Everyone respected Katherine. What was he up to?

121

The midwife leaned a little closer. 'Don't let him wind you up. He does it sometimes, just to hear his own voice.'

Rose nodded, glad of the sympathy, but still wondered what was going on. Why would he bother challenging her, trying to make her look bad in everyone's eyes? He was up to something, but she didn't know what it was. Yet.

CHAPTER TWELVE

Katherine was back at work the next day, insisting to everybody that she was feeling better but, to Rose's eyes, still looking pale. Usually her cheeks had a healthy pink glow, but that was absent now. Rose waited until there was a quiet lull on the ward, or as quiet as it was liable to get, so that she could ask her senior colleague directly. She was anxious that there might be something more seriously wrong than a bout of food poisoning, and dreaded what the sister might have to say.

'Well.' She handed Katherine a cup of tea, and they both sat at the central nurses' station. The general buzz of noise from the ward gave them some privacy. 'Are you sure you should be back yet? I know what you told everyone, but are you really feeling better?'

Katherine met Rose's gaze and pulled a face. 'I should have guessed you'd notice something,' she said, cheerfully enough, but she sounded tired. But then again, they were all tired. It might not mean anything. Still, Rose was concerned.

'Out with it,' she urged. 'Tell me, are you really sick? If there's anything I can do . . .'

Katherine laughed. 'No, there's nothing you can do, or not in that way, anyhow. You're right, it's not food poisoning after all.' She paused, looking around to check that there was nobody within hearing distance.

Rose gasped in alarm and then sat back a little, narrowing her eyes as an idea began to form. 'Hang on. You were sick yesterday, weren't you? And now, you are white as a sheet – sorry, but you are. Oh. Let me guess. You were sick again this morning.'

Katherine shrugged, as if there was no point in denying it.

'And you're tired, more than just from the latest raids.'

The sister nodded. 'I certainly am. You've got it, haven't you?'

Rose took a moment to take in the news and then smiled broadly. 'Well, that's a surprise – or rather, it isn't really. Congratulations.'

Katherine's eyes glittered brightly with pleasure. 'Thanks. But don't tell anyone, please. Nobody at all. It's such early days. I haven't even written to Richard yet. I want to be sure. I would hate to raise his hopes for nothing. He's wanted to be a father for so long.' She looked down at her hands and twisted the gold band on her fourth finger. 'And you know what some people will say.'

Rose cocked her head. 'No, what? What could they possibly say?'

Katherine tutted. 'That I'm too old. Too long in the tooth to start a family. I know perfectly well what certain people round here said when I got married. That I'd been left on the shelf and what a surprise it was that someone was prepared to take me on.' She shook her head.

Rose sighed. 'That's nonsense and you know it. You've not that long turned thirty.'

Katherine sat up straighter. 'Yes, of course. But that's what some people are like. So I don't intend to give them any ammunition. Give me a few more weeks and then I'll be more sure. We'll just carry on as if we haven't had this conversation, and if I'm a little slower than usual you'll know why.'

Rose reluctantly got to her feet. 'Yes, of course. I'll cover for you if you need me to, you know that.'

'Thanks,' Katherine said again. 'Actually, I think I'd better get to the bathroom right away. Sorry – can you see to the trainees?'

Running was strictly forbidden in the wards and corridors but she moved away pretty sharply, Rose observed, hoping she made it in time.

Well, that bombshell had put paid to her plans to ask the sister about the peculiar behaviour of Mr Prendergast in the meeting. She'd have to pick another moment to see what Katherine thought, or if she'd had the same humiliating experience herself. Now was not the time. Because, of course, one of the people she had referred to was none other than the surgeon himself. He'd made those very same disparaging comments at Katherine's engagement party.

It made Rose hot under the collar with anger at the way he could come out with such casual cruelties. He was far from young himself, and no oil painting, with his growing paunch and thinning hair. Yet he thought he could make demeaning remarks about a senior nurse, throwing doubt on her future happiness. Odious little man.

Rose sighed with frustration and then gathered herself together. It would have to wait, and it was not the most important item on her to-do list. She glanced around to see if any of the trainees were nearby. Ever since she had resolved to speak to Effie the girl had been nowhere to be found; perhaps she had lectures and Rose hadn't remembered. In that case it was time to check the latest round of burns victims. Katherine, Effie and the surgeon could be dealt with tomorrow.

'Hello! Hello, can any of you hear me?' Faith's voice echoed down the stairwell of the house. She had taken Artie up to her bedroom, which was even more luxurious now. Vera had installed a peach velvet chaise longue, to match the furnishings. Heaven only knew how she had got hold of such a beautiful object. Faith loved it as she could stretch out, holding the baby, and soak up all the admiration that was her due.

Joy skulked along the ground-floor corridor, past the area under the stairs where Artie had put in his first appearance.

'I can hear your footsteps. I know you're there,' Faith's demanding tone continued. 'Bring me up a cup of tea.'

'For God's sake,' Joy muttered, edging towards the front door. Then she caught sight of Hope, trying to read a first-aid manual in peace at the dining-room table. 'You go. I've done it twice today already.'

Hope pointed to her book. 'But I have to learn . . .'

'Tea! I should like some tea!' The voice was getting louder.

'You go. You've got nothing better to do,' Hope insisted.

'I have. I'm going out.' Joy dashed away, leaving Hope fuming.

Never mind that she'd promised herself to read the whole chapter before her next shift at the depot. She was keen to impress the nurses who were leading the classes, but when it came to the baby, her plans always came second-best in this house.

'Tea! If you think I can make my own, well, I can't!'

Hope gave in to the inevitable. Faith was not going to shut up until she got what she wanted, just as had always been the case since they were little. Now she had the perfect excuse to be waited on hand and foot.

'Hold your horses!' she called back.

'Keep your voice down, you'll wake him!' Faith shouted, twice as loud.

Hope dragged herself to the kitchen and put on the kettle, unsurprised at the way things were turning out. Why had she ever thought that motherhood would be the making of her big sister? That after a lifetime of expecting everyone else to do as she wanted, she'd have a change of character? If anything, it had made her even worse.

Still, she didn't want to wake the baby. If Artie started one of his crying marathons, she'd have no chance to finish her chapter. Gritting her teeth, she sloshed hot water onto the tea leaves and plonked the teapot onto a tray, alongside a pretty rose-pattered cup.

Then she dragged herself upstairs, resenting every step.

By the time Rose managed to grab a private word with Effie, the girl seemed to have returned to her usual quiet but eager self. Rose wondered if she had imagined the worried expressions of just after the raids. After all, everyone had been anxious, especially those who had dared to hope that the Blitz might be over.

Effie was plainly flattered that Rose had taken precious minutes out of her busy shift to check that she was all right, and protested that there had been nothing wrong.

'Are you sure?' Rose quizzed.

Effie nodded, but then decided to add a little more. 'Honestly, I am fine. I just got the wrong end of the stick, that's all.'

Rose paused in her rerolling of some bandages, which had come loose when being transferred from the store to the ward. 'Oh, in what way? That's if you want to tell me, of course,' she went on, knowing that the trainee might have personal matters to keep to herself.

'Well, like you said, it was the night of the big raid, when I went to my auntie's shelter down Chatsworth Road.' Effie shrugged slightly. 'Mr Prendergast was ever so kind, walked me all the way there, wouldn't take no for an answer when I said I knew the way and he could leave me at the corner.'

'I see.' Rose was immediately on alert.

'Yes, he took me right to the door of the church hall. He was determined to see me all the way there, to make sure I wasn't lost or anything like that. He even took my arm for the last bit, where you have to leave the main road and go down the side street. It's ever so dark there.'

Rose had to steel herself not to react. 'I see. I can imagine,' she said neutrally, wanting the girl to go on, to say if anything had actually happened.

'Yes, he didn't want me to fall off the kerb – you know you can't see them properly no more.'

Rose nodded. Like just about every nurse, she had treated people who had had accidents owing to the blackout, and falling from or tripping over a kerb was one of the commonest.

'So he was a real gent, he held my arm very tight. I said to him, "It's all right, you can let me go now," once we got to the hall door. And that was what I thought was a bit strange, 'cos he didn't want to. He brought his face up real close to mine and said, "You should thank me properly," and then my auntie's neighbour come up behind us and he let me go. So he was just looking after me. I understand that now.'

Rose let out a breath she hadn't realised she had been holding. 'You're sure he didn't try anything else? He, er, didn't hold you anywhere except for by your arm?'

Effie gave her a disbelieving look. 'Of course not. I said so, didn't I? No, he was a gent, and I just got it a bit wrong. He's just a kind old man.'

Rose shook her head. 'Well, maybe. But I'm sorry

if he made you uneasy. I won't ask him to escort you anywhere again. You trust your instincts, Effie. Sorry, Nurse Jenkins.'

Effie nodded cheerfully and reached for the bandages. 'You let me do those, Nurse Harrison. You got more important things to do. Besides, for the next few days I don't need no old doctor to see me home safe. My brother's back on leave – do you remember, I told you I had one in the merchant navy?'

'Oh, yes. That's good news.' Rose handed over the box.

'Yes, we're so glad to see him back in one piece, even if he's not here for long. He's going to meet me after my shift and see me back to Limehouse. He likes looking after me, always has. Aren't I lucky?'

Rose smiled, and thought that Effie was indeed lucky; she'd love to see her own brother Peter. But Effie was obviously used to men keeping an eye out for her, relying on them for her safety. With her brother, that sounded like a good thing. When it came to the surgeon, though, Rose was far from convinced.

CHAPTER THIRTEEN

Hope shivered and drew her ambulance-service-issue coat around her. At least she had one that fitted better now. The one she had grabbed on her first outing, that baptism of fire, had been too big and she'd exchanged it as soon as she could. To think that it wasn't even two weeks ago. Already she felt like a veteran.

She was in the passenger seat once again, as officially she was still in training, learning to drive the cumbersome vehicles by day. By night she was on duty when needed, and she was needed tonight. The sirens had begun not long after dusk and now the capital was ablaze once more. Even though bombs were falling over Hackney, the crew had been alerted to a major strike in the City of London.

'Off you go,' Jimmy had said, passing her the little bag that held her gas mask. They'd been sharing a pot of tea at the depot when the instructions had come in. 'You'd better take this – no knowing what you'll find at the other end. I'm not rostered with you this evening, so you'll have a different chauffeur.'

'Oh?' Hope had got used to the idea that her daytime driving instructor would also be her partner when the call-outs happened. 'What's going on?'

Jimmy smiled grimly. 'I'm off to a bunch of

high-explosive strikes over towards Stoke Newington. Can't say I'm looking forward to it – my sister and all her bunch are over that way. But maybe her road'll be all right. No, you get the joys of our Mr Macleod. He's just joined us from one of the North London depots, so still finding his way around. You can direct him,' he added, patting her shoulder. Then he leaned in and whispered, 'You'll be all right. His bark is worse than his bite.'

Before Hope could ask him what he meant, Jimmy had gone, moving nimbly across to the parked ambulances.

So now she found herself stuck in the cab with a stranger, who had grunted that he was Ian Macleod but had said little else.

To begin with, Hope had tried to make conversation. 'Oh, you're Scottish. Fancy you being down here in London.' She'd scoured her brain to make any further connections. 'I know a Scottish nurse in Dalston – have you met Fiona Dewar? She's the superintendent of the district nurses' home; she's very important.' Hope had met her briefly in her second week of first-aid classes, when the diminutive Scotswoman had come to check that all was going to plan. She was evidently Nurse Lake's boss, and was quietly impressive.

The only response from Mr Macleod had been another grunt. Hard to say if that was a yes or a no. Hope had decided not to pursue it. She'd studied him covertly by glancing sideways but his expression gave little away. His face was thin, almost gaunt, his chin stubbly as if in need of a shave. He wore a knitted round hat, not exactly regulation but useful against the cold. Hope wondered if he was bald underneath it. It was hard to guess his age.

All around, the fires were catching hold as the ambulance raced down the main road towards Liverpool Street. Hope remembered how shaken she had been on that first call-out, and how now it felt almost normal. Good job her mother couldn't see her, she thought. Vera would be having kittens, as flaming debris fell all around, a clank from just behind her sounding out as a chunk hit the roof of the vehicle. Again, the smoke was pungent and sometimes threatened to obscure the way. Hope tried to work out how she'd drive in such conditions, and was quietly glad it wasn't up to her just yet.

'Bloody hell.' The Scotsman's first words were muttered but furious. 'What's gone on here?'

The road ahead was blocked, the fires fiercer still. An ARP warden ran towards them. 'The road by the main station's been hit. You'll have to go round.'

'And how the hell am I meant to do that?' Macleod demanded, but Hope intervened.

'It's all right. I know the side streets here. If we can find a right turn I'll sort something out.'

'Excellent, on you go, then.' The warden was needed elsewhere and dashed off.

Macleod turned to her. 'You'd better know what you're talking about. He's left us stranded otherwise.'

Hope was offended. She'd had her fair share of being talked down to or ignored because of her sex and age, but had expected better from a fellow ambulance driver.

'Of course I know,' she said from between clenched teeth. 'I've lived around here all my life. This is our nearest main station. I could walk it blindfold.'

'Good, because we're driving blind, or as near as. Over to you.' He said it like an insult.

Hope took a deep breath and gathered her thoughts. If the usual approach to Liverpool Street was impassable but they had somehow to get to Bank, she'd have to come up with something clever. 'Turn right here. Exactly here. I know it looks like an alleyway leading to nowhere but, take it from me, it isn't. It should be just wide enough for us to get through,' she said with her fingers crossed. She'd only ever walked it, never attempted to drive down the tiny street. But it was their best chance.

Macleod might be a miserable companion but he was a more than decent driver, manoeuvring the ambulance between bollards, narrowly missing an old building that jutted out onto the pavement. All these ancient terraces, with historic churches and houses, their once-impressive stones now lit by the ominous orange glow – what they must have seen in the hundreds of years for which they'd stood, Hope thought. And now their windows were shattering and their roofs collapsing under the onslaught from above. She caught sight in the wing mirror of a huge wooden beam falling into the road behind them, sparks flying brightly upwards. So that was it: they would have to get out of this alley by driving onwards. Any attempts at reversing would be blocked. She fervently hoped she could remember the sneaky diversion.

'Left here.' She pointed to another narrow gap between buildings, even though it was so dark at this point Macleod could scarcely see where she meant. Still, he plunged into the new alley, the ambulance's covered headlamps just about picking out the twisting way forward, above them the faint stripes of AA searchlights, and everywhere the noise of burning buildings. She had to shout the next instruction.

'Now right again, that's it.' She pointed once more, not that it was much use. Somehow he understood and swerved around what had been until recently a pub, but now was more of a shell. Hope turned her head from side to side, nervous as they were almost there and she had one last tricky turn to make. 'Over there. It looks like a passageway but it'll be just wide enough.'

'Are you sure?' he half shouted.

'Trust me.' In for a penny, thought Hope, and it was too late to turn back now. This was the final dodge around the major diversions and there, thank the Lord, was Bank station. Or rather, where it had been.

ARP wardens rushed forward to direct them to the safest place to park. 'Oh my God,' Hope muttered, taking in the devastation all around. A direct hit on the tube station, a massive pit in the road. If they'd tried to approach by any of the usual routes they could have gone straight down into it. She shook her head – she couldn't think about that at this moment.

'Come on, get a move on,' Macleod snapped, jumping from the driver's seat. Hope wanted to shout back at him, but there was no time. They grabbed a stretcher from the back and then ran to where a warden was indicating, to what appeared to be a heap of old coats.

Hope gasped as one of them moved and moaned.

Not coats, then, but bodies.

'Right, we load the back with as many as we can,' Macleod said gruffly. 'You've done this before, I take it?'

Hope stood up straighter. 'Of course.'

'When did you start?'

'Two weeks ago.'

'Bloody hell, they've given me a beginner,' he snarled.

'And I've had nothing but practice ever since,' Hope replied with fury. 'So I know not to drag these poor people about without checking on their injuries first. Such as, broken bones or, in particular, back, neck and head injuries.'

He ran onwards as he spoke. 'You needn't quote the nurses' bible at me,' he shouted. 'Just prove me wrong. That woman first. You take the arms, I'll take the legs.'

The heat was unbearable and the noise of the blazing buildings terrifying, punctuated by rumblings as more walls collapsed. Hope didn't speak, simply went into automatic, lifting and shifting and settling as many casualties as she could before the van was full.

'Take 'em to Barts,' said one of the wardens, and Macleod looked at her blankly.

'Barts. The hospital. St Bartholomew's,' Hope explained.

He nodded but still continued to stare. 'And how do we get there?' he demanded.

Good question, thought Hope. Normally it was no

distance at all. You could walk it easily – not that any of their passengers could take two steps, let alone the few minutes' walk it would usually require. Tonight, though, the roads were full of new holes and the surfaces strewn with bricks and blocks. Well, she'd just have to come up with something.

'Get in, and turn round,' she decided. 'We'll cut along the back. It might be a longer distance but at least it's away from this.'

This was a hellscape of pure horror. She couldn't get it out of her mind as they set off again, curving around in a tricky diversion. The gaping pit where the ticket hall had stood, the destroyed escalators, the platforms now submerged in rubble, all of which had been full of people, sheltering or trying to catch trains.

She fought to banish the images, and the sounds of people crying for help or screaming in pain. Perhaps worse were the ones who sat or lay amidst the rubble and made no sound at all. She'd think about it all tomorrow, but for now she had to help these desperate wounded patients to safety in the hospital, and then return to do the same all over again.

Macleod obviously thought she was a waste of space, but she'd been asked to do this work tonight and she could not back away. She held on to what that senior warden, Mr Banham, had said on her first night. He'd praised her, surprised that she was so inexperienced. If he thought she was up to the job, well, that was enough. Macleod was plain wrong.

After a while she lost count of the number of trips they made, from the site of the explosion to the hospital and back again. Other ambulances cottoned on to their diverted route and began to follow them, realising it was a good way to transport the wounded. Hope didn't recognise any of the other crews; from the occasional remark she understood that they'd come from far and wide as, even for a city in the midst of the Blitz, this was a notably bad incident. She went from tired to exhausted to out the other side, beyond caring. She stopped wondering why Macleod was so grim and silent. If she didn't have to make conversation with him, then so much the better. She could save what little energy she still possessed for the task in hand.

Finally, when the first streaks of a dull dawn appeared in the smoky sky, the warden in charge approached them. 'Best be off. We've saved everyone we could reach so far,' he said, his words as flat as the way Hope felt. 'We'll need heavy lifting equipment for the rest. The day shift can take over. You get yourselves back to the depot.'

Moving like an automaton, Hope picked her way back to the street corner where they had left the vehicle. Macleod turned to her. 'Think you can get this thing back?' he asked.

Hope was not too tired to be surprised. 'Really?' This was her chance. If only she was more awake to enjoy it.

'You know the roads round here better than I do,' he said. 'If there's any further problem then you can work out a new route. Don't know about you but I just want to be away from here as soon as possible.'

'Of course.' Hope snapped into action and hoisted herself into the driver's seat, swiftly adjusting it to the right position. Macleod had to be close to six foot, far taller than she was.

She gritted her teeth and started the engine, remembering to double declutch as she moved into gear, feeling the crunch of new rubble under the worn old tyres. She didn't need to attempt the narrow alleyways now, as some of the bigger roads had been half cleared. There was a grimy procession of emergency vehicles making their way north, overtaken by messengers on bikes, and she joined it, chugging along, keeping her eyelids open by sheer willpower. Everything about her felt gritty and itchy with dust, but there'd be time enough to clear up when this gruesome journey was over.

At last they pulled off the main road and trundled back to the depot, and Hope sensed every last drop of energy leave her. She didn't care if she parked accurately or not, just staggered the final few feet as close as possible to the open depot door. 'Here we are,' she managed to force out, and then saw why her passenger did not reply. Macleod was sitting at an angle, his gaunt face pressed against the window, his mouth open a little. He was fast asleep.

CHAPTER FOURTEEN

Hope had got as far as the first set of tables and chairs in the ambulance depot, sat down, rested her head on the table in front of her and gone straight to sleep. The clatter of the day shift, the other trainees and instructors arriving and everyone talking nineteen to the dozen had failed to rouse her. It was nearly dinner time before she came to, realising her neck was very stiff, and then that she was still filthy from the night before.

'If it isn't Sleeping Beaty,' Jimmy commented, setting down a cup of tea at her elbow. 'This is for you after you've gone and had a wash, young Hope. Look at you, you're a health hazard and a half. I trust you have a clean set of clothes in your locker.'

Hope dozily sat up and stared at the state of her clothing. Now it was daylight, she could see just how bad it was. Covered in dirt, yes, smelling of smoke and singed at the hem, but also with streaks of blood, deep reddish brown against the grey twill. 'Oh dear.' She swallowed hard.

'Off you go, get smartened up. I'll save your seat and make sure nobody runs off with your tea,' Jimmy assured her.

Hope nodded, recognising the kindness behind his bluff words. Ten minutes later she was back at the rickety table, feeling altogether more awake and noticeably cleaner. She had shoved her dirty clothes from the night before into her bag, wanting to smuggle them back into the house and launder them before her mother or sisters saw.

'Well, I hear it was a bad one last night,' Jimmy began.

Hope nodded, gulping as she remembered. 'Yes, it really was. Have you heard anything on the wireless or in the papers?'

Jimmy nodded sadly. 'Over fifty people killed at Bank – they aren't sure of exact numbers yet. And then there'll be more deaths in the hospitals, I dare say.'

'Barts was rushed off its feet,' Hope said.

'I'm sure it was. The London took in plenty of casualties from there too, you know, the big place at Whitechapel. And heaven only knows how many are still to be found. They're saying they can't even repair the road. They'll have to put a bridge over the pit. Sorry, that's bringing it back, isn't it?'

Hope thought for a minute that she was going to cry, but took a deep breath and stopped the tears from falling. 'It was pretty bad,' she whispered.

Jimmy nodded again. 'Well, I know it's not in fashion, but I say it doesn't hurt to talk about such things. We're doing reversing around corners later and I don't want you overcome with memories in the middle of that. It's a tricky manoeuvre. So suppose you tell me all about it before we go out. Here, I'll top up your cup with a drop of hot water, make it nice and fresh again.'

Hope nodded dumbly, glad beyond measure that

she had such an understanding instructor. There would be nothing she could say that would horrify him. He'd seen it all, been in the thick of it for the entire Blitz, and the previous war, and all the accidents and emergencies in civilian life in between.

So she waited while he refreshed her tea and fetched a cup for himself while he was at it. She saw him exchange a few words with a nurse she didn't know, who was marshalling people for the next first-aid session, and he shook his head firmly. Good, so she wasn't expected to join in the class. She was sure she wouldn't remember a thing. Her brain was still protesting at all the images it had been subjected to last night.

'Here we are.' Jimmy settled back down opposite her, carefully placing the cups without spilling any hot liquid. 'Don't want to burn your hands,' he said with a slight smile. 'Can't have it said that you got through a raid unscathed only to pick up an injury at the depot.'

'No, that wouldn't do at all.' Hope smiled back and felt a bit better.

'Right, so, begin at the beginning.'

Hope took a sip and then told her tale, starting from the moment when Jimmy had left her to get into his own ambulance.

'... And then I drove back,' she finished. 'Me! Driving the ambulance on those awful roads. I don't know how they'll ever get the buses running again around there. And I double declutched and everything.' She sat back, as it hit her just what she had achieved the night before. 'I didn't stall it, I didn't hit anything. I remembered everything you taught me and – well, it worked.'

Jimmy beamed in delight. 'See! I said you were a natural, that very first day. Now you've proved it. Oh, you'll pass with flying colours, you will. Keeping a clear head under such conditions – well, let's just say not everyone can do it. But it will serve you well, you mark my words. If ever in the future you come to doubt yourself, just you remember how you coped under fire. Even if you did fall asleep in your filthy clothes after.'

Hope grinned and then realised she hadn't asked how his night had gone. 'And what about your sister? How did she and her family get on?'

Jimmy pushed his cup away and took a moment to reply. 'She's all right, thanks.' He paused. 'Though her neighbours aren't. Their place caught fire. Lost half the house, they did. When we're finished here I'm going over to make my sister's house secure, against those useless chancers who think it's fair game to go looting. Then they'll all move in with me for a bit, till we can get their place cleaned up again. It don't half stink from next door's fire.'

Hope shook her head, sickened beyond words that some people would stoop so low as to rob the houses of those who'd escaped the raids. But it went on all the time, everyone knew that, even if they preferred not to say.

Jimmy rubbed his hand over his forehead. 'The cemetery, you know, Abney Park, well, that got hit by a high explosive. So it don't look so good at the moment. Still, you can only die once.'

Hope felt for him, a man of his age and experience having to have his home life turned upside down.

At least his sister was alive, even if her house was not in great shape.

'Well, guess what, while I was driving back, that man I was rostered with fell asleep against the window! Imagine that! In all that noise and the ambulance shaking from the potholes and whatnot. That's one better than me passing out at the table.'

Jimmy smiled again, which had been her intention. 'Ah, yes, how did you get on?'

Hope made a face. 'We didn't. Or rather, I couldn't tell as he barely spoke. He was pretty rude when he did, to tell you the truth. Didn't think I could find my way or know how to deal with the wounded.'

'But you did.' Jimmy's voice brooked no argument.

'Yes. Yes, I did. So he didn't have a cause for complaint.' She paused, a sudden thought hitting her. 'He hasn't complained about me, has he? What's he gone and said?'

Jimmy smiled more broadly and his eyes crinkled with amusement. 'Calm down, no, nothing like that.' He chuckled. 'In fact, after someone had woken him from where he'd had his kip in the ambulance, he said you were good. That he was surprised. There, what about that?'

Hope was too stunned to speak. She could more easily believe that he'd filed a complaint than paid her a compliment. 'He did?' she finally managed to say.

'He did.' Jimmy rose to his feet. 'But then, you didn't have to reverse around a corner, did you? So off we go. Remember, you have to use your mirrors . . .'

144

CHAPTER FIFTEEN

'Can somebody take him? I'm so tired.' Faith tried smiling at her sisters, and then glaring when they didn't respond. 'Look, he weighs nothing. He's no trouble.'

Joy glared back. 'If he's no trouble then why don't you hang on to him? He's your baby, after all. We didn't ask for him to live with us.'

Faith rounded on her. 'You'd better not let Mother hear you say that. She'll be down on you like a ton of bricks.'

Joy tossed her hair back and stood her ground. 'Well, she isn't going to, is she? She's gone shopping. Probably queuing to get more nappies for your blessed baby. Like what we never see you do.'

Faith was having none of it. 'What do you know about it? I'm worn out from feeding him. I can't be expected to be on my feet all day, going from shop to shop in case one of them has what we want.'

'Oh, of course not. It's way beneath you, we all know that. It's all right for Mother to go, even if she's always saying she's got aches and pains. What happens when she gets worn out, then? Are you going to start doing the shopping for your own baby at last?'

Faith squared her shoulders, or as well as she could from where she was reclining on the sofa, and Artie began to cry. 'No, because that's where you come in. Face it, Joy, what else are you there for? I don't see you going out to work, or helping around the house, or volunteering for anything useful. You might as well get in some practice, in the unlikely event that some poor man falls for you and you have your own family. I know that's pretty well impossible—'

Joy jumped to her feet. 'You take that back, you smug—'

'*Stop it!*' Hope gave up trying to read the *Radio Times* and got to her feet. 'I don't know what's worse, the baby crying or you two at each other's throats again. I'm sick of it. Sick and tired. And I've got a bloody good excuse for being tired, if you hadn't noticed. I work and train all day, and then, when I try to get a decent night's sleep, either the baby or the Luftwaffe wake me, or both. Give him here. I'd rather walk the streets with him in the pram than listen to you two, and that's saying something.'

Joy was momentarily silenced by her sister's uncharacteristic outburst, but Faith was straight on her high horse.

'Oh, Hope, we all know you're such a saint. We know you've saved the world since you started on the ambulances, or at least this corner of London. What a pity you can't sleep because of the baby, who, let me remind you, is your nephew, and of course he's doing it just to annoy you. Don't you worry about me being the first to wake up when he cries all night every night. Don't you worry about me being so tired from feeding him . . .'

Hope ignored the barbs and reached for Artie, whose little face was growing redder by the second. 'Come on, then, let's wrap you up warm and find your woolly hat,' she said resignedly. 'Just what I had in mind for my first afternoon off for a week. A little stroll in the lovely freezing wind. At least you'll be sheltered in your pram. That's it, now off we go. Leave these two to it.'

She shut her ears to the continuing argument between Faith and Joy as she carried the wailing baby to his pram in the hall. It was a Silver Cross – nothing but the best for Faith – and as she settled him under his soft wool blankets he looked tiny. She shrugged into her thickest coat, hanging on the hallstand, and dug her knitted gloves from its pockets.

'Come on then,' she muttered, dragging open the front door. 'Let's see if Auntie Hope can get you down the front step without tipping you over.'

She just about got him to the front gate without mishap and set off along the pavement, which the rescue services had more or less cleared of broken bricks and debris. The air was bitterly cold and she could feel her nose turning red, but Artie didn't seem to mind. The rhythm of the moving pram started to work its magic and his cries gradually subsided, until finally they were nothing but gentle snuffles.

I must be doing something right, Hope thought, still resentful that her planned afternoon had changed direction. It was too bad that Faith was so lazy and reluctant to take responsibility for the baby. She handed him over at every possible opportunity, and only really seemed to enjoy him when there was an audience. Then she could play the part of a doting young mother, beautiful and serene. Hope could have snarled in fury if there hadn't been passers-by on the other side of the narrow street. She'd thought that Faith might rise to the challenge of motherhood and have a character transformation, but there was little sign of it so far.

She wondered if she should take the chance and do some shopping, but nearly every doorway had a queue outside it. Then she realised she had left her purse on the dining-room table. For a moment she was disappointed, but she told herself she didn't really need anything. Better to save her hard-earned money and coupons for when she genuinely did.

By now, the skies were heavy with deep grey rainclouds and she didn't fancy being caught outside in a downpour. 'It's all right for you, Artie, you've got your pram hood,' she told him.

She swerved the heavy pram around the corner and onto the main road. A good job she'd built up her arm muscles steering the clunky ambulance and wrestling with its gearstick. Pushing a pram turned out to be much trickier than she'd realised. She'd seen women out in the park and the things seemed to glide along, but that was an illusion. You had to put in a fair bit of work to keep it going and make sure it was smooth. She dreaded hitting a pothole or piece of stonework and waking Artie. She didn't think she could stand it if he began to cry again.

Now and then she noticed women, usually older ones, smiling indulgently and nodding in approval as they went by, sometimes looking into the pram. Hope gritted her teeth. She wanted to tell them he wasn't hers, that she was only pushing him around in the cold because it was better than enduring still more bickering between his actual mother and other aunt. If he hadn't arrived, then Faith would still be living it up in the West End, Joy would be sulking quietly somewhere and she would have been free to read or listen to the wireless as much as she liked. But he *had* arrived – and that was that.

Oh, no, here came the rain. Freezing drops fell like stair rods and the shoppers began to scatter, the ones in queues putting up umbrellas and huddling close to the shop windows or walls for protection. Hope had forgotten her brolly in her haste to get out of the house. She pulled the pram hood into place and settled the waterproof covering over the woollen blankets so at least Artie would be dry.

Hope wiped her forehead with her glove so that she could see properly and then it dawned on her that they were close to the greengrocer's where Aunt Patty worked.

'Right, Artie, prepare for a bit of a dash,' she muttered, putting her head down and speeding along the pavement, abandoning the idea of a smooth ride for the baby.

He woke up and began to protest, but Hope didn't care. Here was the doorway, and by a miracle there was no queue outside. Desperate for warmth, she bumped the door open by shoving it with her shoulder and dragged the pram into the shop.

Instantly the contrast hit her. There was that smell of fresh earth, with something else in the background, sweet and welcoming. She sighed in relief, wiping her dripping face as Patty hurried forwards.

'Hope! How lovely. And you've brought Artie to see me. It's his first time here. Hello, young man, are you all tucked up?' Patty helped bring the pram through the front aisle and down by the counter, expertly collapsing the hood and taking off the waterproof covering, propping it against a shelf so that it could drip-dry out of the way.

'Now, then,' she said cheerfully. 'You've timed it well. We've just boiled the kettle. Daisy's here, out the back. Daisy! Your cousin's brought Artie on a visit. Bring an extra cup.'

Hope sank gratefully onto the stool by the counter and allowed her aunt to take her damp coat. 'Something smells good,' she said appreciatively.

Daisy came through from the storeroom, bearing a tray of three mismatched but steaming cups. 'Look, we've got cocoa – and with sugar!' she beamed. 'I did a swap with one of the WVS helpers at the station. Ma had extra swedes and this woman wanted some for her Sunday roast, and we got this in return. How about that?'

Hope could have cried with relief. It was such a little thing, given what was happening in the world outside, but at this moment she could not imagine anything better. Teeth chattering but grinning broadly, she accepted a cup, and warmed her chilly fingers on it. 'That's wonderful,' she breathed. 'I haven't had any proper cocoa for ages. We've got a sort of substitute you make with water at the depot, but this is the real thing.'

Patty nodded happily. 'It's a treat, but you deserve it,' she said. 'We heard what you did the night Bank got hit. It's the least we can do.'

'Right now, it's the best possible thing you could give me,' Hope said honestly.

'Well, drink up.' Patty raised her cup and took her own advice. 'And look at you, taking little Artie for a walk. Are you getting used to him?'

Hope raised her eyebrows. 'Not really. But it's better than sitting at home with my arguing sisters.' She glanced across at the pram. 'I tell you what, Aunt Patty, I'm never having a baby of my own.'

Patty laughed. 'Oh, you'll change your mind when you're older.'

Hope shook her head. 'No,' she replied solemnly. 'Never. There's more chance of me flying than having a baby. I'm just not going to do it.'

CHAPTER SIXTEEN

'You sure you don't mind coming all this way for a lemonade, Daze?' Sam teased as he swung open the door to the riverside pub. 'I know it's a bit out of your usual stomping ground. But I like it. When I was driving the number 15 for a bit, I got to know it and I thought, soon as the evenings start getting lighter, I'll go back there.'

Daisy shrugged, pulling her work jacket more tightly around her. The evenings might be getting slowly lighter but the warmth of spring was yet to show itself. 'No, my brother Peter used to come here now and then. He always liked being able to see the river. That was before everywhere around got badly bombed, of course.'

'Of course.' Sam steered her to a table from where they could see the water, and if they squinted in the low early evening light, the damaged warehouses on the southern shore. 'But it's a change, ain't it? Got to get you away from Manor House or you'll only talk about work.'

Daisy nodded and watched her friend's back disappearing towards the bar, where a group of young men in rolled-up shirtsleeves were gathering. Dock workers, glad to have finished their shift, she supposed. She'd taken the early shift today as well, and was glad to get away. How she wished Sam was still there alongside her in the ticket hall to laugh and joke with. Never mind, she chided herself, he was here now. Sylvia would be along a little later, as she still worked nine to five in the ATS stores in the centre of town. Depending on which tubes or buses were running, it might take her a while to join them.

'Here we are.' Sam set down her drink and a pint for himself. 'I'll get one in for Sylvia a bit later. I know the 15 is on diversion again, so don't expect to see her yet.'

Daisy cocked her head and smiled. 'You're really keen on her, aren't you?'

Sam blushed, which he hardly ever did. 'Might be.'

Daisy tapped him on his forearm. 'Go on, admit it. It's been, what, about six months? That's a record for you, isn't it?'

Sam wiped the foam from his beer from his top lip. 'Might be.'

Daisy gave him a stern look. 'Well, I hope you aren't messing her around. My sister Clover would not be pleased to hear it and, take it from me, you don't want to annoy her. She's not someone to cross.'

Sam smiled back. 'So I understand. Sylvia said much the same thing, And no, before you ask again, I'm not messing her around. But it's hard to know what to do, ain't it? I know we're lucky: we're both living and working in London and don't have to put up with month after month of separation, like what you and Freddy do. We're young, we like to have fun, we share interests and it's all going well – but how could we settle down, if that's what we wanted to do? You can't get a house now. They're in terrible short supply, what with all of the ones damaged in the raids. I don't think my old dear would take kindly to me asking Sylvia to move in and we don't have room to swing a cat. Sylvia's the same. She has to share a room with her sister as it is; there's no spare space. And she lives in Tottenham – who'd want to live there?' He mock-shuddered.

Daisy replied instantly, 'Well, you would, if you could get a place of your own.' She felt quite heated suddenly. It was the mention of Freddy, when she had no way of knowing when she would see him again. The pain of separation was real, every day, and it got no better as time went on.

'Fair enough.' Sam wasn't going to argue about it. He could see she was upset.

'Sorry.' Daisy saw that her answer had changed the mood and didn't want to spoil their evening. 'It's just . . . well, like you said. I know I'm lucky. I like my job and I love my family, and we're as safe as anyone can be with what's going on – but I miss him, Sam, I do.' For a moment she couldn't go on. If she stopped to think about it, it was too much. Then she caught sight of Sylvia coming through the big outer door and pulled herself together. She didn't want to cry in front of the young woman who'd done nothing but show her kindness.

Sam stood up at once and gave his girlfriend a peck on the cheek, which caused a few of the dock workers to go 'oooh', from where they stood a few yards away. Sylvia pointedly ignored them as she settled into the chair Sam had held for her. 'Sorry I'm late. Diversions,' she said, not that she really needed to explain. It was what they were all used to, after all.

Sam eagerly began to regale them about the best diversions he'd had to drive recently, and he made them sound like adventures rather than the difficult journeys they must really have been. 'Then we realised this old woman was totally lost but, what do you know, it turned out we'd delivered her straight to her granddaughter's house. Door-to-door service. How about that?' He lifted his pint in conclusion and both young women laughed and congratulated him. Any sign of a silver lining in the ongoing transport troubles was very welcome.

'You've almost finished that.' Daisy nodded towards Sam's pint. 'How about another? And you, Sylvia? I'm having a ginger beer, if they've got one.' She stood, taking off her jacket and carefully setting it on the back of her chair. With an increasing press of people the place was becoming warmer.

The cheerful friendliness of the dock workers was now underlaid with a more strident note, Daisy observed as she edged closer to the bar and caught the eye of the landlord. They'd obviously been in here longer than she and Sam had. No doubt some would have been hard at work before dawn, unloading the cargoes to make room for any new consignments that had dodged the bombs and reached the warehouses at the start of the day. She couldn't blame them for taking advantage of a few hours off.

Now, though, one seemed intent on making her acquaintance. He was about her age, dark-haired, cheeks flushed from drink. His sleeves were hitched up and revealed a gleaming watch – so somebody who liked to flash his style, she thought, politely nodding and then immediately placing her order for the drinks.

He didn't take the hint. 'Haven't seen you in here before,' he started. 'What's your name, darlin'?' His words were slightly slurred.

Daisy stepped further away from him and didn't answer.

'Here, I'm talking to you.' Not quite so friendly now. 'You there, with the pretty face. I seen you come in and thought you was with your fella but he's with your mate, ain't he?' He leered suggestively and she caught the whiff of the stale beer on his breath.

'Steady on, Des,' the landlord said, giving him a look. But then his attention was distracted by another customer, and he moved to the far end of the gleaming wooden bar.

Des was encouraged and stepped up his efforts to get to know Daisy. 'Why don't I buy you something nice to drink a bit stronger than what you got there? All you girls say you like lemonade and whatnot, but you don't know what you're missing. How's about a port and lemon? Nice, that is, all sweet, just how you like it. I know about these things. Make you all relaxed, it will.'

Daisy shuddered, hating the memory of port and lemon. She hadn't had it since . . . she preferred not to think about that evening. That had been a narrow escape and she would never be caught out like that again.

'No, thank you,' she said, not looking at him.

Des grabbed her arm and managed to spill some of his drink on her pale blouse. He didn't notice. 'Oh, think yer too good for the likes of me, is that it? Don't want to be seen having a drink with an honest working man? Bit stuck-up, are yer? Well, I know how to take you down a peg or two.' With that he lunged at her, and Daisy had to step quickly out of the way, more beer sloshing onto her and onto him. He was too far gone to be accurate and he caught the edge of her shoulder before staggering, and nearly falling, slipping on the beer he'd spilt on the wooden floor.

'Here, that's enough.' One of his colleagues stepped in, grabbing his drunken friend around the top of one arm. 'You leave her alone. You don't know what you're like when you've had a few.'

The young man was shorter and slighter than Des, but sounded as if he'd had fewer drinks. Still, his eyes were glittering with fury and Des rounded on him.

'You stay out of this, Perce. None of your business. Don't want me to remind you of who's the best fighter on our crew, do you?'

'Drunkest on our crew, more like.' Perce was not put off. 'You go on, miss, get out of his way. He gets like this and it ain't pleasant—'

Before he could go on, Des had swung his right arm back and hit the other man in the face. Bright red blood spurted from his nose and Perce's hands flew to his injured face. 'You bastard,' he grunted, and then gave Des two swift upper cuts, both hitting their target and drawing blood as well. He would have continued but the landlord had raced back to this end of the bar and intervened. 'Desmond Hallett, out of here now. You're banned. Don't make me throw you out myself.'

'Yeah, just you try it,' Des started, but two of his other colleagues grabbed him, one under each arm and half walked, half dragged him to the door. 'Bit of fresh air is what you need, mate,' one of them could be heard saying as they took him away, with the entire pub staring after them.

The landlord handed a bar towel to the furious Perce. 'Best clean yourself up, lad,' he advised. 'That was brave but stupid. You know what he's like more than any of them. You all right, miss?'

Daisy looked down at herself. Her lovely blouse was now dripping and filthy. But she felt angry that she hadn't had a chance to deal with the drunken advances herself. She knew what to do now. She'd never be in that vulnerable position again, not after what Ted had tried to do to her. She was no innocent.

Now Sam and Sylvia were coming over, their faces a mix of anger and concern. 'Come with me,' Sylvia said. 'I've got a spare cardie in my bag; you can wear that. I always keep one in case it gets messy at work.'

Daisy took a deep breath, knowing that she'd have to change out of what she wore as it was wet and horrible. 'Thanks,' she said, and Sylvia led her away to the ladies, out of the curious gaze of the other customers. That was their evening entertainment, she thought, and they'd all go home and tell their families about the fight. Not much she could do about that.

She was still quietly seething ten minutes later as she came back to their table, having had a basic wash down in cold water in the chipped sink. It was not perfect but it would have to do. She'd dabbed at her vest and Sylvia had helped check her back, and also her hair. 'Beer's meant to be good for washing your hair, but maybe not like this,' she'd commented, and Daisy appreciated that the other woman was making an effort to cheer her up. She was also glad of the borrowed cardie, a serviceable fawn one with plain buttons. 'Keep it as long as you like,' Sylvia had said.

Now the other punters had lost interest and paid her scant attention. 'Landlord's given us all drinks on the house,' Sam said.

'That's good of him,' Daisy said, 'but do you mind if we go after that? I just want to have a proper hair wash. Honestly, some people shouldn't be allowed to roam the streets. That man's a menace.'

'Well, he won't be allowed back in here in a hurry,' Sam pointed out. 'Oh, look, here comes his friend. The one who tried to save you.'

'I didn't need saving, I'd have sorted him out myself,' Daisy snapped, but the young man was coming over, still holding his nose.

'Sorry about that,' he lisped.

Daisy had to feel sorry for him, despite everything. When Sam pulled out a stool for him she made way, shifting over towards Sylvia. Sam gave him some of his free pint in a spare glass.

'Thanks. I'm Percy,' he said, looking even slighter as the daylight began to fade from the river-facing windows. 'Percy Jenkins.' He nodded at each of them, wincing as he did so.

They introduced themselves and Daisy cast a worried glance at his nose once he'd dropped his hands away from his face. 'You should get that seen to at a hospital or first-aid point,' she said.

He shrugged, as if it was not a manly thing to do. 'It'll be all right. I've had worse.'

Daisy wanted to scream. He was putting on a show for her, thinking that's what she wanted to hear. 'No, really, because if it's broken they can check it properly, make sure you can breathe.'

He took a cautious sip of beer. 'Well, maybe. I'll ask my sister, that's what I'll do. She's training to be a nurse,' he added proudly. 'My little sister, going to be a nurse, who'd have thought it?'

'That's a good idea,' Sylvia said, smoothing things over. 'Daisy here can do first aid, you know. And her sister's a nurse too.'

Percy sat up straighter. 'Oh, where? Is she with the forces? Or local, like? My sister's at the Hackney Hospital over in Homerton.'

'Small world,' said Daisy. 'So's mine.' She didn't add further details, knowing there were so many nurses on the staff there. And also, she didn't really want to get any friendlier with Percy Jenkins, even if he'd taken a blow to the face in defending her. Why did men always want to fight?

'Perhaps they know each other,' he went on. 'You ask her, does she know Effie Jenkins. Not long started, but she's going to be ever so good. She's a hard worker, our Effie.'

Daisy nodded, and promised to make a note of the

name, as Sam drained his glass and stood. 'Best be getting back. We've got a way to go, this not being our local,' he said brightly, recognising that both Daisy and Sylvia were more than keen to leave.

'Thought I hadn't seen you down this way before,' said Percy. 'Well, thanks for the beer. I'll stay on for another. It'll numb the old nose here.' He smiled lopsidedly as the others nodded and left him to it.

'Blimey, I hope his sister's not as keen to use her fists,' Sylvia commented as they stepped out into the dusk. All around, blackout blinds were being put in place. 'Nurses fighting – that's all we need.'

Daisy tried to smile but the joke was hard to take. Still, she'd have no trouble remembering the name of Jenkins.

CHAPTER SEVENTEEN

However, Daisy did not have the chance to raise the subject when she got home. Her house was in excited uproar, thanks to an unexpected arrival. When she pushed open the door to the kitchen, there sat her sister Clover.

Daisy gasped in surprise. There had been no letter to say she was coming, no telegram. As far as they all knew, Clover was still on her army base somewhere near the south coast, charged with aiming the massive anti-aircraft searchlights. Yet, here she was. Daisy took a moment to adjust her eyes, to check she wasn't imagining things.

'Daisy! Where have you been?' Clover leapt up and gave her sister a hug. Not so long ago the two of them had been at loggerheads every second of the day, but after a period of separation that was all in the past. Daisy hugged her back, laughing.

'Ugh! You smell of beer.' Clover held her at arm's length.

Daisy could see now was not the time to explain the events of the evening. 'Oh, I went for a drink – with Sam and Sylvia, as it happens. Someone tripped and spilt their pint.' That was close enough to the truth for now. She wanted nothing more than to wash her hair and rid herself of all traces of the horrible Des, but that would have to wait.

'Oh, that's too bad. Now come and sit down and hear your sister's news. She's not long got here,' Patty said, fussing around in delight as she had another of her beloved children safe under their own roof, even if it was briefly.

'I'll just go and get changed out of my work clothes,' Daisy said, and hastily ran upstairs. Of course she wanted to hear what Clover had been up to and why she was home so suddenly, but she could not stand one more minute inside these garments, all bearing the imprint of the incident with Des at the pub.

She carefully folded Sylvia's cardigan and then pulled on whatever clean things she could find. It didn't matter if nothing matched. There was her big, baggy green jumper, and that would hide everything. Feeling better and more like her usual self, Daisy ran back down the stairs to the kitchen, where Patty had magicked up a spread of ham sandwiches and a rhubarb tart. Daisy felt her mouth watering – it had been a long time since lunch.

'I'd have made a proper roast dinner if I'd known,' their mother was saying as she passed around side plates. 'We just had the end of yesterday's pork pie. Never mind, this will fill you up. Tuck in, everyone.'

Robbie's eyes were huge as he looked at the tart. 'Glad you came home, Clover,' he said.

'Well now, this is a treat,' said Bert, easing himself into a chair. 'You must have been travelling half the day, Clover. What were the roads like, or did you come by train?'

Clover helped herself to a plateful of sandwiches, and reached for the jar of home-made piccalilli that usually appeared only on special occasions. 'They let several of us catch a lift in an army lorry,' she said. 'Those of us that wanted to come to London. The others have gone by train.'

'To where?' Bert paused with a sandwich halfway to his mouth, asking the key question.

Clover took a bite of sandwich and pickle, then nodded. 'Yes, well, that's why I'm here. A group of us have been given a new posting – to North Wales.'

Patty gasped and her hand flew to her collarbone. 'North Wales? But – but that's miles away. I mean, I know you've been away for a while, but that's so far. What do you think you'll be doing up there?' She sat down beside Bert and took his free hand.

Clover looked soberly at her parents. 'There's a base there where they can give us specialist training. There's a limit to what we can do where we are now. There's not a great range of equipment. They need us to be able to handle more types, from the old ones to the state-of-the-art lights that are only now being developed. It's a big thing, to be chosen for this. I couldn't say no.' She put down her plate and glanced at it, blushing a little. She wasn't one to blow her own trumpet, but obviously she had been singled out in some way.

'Well, no, of course you couldn't,' Bert said at once. 'You must have done very well for them to have thought of you. But we're concerned as well as delighted. That's only natural.'

Patty nodded in agreement, her face pale despite the heat from the oven.

Daisy turned to her sister. 'So how long are you here for? Is this a stopover in between the south coast to North Wales?'

Clover gave a small smile. 'I'm afraid so. It's just one night. I've got to be at the station by mid-morning. There will be several of us travelling together so you needn't worry. Hope you've not covered my bed with all your clothes, Daisy.'

'Of course not!' Daisy replied at once, even though she had.

Patty cut the tart into generous slices and started to serve them up. 'Here, Robbie, I can see you didn't want any sandwiches and were waiting for this.'

'Is there any cream or custard?' he asked hopefully, and was met with a glare from his mother.

'No, I'm afraid there isn't,' she said firmly.

'Nice try, though,' Clover added, and Robbie grinned at his middle sister.

They all fell silent while they ate.

'I suppose Rose is working?' Clover asked, having finished first, being the hungriest.

'Yes, she's on lates this week,' Robbie piped up, and Daisy remembered Percy Jenkins and how proud he was of his sister. She'd ask Rose about her.

'So you won't see her. She'll be sorry to have missed you,' Patty added, her face falling at the idea. There was nothing she loved more than having as many members of her family together as possible.

Clover nodded. 'I didn't expect to see everyone.

There was no time to send a message to warn you – it happened very fast. Then there was a truck leaving and three of us got on. We only just managed to pack. I've had to leave some things behind and my friend Marigold will bring them with her.' She scraped the last trace of the rhubarb from her plate. 'Lovely tart, Ma.'

Patty's face relaxed and she beamed. 'The least we could do,' she said. 'We were lucky to have some rhubarb all the way from Yorkshire. One of our delivery people got hold of it. He didn't say how and I didn't ask. What good timing that proved to be. And yes, Robbie, I wish we'd had a way of making custard but I didn't have any eggs.'

Clover laughed. 'I didn't expect it. I know how hard they can be to get hold of. We're hoping for some friendly farmers in Wales.'

'Not too many of those in Dalston,' Daisy chipped in, and they shared a grin.

She thought about what Clover had been like before the war and how they'd argued non-stop. How different she was now. That was what responsibility did to you. It occurred to her that it had made things more difficult for her sister, detouring via London rather than going straight from camp to camp. But Clover would have known how much it meant to their mother to see her, even if it was just for the one night.

'How's the new baby?' Clover asked, changing the subject. 'Sounded like he picked a terrible time to arrive. You must have had your hands full, Ma.'

'Yes, it was a bit of a pickle,' Patty admitted. 'But

Rose was there and so we knew everything would be all right. Hope helped out – she's on the ambulances now, you know.'

'Yes, you said.' Clover spoke as if she knew what it would have been like, that night under the stairs. Of course, she'd witnessed the medics in action on the army base, when those poor pilots had crashed during the Battle of Britain.

Daisy chuckled. 'We saw Hope the other day, swearing blind that she'd never have a baby herself. I reckon Artie has put her right off. Looks like Faith lets everyone else take care of him and Hope's pretty fed up.'

Clover raised an eyebrow. 'Surprise, surprise.'

'Don't talk about your cousin like that,' Patty said, but Daisy persisted.

'Ma, you were there. Hope has had enough, and Faith isn't pulling her weight, just like we all thought would happen.'

Patty began to stack the empty plates. 'Yes, and I was also there when Artie was born, like we just said. I can tell you that Faith loves her baby. There's no question about that. It's hard being a new mum, and you're tired all the time – no wonder she looks to others to help out now and again. I know it's tough on Hope, what with her job now, but you wait and see. It's hard to describe till you've had one of your own.'

Daisy made a face, and Robbie laughed and pointed. 'Daisy doesn't want a baby either.'

Daisy turned to him. 'No, because I remember what you were like when you arrived, you little horror. Kept us all up at every hour of the night, nothing but a nuisance.' She reached to tickle him, to soften her words.

'I'll put the kettle on,' Clover offered, clearly keen to avoid being drawn in to the discussion on her one night at home. 'Looks as if I'll just have to meet my new cousin another time. They won't thank me for turning up at this hour, that's for sure.'

Patty moved into the back kitchen to begin the washing-up and soon Daisy could hear the murmured conversation between her mother and sister as they fell into the familiar routine at the sink.

She leant back and stretched her arms above her head, ignoring Robbie's attempts to needle her. She was glad Clover had made the effort to come home; she'd missed her more than she would usually care to admit. They were so close in age and for years had done everything together; it was strange to be apart now. That was war for you.

Robbie was eventually persuaded to go to bed, Clover having promised to have breakfast with him before he went to school in the morning. Then they sat round the warmth of the range, drinking more tea and exchanging news on more grown-up subjects that they couldn't raise in front of the young boy, until Patty regretfully admitted that her eyes were closing and she couldn't stay up for a minute longer.

'So . . .' Clover sat on her old bed, for once not making a fuss about Daisy having to remove a heap of her clothes from the middle of it. 'How have you been? What's going on at work? And how's Freddy?'

At that, Daisy collapsed on her own bed. 'I try not to think about him too much,' she said slowly, 'or I couldn't bear it. Now and again it hits me, being apart from him for so long, but there's nothing to be done. We write lots of letters.'

Clover nodded in the dim light of their old room. 'I thought he was nice,' she said.

'He was. He is.'

Clover kicked off her sensible flat shoes. 'You been reading the papers or listening to the wireless much recently?' She said it casually but Daisy could tell there was more behind her words.

'Not really. I leave that up to Pa and Rose.' Daisy hunted under her pillow for her nightdress, and then placed her siren suit rolled up under the head of her bed, in case the alarm sounded in the night.

'Yes, they always keep on top of the news,' Clover said. Then she spoke more seriously. 'It's true that we're going to Wales for further training. They've got all manner of machines on the base where we're headed to, so that's the reason they give. But you know that since all the activity on the south coast died down, the war's changing a bit? Like, you've been in the Blitz, and plenty of the other big cities have been hit. And now they say the action is going to heat up in the Western Approaches.'

Daisy nodded, not trusting herself to spell out what that meant.

'You know where that is, right?' Clover flashed her a look. 'All the western side of the country – everything facing the Atlantic.'

169

'Where the ships come in bringing all the supplies from America,' Daisy answered dully. It made her feel sick to think about it.

'Yes, that's what we're relying on. You think that rationing is bad now . . .' Clover swallowed and then sat up. 'I didn't come here to depress you, sorry. But just wanted to say – I'm heading up that way because they reckon people like me will be needed on shore, and then there's the likes of Freddy at sea. He's going to be pretty busy, I'd say.'

Daisy pulled on her nightdress and rolled up her worn stockings in a ball. 'That's sort of what he says. Although of course he can't say much directly.' She shivered. 'Oh, Clover, I'm scared for him and proud all at once.'

Clover sank back on her old pillow. 'Sounds about right,' she said steadily.

Daisy picked up her own pillow and hugged it. 'He might get leave,' she said, more in hope than with conviction. 'He hasn't had any since early in the autumn, when you met him. He must be due some soon.'

Clover sighed. 'It's not so much a matter of if he's due some, it'll be a case of all hands needed for the forthcoming fight.'

'I know.' Daisy reached to put off the gaslight. 'And, Clover . . . you will be careful, won't you? It's bad enough with Freddy up there. Now you too.'

Clover cleared her throat, although it was too dark for Daisy to see her expression. 'Of course,' she said softly. 'And you too, Daisy. I know it's been bombs everywhere around here. So you take care too.'

CHAPTER EIGHTEEN

Rose was sorry to have missed Clover, but knew she'd had little choice. Although there had been no air raid that night, her ward was still full with victims of earlier bombings. As evening fell, some of the older patients became fearful and confused, which meant she had to dash from bed to bed, seeing to their medical needs but also comforting them when she could. She didn't blame them – they were only expressing what plenty of other people were feeling. It was tiring work, though, especially when it came at the end of a long shift. Her feet ached all the time and there were moments when she could barely keep her eyes open.

But now she was on the morning shift again, and that always made her perk up. She'd always preferred to be up with the lark, enjoying the bright early light. Now there was a real sense of spring in the air. With luck the longer hours of daylight would mean fewer hours when the Luftwaffe could fly across the capital spreading their destruction. She'd hang on to that hope, she decided, as she pushed open the big doors to her ward.

Katherine was already at the nurses' station, looking up with an expression of relief to see Rose approaching. 'Good morning!' she said cheerfully, and then, more quietly as Rose came closer, 'and I'll just quickly pop to the bathroom. See you shortly.'

Rose nodded, thinking that Katherine's morning sickness had shown no sign of abating. If anything, it was extending into afternoon sickness as well. She had lots of sympathy for her colleague, as she must be twice as tired as everyone else, and yet she was determined to keep going.

She checked the notes from the previous shift to see if any patients needed urgent attention, or if there was any change of medication. One old man had been moved to the convalescent ward – her request for prompt alerts when a bed became available seemed to be working. Well, that was one thing she'd managed to sort out, at least.

Katherine came back after a while, her face showing a mixture of embarrassment and anxiety. 'I think my secret may be out,' she murmured, as Dr Edwards came onto the ward ready for his morning round. 'I'll tell you later. You go with the doctor and explain to him I've got a meeting to prepare for or something.'

Rose nodded and snatched up her notepad, wondering what had just happened. She had to fight to concentrate on what the doctor was saying as they walked down the broad aisle between the beds, pausing at the foot of each one. She usually enjoyed working with him as he never stood on ceremony. He was experienced enough for her to learn from, but actually not very much older than she was. Bad eyesight had stopped him from enlisting. Now he was requesting her opinion, and she had to ask him to repeat what he'd said.

'Everything all right, Nurse Harrison?' he queried in surprise.

Rose cleared her throat. 'Yes, yes, of course. I was . . . was just wondering if we still have enough gauze for all the burns patients. But now I remember, we had a delivery yesterday and so we will be fine.'

'Good, good.' All the same he cast her a sideways glance as if he knew she was making excuses. 'Right, on to Mr Wallis. Complications from a fall, wasn't it?' He looked kindly at the elderly man, who brightened at the doctor remembering.

'Yes, I was coming out of me house and this nipper on a bike goes whizzing round the corner . . .'

Rose tuned out as she'd heard the story several times before, and was only thankful that it wasn't Robbie who'd done the damage.

The round seemed to take twice as long as usual, even though when she checked her nurse's watch she could see that was all in her imagination. All the same, she was glad when it was over, for once. She assured Dr Edwards that all his instructions would be followed to the letter, and then she rushed back to Katherine, still whey-faced at her desk.

'Tell me!' she urged.

Katherine sat back and pursed her lips. 'I had to get to the bathroom sharpish, as you know. I thought I had it to myself but I was wrong. When I went to wash my hands I looked up and there in the mirror was – guess who.'

'No idea.' How bad could it be, Rose wondered.

'Only the chairwoman of the big meeting, Mrs

173

Gleeson. She didn't say anything, but she gave me such a look. She'd heard me being sick, no doubt about it. And they say she's got two sons, so she'll know all about it.'

'You could say you had a tummy upset,' Rose suggested.

'But then why would I have come to work? That would be very unprofessional. I might be infectious if that were the case. No, she knows, and she knows I know. The question is, who will she tell?'

Rose sat down heavily on the little filing cabinet beside the desk. 'Perhaps she'll keep it to herself.'

'Perhaps. But she might think it's her duty to inform the powers that be.'

Rose sighed. 'I suppose you could be right.'

Katherine stood up. 'I am right. Anyway, I realise it was always going to come out at some point. I had counted on being able to hide it for a bit longer but, to be honest, I'll start to show within a matter of weeks. It's only bringing forward the inevitable.' She squared her shoulders. 'Well, no time like the present.'

Rose was alarmed. 'To do what?'

Katherine's gaze was steely. 'To tell Matron. Best if I get there first, before the chairwoman says anything. Right, you're in charge here for the next few minutes. Wish me luck.'

Rose took a deep breath. 'Of course. You won't need it. Matron will understand, more than anybody.' She hoped that was correct.

'I hope so. Well, I'll find out soon enough,' said Katherine grimly, and then she was gone.

174

'Nurse Harrison, a word, if I may.'

Rose started, as she had not heard anybody coming up behind where she was standing, hastily searching for gauze dressings in the corner cupboard of the ward. She set down the packets, and smoothed her uniform when she saw who it was. A small, stout woman whose own uniform had such sharp creases they looked as if they could cut through paper. 'Matron. Yes, of course.'

Matron rarely came onto this ward, and Rose took it as a compliment. The head of the hospital's nurses concentrated her time on areas that were in need of supervision and improvement. She liked to think that their ward was well enough run not to require that kind of scrutiny. But that had been on Katherine's watch. One way or another, change was bound to be in the air.

Matron regarded her steadily. 'I have just had a conversation with your ward sister. Katherine.'

'Yes,' said Rose, realising there was no point in pretending that she didn't know.

Matron was brisk. 'Obviously she will have to stop work soon. I am aware that plenty of women carry on well into their pregnancy but I fear Sister will not be one of them. Her morning sickness is depleting her reserves of energy. I can see that for myself.'

Rose felt obliged to defend her friend. 'It's not affecting her work; she wouldn't let it,' she said staunchly.

'No, I'm sure you're right. However, she's past the

point where nausea often stops. You may not be aware, as her bump is far from obvious as yet. Now, don't look alarmed. I'm very reluctant to lose the skills of such a trusted member of staff.'

Rose nodded, wondering where this conversation was heading.

'I do not intend to order her home for bed rest or anything like that. She wants to keep working, as much for her own health as that of the patients. As long as she can do so without compromising standards on the ward or making her condition worse, I am happy.'

Rose nodded again.

'But we have to face the fact that she won't be able to for much longer. She knows this as well as I do. Therefore I need to have a plan in place, as we cannot say for sure when she will have to cease working. It could be any time, and I have to be certain that this ward is in good hands.'

Oh no, thought Rose. She's going to bring in another sister, maybe one from a different hospital. What if we don't get along?

While she knew it was important to be able to work with everyone, it made life so much easier when your immediate superior was also a friend – and possibly the best nurse in the building.

'And so, Nurse Harrison, I have to ask you . . .'

Here it comes, thought Rose, a heavy feeling of dread settling deep in her stomach.

'. . . if you will be acting sister on this ward, until such a time as Katherine can return to work, as she has indicated she fully intends to do.'

Rose was so surprised that she could make no response, but just stood on the spot with her mouth hanging open.

'Nurse Harrison?' Matron peered at her over her wire-rimmed glasses.

'What – me? Are you sure?' Rose couldn't believe that she had understood properly.

'Well, yes, you. Of course you. Who else knows this ward as well? Or how to run it? I have seen for myself what a tight ship you operate. I strongly suspect you have been doing more than your share recently, to cover for your friend. I'm not saying that as a criticism, far from it. It is admirable that, between you, you have kept it going in the most testing of circumstances and while one of you has not been feeling one hundred per cent. So of course I am asking you to step in. Have you any doubts? If so, you should tell me now.'

Rose pulled herself together. If Matron thought she was capable then she must be. The woman would not have made the suggestion otherwise. Besides, if another sister was brought in, she might not want to stand aside again when Katherine returned. Katherine might resent a new rival. And, if Rose was honest with herself, she didn't want another boss. Nobody would be as good as Katherine.

'You'd be called Sister Harrison, of course. You'd need that title so that the other members of staff would accord you the proper respect.'

Rose stood a little straighter. Sister Harrison – it had a definite ring to it.

'In the fullness of time you have every prospect of

becoming sister in your own right. This has all been somewhat hurried this morning and I've had no chance to make formal arrangements, and so that might take a while. Forgive me, we will see to it at some point.'

Rose nodded, at first hesitantly but then with more certainty. 'Yes, of course, Matron. I'd . . . I'd be happy to accept.'

Matron smiled, her face losing its sternness for once. 'I'm afraid it will come with all the inevitable administration duties. The regular committee meetings, for example. But I know that you have already deputised for Katherine there.'

Rose did not let her feelings about those meetings show on her face. 'I have, Matron. I know that they are vital to the smooth running of the hospital.'

Matron's smile widened. 'I know that they can seem onerous, but they are excellent experience if you intend to rise up through the ranks, Nurse Harrison. You have all the makings of a senior nurse. You may not know it but I have been watching you.'

Rose's spirits soared. She had had no idea. Matron was not known for saying anything she did not mean and so this was extraordinary praise.

'Thank you,' she said as steadily as she could. 'I'll do my best to repay your faith in me, Matron. I won't let you down.'

Matron nodded, back to her brisk self. 'I must return to my office,' she said. 'But thank you, Nurse Harrison – soon to be Sister Harrison. I know full well you won't let us down.'

CHAPTER NINETEEN

'Such a shame it's only for twenty-four hours!' Vera fussed, bustling around the little side table to the best easy chair. There sat the unexpected guest of honour, Martin, in his naval uniform, minus the heavy coat in which he had turned up. 'Won't they make an exception, as you have so recently become a family man?' She put down some biscuits, carefully arranged on a small plate to disguise how few there were.

Martin did his best to smile. 'No, I don't think they would consider that as important as me escorting the Canadian officers back to base. I'm only here because they've been called to a meeting at the ministry. I'm just their guide, really.' He brushed the sharp seam of his dark trousers.

'Oh, I'm sure you're much more important than that,' Vera insisted. 'Isn't he, Faith?'

Faith half sat up on the sofa, artfully swishing her hair. 'Bound to be,' she beamed. 'You play your cards right if you meet the top brass and you could be in for a promotion, Martin. Just you see.'

Martin attempted another smile, although his expression rather gave away that he knew this was not how the navy worked.

'Well, how's everything here?' he asked, clearly

179

wishing to change the subject.

Vera looked pointedly to Faith, indicating that it was her place to respond to this man who was, after all, now her husband.

Faith sat up a little straighter. 'We're all doing terrifically well,' she replied. 'Artie is a beautiful baby and so well behaved. Of course he's very tiring, but I do my best, I really do.'

Martin nodded. 'I'm sure you do – and that your mother is a great help.'

Vera beamed at the recognition of all her hard work and Faith's mouth tightened at the corners. 'Yes, everyone is very kind,' she acknowledged graciously. 'Of course they all love him. He's such a little darling, who wouldn't? He's sleeping now, but you'll get your chance to hold him later,' she added, checking for her husband's reaction.

Martin nodded. 'One of the reasons I came,' he said.

'You can change his nappy,' Faith suggested.

Martin nodded again. 'I'd be happy to. I've had recent practice. Did you know my best man's wife had a baby not long after Christmas? She lives near the base, and so they've made sure I know exactly what to do. How about that?'

Vera was visibly impressed. 'Now, isn't that marvellous? Not many young men would take the trouble.' She looked sharply at her eldest.

Faith beamed in delight. 'That's wonderful news, Martin. Do congratulate them from me. And you can change as many nappies as you like now you're here.'

Vera gave her another sharp look, but Faith continued

to smile. 'Would you be an angel, Martin, and pass me the biscuits? I do find I'm ravenous. Feeding Artie really is simply exhausting sometimes.'

Martin did as he was asked, despite not yet having had one himself. 'I'm sure. You must take proper care of yourself.'

Vera sat down beside Faith, taking up the conversation as her daughter tucked in to the biscuits. 'Oh, she does, we see to it. And her sisters help too; in fact, we all do. Don't we, Faith? And you'll want to know the rest of the news . . .'

Vera chattered on, describing what had happened since the hasty wedding, and Faith polished off the biscuits, delicately dabbing a beautifully manicured finger in the last of the crumbs. Martin looked on, with the look of a man realising just what he had let himself in for.

'I'm never going to get the hang of this,' Hope groaned, staring under the bonnet of the vehicle. The old ambulance stood in the small yard at the back of the depot, where barely any sunlight fell, even though the first buds of spring were out. There was a strong smell of rusty metal and rancid oil. She wiped her hands on a filthy rag and stood up, arching her sore back.

Jimmy grinned and shook his head. 'You always say that, and usually just before you get it right. Nobody expects you to be able to do it to start with. Don't be so hard on yourself.'

But Hope *was* hard on herself. She hadn't expected it to be this difficult. The problem was, as she very well knew, that the driving side of the job had come easily. 'Water off a duck's back,' Jimmy had said proudly, as she mastered reversing into narrow spaces with no trouble at all. She'd picked up the first-aid instructions with barely a hesitation. She'd proved she could deal with horrific situations without falling to pieces.

But the mechanics: that was an entirely different matter.

'Take a moment or two and try again,' Jimmy said encouragingly. 'Think about what you do when you're in the driver's seat – what happens when you speed up? Slow down? Change gear? You hear all those noises. Now look, here's where . . .'

Hope tried to pay attention, but nothing was going in. She had to face it: engines made no sense to her. Yet she could not avoid this part of the job. If she was out on a call and the vehicle broke down, it would be up to her to fix it.

'Hope, you're not listening,' Jimmy scolded. 'Watch what I'm doing. All right, you might get your hands a bit dirty but that's never bothered you up till now. That's it, that tube thing. Pull it out, see how it joins the rest of the engine.'

Hope did not want anyone to think she minded getting covered in oil and so she had a go, but really had no idea of what Jimmy was on about. It was all well and good with him standing there, showing her exactly what to do. What if he wasn't there? Still, she wanted to do her best for him, as he was taking so much care to teach her well.

'Like that?' she asked dubiously.

Jimmy shrugged. 'Better. Definitely better.'

He was humouring her, she could tell.

'Let's take a break and have a cuppa,' he suggested. 'Always good to try something tricky after you've had a chance to warm up. That'll be half the trouble, cold hands. You've got to feel what you're doing, sense it. Like when you drive, you listen to the engine without even thinking about it. Well, fixing it is the same sort of thing.'

'If you say so,' Hope said, trying not to be defeated, but it was an uphill battle.

They wiped off as much oil as they could and stepped inside the depot building, which was buzzing with people as usual: drivers changing shifts, messengers bringing requests from the ARP, and first-aiders signing up classes. There was a queue for the tea urn.

'You get one for me. I just need to check something,' Jimmy said, and left her standing behind a warden she didn't know. The instructor was coughing, trying to clear his throat. Well, he deserved his cup of tea, Hope thought, shuffling forward.

Someone came to join the queue behind her and she glanced around. 'Oh, hello.'

It was Ian Macleod, whom she'd hardly seen since the night of the Bank disaster. Now that the weather had improved he was no longer wearing his woollen hat and she could see he was not in fact bald. His hair was close-cropped, almost as if he was in the services, but she had to admit he was younger than she'd thought that first night. Perhaps in his thirties.

His eyes tightened and for a moment she thought he was going to pretend not to recognise her.

'Hello. Miss Potter, Hope, isn't it?'

'Yes, that's right.' He was obviously still not keen on conversation. All the same, it was against her instincts to give up. 'How are you? Haven't seen you for a while.'

'Oh. Well, no. Maybe not.' He stood awkwardly, shoving his hands in the pockets of his drill overalls.

'Keeping well?' she persisted.

'Can't complain.'

This was like getting blood out of a stone. One more go and she really would give up.

'I've been having my first motor mechanics lessons,' she told him. 'I've never done anything like it before and it's not easy.'

He nodded, and perhaps there was a small glimmer of interest in his intense blue eyes – she couldn't be sure. 'Aye, well. It takes time.'

'Right.' She could see Jimmy making his way back towards them, and they'd reached the head of the queue. With relief, she reached for two cups.

'A-ha, Mr Macleod. How are you today?' Jimmy was his usual friendly self and surely the reticent Scotsman could not resist that.

'Can't complain,' he said again. Then, to her surprise, he went on: 'Hope says she's having trouble with the mechanics.'

'Early days yet.' Jimmy defended her at once.

Macleod nodded. 'Got to start somewhere, eh?'

Hope nodded and smiled, taken aback at the comment. It was as close to small talk as she'd ever heard from him. 'I'm not going to let it beat me,' she assured both of them.

'Exactly, that's the spirit.' Jimmy accepted his cup of tea and led them to a side table. 'Can't expect to be a natural at everything, young Hope. You've got to accept that you're sometimes like we normal folk: have to put in a bit of effort now and again.'

From anyone else this would have sounded like a criticism but he said it so lightly that she did not take offence. 'I'm happy to do it,' she stated, more for Macleod's benefit than Jimmy's. Even if he was a miserable so and so, she didn't want him to think she was skiving.

Macleod stood hesitantly while she and Jimmy sat down, as if unsure whether to join them. 'Tell you what,' he said suddenly.

Before she could ask what he meant, Jimmy looked up with interest. 'Ah, what's that then? Do you have an idea?'

Macleod put his tea on the table, even though he still did not sit down. 'Yes. I'm going to be rostered here for some daytime hours this week. Usually I just do evenings. How about I help out? I could teach you some of the theory, if that would be useful.' He paused, then rushed on, 'I'm an engineer. I understand these things.'

Hope was flabbergasted. Up to now he'd given every appearance of trying to avoid her – well, her and everybody else. Now he was volunteering to teach her mechanics. She was part intrigued, part horrified. 'Oh, I wouldn't want to put you out—'

Jimmy jumped in. 'What a good plan. Hope, Mr Macleod here is being modest. He's head engineer at one of the local factories. We can't say what you're

185

manufacturing now, can we? War effort, top secret, all that. But he's the best qualified person in the whole station when it comes to these things. You should make the most of the offer, young Hope. He can teach you far more than I can.'

Hope blinked. 'Really?' If Jimmy said so, then it must be true. All the same, she was far from certain that she wanted to. She could see it now: hour after hour of Macleod saying hardly anything; grunting now and again, maybe. And then probably complaining. It would be the exact opposite of learning with Jimmy.

'You don't have to. It's no bother.' Macleod was retreating again. Boy, he was touchy.

'No, I want to.' The words were out before Hope had a proper chance to think about it. 'I need to learn how to mend those engines or I won't be able to do the job. So yes, please.'

Macleod nodded briefly. 'Good. We'll make a start tomorrow. Three thirty, in the yard.' He drained his cup and turned on his heel, marching away.

Hope stared after him. 'What have I let myself in for, Jimmy?'

Jimmy for once was almost as stunned as she was. 'I've never known him to make such an offer,' he admitted. 'It's a great chance for you, Hope. He can teach you more than I ever could. You mustn't mind his manner. Say you'll try. I know you can do it. Don't let his funny ways put you off.'

Hope made a face. 'But he doesn't like to talk much, does he?'

'We can't all make sparkling conversation,' Jimmy laughed.

Hope smiled. 'Well, I've agreed now and I can't back out of it.' She drained her cup. 'If I try to kill him I'll say it's your fault, though. You have to take the blame, fair and square.'

Jimmy finished his own cup. 'That's enough slacking for the day, young Hope. Now we've got nice warm hands, it's back to the mysteries of the ambulance engine. Between the two of us, Mr Macleod and myself will make a mechanic of you yet.'

Rose rushed round the corner where Ridley Road met the high street, her mind on the new buttons she had managed to find on a market stall. She hated it when you couldn't wear a favourite old cardigan because it wouldn't fasten, but hunting for a couple of lost buttons at the hospital was a loser's game. They'd have been swept up almost as soon as they fell, or somebody might have claimed them with delight. Either way, she was pleased to have found replacements, and in a nicer blue too.

'Rose!'

She hadn't seen him, but now he was right in front of her, in his full naval uniform, no less. 'Martin!' she exclaimed, slightly breathless. 'I . . . we didn't know you were back.'

He smiled down at her. 'I didn't tell anyone – it's a fleeting visit. I'm just on my way back to your cousin's house to say goodbye, then I have to be off again. Only barely got a chance to say hello to my own folks.'

She grinned up at her old school friend. 'You sound as if you're in high demand.'

'Hardly.' He raised his eyebrows. 'I'm a glorified tour guide for a bunch of Canadian officers for a few days. Makes a change, but it's not going to alter the face of the war.'

'Pity,' said Rose, heartfelt. 'Still, it must be nice to see everyone. Did you hold Artie? Isn't he a sweetie?'

Martin's expression changed. 'Oh, yes, I held him all right. He's a lovely little fella, isn't he? In fact, they had me changing his nappy almost as soon as I was over the threshold.' He paused for a moment. 'Is it just me, or is Faith not taking to motherhood? I mean, she says all the right things, but it's as if she can't be rid of him soon enough. Whenever a new pair of hands appears, she offloads the baby at once. Or, maybe I'm wrong. I've been there less than a day. You'd know more than me.'

Rose looked away, gazing towards the oncoming bus for Liverpool Street, which was heavy with passengers. 'Hard to say.' She wanted to dodge the question but felt she had better not. 'I mean, she does feed him, but she's happy for others to help out. Auntie Vera in particular, but then she'd want to anyway.'

'Of course.'

'And she's bound to want you to get to know him, even more as you're here for such a short time. I expect that's it.' It sounded plausible.

'Maybe.' Martin shuffled his feet, smart in their uniform shoes. Then he changed tack. 'I don't think you'd behave like that, though, Rose.'

Rose glanced up sharply. 'Well, I'm not in that position.'

He shrugged. 'I didn't mean it like that. But . . . but don't you ever stop to wonder, what if? What if it wasn't Faith—'

Rose interrupted at once. 'But it is Faith, Martin. You're married now. That's it, the decision's been made. And . . .' she went on, as his face fell, 'you know that it wasn't on the cards for us. We were friends – good friends, yes, of course – but that was all it really was.'

He held her gaze. 'Are you sure, Rose? Because, being away for so long, I've had time to think—'

'No.' She cut him off again. 'I'm sure, and you've married Faith. That's all there is to it. No what ifs. Sorry, but you can't seriously expect me to say anything else.'

Martin stared at the ground for a moment and then composed himself. 'No. No, of course not. Well, I'd best be going. Don't want to keep them all waiting. Nice to see you, Rose.' For a moment she thought he was going to reach out to her and pull her close, but to her relief he let his hand fall and turned it into a brief wave, as he spun round and headed for the side street leading to the Potter family home.

Rose stood still and shut her eyes for a second. She'd hoped he'd abandoned any thoughts of them getting back together – or his version of it – as in her mind they had never been together in the first place. Perhaps she should have mentioned Philip. Then again, if he was still harbouring ideas despite being married to Faith, it would most likely have made no difference.

She shook her head. He was going back to his base soon, he'd said so himself. This would all be a reaction to meeting the baby, officially his son, for the first time. He'd get over it. He'd have to.

Patty knew it was early in the year for seeds to germinate but she could not wait any longer. There was nothing quite like the first moment of planting in springtime. She'd chosen carefully, and gone for a kind of radish that she'd been told would cope with the temperature, which was far from warm.

She always found a huge satisfaction when she managed to succeed in growing anything her family could eat. She knew they were lucky, as with her job at the greengrocer's they would not go short, but it was extra special to provide a little additional treat. Fresh radishes dipped in salt – the very idea made her mouth water.

Another good thing about radishes was that they did not need much room to grow. Patty would have liked to try all manner of fruit and vegetables but there simply was not enough space, even less now that they had the shelter in the back yard. Never mind, she told herself, just work with what you have got, rather than what you would like to have. Her dreams of a big garden full to bursting with edible produce, and beautiful flowers surrounding the vegetable beds, were exactly that: mere dreams.

A kind neighbour had brought round an old kitchen sink, left in the ruins of a house a few streets over. It would never be a sink again; it had a big crack all along the bottom. But to Patty this was an advantage, as it would help the drainage. Carefully she took some half bricks and positioned them next to the door of the shelter, which would otherwise have been wasted space. Patty hated waste of any sort. Then she lugged the heavy off-white sink across from the corner where she'd stored it and balanced it on the bricks. A good job that she had strong muscles from moving vegetables around all day at the shop, she thought. Plenty of women would not have been able to lift the sink.

Next she placed a few pieces of rubble in the base, to act as further drainage. There was no shortage of material as so many houses had been destroyed. That was how she'd come by some decent soil; where back fences and walls had been demolished, there was access to other yards and tiny gardens. If the earth was not contaminated by bomb debris or substances such as oil, people would take it to use for themselves.

Patty had persuaded Daisy to help her, and they'd gone out with a wheelbarrow and filled it with the best earth that they could find. It might not have suited the professionals down at Kew Gardens, but it would do for what Patty had in mind.

Then came her own magic ingredient: compost. None of the Harrisons dared to throw away anything that could be composted, as Patty diligently took every scrap that she could to her home-made bin, tucked into another corner of the yard. She would bring back wilted vegetables from the shop as well. The only exceptions were those put aside to feed Robbie's rabbit, who was watching her right now from his hutch, his twitching nose pressed up against the wire mesh at the front.

To begin with, Patty had been very much against the creature joining the household. Just about everybody they knew had had to get rid of their pets early on in the war, as they were hard to feed and look after. Then Robbie's friend had got a rabbit, which had gone on to have babies, as was the way with rabbits. Robbie had fallen in love and had sworn he would help to feed it and build the hutch.

To be fair, he had helped Bert, who had maintained it was never too early to start to learn carpentry. Also, it was much easier to feed a rabbit than a cat or a dog. It loved carrot tops and the outer leaves of cabbages, which no customers wanted. Patty would never admit it to her youngest child but when there was no one else around she found herself talking to Snuffles, and even on occasions tickling his silky ears.

She added a precious few handfuls of the dark and crumbly compost to the sink, and mixed it in with her small trowel. 'Now we make a line in the compost, just a shallow one. Then, a hand's breath away, another one alongside.' She ran the tip of the trowel across the surface. 'We water it, and then in go the seeds. See how careful I'm being, spacing them out so they all have room to grow.' She gently pinched the seeds from her palm and dropped them onto the wet soil. 'Then we cover them up – only lightly, mind – and press them down. After that we water them in again.'

Patty tucked the remaining seeds into their twist of paper and put that in the pocket of her old coat, the

one that was too far gone to be mended any mo. could use those for a later sowing as long as the did not get wet.

She stood up and stretched, testing her back to ch if lifting the sink had done any damage, but it was right. She sighed out in pleasure. The beginnings of new gardening season: it might not be a big vegetable patch but she took great pride in it nonetheless. Perhaps one day she would put her name down for one of the allotments that were springing up in the local parks. Then she would have as much space as she could ever want. Yet it would take time, and she never had much of that. She'd have to be sure that everyone else would play their part – although they all worked so hard as it was.

'Not this year, then,' she said to the rabbit, pushing a small carrot peeling through the mesh. 'We can't ask them to work all the hours God sends, now, can we? Heaven knows they do close to that already.' She brushed wet earth from her hands, then dried them on the coat, already streaked with mud. Bending over th hutch, she reached in and stroked the rabbit, enjoyin the feel of his soft fur. 'Listen to me. People would thin I was going crazy if they could see me now, talking you.' The rabbit leant towards her hand, seeking t warmth. 'Must be the lack of sleep that's doing it,' Pa went on. 'When did we last have a week of uninterrup nights in our own beds, can you remember? I ca Well, it's all right for you, you can doze off whenev takes your fancy. The rest of us have to keep going matter what.'

She drew her hand back and stood again, gaz[...] at the sky. 'Well, that blooming Hitler had bette[...] well away from my radishes. I haven't gone to all this effort just so that he can drop one of his blooming bombs on them.' She scraped the mud from the end of her trowel into a window box that stood ready for the next bout of planting.

She caught the distinctive sound of the front door banging shut and then a call from the hallway. 'Ma, I'm back. Are you in the kitchen?' Daisy was home from the station, not working late for once.

'Coming in a minute,' Patty shouted, turning to look at her handiwork one more time. 'Well, thanks for listening, Snuffles. You shall have your reward when these come up in a few weeks. All those green leaves that are too bristly for our salads – they're for you.'

CHAPTER TWENTY

'Oooh, you never did!' Effie's scandalised giggle caught Rose's attention as she entered the busy ward ready for her next shift. The young nurse and her Welsh friend were loading the trolley ready to be pushed around the beds, but quite how diligent they were being was open to question. Rose deliberately moved away so that she could observe them without putting them off. If they were being sloppy, she would have to intervene.

'I did. I just couldn't resist him. It's been so long since I saw him. I never get enough leave to go home and back – it's too far. But when he said he had several days and could come up here, well, I nearly burst with excitement, I can tell you.'

Effie's eyes grew wide. 'Oh, it's ever so romantic, Coral. To think he came all that way just to see you. That's true love, that is.'

Coral grinned and raised her eyebrows. 'Well, it's true something, at any rate. He makes me feel really special. I've missed him something dreadful, I have.'

Effie put the bottles of iodine and calamine lotion into a neat row on the top of the trolley. 'Oh, I can just imagine. Someone to look after you, care for you. You're lucky, you are.'

Coral nodded and her red hair began to tumble out

of its bun. She automatically tucked a curl behind one ear. 'I reckon I am. He's one in a million, my Jonnie. So when he said he'd got this hotel room and it wasn't far from here – what was I to do? Ever so nice, it was, clean as anything, big thick curtains like you see in the films – and a great big bed. Such lovely sheets . . .'

Rose thought she'd heard enough. If she could pick out their conversation from across the aisle, then so could any of the patients. Although, strictly speaking, the ones nearby were all rather deaf and so Coral's exploits might remain private.

'Now, are we all set to go?' Rose decided not to challenge Coral, who must have broken the nurses' home curfew, but to get back to the business of nursing.

The Welsh nurse blushed a little but to her credit she nodded and showed that the trolley was fully equipped. 'We are, Nurse Harrison. Sorry, I meant Sister.'

Rose smiled generously. 'That's all right, it will take a bit of getting used to. I still find that, myself.'

Effie gave the last bottle a quick wipe. 'It's all there, Sister. I checked against the list and everything.'

Rose nodded. 'Quite right, Nurse Jenkins. Not that I would have expected anything else.' She met the young woman's gaze and hoped that her own brisk efficiency would bring out the same attitude in the trainee. But Effie's expression showed that she was still dreaming of romance. Ah well, thought Rose, she'll snap out of it soon enough. Just at that moment a patient from the far end of the ward cried out that he needed help, and Rose indicated to Effie that she should go. To give her her due, Effie didn't hesitate and hurried to find out what the problem was.

Coral had got her hair back under control and stood up straight. 'We need more cotton wool after this lot,' she said. 'Will they let us have it?'

Rose pursed her lips. 'I'll see what I can do.' It was a constant battle between the wards to keep supplies stocked up, but from now on, she was one of the 'they' that Coral had referred to.

Katherine was still working, even though she was in effect simply handing over to Rose, making sure that she knew all the small details and practices that somehow never got written down but existed in the senior nurse's well-organised brain. Rose was pleased that her friend had offered to take charge for an hour to enable her to go for a proper lunch break in the canteen. Rose knew that she had to prepare for the next meeting, and it would include the request for extra supplies.

There was a tempting aroma of beef stew as she entered the canteen, and she could see that there was a steamed sponge pudding for after that. Of course, it wouldn't come close to her mother's cooking, but it was very welcome nonetheless. She took her tray to a small table next to the window, overlooking the courtyard. For a moment her train of thought was derailed as she remembered sitting out there with Philip, just after he had started to recover. That magic moment when she realised she hadn't been imagining things – and he recognised her voice even though he had been in a coma all the time she'd been speaking to him. For a wild instant she wondered if she could get away, just like

Coral's Jonnie had done, and visit him on his air base. She wouldn't have the nerve to book a hotel room . . . No, she told herself, don't even think about it. You've got an hour away from the ward; you have to use it to prepare.

Because, of course, she did think about him often, and what their relationship might bring. Something in what Coral had said had touched a nerve. The young nurse's delight in seeing her boyfriend had made Rose long for something similar. When would she ever feel Philip's arms around her again? This separation felt as if it was going to go on for ever. She tried not to mind, to lose herself in her work, but deep down she yearned for him constantly.

She brought her gaze back to the busy canteen. It was full of chatter and the sounds of cutlery on plates. Hungrily she took a mouthful of beef stew. Not bad, considering the pressures that the cooks were under. Lots of carrots helped to bulk it out. She smiled as she remembered the posters that had sprung up everywhere, proclaiming that carrots helped you to see in the dark. She doubted that was really true, although they were full of vitamins, and didn't one of those help the eyesight? One of the most successful air-force pilots had claimed carrots had helped him spot enemy planes as they tried to fly in on raids. She took another mouthful. If it helped her to navigate in the blackout and not fall over the kerbs, she'd be grateful.

Looking up, she noticed that Effie had also taken a lunch break, sitting at a table on the opposite side of the busy room. For a moment the queue for the stew obscured who she was eating with. Then a group of midwives moved out of the way and sat together at one of the long tables and the view was clear.

Suddenly Rose felt the food grow heavy on her tongue. Effie was sitting with Mr Prendergast, and laughing at something he said. She couldn't imagine the horrible man making a joke, but the trainee was behaving as if he had. Perhaps he was not so bad after all – but Rose doubted it. Then he leant in closer to the young woman and put his hand on her bare forearm. Rose shuddered, but Effie did not seem to mind. It was only for a moment, but it made Rose squirm.

The surgeon looked up and met her gaze. He knows that I've seen him, Rose thought, and was tempted to look away. Then she steeled herself to gaze levelly back. Let him know that she did not approve and would not back down. Effie seemed to have forgotten his dubious behaviour on the night of the big raid, but Rose had not. Effie was her responsibility now. Let him realise he was being watched, and wonder what she was going to do about it. Perhaps it would put him off.

If Rose hoped that Mr Prendergast would change his spots, she soon found that she was wrong. As she took her place at the meeting the next morning, he was already there, eyeing her in his predictably creepy way. Rose sat next to the kind midwife, knowing that this would give her confidence. She set down her notes and tidied them so that all the edges lined up. A small thing but it made her feel better.

She knew that the onus was on her to represent

her ward. She was no longer standing in for Katherine at a one-off event; now it was all down to her. On the one hand, it made her feel more nervous. Yet on the other, it buoyed her up: here was her chance to see if she was up to the mark. All the work before and after would be her own, for good or ill.

Matron herself was also at the meeting, taking the seat to the right hand of the chairwoman. Rose could not decide if that was good or not. Well, she had better get used to Matron's direct scrutiny. There would be no Katherine in between to act as a buffer.

The meeting followed its usual pattern of each member in turn giving their report, as Mrs Gleeson's attention moved around the room. The midwife spoke about the difficulties of women reaching the hospital in time, owing to the blackout, and their understandable reluctance to venture out of the shelters during the raids. 'Perhaps we should liaise more closely with the ambulance service,' suggested the chair, and Rose thought of Hope, now apparently learning how to fix engines, along with all her other accomplishments.

'Sister Harrison, let's hear what you have to say.' The chairwoman was businesslike as ever, and Rose took a deep breath. Matron was looking at her over her wire-rimmed glasses, but with an encouraging expression. Rose gave what she hoped was a professional but warm smile and began, explaining about their need for supplies. She knew it would not be popular with other sisters who had the same problem, but it was necessary to set out the issue. If she did not, then nobody would.

Sure enough, the sister from the children's ward

spoke up and said she had the exact same worry, and why should extra supplies not go to her patients instead? Rose acknowledged she had a point, but she could not let her own charges go short.

The chairwoman cleared her throat. 'It seems to me that this is a problem not restricted to one ward. It might be time to change our supply requirement all round. Leave it with me.'

Rose nodded in relief, as she had no wish to make an enemy of the other sister. Then she gave the rest of her report, which was far less troublesome.

Just as she thought her ordeal was over, Mr Prendergast raised one bony finger. 'If I may,' he said, smarmy as ever. 'Are we to take the men's general ward figures at face value? I have to remind you that there was a query hanging over them before. When presented by the same nurse, as it happens. That cannot be a coincidence.' He smiled genially, as if he had only pointed out the obvious.

Rose inhaled sharply – how dare he? – and the kind midwife patted her arm beneath the table so the others would not see.

Before she could reply, Matron turned to the surgeon. 'You have me at a disadvantage, Mr Prendergast, as I was not in attendance at the meeting to which you refer. However,' and her voice grew in strength, 'I have no reason to doubt those figures. I had sight of them before and I can assure you that they tally exactly with the ones I myself had put together. In fact, frankly I find it astonishing that you should doubt them.' She fixed him with her beady eye.

Rose could feel her shoulders relaxing in relief. She knew that she could not have spoken so directly, and her anger might have caused her to be rash. But there was no need. Matron had her back, and agreed with her figures. Matron had put the odious little man well and truly in his place.

'In that case, let us move along.' Mrs Gleeson obviously had no intention of wasting any more time on a false accusation.

Rose paused in the corridor as she left the meeting room, to catch a few words with the midwife who had been quietly supportive. 'That's twice you've done that – thank you,' she said, heartfelt, as the middle-aged woman approached, carrying a heavy file.

'Oh, think nothing of it.' The woman smiled and Rose was certain that she was excellent at her job, reassuring anxious women as they laboured to give birth to their babies.

'Well, I appreciate it.' Rose wanted to emphasise her thanks. It was in one way a small thing, and yet it had made all the difference to her confidence at those crucial moments.

The midwife looked back over her shoulder. 'That man's a menace,' she said. 'The first time he did it, I was certain it was just him being his usual self, wanting to hear his own voice. But he's done it again, and so blatantly too. What's he got against you? Have you offended him somehow?'

Rose shook her head. 'I try to have as little to do with him as possible.'

'Of course. Who wouldn't?'

Rose sighed. 'Well, one of my trainees doesn't seem to mind him, in fact quite the opposite.' She decided to explain a little more. 'He's trying to take advantage of her, I'm pretty sure. I can't keep my eyes on her all the time. I've told her to trust her instincts, but, well, I'm not sure how well developed they are as yet. She's the youngest on our ward. But I'm on to him.'

The midwife's mouth turned down at the corners. 'You're on to him and he knows it. Well, that's it, then. He's wary of what you might say, so he's trying to discredit you.'

Rose nodded. 'That's exactly what my ward sister told me the last time. Once she said that, it made complete sense.'

The midwife grinned. 'I have to be off, but glad we know what he's up to. And it won't work, will it? Matron was down on him like a ton of bricks. People know you now, and trust what you say. It won't be so easy for him to make them doubt you. You're not a junior nurse any more.'

Rose realised the woman was right. Her new position not only came with heavy responsibility, it gave her power. She was not perhaps as vulnerable as she feared.

'Good luck,' said the friendly midwife, and headed off back to the labour ward. Rose gave her a cheery wave as she disappeared around the corner of the hall.

Then she nearly jumped out of her skin as she turned to make her way back to her own ward. Mr Prendergast had done it again, crept up without making a sound.

He stood in her way, anger radiating off him in waves.

'Don't think I don't know what you're up to,' he hissed. 'Getting Matron to insult me in front of everyone. I shan't forget it.'

Rose would have crumbled in the face of such hostility only a short while ago. Now, though, she saw it for what it was: empty bluster. He was trying to intimidate her but he would not succeed.

'Don't be ridiculous,' she snapped. 'I'm not even going to argue with you. Now please stand aside.'

His eyes bulged so much she thought they might pop.

'Very well, Nurse Harrison,' he said between gritted teeth. 'But don't expect me to call you Sister. You are nothing but an imposter. You're no kind of sister.'

Rose strode away, her cheeks burning but her head held high. Let him call her what he liked. That was up to him, and his refusal made him appear even more petty. He was digging his own grave.

CHAPTER TWENTY-ONE

Hope looked at herself in the rather mottled mirror in the depot's cramped toilets. She'd been issued with a set of cotton drill overalls in an unflattering sludge colour, but she supposed that didn't matter as they would soon be covered in oil anyway. To think that she used not to care in particular what she wore – that was the sort of thing Faith worried about. Now she longed to add a splash of colour: a scarf or belt or anything.

'Young Hope! You ready or what?' Jimmy was calling her from outside, as close as he ever got to being impatient.

'On my way,' she shouted back. Still she hesitated. It was her first lesson with Ian Macleod and she was nervous. It annoyed her that she felt so shaky, but she couldn't calm her nerves no matter how hard she tried.

There was nothing for it but to go out into the yard and get on with it. Jimmy was waiting for her, a look of concern on his face. 'You all right?' he asked gruffly, stifling a cough.

'Of course. Well, a bit tired. The baby kept us awake half the night,' she replied. 'More to the point, are you all right? Have you got another cold? You only just got rid of the last one.'

Jimmy stuffed his large handkerchief back in his

pocket. 'Don't mind me. It's me sister's nippers – they bring their little friends home and they've all got colds. They pass them round at school. So we always end up getting them as well.'

Hope nodded, thinking grimly that her own family had that joy to come, if Artie was still living with them by the time he was big enough to go to school.

'Well, then, you're over there. He's just finishing his cup of tea.' Jimmy inclined his head towards another old ambulance parked up beside the depot's back fence, its bonnet already propped open. 'Cheer up, he won't eat you alive. He's all right really, you know that.'

Hope was cross with herself that she'd let her true feelings show. Jimmy could read her like a book by now. 'Of course.'

Jimmy fixed her with a steady gaze. 'He's doing you a favour. Well, all of us a favour. You make the most of it, that's my advice.'

Hope nodded, unsure of what she could say that wouldn't betray her anxiety.

'Right, now I have to be off. I'm rostered with that new woman, what's her name, Geraldine. Think I'll let her do the driving.' He gave Hope a little wave and then was gone, leaving her still worried, and slightly jealous of Geraldine, whoever she was.

There was nothing for it but to cross the yard and await her fate. As she did so, the tall figure of Macleod came through the back door, a tool bag in one hand. He'd seen her. There was no escape.

Hope pinned a bright smile to her face. 'Hello again.'

'Good day to you, Hope. Are you ready to start?'

He set down the tool bag, hitched up his sleeves and glanced towards the old vehicle. So there was to be no small talk, no easing their way in.

'I . . . I . . . yes, let's get going.' He's doing you a favour, she reminded herself. You're not here to make friends. Just concentrate, and learn whatever you can.

'In that case, why don't you show me what you've learnt thus far?' he suggested, and Hope's mind instantly went completely blank. She approached the ambulance and stuck her head under the bonnet, trusting that something useful would occur to her. But it did not.

'Ah, I see.' She couldn't tell if he was being sarcastic. 'Well, never mind. Let's start from the basics, eh? This engine, now, you know how it's powered . . . ?'

Hope dug her fingernails into her palms to make her concentrate, to try to understand what he was on about. 'Yes, er, you have to put fuel in. Petrol – at least when you can get it.'

Macleod nodded with perhaps the ghost of a smile. 'Indeed. Well, we'll imagine that we have got hold of some. So what happens when you start the engine?'

Hope squeezed her eyes shut to try to recall the sequence. Jimmy had told her this. What had he said?

'Never mind. I'll point out the main parts, you watch.'

Hope stood back a little to allow Macleod to get fully under the bonnet. Slowly she found herself relaxing, and as she did so, more of what she'd learnt with Jimmy came back to her. Perhaps what the man was saying made a little sense after all, rather than total mumbo jumbo.

'Ah, the carburettor!' she said proudly, and felt a small fizz of excitement when Macleod nodded in approval.

'The very word I would use myself,' he said, and Hope realised he was being drily humorous, or as close as he got. It was a little like learning to translate a foreign language, she decided. Not that she'd ever had much chance to try that, but this must be what it would be like. You had your own way of expressing things; other people did things entirely differently.

'Now come a little closer to get a good view of what comes next.' He shuffled sideways and Hope edged towards the smelly engine. She had almost to brush against him as she did so, the over-large sleeve of her new overall flapping against his similar, well-worn one.

'Don't be afraid to get close,' he went on, and she was shocked for a moment – but of course he meant to the engine. She stuck her head fully under the bonnet, not wanting to come across as one of those girls who volunteered for the service and then recoiled at anything more grubby than neatly rolling bandages.

'Put your hand there, see how it gets warm.' She did so and oil leaked all over her, up to her wrist, its pungent smell filling her nostrils. A few months ago she might have found it annoying, but now she suddenly saw the point: that part was heating up because the engine was working.

'Don't keep it there too long and never do it when the engine's been running for any length of time. This is just to demonstrate, you understand? You wouldn't do that out on a call. You'd be badly burnt and no help to anybody. While I'm on the subject, always wait to open the radiator cap . . .'

Hope felt overwhelmed at the big list of dos and don'ts but now they seemed to fit into a framework and made more sense. When he handed her a rag with which to wipe her hands she was almost sorry that the practical side of the lesson was over. It was her nerves that had prevented her getting the most out of the lesson to begin with. She could see that he was making a special effort to explain everything and was pretty good at it.

'Now we'll go in and have a cup of tea,' he went on. 'Well done. Do you begin to get the picture?'

Hope astonished herself by saying, without even thinking, 'Yes, it made more sense this time.' She flushed red, knowing that she'd blurted it out. He would think she was one of those silly, gushing girls after all.

'Excellent. Then we have made some progress.' He didn't wait for her and plunged back across the yard towards the door.

She was left to follow him, noticing his broad back and trim physique almost by accident. Perhaps he kept himself fit. That would be a good thing, working on the ambulances. She'd already found that she could do with more strength when it came to lifting heavy stretchers, but she didn't think she'd be asking him for any help with that.

'Over here.' By the time she caught up with him he had bagged a table. 'You go and clean yourself up and I'll fetch us tea. Then we'll go over what you saw under the bonnet. Sometimes knowing the theory behind it all helps it to stick in the mind.' He gave her a solemn look as if to impress upon her the seriousness of his words and she nodded, noticing his eyes were not ice cold as she had first thought. They were deep and intense, certainly, but not openly hostile as they'd seemed on the night of the Bank station disaster.

Back in the small toilets she looked once again at her face in the mirror. There was a dark smear of oil across her forehead and what seemed to be rust across one cheek. How long had that been there? She coaxed the scrap of coal tar soap to foam up under a trickle of cold water, and then vigorously washed her face. Not perfect, but better, she decided, attempting to tidy her hair.

Her mother would have forty fits if she could see her now, but that didn't matter. Hope felt an odd sense of satisfaction. This was without a shadow of a doubt the hardest part of the job, but she had not made a complete mess of it for once. Despite her fears, she might yet master the mechanics of the ambulance engine.

If she did, she had to admit, it would be in no small part down to the man who was waiting for her with a cup of tea in the busy depot hall. Just a couple of hours ago she had been dreading the thought of having to spend more time with him, under his unforgiving gimlet gaze. Now, though, she found she didn't mind as much. He was her route into understanding a whole new world, and if she was not careful, she might even enjoy it. Smiling properly for the first time that day, she smoothed her hand through her hair one last time and went through the badly painted door to see what he had in store for her next.

'I don't see why we have to have this done!' Mr Rathbone was most put out. 'Let the central tube stations go ahead – I can see the reasoning behind it there – but we're far to the north. We surely don't need any more disruption.'

Daisy sighed and made an apologetic face to the woman from the Tottenham branch of the WVS, who had just come down the stairs from Seven Sisters Road into the ticket hall. 'Yes, but people don't live in the very centre,' she countered. 'Or not very many. It's mainly shops and offices. People go there to work and then come home in the evenings, and that's when the raids happen. We have to provide for people where they actually are, rather than where we'd prefer them to be.' She bit her lip, wondering if she'd overstepped the mark, speaking to her boss like that.

Mr Rathbone sighed. 'You may be right, but it's so messy! Our passengers expect a decent level of order . . .'

'But also a decent level of hygiene,' Daisy pointed out. 'You know that's been a problem. Now it's spring, all those mosquitoes are waking up. I told you what my sister Rose said about them: they aren't a killer in this country but you get any bites and then they get dirty, you run a risk of infection. Crowds of bodies, not all able to keep very clean – it's asking for trouble.'

Mr Rathbone frowned and turned on his heels to go back to the safety of his office. Daisy shrugged. Whether or not he agreed, the London Transport board had decreed that stations used as shelters should be sprayed with disinfectant. They had put aside any remaining habits of expecting the local authorities to organise everything. Today they were delivering the equipment, with strict instructions that it should not be used on people when they were sleeping but to commence the next morning.

'They call that the "coughing period",' the WVS woman had explained. She and some colleagues had come along to help with other arrangements, such as buckets in place of lavatory facilities. 'They got Elsan chemical lavvies down at Holborn but they can't give those to all the underground shelters, so you got to make do with buckets,' she'd said, not unkindly.

Mr Rathbone would be dealing with the special tickets that admitted people to the shelters but not for any kind of onward travel. Daisy could tell that this was against everything he held dear, but it was a practical solution to a growing problem. To begin with, everyone had simply bought the cheapest travel ticket and then they could not be denied access to the platforms. Now the powers that be had come up with the idea of special reservation tickets. Daisy thought it was a good idea. The Board had realised they could not stop people coming, so they'd devised a way of controlling numbers. Never pass up a chance to create more paperwork, she thought. It should be her boss's cup of tea, although it would take him a while to get used to it.

Last month's staff magazine had brought him out in conniptions. The Board was allowing entertainments down on the platforms – even encouraging it. Gramophones were being taken down there, and those taking shelter were asked to bring along their records, as long as they took them away again in the morning. There were even musical and drama societies. A whole underground world was happening beneath their feet. Daisy knew they could not pretend it wasn't there. They had to become part of it, and patrol it for everyone's safety. The new tickets had the rules clearly printed on them: no admittance before six thirty; leave again by seven the next morning; don't stand near the edge of the platform; supervise children. All very sensible stuff, but Mr Rathbone grew pale every time any of it was mentioned.

Now the WVS woman set down her pile of buckets. 'My old man has a gramophone he wouldn't mind bringing along, if it would help,' she offered. 'I know his nibs in there won't like it, but it would keep the kiddies happy, and then later on the grown-ups could have a bit of a singsong. What do you say?'

Daisy felt it ought to be her boss's decision, not hers. But Mr Rathbone was still shut away behind his desk. Once again it was down to her.

'Yes, please,' she said decisively.

CHAPTER TWENTY-TWO

'Good of you to find the time to come and visit, now you're so important,' Daisy teased her big sister, grinning as Rose shut the front door behind her.

Patty came through from the kitchen, wiping her hands. 'What a thing to say to your sister. Come through to the kitchen. I've made biscuits!' She hurried back through the inner door and an irresistible scent of baking wafted out into the hallway.

Rose followed as soon as she had hung up her heavy navy coat, with Daisy trailing after.

'Sit down, put your feet up.' Patty was welcoming as ever, but Rose could detect an edge of worry in her mother's voice. She hastened to reassure her.

'That sounds lovely,' she said, 'although you mustn't think this is the first time I've had a chance to relax since Katherine left. They do let me have the occasional hour off, you know.'

Patty reached into the warm oven and took out a tray of golden biscuits. 'Daisy, reach on top of that cupboard and find my special tin. Yes, you'll have to stand on a chair, but this is an important celebration. We'll put some of the sugar I saved from before rationing over these biscuits. We have to mark the moment Rose becomes a full Sister. Imagine! Our Rose, with such a promotion!' Her eyes were almost brimming over with emotion.

Daisy dragged a chair across to the cupboards and stood on tiptoe to reach the secret tin, which even Auntie Vera did not know about. Rose stood up again to hold the chair steady. It would be no sort of afternoon off if Daisy fell and injured herself.

Patty carefully set the biscuits to cool on a wire rack, placing a plate under them to catch any sugar that fell through the gaps. 'Here we are,' she said, half to herself, as she took the tin from Daisy, reached in for the precious packet, and sprinkled the granules over the top. 'We'll just let them cool down, while I make the tea. No, you two sit back down. And, Daisy, don't forget that we've had some news.'

Rose looked at her mother to try to work out if this was good or bad. Daisy laughed, and took an envelope from the table as she sat opposite her sister. 'I'm an idiot – I nearly forgot. Yes, look, it's a letter from Clover.'

Rose leant forward. 'What does she say? I was so sorry to miss her. Has she settled in? Does she like North Wales?'

Daisy took out the flimsy sheets of paper, covered in Clover's distinctive broad scrawl. Rose thought that her middle sister would have struggled in nursing, having to fit her handwriting onto the narrow forms. 'Here, see for yourself.'

Rose ran her eyes down the first page, and then read it again more closely. 'Well, this sounds good,' she said cautiously, before moving on to the next page. 'Oh – better than good. She's really taken to the place, it seems.'

Patty set down the teapot and cups on the table and joined her daughters, looking over Rose's shoulder to see which part she had got to. 'Yes, who'd have thought it? Clover was always such a city girl. She did her best to be interested in the fruit and veg when she worked at the shop with me, but her heart wasn't in it. Plants and growing things didn't appeal at all.'

'And now here she is, loving the mountains and hills,' Rose laughed, trying to imagine Clover hiking up the slopes for the views. 'It's hard to picture it.'

Daisy pointed to a paragraph. 'See, she says we should go up and visit,' she said.

Rose gave her a direct look. 'I can't see how that will happen. I mean, come on, really? Even if we could get enough time off, how long would it take on the train? How many changes would there be? No, it's nice of Clover to invite us, but honestly. She must know it's impossible.'

'Spoilsport.' Daisy stuck her tongue out. 'Things might change. They might sort out the trains, or alter our leave, or something. We can dream.'

Patty sighed regretfully. 'It would be nice, wouldn't it? To see where she works, and all these places she describes. It would be such a change of scenery. But no, Rose, of course you're right.' She poured the tea and then stood to fetch the biscuits.

Rose turned to her sister, a sudden suspicion forming in her mind. 'Hang on, Daisy. You're the transport queen. You've been checking the routes, haven't you? And I've just worked out what the other reason is you're so keen.'

Daisy looked down at the table top. 'All right. I know it's a long shot, you needn't make that face.'

Patty glanced back over her shoulder from where she was gently laying the golden biscuits on a delicate plate, one of her best. 'Now what do you mean, Rose? Daisy, you haven't said anything.'

Rose chuckled, pleased that she'd guessed right. Daisy's expression told her that much.

'To get to North Wales I reckon you have to travel up to, I don't know where exactly, maybe Crewe? And then change for another train going towards the coast and into Wales. No, Daisy, I don't know how many trains. But you'd be closer to Liverpool, wouldn't you? And who is now based in Liverpool, I wonder . . .'

Patty brought the delicious-smelling biscuits over to them, smiling as the penny dropped. 'Oh, Daisy. You thought you'd be closer to Freddy. Well, yes, I suppose you would be. But it would take a small miracle to work it all out, wouldn't it? Not only trains, but everyone being on leave at the right time? Oh, my poor girl. There, don't look upset. I know how much you want to see him, and you will, you will.' She took her youngest daughter's hand briefly, giving it a squeeze. 'Maybe not just yet.'

Daisy squeezed her mother's hand back. 'I know I'm being silly. It was just a daft notion. In peacetime it wouldn't be so far-fetched . . .' She gave a quick shake of her head. 'And in peacetime they'd have no reason to be there in the first place. So, no, I won't get my hopes up. Still, I can dream, can't I?'

'Have a biscuit,' said Rose hurriedly, worried that

217

Daisy was going to become really upset. She regretted teasing her. If anyone knew about the pain of separation her sister was going through, it was her. What a pickle they were both in.

Daisy sat up straighter, rallying quickly. 'I'd love a biscuit, but they were baked in your honour, Rose. We should have a toast – a biscuit toast. To Sister Rose Harrison, now in charge of the men's general ward.' She laughed and raised a biscuit in the air.

'Better than sherry any day of the week,' Rose grinned.

'Yes, congratulations, Rose. We're so proud of you. Your father would say the same, only he won't be back for a while yet.' Patty smiled and gazed at her eldest with pride and love. To be promoted to such a role, and Rose still in her mid-twenties – it was no small achievement.

Rose took a bite and beamed in delight. 'Ma, these are the best yet. Thank you, and thank you for never doubting me.' Suddenly she had to pause, knowing that she would never have been able to do what she had done without the support and encouragement of her family. Yes, her sisters drove her mad at times but then, in fairness, she'd done the same to them, especially while they were all younger. Her mother had never been less than a rock, telling her that she was every bit as good as anyone else, and if she wanted to try nursing then she should do so. Not every young girl from their background had been so lucky. But Patty had always aimed high for her children, and Rose had reaped the benefits.

Patty's eyes glistened. 'No, thank you, Rose. We know it hasn't always been easy, what with money often being short, and then you having to work such long hours. But we say that the hospital is blooming lucky to have you.'

Rose didn't know what to say for a moment. Then she met her mother's gaze. 'No, I'm the lucky one,' she said simply. 'I love my job. Yes, it's hard sometimes – and when it is, I can come back here. So it doesn't matter about the money. You can't buy what we have.' Her thoughts flew to Philip, as ever, and then to his home: all those lovely things, a maid to clean and cook, but a coldness at the heart of it all. The warmth in this kitchen was beyond price.

Daisy nodded. 'It's true. But they are lucky to have you, Rose. And, to top it all, Ma's made these biscuits to mark the moment.' She grinned again. 'So hurry up and get promoted again, if you don't mind? What's next? Matron?'

Rose set down her biscuit and cup and snorted. 'Ha! I don't think so. That would be a very long way off, and the positions don't come along very often. It's going to be tricky enough finding my feet as a sister. Everyone looks at you differently. You're not really one of the general nursing staff any more. All those young recruits and trainees expect me to be some kind of expert on everything, and I'm not.'

Patty nibbled on a biscuit thoughtfully. 'Well, you're like that in their eyes, I dare say,' she said. 'Consider how you've changed since you were in their situation. It's a world of difference, when you come to think about it.' She finished her biscuits and stood. 'I'd better fetch that torn shirt of Robbie's while I remember, and bring it down to be mended. Honestly, they never last two shakes. He's always ripping them on something or other.'

'Ma, sit down for a minute,' Rose protested, but knew it was no good. Patty could never fully rest during daylight hours; there was always something else urgent to be done. She could hear her footsteps now, going up the stairs.

Daisy drained her cup. 'Oh, yes, that reminds me.'

Rose looked at her. 'Of what?'

'When that letter came from Clover, it made me remember what happened that night she got home. And then when you said about your trainees . . . You weren't here, of course, but I got back from meeting Sam and Sylvia for a drink and I'd had a drink spilt on me, so I was soaking wet. Nobody paid much attention, though, as Clover was here, and we all forgot about it. I don't think I even told anyone the full story.'

Rose cocked her head. 'Oh? Was it something horrible? Did someone do it deliberately?'

Daisy pursed her lips. 'Sort of.' She cast her mind back to the evening in the Limehouse pub, and recounted what had taken place.

'So what made me think of it was, the one who stepped in, he said his name was Percy Jenkins and he had a sister who was a trainee at the Hackney Hospital. I don't suppose you know anyone with that name?'

Rose had rather lost her appetite on hearing about what her sister had had to put up with, and pushed her plate away. 'That is terrible, Daisy. Were you all right?'

'Yes, yes, of course, or you'd have heard all about it by now.' Daisy smiled ruefully. 'But does that name ring a bell?'

Rose leant forward a little. 'Jenkins – it's not uncommon, is it? But actually, if it's a family by that name and from around Limehouse, well, yes. There's a young woman on my ward whose name is Effie Jenkins. Also, she sometimes talks about her brothers. One's away with the services but the other works on the docks.'

Daisy nodded decisively. 'That'll be him, then. He was a dock worker, I think. Certainly he and his friends looked as if they were. Tell you what, I wouldn't want to get on the wrong side of him. He was kind enough to me, I can't deny it, and he wasn't exactly big, but blimey, he's got a temper. He can land a punch when he has a mind to.'

Rose raised her eyebrows. 'Effie always says her brothers are very protective. Yes, it does sound as if it's the same one.'

Later on, walking back to her room at the hospital, Rose's thoughts turned to the conversation once again. She'd been worried for Daisy, but her sister had assured her it was nothing to be concerned about and she'd been in no danger. Besides, Sam had been there. Still, it couldn't have been pleasant. If Clover hadn't arrived home unexpectedly and distracted them from Daisy, the family would have been up in arms.

In some ways, it was good to know that Effie had

someone at home to watch over her, that she hadn't been exaggerating. Docklands could be a rough place for a young woman, and Effie still had that air of vulnerability about her, despite her months of training on the ward. She'd need a brother who kept an eye out for her safety. But in other ways, he sounded as if he was a bit of a liability. It wouldn't be good for Effie to rely on someone like that.

Rose sighed. This was taking her responsibilities too far. She couldn't change the home life of her junior staff, no matter how much she might like to.

They weren't all lucky enough to have a home like hers, she reflected as she reached the door of the modern nurses' quarters, pushing it open, automatically checking the time as she did so. And she knew she'd never have got to this place without her loving family, trusting her every step of the way.

CHAPTER TWENTY-THREE

'Ugh, you smell.'

Hope put her bag down in the hallway and sighed. She glared at her younger sister, who was hanging around the foot of the stairs, the big Silver Cross pram separating them. 'So would you if you'd been up to your elbows in motor oil for half the day,' she snapped. 'Not that you show any signs of doing anything as useful.'

Joy glared back. 'Don't they let you wash properly? And look at your hands. They're all black under the nails. Don't let Mother see you like that – she'll have forty fits. And you'd better not touch anything. If you make any marks on her new three-piece suite she'll be furious.'

Hope knew that was true. Sometimes she wondered if their mother loved the new furniture more than her daughters. To her eyes, it was twee and ugly, but then again she hadn't been asked for her opinion. 'Well, get out of my way and I'll go and wash properly. They don't have a decent nail brush at the depot,' she added.

Joy gloomily stepped aside but before she could go any further, Faith came through from the kitchen, holding Artie. 'Quiet, the pair of you. He's only just dropped off. Don't you dare wake him,' she hissed. 'Here, one of you can hold him while I change my cardigan. Ugh, Hope, no, on second thoughts, don't come within a mile of him. Your nails are filthy, and what's that strange smell?'

'Motor oil,' Hope said, wondering why Faith made such a fuss when she'd demanded silence from her sisters.

'You'll have to take him, Joy.' Faith held out the baby, but Joy recoiled.

'Um, no, I never know what to do with him. I might drop him.' She had not exactly taken to being an auntie.

'Oh, for God's sake.' Faith flounced in fury and the baby started to make soft but discontented noises. 'Now look what you've done.'

Hope groaned in frustration. All she really wanted was to get properly clean and grab a cup of tea and perhaps five minutes with the wireless, but now she was caught in a standoff between her sisters. 'Put him in his pram, I'll push him to and fro and you go and get changed,' she suggested.

Faith flashed her a grateful glance. 'Thanks, Hope. Even if you do reek of that horrid stuff.' She hastily settled Artie in his pram without disturbing him further and ran up the stairs.

'I'm going out,' Joy said.

Hope raised her eyebrows. 'Where? It's nearly tea time.'

'I'll find Mother. She went to the market.'

This was a new development. For ages Vera had despised women who relied on the cheaper prices at the market, and had insisted upon going to what she called 'proper shops'. It had infuriated Patty and the Harrison girls, who all shopped at Ridley Road's stalls, and had done for all their lives.

'Well, she could probably do with help queuing,' Hope agreed, wiping her hands as best she could on her hanky and then gripping the pram's handlebar, jiggling it gently to soothe the baby.

'I hate queuing,' Joy complained.

'Then don't go.'

'It's better than having to mind him,' she said, nodding towards the pram. 'Faith shouldn't even ask us. It's her damn baby. Nobody asked us if we minded him living with us.'

'I know,' Hope agreed, as she frequently felt the same herself, even though she knew it was mean-spirited. If Faith would only acknowledge the difficulty she'd caused, it would have been more bearable, but this afternoon was about the only time she'd said 'thanks' that Hope could remember.

'Is it cold out?' Joy asked, pausing by the hall stand. 'Do I wear my big coat or my jacket?'

Hope shrugged. Her younger sister relied on everyone else to make decisions and then moaned about it. 'I was cold earlier. Wear your coat.' She knew she shouldn't give in and play Joy's games but she'd gone along with it for the best part of twenty years.

'See you later then.' Joy dragged her heavy coat from its hook and was out of the door, her face longer than ever.

Hope peered into the pram. Artie was sleeping and she had to admit he did look sweet, his little face rosy and peachy-smooth. 'It's not your fault, I know it isn't,' she sighed. But how she wished Faith would take more responsibility, and Joy too, to play her part in what was going on in the outside world. 'You know what, Artie?' she went on, speaking very quietly so as not to wake him. 'Sometimes I think I'm the only sane person in this whole house.'

'You look very happy, Effie,' Rose observed, as the young trainee approached her from the far end of the ward. 'Are they the handover notes? You started early, didn't you? It must be time for you to clock off.'

Effie nodded cheerfully. 'There's only the one new admission this afternoon,' she said, pointing at the corner by the end window.

'Makes a change,' Rose smiled.

'Yes, he had ever such a nasty fall. Not even because of the blackout or anything. Said he was waving at a friend and lost his footing on the back platform of a bus. Now he's had to have an operation on his leg, poor fellow.'

Rose raised her eyebrows. It was an unwelcome reminder that all the old injuries could still happen. One misstep, one unlucky move, and you ended up in hospital. 'That's a shame for him. Still, he looks younger than lots of our patients. He should heal faster.'

Effie glanced back at him. 'I hope so. That's what Dr Edwards said as well.'

'Yes, you'll find that as you come to have more experience nursing different age groups. You've worked on the children's ward – you'll have seen how quickly many of them bounce back, even after major illness or operations. Now you've seen plenty of elderly patients and how long it can take them to shake off what a child would get over in no time at all. The age group you've seen least of is that of young and middle-aged adults, and that's because so many of the men who fall into that category are away in the services.' Rose halted, realising that she was giving the trainee a lecture that she had not asked for, and was delaying her chance to leave in good time for once.

'Doing anything nice with your extra few hours off?' she asked lightly.

Effie checked her nurse's watch. 'Yes, if there's no raid I'm going to a concert. Imagine! It's only at a church down in Limehouse, but they got some lovely singers, my neighbours said. They were selling tickets. It will make a change. I don't usually go out, or not when one of my brothers aren't about.'

Ah yes, Rose thought, the famous Percy. She held her tongue.

'Well, that sounds lovely. I enjoy a good concert myself. I wish I'd heard about it sooner.'

'Oh, Sister Harrison, I should have said!' Effie was stricken and Rose was instantly mortified.

'No, no, I didn't mean it like that, Effie. I don't want to spoil your enjoyment. I only meant it's the sort of thing I like too, and so I can see why you're so pleased. Besides, as you know, I'm on duty for hours yet. No, you go off and have a nice concert, and you can tell me all about it next time we're rostered together.'

Effie brightened. 'I gave my other ticket to Coral. I'll meet her outside later 'cos she's on the maternity ward this afternoon. She'll need a bit of nice music after all the crying babies, I bet.'

Rose thought of Artie and how his presence was turning her cousins' house upside down. 'That's babies for you,' she said with a shrug. 'That was kind, Effie, getting her a ticket.'

'Oh, no, she's my friend. I like going out with her,' Effie assured her. 'Not that we usually go far, like I said. Just the teashop down the road and places like that. But, she won't mind me saying, she's a bit down at the moment.'

'Oh? Why?' Rose hoped she wasn't going to regret asking. But she could hardly not, or not without sounding callous.

Effie took a breath. 'Well, she's got a young man. They were walking out together for ages when she lived back home in Wales. He's there still; he's a miner. He came up and visited. It's ever so romantic and he really must love her to do that. Now he's gone she's missing him ever such a lot. So I wanted to do something to cheer her up.'

Effie really was a kind-hearted soul, Rose thought. 'Well, that's a lovely idea. It's very hard when you've met somebody and then you can't be together,' she said, perhaps giving away more than she meant to. But Effie probably thought she was too old and sensible to have a boyfriend who she missed so intensely, every day.

'That's what Coral thinks,' the girl said sombrely. 'It's miles away, Wales. I've never been, but Coral told me it took her five hours on the train to get here and that was before the war, even. Can you imagine? So no wonder she's a bit down in the dumps.'

'Yes, I can see that.' Rose noticed one of the patients across the aisle from the nurses' station, trying to catch her attention. 'Well, you'd best be off, Nurse Jenkins, and make sure you have a lovely time. Tell me everything tomorrow, like I said.'

'I promise,' said Effie, and dashed from the ward, like a schoolgirl in her eagerness. Rose went over to the elderly man who had managed to lose his pillow down the side of his bed and was too dizzy to reach it for himself. 'There you are, let me plump it up for you,' she offered, automatically checking that the man would be comfortable and that he had not dislodged anything else. She thought ruefully that the two young nurses would be having a more exciting evening than she would.

The elderly man was not dangerously ill but he was dangerously clumsy, Rose found out, not much later. He'd now contrived to knock over his water jug. As she turned to take it for refilling, he reached out to his bedside cabinet and over went a bottle of cough linctus, its bright red liquid oozing over Rose's arm. So once she'd cleaned up, accompanied by his fulsome apologies, she hurried to the cloakrooms to wash off the sticky mess.

'Nurse Palfrey, you're in charge,' she called to an experienced nurse who'd begun to work on the ward more frequently. Rose liked her. She was very practical and could sort out just about anything.

Fortunately, the linctus had not gone all over her uniform, Rose thought. She checked herself in the mirror to make sure it hadn't dripped on the side or back of the skirt, but she was in luck. She really did not want to have to run up to her room to change, and have to sort out laundering this one. Nobody had many spare sets and it was always a juggling act to appear clean and presentable. You got used to it – but one unlucky spill could upset the balance.

'Right, you're all set to go,' she murmured to herself, straightening her collar.

As she turned to leave, the door to the corridor swung open and a young nurse came in. She did not make eye contact and headed straight into a cubicle. Rose did a double take. Even though she had been concentrating on neatening her appearance, surely she could not have been mistaken. There was only one nurse with hair that wonderful shade of red working in Hackney Hospital. But hadn't Effie said that she was meeting her outside before they went to the concert?

Perhaps there had been a misunderstanding or something had gone wrong. Rose looked at her watch. She would wait a couple of minutes, to see if all was well. She didn't like to think of Effie being disappointed, not when she'd been looking forward to her evening. Nurse Palfrey was more than capable of holding the fort for a little longer.

After a short while the cubicle door opened and Coral came slowly out into the area beside the wash basins and mirrors.

'Everything all right?' Rose asked lightly. Not that

Coral was under any obligation to answer her; she might well think it was none of Rose's business. Rose turned to face the row of mirrors over the basins as Coral swiftly put her hand under the cold tap and scooped up a palmful of water, which she hastily drank.

The young nurse simply nodded in reply.

'Oh, good. It's just that I spoke to Nurse Jenkins a little earlier and she said she was meeting you outside, before going to a concert.' Rose caught Coral's gaze in the mirror.

Coral sighed and her shoulders slumped in dejection. 'Yes, well, that was what we had planned.' She stared at Rose's reflection as if deciding how much to say. 'Effie got me a ticket, I expect she told you.'

Rose nodded.

'It's not that I didn't want to go, it's just that I felt a bit off colour. Not bad enough to go up to my room or anything, but it put me off the idea. The thought of sitting in a crowded church, listening to I don't know what . . . I didn't like to let her down but I really didn't fancy going any more.' She was getting into her swing now, sounding more convincing. 'Besides, all her neighbours will be there, and it's more her sort of thing than mine. You know, growing up in Wales, I've had a lifetime of sitting in cold chapels listening to people singing. I won't mind missing this.'

Rose gave a small smile. 'Well, yes, I suppose you must have. I thought it sounded like a good night out, myself.'

Coral splashed cold water on her face, and gave a slight shudder. 'Effie thought so too. If I'd felt better

231

I'd have gone along, but more to keep her company, you know. I'll have heard all the music fifty times over. I'd rather go to the cinema, to be honest, but like I say, she'd got those tickets.'

Rose made a sympathetic face. 'Well, that's what happens sometimes. We all get ill now and again.'

Coral nodded. 'That's it, and I did go to meet her, and told her I wasn't up to it. She understood. She said she'd see if someone else wanted the ticket. Shame to waste it.'

'That's true. Well, I'm glad you sorted it out. Now I must be going back to the ward.'

'Yes, Sister. Thanks for asking.' Coral reached for a towel to wipe her face as Rose turned once more to leave.

Once the big door to the cloakroom had swung shut, she paused for a moment in the corridor, which smelt as always of pungent disinfectant. Perhaps Coral had felt a little out of sorts and used it as an excuse not to go out. But she and Effie were thick as thieves, anyone could see that. Rose didn't think Coral would let her friend down without a good reason. And, in the bright lights of the cloakroom, she'd noticed the pallor of the young nurse's skin.

There could be a hundred and one reasons behind that, of course. She, as a senior nurse of all people, knew not to rush to assume a diagnosis. But the noises behind the cubicle door, the tired expression on the face of the usually lively nurse – they brought to mind somebody else she'd seen looking similar, and not long ago either. Katherine, before she'd confessed her pregnancy.

Rose knew that her long-term boyfriend had been visiting recently, and there'd been that conversation in the ward that the young nurses didn't know she'd overheard. Rose could not help the growing suspicion that Coral's sickness had more to do with the consequences of the young man's visit than being fed up of chapel concerts.

She took a deep breath. In so many ways it was none of her business, but the young nurse was far from home and might need someone to turn to. So Rose pulled open the heavy cloakroom door once more and was glad she had returned. Coral was leaning over the basins, her face even paler.

'Coral, you can tell me to go away if you want to.' Rose made her tone as unthreatening as possible. 'But is there anything you'd like to tell me? I can put two and two together, you see. I'm a nurse, after all.'

The young woman met her gaze in the big mirror above the basins, and her face showed a trace of relief. 'Well . . .' she began. 'Yes, yes, there is.'

CHAPTER TWENTY-FOUR

Hope bit her lip in concentration, knowing that she had to get to the hospital as fast as possible. The woman in the back of the ambulance was on the point of giving birth, but the baby was breech. The trick was to drive quickly but not so fast that she crashed the vehicle, or threw the passengers around too much.

'Bit slower.' Jimmy rarely told her off these days but Hope took his advice as they approached the last corner before the big main building of the hospital came into view. She gripped the steering wheel tightly, waiting for a bus to lumber its way past the entrance before she could swing the ambulance as close as possible to the wide doors.

Jimmy jumped out of the side door to help unload the patient and Hope collapsed back into the driver's seat in relief. That had been touch and go. She could hear the woman's cries as she drove, and realised they meant the contractions were coming faster. She really had not wanted to attend a breech birth at the side of the road. She shuddered at the very idea of it.

While Jimmy escorted the young woman into the hospital, wheeled in a chair by a porter who had been waiting, Hope gazed around at the busy place. This was where Rose worked, she knew, although her cousin would be inside on one of the wards. Staff were coming and going, singly or in groups, huddling in their coats flung over their uniforms. It might be spring but it was still cold. Other people must be visiting friends and relatives; some carried flowers, or parcels.

Hope watched as a young boy on a bicycle came cycling up to the porter's lodge, delivering a message of some kind. He must be old enough to have left school, she decided, but too young to enlist. That could be Robbie in a few years. She turned away; she didn't want to think of the war going on that long.

Across the road, two young women in nurses' uniform were standing close together, talking earnestly. Hope squinted so that she could make out their expressions more clearly. One, taller, and with stunning red hair visible around the edges of her cap, looked upset. Hope wondered what could have happened. Then the shorter one, more slightly built, began speaking and Hope decided she looked upset as well. Perhaps they were comforting one another. Maybe they had had a difficult shift, losing a patient they'd come to know or something like that.

Hope could sympathise. It was another thing that she didn't like to think about: when you did your best but the patient died anyway. It hadn't happened often, but when it had, she'd found it hit her very hard. It turned out that she could deal with all manner of medical emergencies, broken bones and blood, but the real difficulty was coping with deaths, especially unexpected ones. She'd known it would be part of the job but had yet to find a way to manage the grim reality of not being able to save everyone.

The sound of the passenger door opening brought her out of her wandering thoughts. Jimmy hopped back onto the front seat, rubbing his hands for warmth. 'That was a close one,' he exclaimed. 'Never seen a porter move so fast. They got her straight into theatre and one of the doctors told me that another few minutes and it would have been too late: she'd have given birth in the back. Bet you're glad we didn't have to see that, eh?'

Hope shuddered. 'Poor woman. But we got her here, that's the main thing.'

'We did. Though I thought we were all going to be goners at one point. You didn't half hit that accelerator pedal, young Hope.'

She glanced sideways to see if he meant it as a criticism or not. 'If I hadn't we'd still be stuck on Mare Street,' she pointed out. 'Wouldn't want that on the certificate, would we? Place of birth: the bus stop, opposite the town hall.'

Jimmy stuck his hands in his pockets. 'Well, you got us here in one piece somehow or other.'

A horn sounded from behind them. Hope looked in the mirror to see another ambulance waiting to unload its patients. She hastily started the engine and moved off, waving at the other driver in acknowledgement. 'Busy today, even without a raid last night,' she observed.

'Yes, babies still arrive, no matter what else is going on,' said Jimmy cheerfully. 'Now we'd better be getting back to the depot. I do believe you have another of your lessons this afternoon.'

Hope nodded apprehensively. Mr Macleod had taken

her through several sessions since the first and most terrifying one, but she had still to find out much about him other than he was a top-notch engineer. 'Yes, and I don't know what's worse,' she said. 'Mechanics sessions or babies almost arriving on the way to hospital.'

Jimmy smiled, refusing to be riled. 'Lucky you – you can have both on the same day.'

Hope drove more slowly on the way back to the depot, glad that she didn't have to put up with the woman's cries any longer. They had shredded her nerves more than she wanted to admit. The longer she did this job, the more convinced she was that she wanted nothing to do with babies. When she'd been at school, plenty of her friends had talked about the families they would one day have, and Hope had had no strong opinion one way or the other. But since Artie's arrival, combined with mornings like this one, she was fully convinced. She was never going to have one.

She'd said as much to Jimmy, and at least he hadn't replied as most people did, that she would change her mind when the time came. She didn't think she would. But he loved children, happy to have his sister's kids sharing his house while they tried to find somewhere permanent to live. As housing got more and more scarce, owing to the bombings, it was not going to be easy. Jimmy was making the most of it, swearing that they kept him young. He'd explained that he was the eldest of seven siblings and his sister was the youngest, and so her kids were almost like grandchildren to him.

Hope scowled as she remembered. Having Artie in

the house made her feel as old as the hills, grumpy with lack of sleep.

At least Macleod did not make endless enquiries about her private life and offer unwelcome advice. He always seemed completely focused on the lesson. Today he nodded briefly when she pulled into the parking bay, leaving the vehicle ready for whoever was due on the next shift. 'I'll be waiting at the back,' he said, and strode away.

Good, thought Hope. She was not inclined to make small talk today. She was free to keep silent and he wouldn't keep asking why. She went through the routine of changing into her overalls and fastening her hair out of the way, secure in the knowledge that she did not have to impress him with the way she looked. Faith would have spent ages brushing her hair and checking her eyebrows before a one-to-one lesson with a man, but Hope had never paid much attention to such things. The only reason she wanted to impress him was to show she was serious about learning what he could teach her, she assured herself.

'Ah, good, we'll begin straight away,' he announced, opening the bonnet before she was even halfway across the yard. 'I shall have to leave promptly so we had best make the most of the time we have.'

Fine by me, thought Hope, and hitched up her sleeves.

The lesson was even more dense than usual, as if Macleod was determined to pack in as much information as he could, although they had less time than normally.

As before, there was the practical side, out in the yard, and then it was back into the depot building for the theory. He'd suggested skipping the accompanying cup of tea, but Hope was not having any of that.

'I'm freezing cold from being out there and I can't feel my fingers properly,' she'd protested. 'I'm having a cuppa even if you're not.'

'Very well. But make mine a small one,' was his compromise.

Hope hurried to fetch the cups and return to their table before he could suggest giving up anything else.

'That's better,' she said, warming her hands on the china. 'Honestly, the combination of chilly wind and having little sleep does me no good at all. It's a miracle I learn anything.' Then she stopped, remembering who she was talking to. He wouldn't be interested. And anyway, she shouldn't complain.

To her surprise he did not ignore her throwaway comment. 'You learn very well, I hope you realise,' he said, as he positioned his cup exactly so.

Hope's jaw dropped. Had he really praised her? She must have misheard.

'I'm sorry to hear you slept badly,' he went on, even more surprisingly.

'Well, yes. If it's not Hitler doing his worst, it's the baby. My sister's baby. They're living with us at the moment and it cries all night, or it feels like that. Enough to put you right off children,' she said, aiming for light-heartedness but realising she probably sounded as if she meant it. Which of course she did, but she didn't want Macleod to know that.

'Ah, yes, they do that,' he observed.

Hope nodded, taking a gulp of her tea. She had better hurry up and finish it so as not to delay this next part of the lesson.

Macleod pointed to a new diagram and Hope did her best to take it all in.

There was an old enamel clock on the wall, ticking loudly. Eventually, Macleod glanced up at it and then checked his watch against it. 'Right, that's it for today,' he announced, tidying the sheets of paper into a precise pile, folding them and placing them in a side pocket of his tool bag. 'Someone has forgotten to adjust that clock. It's running two minutes behind. I can't be late.'

He stood and tucked his chair neatly beneath the battered little table.

'No, of course not.' Hope stood as well, disappointed the lesson was over. She could have gone on much longer, having these new ideas explained to her. But naturally he would have other demands upon his time. He most likely had to get back to the factory, producing whatever it was that he wasn't allowed to talk about. 'They must value you very highly, and rely on your specialist skills.'

He looked at her askance. 'Well, something like that. Although I'm not unique in those skills.'

'But the way you're teaching me . . .' Hope's sentence petered out, as she sensed they were talking at cross purposes. 'Your workplace, I mean . . .'

'Oh.' His expression changed, and if she didn't know him better she thought it could almost have been a smile. 'Now I understand. No, I'm not needed at the factory this afternoon. I have to be at the primary school before it closes for the day. My children need collecting. Their aunt usually takes them but she's unable to for once. So I must be off.' With a nod, he was gone.

Hope sat back down with a bump. Macleod had children? That was a surprise. He'd never given any indication of that before. Of course, he hadn't given much indication of anything. But it was such a big thing not to have mentioned. And then she clapped her hand to her mouth, remembering what she'd said about how babies and children were a nuisance. What must he have thought of her? She would check with Jimmy. Unreasonably, she blamed him for not warning her, even though she knew that was unfair.

Then her face grew a little hotter. If Macleod had children, then they must have a mother. He must be married. He'd never said anything about that either. She had noticed that he did not wear a wedding ring, but then again, plenty of men did not. Also, he was here to show her how to mend an engine – he could well have left his ring at home rather than get it caught in the wires or lost in the maze of parts.

Anyway, it could not possibly make any difference to their lessons. It was hardly going to change the way he taught or whether she understood or not. Somehow, though, she felt the ground shift. It did make a difference to her, she just wasn't sure why. And she'd made herself look uncaring by that throwaway comment about babies. She didn't want him to think badly of her.

She could try to explain next time, but that might only make it worse.

Rinsing her cup at the ancient sink, she felt her heart was pounding uncomfortably. She could not work out what was going on. She had not been lied to; the subject had never arisen. She'd jumped to the wrong conclusion somehow. Well, there was nothing to be done about it. It ought not to make a difference to her one way or the other – and yet somehow it did.

CHAPTER TWENTY-FIVE

The woman was perfectly turned out, from her stiff coat collar at just the right angle to her immaculately coiffed hair. Her gloves were soft leather, evident even from a slight distance, and their olive shade matched her shoes. Mrs Sutherland looked as if she had just stepped out of a magazine, not like someone dashing to work to make the start of her shift.

Rose debated pretending not to have seen her as she hurried along Mare Street, but the idea of Philip's mother realising she was avoiding her was even worse. There was nothing for it – she would have to greet her and keep the encounter as short as possible.

She forced herself to slow down and took a deep breath.

'Hello, Mrs Sutherland. How lovely to see you.' There, she'd done it, and sounded as if she meant it as well.

Philip's mother looked up and took a fraction too long to show she recognised the young woman in nurse's uniform standing in front of her.

'Ah, Nurse Harrison. Rose. Well, this is a surprise.'

Rose thought that was a bit rich, as she obviously lived nearby, but she let it go.

'How are you? Thank you so much for welcoming

me just before Christmas. That was very kind.' Rose kept smiling.

Mrs Sutherland inclined her head. 'Indeed. How time flies.'

Hard work as ever, Rose thought, but she persevered. Philip would want her to, she knew. 'And how is Charlotte? Has she settled into the WAAF?'

Mrs Sutherland pursed her lips, slicked with a little subtle gloss. 'I'm pleased to say she seems to be loving it. She's made some good friends, all girls from suitable backgrounds, which is a great relief.'

'I'm sure.' Rose refused to be provoked. She could tell that was a direct criticism but she would not let it upset her. What else did she expect?

'Yes, it's quite the best choice she could have made, under the circumstances. I see you are about to return to work.'

Rose smiled again. 'Yes, I am. In fact I am running a little late.'

The woman seized on the advantage. 'Well, we can't have that. Good day to you, Nurse Harrison.'

Suits me fine, thought Rose. But she couldn't resist one last dig. 'Actually, it's Sister Harrison now.' Then she turned and made off, resisting the urge to check Mrs Sutherland's face.

Honestly, that woman would try the patience of a saint. She reminded herself that Philip knew what she was like, and was keen for her to make the effort anyway. Rose clenched her jaw as she walked on, dodging other shoppers, laden with whatever was available. It was Philip that she loved, that she wanted to be with. Not his mother. There was a big difference, and she would just have to live with it.

Manor House tube station was bustling in the early evening, and it was not yet dark as the local residents queued with their tickets, reserving space on the platforms. People were laughing and joking, as the frequency of the raids had decreased. Once again some were daring to hope that the bombings were a thing of the past.

'I come here for a bit of company,' one elderly lady confided to Daisy, who was keeping a close eye on who had the right tickets and who didn't. 'We don't need to shelter no more, not really, do we? But I'm in my house on my own, so I come here to see some friendly faces.'

Daisy was somewhat distracted. 'Yes, that sounds like a good idea,' she said politely. But her attention was on a group of young lads, maybe about fifteen years old, messing around at the top of the escalator. They probably meant no harm but all it would take was one of them to stumble and people could end up falling down the whole thing like ninepins.

The woman's chin came up as she saw who Daisy was looking at. 'I don't like them young 'uns,' she said at once. 'They're nothing but trouble, they are. What do they think they're doing here anyway?'

Daisy could sense that there was an old grievance behind this and so moved to nip it in the bud. 'I'll have a word,' she promised.

'Yes, you do that, dearie.' The old woman pursed her lips.

Daisy decided she'd dealt with her former colleagues at the factory when they weren't much older than these lads, and despite their bluster they were just kids underneath the swagger. She put a friendly but steady smile on her face as she approached them.

'Everything all right?' she asked.

The one closest to her couldn't meet her eyes, but went bright red. 'Yep,' he mumbled. One of his friends nudged him.

'He wants to know if you'll walk out with him, miss,' he chuckled.

Daisy fixed him with a steady glare. 'You don't want me to be walking you out of the station because you're being a nuisance, now do you?' she said. 'After all the effort you've gone to, to buy reservation tickets? If you want to fall down the escalator then be my guest but we can't put the general public at risk, so you'll have to wait above ground till they've all gone on ahead of you.'

The first boy looked startled. 'But then . . . then we won't be safe if there's bombs,' he protested.

'And all the good spaces on the platforms will have gone,' added the third, which left the second one deflated and outnumbered.

Daisy stood with her hands on her hips. 'Well, exactly. So why don't you just make your way down there without pushing and we'll all be safe in the event of a raid?'

She watched as they turned to do as she asked, and waited until the tops of their heads had disappeared into the crowds below. She'd have a word with the WVS volunteers who stayed later than she usually did, to alert them to be on the lookout for trouble; but in fact she thought the boys would probably behave from now on, having had their moment of fun.

'Nicely handled, Miss Harrison,' said one of the Tottenham ladies, who always reminded Daisy of her aunt Vera: stout, fond of bright colours, and who liked to organise everyone else. Mrs Nicholls had a good heart, and her ability to organise was much valued at the station. She and her team had set up a tea stand, so that everybody could have refreshments in the long raids.

'I've got two brothers,' Daisy replied. 'And I worked in a factory before I came here. I'm used to it.'

She stepped out of the way as another band of ticket holders came down the steps from ground level, carrying their bedding and bags of other overnight essentials.

'Yes, I thought you were no shrinking violet,' Mrs Nicholls told her. 'Cheeky lads, those ones, but no real harm in them.'

Daisy nodded and left the volunteer to carry on setting up the tea stall. She did not want to give away her feelings, but the silly comment about the boy wanting to walk out with her had struck her Achilles heel. Several times a day the sensation of missing Freddy would all but knock her sideways. It was getting worse, not better. It was not helped by news from the Liverpool area. Strikes on merchant ships were increasing as the Nazis targeted provisions headed for the British Isles. He'd be out there on the high seas, defending the trade routes, and heaven only knew in what sort of danger.

Back in the office, she reached under her desk for the cardboard box kept there during the daytime.

Mr Rathbone frowned. 'I wish you did not leave those blessed records here,' he complained. 'If anyone from Head Office comes and does an inspection, we are done for. The new regulations particularly state that all items brought in for shelter entertainment must be removed when normal morning tube services resume.'

Daisy had heard it all before. 'Yes, but Head Office have got better things to do than come inspecting under my desk,' she pointed out. 'They have a lot on their plate.'

Then she stopped, realising how rude that sounded, and to her boss. But she was too upset by the idea of Freddy being shot at on board his ship to rein in her impatience.

Mr Rathbone sighed, spreading his thin hands across his desk, which was as always covered in stacks of reports and accounts. 'You may be right,' he said mildly. 'All the same.'

Daisy dipped into the box and drew out some 78s, in their paper covers. 'Don't tell me you don't like these,' she said, trying to regain her good humour. 'Look, we've got Glenn Miller – "Tuxedo Junction", remember that from last year? And Frank Sinatra. You must like his voice. Or how about the Tommy Dorsey Orchestra?'

Mr Rathbone relented. 'Well, all right, they aren't bad. My Poll does enjoy a bit of Frank Sinatra when he comes on the wireless. She sings along. Not that I ever do. I'm tone deaf, I believe.'

'No such thing,' Daisy said staunchly. 'I bet

248

you've got a lovely voice. You just don't want to boast about it.'

Mr Rathbone laughed, and Daisy felt her tension relax. Everything was better when he was in a good mood, as he always used to be in the old days. She ought to be more forgiving. He was having a difficult time, anyone could see that.

'I really do not,' he maintained, and she was just about to tease him again when a scream came from outside the office. Quickly she set the records on her desk and dashed out to the crowded ticket hall.

'Quick!' Mrs Nicholls shouted, rushing around the tea stall. 'That came from the escalators. Please, make way, make way,' she shouted with authority and, to Daisy's relief, people did. She dreaded facing the sight of the young lads, either having caused an accident or having come to harm themselves.

It was nothing to do with them, though. It was only too clear what had happened. Somebody with a larger than normal pile of bedding had missed their footing halfway down the escalator and fallen forward, becoming entangled in the blankets, and taking several other people with them.

A member of platform staff had had the quick-wittedness to press the emergency stop button and the escalator was no longer moving. Without that it could have been an unspeakable disaster. As it was, several people lay muddled in a heap, groans reaching the ticket hall.

'Oh, no.' Daisy stood unable to move for a moment, horrified by what had just happened, and so quickly.

Then she thought fast. She was now a qualified first-aider, but this situation looked as if it was way beyond her basic skills. 'I'll call for help,' she said. 'We need an ambulance.' Then, as an afterthought, 'Mrs Nicholls, please stop the up escalator and then go down there and assess what is most urgent. I'd do it, but getting help can't wait.'

Mrs Nicholls for once was quite pale. She looked almost glad that somebody else was taking charge. 'Yes, excellent idea,' she said. 'I'll see to it right away. You go.'

Daisy needed no further telling and raced back to the office where there was a telephone.

'It's surprising that this hasn't happened before,' said Hope as she jumped down from behind the wheel of the ambulance. 'Us being at the same incident, that is.'

Daisy had been waiting at ground level, at the big crossroads where Green Lanes met the Seven Sisters Road, on the edge of Finsbury Park. Manor House had several entrances and she had waved the ambulance over to the correct one, only to find that it was her cousin in the driving seat. She was heartily glad to see her. She knew Hope would not flinch at the sights awaiting her downstairs.

'This way,' she said, giving the thumbs up to the ARP messenger, who was first on the scene.

Hope waited for Jimmy to fetch the stretcher from the back of the vehicle and then followed Daisy into the semi-gloom of the ticket hall. Once her eyes adjusted to the artificial light, she could see that it was still full of people, some being held at bay by Transport staff, and others crowding the tea stall.

'Down here.' Daisy pointed to the foot of the escalator, which had now been cleared of everyone who was not directly involved in the accident. One of the platform staff waved up at her.

'It's not quite as bad as it looks,' he said, clearly putting up a brave front.

Daisy ran down the last few steps. Three adults and one child were waiting, two of the grown-ups with makeshift dressings made from torn pieces of bedding.

'We had to use what we had,' explained the platform worker, whom Hope recognised as Larry. 'I know we got a first-aid stall at the far end of the southbound, but it was too crowded, we couldn't get through to it. So we did our best. Sorry, miss, as it ain't up to your standards,' he said, noticing Hope and Jimmy.

Jimmy propped the stretcher to one side and instantly began firing on all cylinders. 'You've stanched the worst of the bleeding – good. Now, where does it hurt, sir? I see. Ah, yes.'

A middle-aged man sat holding himself at a peculiar angle, his jacket draped across his shoulders.

'We did that to keep him warm as he's shivering,' explained Larry.

'That'll be the shock,' Jimmy said, as he gently moved the jacket away. 'Right, that looks like a broken arm, and you might have done your collarbone in. Can you stand? It'll hurt, but easier if you can reach ground level under your own steam.'

'I'll help,' offered Daisy, figuring that she would not

251

be much use lifting one end of a heavy stretcher.

She let the groaning man lean on her and slowly they found a balance together. Bit by bit they began to inch across to the up escalator, which was now cleared of people.

'Can . . . would you . . . ?' he gasped, his face pale and clammy.

'It's all right, I work here. I know how to make it start,' Daisy told him, gasping herself as she was bearing some of his weight. 'Hold on, don't want you to fall again . . .' And with a clank it started up once more and they were being borne upwards. She somehow helped him up the final steps, to the last of the daylight and the comforting sight of more ARP staff and another ambulance pulling up.

Daisy handed over the patient to the newly arrived medical staff and then turned and dashed back to the ticket hall. To her amazement, there was Hope, carrying the injured child. The little boy was about nine, and Daisy felt faint for a second, thinking he was not much smaller than Robbie.

'He's going to be all right. It's another case of bad shock,' Hope murmured. 'But he's badly cut, and needs attention right away. I'll take him to the ambulance and make a start, while Larry and Jimmy bring up the most badly injured woman. We need another stretcher down there for the last casualty. I can't lift her.'

'Another ambulance just came,' Daisy remembered. 'Driven by a tall woman with short sandy hair.'

Hope nodded. 'That'll be Geraldine. Couldn't have asked for better. She's stronger than most of the men at the depot. She'll manage this with no trouble.' She gently adjusted the boy's grip around her neck and then hurried up the last stairs to the pavement outside, for all the world as if he weighed no more than Artie.

Daisy zigzagged her way through some of the locals waiting for their chance to take their places on the platforms, who were milling around the edges of the ticket hall. From the top of the down escalator, she could now see that all the casualties had been safely taken away and that soon they would be able to allow everyone downstairs. It had been bad enough, but could have been so much worse.

She ran up the stairs to the pavement level, searching for Hope to thank her. Now it was almost dark, and it took a minute to work out that she was around the far side of the ambulance, taking a swig of tea from a flask.

'How did you do that?' Daisy asked as she came up to her. 'Lift that child, I mean. You got him to safety in no time at all.'

She could just about see Hope smiling in the dim light of the anti-aircraft beams. 'Practice,' she laughed. 'When I first began I could never have done it but I've built up my muscles a bit. Also, I need to be able to change a wheel and they're really heavy. Can't rely on Jimmy being there to bail me out every time.'

Daisy was impressed. 'Well, I'm glad you can do it. I suppose you have to dash off to the hospital now.'

Hope screwed the stopper back on her flask. 'Yes, sounds as if they're fully loaded up and so I'm off. I was going to drop by Victory Walk on the way home as I haven't seen Aunt Patty for ages. I suppose Uncle Bert will be out on fire-watching duty?'

'He's bound to be. Well, tell them I'm going to be late, because I'll have to make sure everything's been cleaned up properly here. But then I'll be back after that. So I might see you later – if there's no raid, of course. But it's been ages.'

'Famous last words!' chuckled Hope as she hopped back into the front seat. 'Don't tempt fate!'

Of course, the city's run of luck had been too good to last. It felt like no time at all after Hope had driven away that the dreaded wail of the siren sounded in the North London air, and a groan went up from everyone still queuing.

Daisy also groaned, realising that this would mean she should not attempt to go home yet. There was still a chance that this was a false alarm and the all-clear would follow at some point soon. She'd be safer taking cover with everybody else rather than catching a bus back to Dalston.

She helped Mrs Nicholls encourage the remaining locals to take their places on the platforms and then popped her head around the office door. Mr Rathbone was still at his desk.

'Come on, we should go down to the platforms with the rest of them,' she said when she registered he had shown no signs of moving.

He shook his head. 'I need to get back to Poll. I nearly always do, no matter what.'

Daisy stared at him in frustration. She knew how

much he loved his wife, but he would be a fat lot of use to her if he wound up dead from stubbornness. She knew her boss had spent an occasional evening here waiting for the worst of a raid to pass, but he'd steadfastly refused to spend a full night underground. She took a deep breath.

'Mrs Rathbone will understand. She wouldn't want you to be caught outside in a raid. Especially when we have such a deep shelter right here to hand.' Daisy was as persuasive as she knew how to be, keeping eye contact as she spoke. 'Besides, it will be good for the crowds here to see the manager is in charge, looking after them.'

He raised his eyebrows. 'The manager and his assistant. I realise you've been holding the fort on these occasions, Daisy.' Slowly, creakily, he rose from his chair. 'Very well. What you say makes sense. So, let's get on with it. And you'd better bring those dratted records too. I am sure I saw somebody carrying the gramophone in earlier on, and it would be a shame if they had nothing to play on it.'

Daisy smiled. 'If you're not careful you might even find that you enjoy it.'

Mr Rathbone shook his head firmly. 'Let's not go that far. I don't know if I'd call it enjoyment. A research opportunity, maybe. So that I can make future decisions based on first-hand knowledge.' He gave a small twitch of the mouth as he picked up his overcoat.

Daisy nodded. If it helped him to think of it that way, then so be it. At this moment she didn't really care how he looked upon it, only that he made his way to safety.

She remembered how kind he had been when she had first started work, after agreeing to employ her when well aware she was not strictly old enough. When it came to the crux she was deeply fond of him, no matter how annoying he had been recently.

He locked the door behind them and they stepped out into the now far quieter ticket hall. Mrs Nicholls was tidying the tea stall, putting the milk back under its ceramic cooler and switching off the big urn. 'I won't keep this open while we're not sure if there are bombers overhead or not,' she told them. 'Once the immediate danger has passed I will gather my ladies and we'll start serving again. For now I shall be going down to the platforms. Shall we go together?'

She was back to her former self, cheerful and efficient.

'Yes, why don't we?' said Daisy, hefting the cardboard box of records in her arms. It was an awkward shape to carry and she had to concentrate as they made their way down the wooden steps of the escalator. As soon as the siren had started, it had been turned off again. She wished her legs were longer – the gap between the steps was all wrong for someone of her height.

She was the last one down of the three of them, but she made it without tripping or dropping the precious records. She set them down at the foot of the escalator and rolled her shoulders, stiff with effort. 'That's better.' Then a thought struck her and she let out a groan. 'Oh, no. I've forgotten.'

Mrs Nicholls turned to her. 'What is it, dear? What have you left up there?'

'My coat,' Daisy explained. 'I know it'll be very

warm on the platforms but I'll need it to sit on, or I'll be on the horrible concrete. I can't expect anyone to have a spare.'

The woman nodded. 'Yes, goodness gracious me, you are right. Best to pop back up and get it, before any raids get fully underway. If we are stuck here for any length of time you will be glad of it.'

Mr Rathbone's face fell. 'So sorry, Daisy, I should have reminded you. After all, I remembered my own. Well, I suppose we could share . . .'

'No.' Daisy was instantly adamant. If this was to be her boss's first adventure sheltering in the underground, she did not want him to suffer on the cold, hard floor. His joints were stiff enough, she could tell from the way he sometimes walked, although he tried to hide it. 'No, I'll run up and fetch it, like Mrs Nicholls suggested.'

He looked dubious, but then gave way. 'In which case, you had better have this.' He took out the key to the office door. 'Be sure to lock it again after you leave.'

Daisy gave him an affectionate but exasperated look. 'Of course.' Then she took it and began the long climb up the now-stationary up escalator, hoping that the Luftwaffe did not choose this very moment to fly over Finsbury Park and let loose their bombs.

Her hands shook a little as she fitted the key in the lock. Quickly she ran to the pegs on the wall where she always hung her coat, and found it more by touch than by the dim light coming from the ticket hall. They had emergency lights, but she did not want to risk the desk lamp. Everyone knew you had to use as little power as possible when the siren had sounded.

Tucking her coat securely under one arm, she shut the office door once more and locked it behind her. Good, Mr Rathbone would be pleased. It was not as if anyone was likely to steal anything from their desks if she'd left it open, but he would worry that the general public might catch sight of one of his confidential reports. Even with bombs falling, that would be uppermost in her boss's mind.

As she turned, a tall figure descended the west stairs from pavement level – perhaps someone who'd bought their reservation ticket but left it very late to arrive. Even if they didn't have a ticket she decided she would not challenge them. It was just the one person and she didn't have the heart to deny them shelter. The person hurried over to her and she thought her eyes were deceiving her. It must be a trick of the emergency lighting, or her mind imagining what it most wanted to see.

Then the person spoke, and it was no illusion after all.

'Daisy? Is that you?'

She stood stock-still, taking in the reality, the wonderful, impossible reality.

It was Freddy.

CHAPTER TWENTY-SIX

In the dimmed lighting he looked more handsome than ever, even more than in the one picture she had of him, which he'd sent her for Christmas. That had grown frayed at the edges from where she'd held it so tightly, so often. Now here he was, in the flesh, in real life.

'What – what are you doing here?' She could hardly get the words out.

He gave his gorgeous grin. 'Well, you weren't at home when I called round, and then your cousin turned up and said you'd be here while the alarm lasted. So I walked.'

'You walked? Outside, while the siren was going off?'

He shrugged and opened his arms slightly. 'There weren't any buses, were there? And I didn't have the foresight to bring my bicycle. Why, aren't you glad to see me?'

Daisy felt as if she was choking. 'Glad? Glad doesn't begin to describe it. I can't believe it, can't believe you're really here.'

Then before her tears began to fall she rushed into his open arms. 'Is it honestly you? Tell me I'm not dreaming,' she cried, holding him as tightly as she could. He held her equally tightly and stroked the top of her head, pulling it close in to his heart.

'You're not dreaming. I'm here. Why would I be anywhere else?' he said tenderly.

For a few moments they stood like that, silhouetted in the strange light, the siren in the background still.

Then Daisy's shock abated. 'But why aren't you on board ship? Or in Liverpool docks, or wherever you usually are?'

He released her a little. 'I got a couple of days' leave but the trains are so bad I didn't know if I'd make it home. So I didn't tell you, in case it all went wrong and you were disappointed. I didn't even tell my family until the very last minute.'

She drank in the scent of his big navy-issue greatcoat, and that wonderful aroma that was his and his alone. How she'd missed it – she'd hardly dared to let herself remember it as it cut her right through to the heart. 'I'm so glad you're here,' she whispered. 'I've thought about you every day, hoping you were safe.'

He nestled his chin over the top of her head. 'I've been doing the same with you. Wondering how you were getting on, while all the bombs fell. I was glad to see your house was all right. Ours has lost the roof of the back shed, but that's all. Pretty lucky, all in all.'

Daisy loosened her hold so that she could look up at him. 'It's had its moments, but we got through it. Well, so far,' she added, as another noise came from ground level. Somewhere nearby, there were explosions.

She turned in his arms. 'We should make our way downstairs to the platforms,' she said reluctantly.

'Yes, we should.' But he made no move to go.

Daisy hesitated and then lifted her face to his. At once he brought his lips to hers and they could at last share the kiss that they had waited for, during those agonising days, weeks and months of separation. She wished that it could go on and on for ever. She willed herself not to think about what might be happening at ground level, the danger they were in by staying here. It was too good to break away, and she allowed herself to be transported, knowing that this was what she had wanted for so long.

But then the sounds of explosions came closer and closer and there was nothing for it. Reality had intruded and broken the spell.

Gasping for breath, she had to move her face away. 'Oh, Freddy. I want to stay right here, just as we are. But I don't think we can.'

He pulled her in for one more tight hug. Then he released her. 'No, you're right. I know you are. I don't want to stop any more than you do although . . .' His next words were drowned out by the nearest bomb yet. Flashes of bright orange lit the tops of the ticket-hall walls.

'Come on.' Daisy picked up her coat from where it had fallen to the ground in her eagerness to hold him. 'This way. Follow me. We won't need much light, but, please – be careful.' She took his hand, and then, with her coat over her arm, used that hand to hold fast to the escalator rail as she led the way once more down the wooden steps. Freddy kept close to her, wobbling a little on the unfamiliar treads.

He squeezed her hand hard to let her know that he

was there and she had not conjured him out of thin air.

At the lower level, it was far hotter than before, and he tore off his greatcoat. 'Can't believe how warm it is!' he exclaimed. 'I tell you, when we've been on night duty on board ship, and it's been wet and windy, we'd have thought we'd died and gone to heaven in this. You get used to spending hour after hour shivering.'

'I wouldn't like that one bit,' Daisy replied, giving him a hug as she longed to do when he was out there in the icy conditions, doing as his duty dictated. Then she had to release him, to guide him through the archway onto one of the platforms. For some reason the northbound was usually less busy, and so she made for that one.

Just inside the archway she could see the bright jacket of Mrs Nicholls, standing with Mr Rathbone. 'Come on,' she said to Freddy, hoping he would not mind the close atmosphere, humid and with a distinct tang of lots of people crowded together. 'It's not so bad when you get used to it.'

He laughed. 'Believe me, if you've ever put up with sailors stuck in their bunks for weeks on end, this is nothing. And like I said, it's a darned sight warmer.'

Daisy hesitated a little before attracting the attention of her boss. Of course, he knew that Freddy existed, and what he meant to her, but she was suddenly shy to introduce them. It was like two separate parts of her life suddenly coming together, and it felt odd.

Then Mr Rathbone turned and saw her, breaking into a big smile. 'Daisy, you are back safe and sound. I thought I caught some loud noises coming from above ground. You had me worried there for a second.'

He paused. 'Ah, I see you've bumped into a friend.'

Daisy thought that was a very polite way of putting it, and plunged in. 'Mr Rathbone, this is Freddy. We worked together at the factory, before the war. Now he's on leave from the navy.'

'So I see.' Mr Rathbone nodded at Freddy's uniform shirt. 'Pleased to meet you. I'm Mr Rathbone and have the honour of being Miss Harrison's manager.'

Freddy held out his hand and the two men shook. Daisy let out a breath – it was going to be all right. Of course it was.

Mrs Nicholls cleared her throat. 'Glad you can join us, Freddy. Maybe you know how to work a gramophone? See, Daisy, I rescued the box of records. My colleague Mrs Everitt over there has her record player. Shall we make a start?' She dropped her voice. 'Mr Rathbone is right – we could hear an explosion somewhere close by, couldn't we?'

Daisy nodded. 'I think so. There have been others – maybe the other side of the park – but one sounded much nearer.'

'In that case, there's no time to lose. Distract them, my dear girl, distract them! We don't want everybody afraid. Let's begin the entertainment.'

Mr Rathbone looked nervous for a moment, but then overcame his doubts. 'Did I hear you say you had some Glenn Miller there, Miss Harrison?' he half shouted, so that people nearby would perk up. All around families were sitting huddled in groups, blankets spread out, children curled up and flasks and sandwiches set out around them.

'We do indeed.' Daisy decided to enter into the spirit of it. Stepping over some blankets and pillows, she handed the first piece of vinyl to Mrs Everitt. 'If you like I'll ask my young man to wind the handle,' she offered, and Mrs Everitt beamed at the thought of a uniformed naval man helping to entertain everyone.

Daisy smiled as Freddy crouched down and worked out how to operate the rather battered gramophone. It was far from an up-to-date model, and his parents most likely had the latest version at home. Then again, he must spend a lot of time on board learning how to operate all manner of machinery, she thought, and this would be no trouble at all.

In no time the sounds of the Glenn Miller Orchestra rose into the humid air and smiles broke out all around. People began to tap their feet. Daisy gazed along the lengthy platform, lit by the occasional spotlight, and noticed that the chatter had died down. Some young women were swaying where they sat, clicking their fingers in rhythm.

Freddy grinned up at her, while Mrs Everitt cleared a little extra room. A family behind obligingly moved their box of food and the son shifted so that he sat cross-legged rather than with his legs stretched out before him.

Freddy patted the empty space that had opened up. 'Come and sit with me!' His smile was mischievous. 'You can choose the records and I'll play them.'

Mrs Nicholls beamed in delight, elbowing her own way through, Mr Rathbone following behind, a game smile on his face.

'Oh, it'll be quite a party!' she exclaimed. 'I do so love it when you young people choose the music. You're so up to date. I never know what anyone likes any more.'

Daisy raised her eyebrows. 'I don't know about that. I don't really pay attention to what's most popular.' She crouched down and then squeezed in by Freddy, leaning as close as she could without knocking the spindly needle of the player. 'I'll do my best, though. All right, what's next? How about a bit of Tommy Dorsey?'

The combination of Daisy's choice of records and Freddy's coaxing the old gramophone to work proved to be a huge success. People were delighted to see the young couple clearly so in love working in tandem to keep the music playing. Towards the far end of the platform some of the livelier ones had got up and started to dance, twirling carefully around the others still sitting down.

Mrs Nicholls watched attentively. 'I know we usually keep the noise down after a bit so that the young children can sleep, but look at them, they're enjoying this as much as the rest,' she murmured to Mr Rathbone. 'That couple over there are really good, look! I bet they've watched a lot of Fred Astaire films. I dare say one, if not both, are home on leave. Well, I for one haven't the heart to stop them. They'll have come home for a short spell of rest and relaxation. Far be it from me to disappoint them, even if they're down here on the platform of the tube and not out living it up in the West End.'

Mr Rathbone nodded cautiously. He still could not

bring himself to approve, deep down, but he could see that everybody was making the best of the situation. As he'd known for a long time, much of this was thanks to Daisy. There she was now, announcing the Ink Spots would be next, which brought a cheer from the group of young women. His wife Poll loved the Ink Spots, he had to admit. The popular group's voices sang out in harmony, and several people joined in. He couldn't remember the words, but he gamely tapped his foot a little. Poll would be pleased with him, that he'd tried his best to join in.

Gradually he began to notice that the smaller children were growing sleepy, their eyes closing and their bodies curling closer to their parents. They didn't seem to mind the noise; he supposed they had got used to it. And at least it was a happy sound, unlike the ones that he suspected were audible above ground. Better that they fell asleep to tracks from the big band orchestras than terrifying crashes and the smashing of glass.

Bit by bit the young women clicked their fingers more slowly and the dancing couples edged their way to where they had been sitting earlier. Daisy announced the final record: another Glenn Miller, saving the best crowd pleaser until last. 'Then that's it for the night,' she announced. 'We've gone through the whole box.'

Freddy glanced over at her and winked. He positioned the stylus and the tune rang out, slightly scratchily. He tapped his hand against his thigh, as he was sitting cross-legged around the base of the gramophone, protecting it from anybody passing close by. Daisy tucked the corners of the record sleeves carefully into their own box, so that they would not be damaged by the crowds. She'd carry them all up before the trains started running again.

Mrs Nicholls and Mr Rathbone had found a spot at the back of the platform, where they could sit and rest their backs against the tiled walls. The big round emblem of London Transport seemed to hang above them, the name of the station emblazoned across the middle of the circle.

Now everyone was quietening down and Daisy moved her box of records so that she could once again be next to Freddy. 'One day we'll go on a proper night out, one that doesn't involve cramming into your family's Anderson shelter or the public platform,' he promised, drawing her close, his arm around her shoulder. It was true: the first evening they had ever deliberately met up on a date had ended in the Victory Walk shelter, not the way Daisy had intended for him to meet everybody.

Of course her family had loved him – she could not think of anyone who wouldn't – but she had planned to take it slowly, to mention him a few times first, explain how they knew one another, and then test the waters to see if her parents approved. They might have said she was too young, or that she should not lose her heart to a young man serving in the navy – as who could predict what dangers he would have to withstand in the future?

All that changed when the sirens sounded for what they now knew was the first night of the Blitz. It had been a new experience for all of them, putting into practice what they had long imagined doing, Patty ensuring everyone took their meal with them, blankets

267

at the ready, and with means of making tea on the old spirit stove. In such mayhem, there was little room for anxiety about Freddy unexpectedly being there. They'd just got on with it.

Daisy recalled how terrified she'd felt, and yet safe too, huddled next to this young man she'd felt drawn to from the earliest days of their acquaintance, but whom she had not dared to dream might share her growing feelings. That first night of bombardment had brought out all the extremes of emotion, from raw fear to deep tenderness. If she had read about it in a story she would not have believed it.

Now here they were again, huddled together, the world they'd once known being ripped apart far above them. Except that this time the bombs weren't new, and the terror, while still there, was an almost daily event and therefore somehow more manageable. Even so, she felt much safer knowing Freddy was here by her side once more and that he was holding her close. She sighed and rested her head against his warm shirt. He pulled her in more tightly to him.

'Try to sleep,' he suggested. 'I wish I could spend all night talking to you, but you need your sleep.'

'And so do you.' Daisy realised he must have been travelling for many hours, and she hadn't even asked him if he'd managed to find a seat for any of the trains. 'We'll talk later. Maybe the all-clear will come soon.'

'But even if it does . . .'

Daisy knew what he meant. Above ground, all would be mayhem, coping with whatever had happened in those big explosions. They would be better off spending the night where they were, no matter how uncomfortable, rather than trying to pick their way home in the chaos, always with the risk of a further raid.

'You're right,' she sighed, partly with sadness as they would not be somewhere private together, but also with happiness that he was here, and there really was nowhere else to be but in his arms.

She didn't think she'd be able to get much sleep, but when Daisy awoke what felt like mere minutes later, she looked at her watch by the light of the dim emergency lamps and realised it was just gone six. She rubbed her eyes, and checked again. Yes, there was no mistake: it was morning. Dawn would be breaking up there in the outside world. More to the point, the tubes would start running again soon and the platforms had to be cleared before then, so that the morning commuters could make their journeys into the centre of town.

And, even with all of that going on, here she was next to the man who meant more to her than anybody or anything else in the world. It was the most wonderful feeling.

Cautiously she shifted her weight away from Freddy, trying not to disturb him, but immediately his eyelids opened.

'Hello,' she murmured. 'You don't need to get up just yet. I have to begin to organise the clear-up, though.'

He smiled sleepily and shook his head. 'Then I'll get up as well. You can tell me what to do. Shall I make a start by taking the gramophone back upstairs?'

She nodded gratefully, glad that he'd understood

what a task lay ahead for her, as the platform was still crowded and everybody had to be gone if they weren't intending to get on one of the early trains.

She could just about make out the shape of Mr Rathbone, who was stretching out his long legs. As she drew closer she noticed he was wincing, his stiff joints most likely protesting at their night on the hard surface. Mrs Nicholls was nowhere to be seen; doubtless she was already in full swing, setting up the tea stall for thirsty commuters and those who'd taken shelter alike.

Balancing the big box of records with her coat on top, Daisy edged her way onto the escalator to go back up, Freddy close behind her with the gramophone.

Daisy made sure that the boxes were safely stowed by the office door out of the way of footfall and that the WVS team had begun their day. Mrs Nicholls insisted they both had a cup of tea before anything else. 'The early shift of the Transport workers are here,' she said. 'They can clear the platforms of people. It's their job strictly, not yours.'

Daisy ran her hand through her messy hair and attempted to straighten her clothes. 'I'll still be on hand at this level,' she promised. 'Mr Rathbone's on his way too. Did you manage to get any sleep?'

The woman gave a small, rueful smile, her vivid jacket now with many more creases and several dark smudges on it. 'A little. Enough. My old bones don't require much.' She smiled more widely. 'And you two? You made a lovely picture there together, but I dare say it wasn't terribly comfortable.'

Daisy laughed and turned to Freddy. 'It was all right.

We don't need much room.'

Mrs Nicholls looked wistful for a moment. 'Ah, I envy you. Youth and the way you can simply bounce back up with bags of energy.' Then she saw a queue was forming by her stall. 'Excuse me. I'm needed at the front line.'

Daisy turned again to Freddy and put her hands on his arms. 'Thank you, Freddy. For pitching in like that, I mean. You could see it made such a difference.'

He shook his head. 'It's nothing. When I see what you people are up against, all day, every day – well, it reminds me of what we're fighting for, you know. Those kiddies falling asleep to the music, that couple waltzing at the far end – it'll sound silly but I was glad to be there, to be part of it.'

Daisy gazed at him. What a thing to say, when he had had every chance of spending the night in his comfortable home with his parents. But she was so glad that he had, that they'd had that time together, no matter how fraught, and always with that underlying layer of dread about what might be happening all around.

'Tell you what,' she said. 'Why don't you go home and catch some proper sleep and I'll do what is most needed here? Then I'm not due on shift again until early afternoon and so maybe we could see each other later.' She halted, suddenly worried that she'd overstepped the mark, that since he'd spent so many hours with her he would want to spend the rest with his family. Then she relaxed as she saw the expression on his face.

'As long as you promise to have some sleep yourself.'

She laughed. 'I'll try. I might be too busy. But if you're

sure – do you think we really could meet up without an air-raid warning going off?'

Freddy shrugged, still smiling. 'We don't have the best track record for that, do we? But we should try. If we don't, we'll never know.'

'Exactly!' she exclaimed and then she was in his strong arms once again, just briefly as the ticket hall was beginning to fill with commuters, but for long enough to know that he really, really wanted to spend his time with her. He kissed her quickly on the forehead and set her free.

'See you later,' he said quietly, and she nodded, before he was borne away on the new wave of crowds. Three short words – but she hugged them to herself, humming with happiness.

CHAPTER TWENTY-SEVEN

Nobody wanted to work the early shift after a night of air raids, but that was what Rose was due to do. She knew she had no choice, and she dragged herself from her warm bed before dawn broke. She dearly wanted to stay in it, to be snug, to catch up on the hours of sleep that she'd missed when the siren sounded. Patients had had to be moved from the upper wards, just when staff and patients alike had hoped they might not have to do it all over again.

Everybody swung into their well-practised routine, and Rose didn't have to think, just followed what she'd done so many times before. It was exhausting, though, lifting and shifting and comforting, all while realising she'd have to be up again soon. Then she'd settled herself in a basement, to snooze sitting up, as her own room was too high up and vulnerable to air attack. Once the all-clear sounded she had hurried back to it, but it had not left her many hours in which to sleep.

Automatically she tidied her hair, checked her uniform was clean and freshly pressed, and her shoes polished to a shine. Satisfied, she glanced at her watch and then hurried down to begin her working day.

As she left the nurses' building, she heard a shout from the front of the hospital. An ambulance had pulled up, just as another one had departed. 'Sister Harrison, could you spare a moment?' shouted the driver. In the lamps that had come on once the all-clear sounded, Rose could make out the tall young woman that she had seen a few times before. 'Won't keep you long.'

Rose checked her watch again. She had a few minutes to spare. She could at least see what the driver wanted.

'It's only to decide which ward this patient should go to,' the driver explained. 'We don't know how old she is, so should it be children's or adults?'

Rose glanced in the back to see a young woman lying unconscious in the lower bunk. She'd need immediate attention.

'Children's,' she said at once. 'Doesn't matter if she's technically a year too old. I happen to know that adults' emergency is full to bursting and she'll be seen quicker on the paediatric section. They can sort out the rest later.' She lowered her voice. 'Were there no relatives or friends there who could tell you her age?'

The driver answered equally quietly. 'None of them made it.' Then she gave a short smile of appreciation. 'Anyhow, thanks so much. That's all I needed.'

Rose smiled back, glad to have been useful with her insider knowledge. It had been a straightforward decision. If only the rest of the day could be so simple. In the meantime, a young girl had been bereaved and didn't even know it yet; another tragedy of the war.

The ambulance crew lifted the patient out of the vehicle and set off for the correct ward, leaving Rose staring towards the porter's lodge and Homerton High

Street beyond. With no streetlights she could not see much in the pre-dawn gloom. It was windy, giving the moment a background rustle of debris being blown along the pavements.

She could not have said what caught her attention. Maybe a faint voice just audible above the rustling and clattering of newly fallen roof slates skittering along the ground. Her ears pricked up and the hairs on her arms rose in a state of alert. She turned her head. There it was again.

A cry, from somewhere over the main road. A female voice, high and faint, but definitely there, not a bird or a pet of any kind. Rose stood stock-still, straining to detect the exact direction it had come from. The correct thing to do would be to go back inside the hospital and find one of the wardens or a member of an emergency service. However, that would take time. And, besides, it might be nothing. Someone having a nightmare, their cries coming through a broken window. She didn't want to report the sound, only for it to be something so mundane.

Before thinking any further, Rose set off in search of whoever was making that plaintive sound. She stumbled on yet another broken slab as she crossed the road, no traffic at this early hour, no ambulances approaching to light her way with their shielded headlamps. She headed towards the church, its shape just about distinguishable in the greyness, smoke from the night's fires adding to the murk.

She slowed, an instinct telling her to quieten her footsteps. The cries had stopped but there was something else. As she drew closer to the corner of the churchyard at the junction of Chatsworth Road, she could just about detect two voices now. One male, as well as the frightened female. They must be on the other side of the wall, in the churchyard itself, where they would be all but hidden from every view.

She could not pick out many of the exact words, but the meaning was clear enough. The man was grunting out his demands, urgent and threatening. The woman was begging him to stop. That came across clearly: 'Stop, please, stop.'

Rose hesitated, wondering what to do for the best. She was sure the man was pressurising the woman, but was he likely to be armed? Would he hurt the woman, or Rose, if she interrupted them? But if she did nothing then she could guess all too well what would happen. It didn't sound like a robbery. No, this man was after something else, and the woman was resisting, though her voice was weak and frightened.

Would just knowing that somebody had heard them be enough to scare him off? Rose drew herself up to her full height, wrapped her nurse's cloak around her for courage, and drew upon her most authoritative sister's voice.

'What's going on? Does somebody need help?' she shouted, her voice sounding steady and confident, although she was shaking in her shoes.

At once there was a sound of a scuffle from the other side of the churchyard wall. The man snarled something that sounded like 'Don't you dare say a word, you filthy bitch.' The woman gasped in terror.

Then, only barely visible, a figure was racing away towards the church gateway, a man, most certainly, but showing very few other distinguishing details. Not tall; dark hair, or a close-fitting hat. Bulky coat, disguising his exact build. Rose couldn't see which way he went, east or west, along the main road.

The immediate danger from him being over, she called out again. 'Hello? Are you all right?' There was no reply, only the faint sound of weeping. 'You don't have to be afraid of me,' Rose went on, more gently now. 'I'm a nurse, I'm here to help.'

She hurried along the church wall and through the gateway. The ground was uneven but she did her best, picking her way towards where she thought the woman might be. 'Hello? I'm coming to find you, don't be scared,' she called.

Then, in the slowly brightening daylight, she saw the figure. And stopped dead in her tracks when the woman cried out, 'Sister Harrison? Is that you?'

Rose was back in her bedroom, having sent a message to her ward that she was delayed owing to an emergency. 'Tell Nurse Palfrey that I'll be down as soon as I can, but something very serious has come up,' she'd told the startled orderly, who had rushed to do her bidding. She was heartily grateful that the competent and experienced nurse was on the early shift too. No harm would come to the patients under her care.

Effie sat across from her, slumped at the end of the narrow bed. She looked dazed and bewildered, as she struggled to hold her ripped frock across her torso.

'My coat, my lovely coat, it's all ruined,' was all she could say for a while. The coat lay on the cheerful rag rug that Rose had brought from home, made years ago by Patty in front of their fire. The coat lining was torn, and it was streaked all over with mud and soot.

Then Effie looked up. 'He pushed me down, see, and there was this big tearing sound, and I thought, that's the best coat I ever had and now it's all ruined.' She sobbed as if that was the worst thing that had happened. 'Will they be cross, Sister? You got to have a proper coat if you're a nurse and this one, this one . . .'

'Hush, Effie, we can see to the coat later.' Rose passed her a clean handkerchief. 'Why don't you tell me what happened out there? There's no hurry – take your time – but you should speak about it while it's still fresh in your memory.'

The girl shuddered and shook her head.

'I know it can't be very nice. All the same, you should tell me. I won't think the worse of you, no matter what. And I'm not easy to shock,' Rose added with a wry smile, hoping to encourage the terrified young woman, who was now shaking.

'Put my quilt around you – yes, that's right. We both know the treatment for shock, don't we? That's it, you go through the phases that you've learnt in the textbook. Do you want to lie down, raise your feet? Up to you, but do keep nice and warm.' Rose was as gentle as she could be, while needing to know what had gone on just a few minutes earlier. If her suspicions were correct, she would have to act, and soon.

Effie's sobs slowly abated and after a while she sat

more upright. 'All right, Sister. I'll do me best.'

Rose sat on her hard chair that usually was placed beneath the desk. She folded her hands in her lap. 'Yes, you try, Effie.'

The young nurse took a deep breath and then began, her voice wavering a little but growing in determination as she spoke. 'There was the raids again last night, as you know. I was on lates. I knew I couldn't get home like I'd planned, but I'm on lates again tonight so I wasn't going to stay in my room here in the nurses' quarters, but wanted to go and see Ma. So there I was, caught outside, and the siren going off, and I thought, well, Auntie is bound to be at her usual shelter. It's only off Chatsworth Road, like I told you before. And they're ever so friendly, her neighbours. I knew I'd be welcome there. So that's what I did.'

She sniffed and a large tear rolled down her cheek, which she'd scrubbed red when she first got to Rose's room. Hardly noticing, she batted it away. 'It was not bad at all, quite comfy. They got tea and biscuits, and Auntie brought sandwiches enough to share. Bit of luck, that was. I beds down with her. It's noisy, what with the bombers, but I slept and all. Then someone's alarm goes off. Her friend's husband has to go to work early in one of them factories over Dalston. So I woke up and thought, I'll come back to me room here, get some proper sleep.'

'Good idea,' said Rose.

'Then I says me goodbyes and go out, only it's still dark. Could hardly see me hand in front of me face to start with, but your eyes get used to it, don't they?

I been eating me carrots. So I start to walk here – it's five minutes, no more – but suddenly he's there, right in front of me.'

'Who?' Rose asked, hardly daring to put the question. But Effie was deep in her memory now and paid no attention to the interruption.

'It's like he's been waiting. Well, he has, that's what he told me. "I been waiting, I knew where you'd be," he says. "I saw you go down that side road and I knew where you were going."' She shuddered. 'He said I owed him, once for when he helped me in the raids before, and once for what I should have given him when we went to the concert. I give him the spare ticket and he goes and tries it on, when I was being nice! I says to him, I don't owe you anything, and he says, oh yes you do. And this time you're going to give it to me. So I tries to get away and that's how my clothes got ripped. Then he drags me into the churchyard. I try to stop him but he's bigger than me and he was so angry. He was all strange, his voice was like breathless and groany, all at once. Then he pushes me and I'm sort of on the floor, sort of against the wall. It was horrid, all sharp and freezing cold.'

She took a moment to gather her thoughts and catch her breath, then sat up still further, pushing the quilt away.

'He got his hands all over me. I don't want to think about it, but I know what he's after and I keep my legs close together. I won't let him do what he wants. I cry out and he tries harder. His breathing's all funny and getting worse. I cry out again and he tells me it's no use, I can't escape him, he knows where I sleep and I'd better

280

give in or he'll make life the worse for me. Then that's when you shouted out. I never been so glad to hear a voice in all me born days.'

The fight went out of the girl and she slumped over again.

Rose knew she had to proceed carefully. 'And he didn't . . . he didn't get what he wanted?' she said, echoing the girl's language.

'No, Sister. No, he didn't. I knew how best to stop him. My brothers always said, you get in a tight corner, you keep your legs together like your life depends on it. They also said I should knee him where it hurts, but I couldn't. He was so strong and heavy, I couldn't . . .' She wept again, her face red with embarrassment.

Rose drew in a sharp breath. Well, that was one thing: he hadn't managed to do what he'd so evidently set out to do. Bad enough he'd got so far. 'You mustn't blame yourself,' she said, knowing she'd said something similar a couple of months ago, and knowing that she would be heaping blame upon herself for not foreseeing it would come to this. 'You can't be expected to fight off someone who's bigger than you. Someone who's taken advantage. It's all his fault, not yours.'

Effie sniffed loudly. 'He was a bastard, Sister, scuse my French.'

Rose gripped her own hands together more tightly. 'Who, Effie? Can you tell me his name?'

She knew, of course. But Effie had to say the words out loud. The silence stretched ominously.

Then the young woman looked up, shaky still, but definite. 'It was Mr Prendergast.'

281

Daisy had the house to herself as she got ready. Her father was at the factory, her mother at the greengrocer's and Robbie was at school. It was unusually silent, but she hardly noticed. Her mind was elsewhere, already reaching into the future, as in only half an hour's time she was to see Freddy once more.

She would have loved to dress up, to show him how much he meant to her, but she would be going straight to work afterwards. That ruled out anything but sensible shoes and serviceable skirt and blouse. She slipped on a pretty necklace with a sparkly pendant at her throat. She could always put it in her pocket if it was too dressy for the ticket office. Then again, she was pretty sure that after last night, nobody would object.

As they were finishing the clear-up, Mr Rathbone had taken her aside. He was as tired as she was – more so, as he was well over twice her age. All the same, he had something like his old manner back. 'A word, Miss Harrison,' he'd said, indicating towards his desk, far away from the office door.

He sat not at his usual chair but on his desk, which she had never seen him do before. It was as close to informal as he would ever get.

'I wanted to thank you,' he began. 'No, let me finish,' he went on, as Daisy started to interrupt him, to say it wasn't necessary. 'I now realise you do this sort of thing all the time – you and the stalwart Mrs Nicholls and her band of helpers. It was, as you might say, an eye-opener for me.' He cleared his throat. 'I'll keep it short, but as you will have noticed, this war has been very difficult. Well, obviously it has been difficult for everyone and far worse for some. However, to begin with we had our routines and that made things slightly easier. Yet when the systems here began to change . . . well.' He took off his glasses and cleaned them with his handkerchief, which was still spotless.

Daisy nodded, not wanting to stop him now, sensing that he had been holding all this in for a very long time. Even if she felt nervous at hearing him speak like this, so unlike his usual self.

'Yes, well, it took me back, you see. To the Great War, when, as you know, I was on active service.' He shut his eyes briefly. 'I didn't have it as bad as some. I was gassed, you know, but no major long-lasting effects, thank the Lord. All the same, all the same . . .' He cleared his throat. 'When our colleague Sam got involved in the Dunkirk rescue it all began flooding back. Then when everyone started to use the platforms for shelter – no, it was the last straw. Such chaos. Like when we ran from the trenches. Not knowing what would happen next.'

Daisy felt a little sick. Her father rarely spoke of the last war, but now she had experience of this one, she could imagine more clearly what he had been through, or at least to some degree. Part of her recoiled, not wanting to know, but she wasn't a child any more. 'Go on,' she said.

'It's not logical, I realise that.' Mr Rathbone grimaced. 'A tube platform is hardly the trenches. People are here for their safety. Still, these things are not always rational. There we are.' He put his glasses back on his thin nose. 'What I wanted to say was, last night made me see the good in what's been happening here. Just how different it is to the horror of twenty-five years ago. Yes, everybody is crammed in together, but the atmosphere last night – it was – now, don't think me a silly old man – it was good for the heart. Yes, that was what it was.' He looked at her and smiled.

'Really?' Daisy was at a loss for words.

'Indeed. The spirit of the local people – it's not to be brushed aside, is it? Their homes might have been being destroyed but they were singing, dancing, joining in. There's a real community on the platforms at night.'

'Yes,' Daisy said slowly, 'I suppose there is. We're making the best of it, that's what it comes down to.'

Mr Rathbone shook his head. 'No, it's more than that. You kept them cheerful, you, and Mrs Nicholls, and that fine young man of yours.'

Daisy could not speak. Part of her was deeply moved that he had admitted how he felt. He was her boss, after all, and not given to long speeches, or discussing emotions of any kind. Part of her was relieved too; she was certain that things would improve now. There was some of that old light of determination in the manager's eyes, the kind spark that got things done.

'You must bring him here again,' Mr Rathbone had gone on, getting to his feet. 'He was an asset, and I wish there were more fellows like him. Do thank him properly from me.'

'Oh, I shall,' Daisy had beamed.

Now she took her coat from the hall, pressing her lips gently together to set the lipstick she had boldly put on. A delicious thrill ran through her. She and Freddy were going to meet in the park, and for once they might manage a full conversation without bombs dropping and disrupting their plans. Full of joy despite the fresh damage to the streets outside, she ran along Victory Walk.

CHAPTER TWENTY-EIGHT

Rose sent Effie back to her room to get changed and cleaned up, reassuring her when the girl protested.

'But I'm meant to be on shift this afternoon. Sooner, if I'm needed,' she fretted.

Rose took hold of her upper arms. 'Listen, Effie. I'm your sister in charge and I can prescribe rest. You see that you take it,' she said sternly, and the young nurse agreed.

Now Rose walked sombrely along the corridor to Matron's office, knowing that she had no alternative. This could not be brushed under the carpet and it was up to her to see that it was not.

'Enter.' Matron was at her desk, clearly snowed under with work, but still with a bright expression. Rose was glad she had made a good impression on the head nurse earlier on; now was the time to press her advantage.

'Thank you for seeing me,' she said, sitting in the opposite chair, and keeping her hands out of view in case they betrayed her nervousness.

Matron cocked her head sideways. 'What is the matter?' she asked, to the point as usual.

Rose had rehearsed how to say this, but the weight of the accusation jumbled her thoughts. She counted to ten. 'I have to report a serious complaint against a senior member of staff.'

Matron's eyes widened, even as she reached for a notebook and pen. 'You'd better tell me everything,' she said, her expression changing to grave in the blink of an eye.

Rose nodded, gulped, and then repeated what Effie had told her as closely as she could. Then she laid out her memory of the early morning, how she'd heard a desperate voice and gone to investigate.

Matron leant back in her chair, the light from the big window picking out the grey strands in her hair peeping from her starched cap. She took a few moments before speaking, and when she did so, her voice was heavy.

'You did not see him for yourself? Not well enough to recognise him?'

'No,' Rose admitted. 'Just someone fleeing the scene. It was too dark to make out all the details. It was a man, and he would have been about the right height and size, but I didn't see his face.'

Matron sighed and twirled the pen through her fingers. 'Then you realise what this will mean. It will be his word against hers. I'm not saying that this is fair, but he is an eminent surgeon of many years' experience, and she is one of our most junior nurses. She's still a trainee.'

Rose had to grasp her hands tightly together not to let her full anger show. 'But that's why he picked on her,' she exclaimed. 'I can see it now. I thought at first he was just doing what he does to all the nurses. Sorry, Matron, maybe you haven't been on the receiving end, but it's how he behaves. Most of us try to avoid him. But Effie – she seemed to think he was kind, even when he came too close. She called him a nice old man. She didn't reject him and he took that as permission.' She wanted to spit in fury.

Matron gave no sign of surprise. 'Yes, he seems the type.' She made a quick scribble on her notepad. 'However, it does not alter the fact that you yourself cannot actually identify him. Just because he has been unpleasant in the past does not prove he did this. This is more than unpleasantness – let us call it what it is. It was an attempt at rape. That is a very serious allegation.'

Rose felt her spirits sink. 'But he can't get away with it. He'll try it again. He's already told her he knows where she sleeps. Of course he does – she has a room here. And she's taken him to her local church – he all but knows her home address. I'm sure he could easily find out the exact house. She's in danger from him.'

Matron considered this. 'I take your point, but I am not so sure he would try again. I would wager he knew that it was you calling out. He would not be so foolish to assume he would win against you.'

Rose shrugged. 'He's tried before. Look how he questioned my figures in the meeting, with not a shred of evidence.'

Matron nodded. 'Precisely. He tried on that occasion and failed dismally. It showed him up for what he was. He knows that if it came to the crux, he would not automatically be believed over you.'

Rose sank her head into her hands. When she'd told

Katherine about it, her friend had said, 'He's trying to discredit you.'

'Has he been planning this all along? Since he first caught sight of her?' she gasped.

Matron pulled her chair a little closer in to the desk. 'It's impossible to say,' she replied slowly. 'It does not help our case to speculate. Certainly, men like that keep an eye out for any likely victims. He probably has a list,' she added with asperity. 'Poor Nurse Jenkins fell smack bang into his lap. She mistook his interest.'

'She's very sheltered, especially considering she grew up near the docks.' Rose lifted her head again. 'Other junior nurses might have cottoned on, told him to sling his hook.'

Matron drummed her fingers on her desk, her face thoughtful. Then she sighed. 'Leave it with me,' she said heavily. 'I cannot promise you will get the result you seek. Doctors do not like to be challenged, as I am sure you are fully aware.'

Rose nodded sadly.

'Meanwhile, tell her to take some time off. I will allocate a replacement nurse to your ward. At least Nurse Jenkins lives locally. She can return home quickly and recuperate with her family.' Matron shut her notebook and Rose understood that her time was up. To her, this incident felt all-encompassing, but to Matron it was one more on the list of matters she had to sort out.

'I'll do that. I shall go and see her now,' Rose agreed, and with a heavy heart turned to leave the bright office, where the sun shone in spite of the dark events.

* * *

Effie had changed her clothes by the time Rose reached her room, which was similar to her own but without the little personal touches. She sat rigidly in her chair, her straight dark skirt and blouse giving the impression she was off to a funeral.

'Matron says you're to have some time off,' Rose began, and then noticed Effie's stricken face. 'It's all right, you won't lose pay. And we'll have a temporary extra pair of hands so your patients won't suffer.'

Effie relaxed a little. 'Thank you, Sister. I should like that. I been worrying about working later, scared I wouldn't do it right. I don't want to mix up the pills or nothing. And . . . and I might have to see him.'

Rose nodded slowly. 'Well, all the more reason to go home and have a change of scenery. You let us worry about the ward.'

The young nurse stared out of her window, which faced the wall of the main building. Not much light came through but enough to show that although she had calmed down, she was still pale and drawn. 'What's going to happen, Sister?' she asked suddenly.

Rose had been dreading this question. She dearly wanted to assure her trainee that justice would be done, but she could promise no such thing. 'I don't know for certain,' she said honestly. 'Matron said to leave it with her. She'll think of something.' She mentally crossed her fingers that this would be the case.

Effie nodded despondently. 'They'll all take his side, stands to reason,' she said, in a tone that made it clear

290

she had expected no different. 'He's a doctor and a nob. And old.'

'Matron won't take his side,' said Rose.

Effie shrugged. 'Anyway, not much I can do now 'cept keep out of his way for a bit.' She hesitated. 'Would you do something for me, Sister Harrison?'

'Of course.' Rose wondered what was coming now.

'Find Coral and tell her she was right. She did warn me, but I didn't take no notice. I thought she might be jealous.' Effie sniffed at the stupidity of the idea. 'She said after that evening at the concert when I got back, she said, he's after you, he is. He's got that look in his eye. I told her no, he's just an old man who's trying to look after me. You find her and say I've gone home for a bit or she'll be wondering. Tell her she was right.'

Rose thought back to her last conversation with Coral, but it wasn't for her to bring that up. Instead she said, 'Yes, of course. She's a good friend, isn't she? I'll go and see her when I have my break. She's on the maternity ward still, I believe.' Ironically enough, she thought, but did not say.

Effie nodded. 'She got her head screwed on,' she declared. 'You can tell her what I said, if you don't mind me language. That bloody surgeon is nothing but a bastard and I don't care who knows it.'

CHAPTER TWENTY-NINE

Patty was busy with the brown tape when Daisy got back from her shift. The overnight raiders had not dropped any bombs on Victory Walk, but one had landed close enough for debris to have caused some damage – minor in the grand scale of things, but enough to be annoying. 'At least they didn't get my radishes,' Patty was muttering, doing her best to cover up the cracks in the back kitchen windowpane.

Daisy guiltily realised that she hadn't even noticed the cracks earlier, she'd been floating on air at the thought of seeing Freddy. 'Let me help,' she offered. She felt bad that she could have done this before leaving, and saved her hard-working mother the trouble.

Patty popped the roll of tape into her apron pocket. 'All done.' She smiled, the wrinkles at the corners of her eyes deepening. 'So, how was it? Not your work, but your walk with Freddy?'

Daisy could not stop a huge smile from spreading across her face. 'Lovely,' she said. 'But then I had to go to work and he's on an evening train back to Liverpool. Which will mean he'll spend the night in a cold siding somewhere.'

Patty looked sympathetic. 'And he spent last night on a rock-hard platform,' she said. 'He's a sucker for punishment, your young man.'

Daisy shrugged, her eyes growing soft at the memory. 'I miss him already,' she murmured.

'Of course you do.' Patty looked fondly at her wistful daughter. 'Believe it or not, I do know how you feel. When your father was away in the Great War it was terrible to be without him – and, of course, Rose was just a baby.'

Daisy's eyes grew wide. 'I never thought about that. You had Granny to help, though.'

Patty nodded. 'I did. Even if she was also helping out with Vera, who had Faith toddling around. Your granddad was a big help too, even though he was working. Used to take the children out on his cart – not that they were old enough to remember all that.'

Daisy berated herself for never considering what difficulties her mother might have faced before she herself was even born. Now she was grown-up and courting, she could see how hard it must have been to be apart from your loved one, let alone having to raise a baby single-handed. She followed her mother into the main kitchen, where it was much warmer.

'Close that connecting door, would you, please?' Patty said, putting the tape into a drawer in the sideboard. 'That wind will come whistling through the new cracks in the back window, even though I've done my best. We'll have to see if your father can get hold of any glass, though it's rare as hen's teeth at the moment, or so I've heard.'

Daisy did as she was asked, then pricked up her ears. 'Is that the front door?'

Patty turned, just as Rose walked through from the hallway. 'Rose! We were just talking about you. Didn't expect to see you this evening. You've been working today, haven't you?'

Rose sank onto the comfiest chair and gave a long sigh, lifting her arms above her head and stretching. 'I have. What a day I've had. I just had to get away from the hospital premises, to clear my head. Boy, oh boy.'

Patty rushed to put the kettle on. 'And you must have had hardly any sleep, just like this one here,' she guessed, nodding at Daisy.

'I got a little, but only after transferring lots of the patients. And then . . . no, do you know what, I don't even want to talk about it. Tell me what you've been doing instead.'

So Daisy eagerly reported what she and Freddy had done the night before, and how Mr Rathbone seemed to have turned a corner and become more like his old self again. Then what a wonderful lunchtime she had had with Freddy, and how she was already longing to see him once more.

Rose sighed. 'Know what you mean,' she said succinctly.

Patty passed her a cup of tea. 'Of course you do. What a pair you are, I do declare. The sooner this darned war is over, the better.'

Rose blew on her hot tea and then sipped it. 'Amen to that,' she muttered.

Daisy rose to cut a slice of bread and smear it with a very thin covering of butter. 'It's all right, I did eat properly, but it was ages ago,' she assured her mother, who was glancing at her anxiously. 'Did you want some?'

Patty shook her head. 'In fact, I'll be off out soon,' she explained. 'I said I'd help out with a seed swap that one of the shop customers has organised. That way I can grow more vegetables this year, if I'm lucky. The more fellow growers I meet, the better, and we can exchange tips too.'

'That sounds like a good idea,' said Rose. 'But do be careful out there. What if there's another raid?'

Patty tutted as she took off her apron. 'Whereas you just walked over here taking the exact same risk,' she pointed out. 'I shall be all right, don't you go worrying about me.'

Rose shrugged, acknowledging her mother had a point.

No sooner had Patty left the room than she was back again, holding the kitchen door open. 'Look who I found about to knock to come in,' she said, and there was Hope, unbuttoning her coat and sliding past her aunt. 'I said you'd look after her, as I'm going to be late if I don't get a move on. See you later, and if you're lucky I'll come back with the wherewithal to grow your favourite veg.'

Hope pulled out a chair opposite Rose. 'I hope you don't mind me turning up,' she said, pushing her hand through her wind-blown bobbed hair. 'I just had to get away from the house. It's not even like home any more. I didn't get much sleep last night, of course. I was out on duty, and then had training this afternoon, and so the thought of spending the next few hours with the baby screaming – and if he's not screaming it's Joy and Faith lobbing insults at each other while Mother pretends not to hear, and Father off out to whatever business drinks excuse he's got this time . . . sorry. Didn't mean to moan.' She slumped forward, elbows on the table.

Rose drained her teacup as Daisy finished her slice of bread and butter. She pushed herself upright from where she had been leaning against the sideboard. 'Sounds as if we've all had a hard day one way or another,' she observed. 'So why don't we go out together? We never, ever do that. How about one of the nearby pubs? The Golden Lion isn't far and it's not bad. You'll have to take my word for it, Rose, as I know you're not really the pub-going type.'

Rose sat up straighter and laughed. 'I've been going to pubs for much longer than you have,' she replied. 'Not very often, perhaps, but now and again. Well, why not? What do you say, Hope? You haven't got to be on duty later, have you?'

Hope shook her head. 'No, it's my turn for a night off. So, yes, shall we? We'll leave a note for Aunt Patty in case she gets back and is worried, Oh, wait, what about Robbie?'

Daisy remembered. 'He's at his friend Ricky's. It's his birthday, and for some reason his idea of a treat is to have Robbie stay over. Each to their own.'

Rose got to her feet too. 'Then it's obviously meant to be. Sorry, Hope, you've only just got here, you haven't even had time to take your coat off, but let's go before the sirens start up again. I might even have a shandy. It really has been that bad a day.'

* * *

Daisy gazed around the busy bar, remembering how she'd come here with Clover, last year when the evenings were long and warm. They'd sat out in the garden and bumped into her former colleague from the factory, Chalky, only to find that he'd narrowly escaped Dunkirk with his life, and a couple of his gang had not been so lucky.

She gave herself a shake. She was in different company now, and they'd have to sit inside, if they could find a spare table. It was still too chilly to be outdoors, and too dark. Lots of other people seemed to have had the same idea, to celebrate surviving another night of raids by going out and enjoying themselves.

Then a group of what appeared to be merchant navy servicemen on leave got up to go. 'Over here, ladies!' one of them called, waving at the newly vacant table. 'Come and take the weight off your pretty pins!'

Rose clenched her jaw at the familiarity, but Daisy took it in good part and smiled her thanks. 'Come on,' she muttered, digging Rose in the ribs. 'They're only being friendly and, besides, they're off now. A comment about our legs won't kill you.'

Rose knew Daisy meant well. 'Just wait till I tell you about what happened today and then see why their remark annoyed me,' she growled.

Daisy gave her a look of surprise. This didn't sound like level-headed Rose. Something really had got under her skin. Hope had forged ahead to buy the drinks, as they'd already decided what they wanted on the way.

Daisy made sure Rose had the best chair and took a wobbly stool for herself, wondering what on earth had gone on.

Once Hope had returned with two shandies and one lemonade, Rose was ready to share her story. Daisy listened almost in disbelief. It was not so much surprise that this kind of thing happened – she herself had been subject to a not dissimilar attack from a man she had foolishly thought admired her. She'd managed to escape, with the major hurt being to her pride, but it could have gone badly, she understood in retrospect. No, the shock was that it was a doctor who was the perpetrator. A respectable member of the community, from a respected profession. You were warned not to go out with strange men, and she'd learnt that the hard way, but you might have thought better of doctors.

Hope was also shocked. 'That poor girl,' she breathed. 'What a horrible man. Someone you should be able to trust.'

'Exactly,' said Rose, and drank half of her shandy in one go, which was unheard of. Then she set the glass down and made a face. 'Anyway, thanks for listening. I feel better, having got that off my chest. I didn't really want to talk about it in front of Ma. She'll be worried it will be me next, but he wouldn't dare. He only targets those weaker than himself.'

'Typical,' sympathised Daisy, outraged on her sister's behalf. 'Well, my day wasn't anything like that. It was lovely because Freddy was here, but now I'm glad you're both here to distract me because he only had those two days of leave and he's gone again.' She glanced at her watch. 'He'll be on the train now.' She could hear her voice was wobbling and she bit her lip, annoyed that she was being so wretched when really it was Rose who'd had the awful time.

But Rose reached out and put her hand on her sister's arm. 'I know, Daisy. I know.'

'Must be miserable,' Hope joined in. 'Sorry, Daisy, but at least you had last night together. Even if it was on a crowded tube platform.'

Daisy shivered at the memory, both of last night and of how Freddy had held her, semi-hidden behind the trees in the park at lunchtime. She could tell that she was blushing. Before, she had never seen why some young women got into trouble, letting themselves get carried away when their boyfriends came home on leave. But now she could readily understand why they gave into temptation. She knew Freddy was a gentleman, and he'd already told her how he respected her and would never do anything to make her concerned – but how she wished they could get away with it, even if just the once.

She nodded silently, not trusting herself to speak.

Hope went on, weaving an amusing story of her afternoon, and Daisy knew it was for her and Rose's benefit, to make them think about something other than their miseries. 'You should see my instructor!' their cousin was saying. 'Honestly, I swear that he wouldn't speak at all if he didn't have to. Talk about dour. Today he was looking at me as if I'd insisted he teach me, when it was him that offered in the first place.' She paused to sip her shandy. 'It was enough to make me nervous, all fingers and thumbs. And there was I thinking I'd finally got the hang of how an engine worked.'

Rose raised her eyebrows. 'Must be hard work,' she said. 'I wouldn't know where to start.'

Daisy was about to agree, when she looked up and opened her mouth in surprise. 'Why, look, there's my friend Sam! Sam, over here!' She could see he was scanning the room for somewhere to sit and there were very few vacant spots.

Sam seemed equally surprised but made his way across to them, taking the chance to swipe a spare stool from a nearby table. 'Fancy seeing you here,' he grinned. 'Only I suppose I should have half expected it as it's near your house, isn't it? I happened to arrange to meet one of the other drivers.' He stopped his chatter. 'Sorry, I'm being rude. You must be Daisy's sister, you look so alike,' he added, turning to Rose.

'And I'm their cousin, only we don't look very alike. Hope. Pleased to meet you.' Hands were shaken and then Sam quickly fetched a pint of beer.

Daisy had briefly explained who he was, which had not taken long because Rose and Hope had already heard of him many times. Hope looked happy to be able to put a face to the name, and Rose was obviously glad of another distraction after her grim working day.

'Well, I deserve my drink!' Sam said, lifting his glass. 'Blimey, Daze, you'd never believe it. Everyone was rerouted yet again. So all the drivers ended up at the wrong depots and I had to do extra hours. I only just finished now. Parched, I am.'

Daisy grinned. 'I bet.'

'And on top of that there was some kind of

dust-up down at Limehouse. Well, you know as well as I do how eager some of those dockers are for a fight. Someone said that was the reason behind it. I couldn't say for sure but I am very, very happy to be here rather than in a depot the wrong side of town.' He quaffed his drink even faster than Rose had. 'I'm glad you're here – lovely to meet you, of course,' he nodded at Rose and Hope, 'but I bet my mate will be late on account of all the disruption. He was on the number 15. Ah, well, you'll just have to tell me how things are back at Manor House, Daze. How's Mr R?'

Daisy beamed. 'You picked the right night to ask. There's good news. Let me explain . . .'

CHAPTER THIRTY

'That's very strange,' said the midwife, who now made a point of sitting beside Rose at the weekly meeting. 'I just can't remember a time when our horrible surgeon friend failed to attend. It means he's missed a chance to listen to the sound of his own voice. It's totally out of character.'

Rose nodded, unsure exactly how to respond. She was not at all sorry that Mr Prendergast had not turned up while everyone else gathered around the big table as usual. She could not tell the midwife what had happened, though. Matron had spoken to her again to double-check that she could not identify the man who had assaulted Effie, as so much rested on it. Rose had sighed. 'I know it was him,' she'd said grimly, 'but I can't lie. I did not see his face as it was too dark.'

So now she sat with a sinking feeling that the surgeon was going to get away with it. When it came to her turn to speak she did so with no trace of nerves, as she was used to it by now, and at least there was nobody to question her figures. She met Matron's eyes as the next person began to talk, and the senior nurse gave a brief shake of her head. Rose sat back in her hard chair, wondering what to do next.

* * *

A couple of days passed and the word went round that the surgeon was ill and had taken a short spell of sick leave.

'He's never done that before,' remarked Dr Edwards as Rose accompanied him on the ward rounds. 'Always made a point of never being absent, in fact. He was downright rude to me after I stayed at home with the flu last year. I said that I had no intention of giving it to the patients or other members of staff, but he carried on implying that I was weak. Takes all sorts, I suppose. I wonder what's wrong with him.'

'I hope it's nothing trivial,' Rose muttered under her breath as Dr Edwards greeted one of the long-term patients as if he was an old friend. This was how doctors were meant to behave, she thought – caring, reliable, knowledgeable. The complete opposite to how Mr Prendergast operated. At moments like this she was reminded of why she loved her job. She always learnt something new from this doctor, and he clearly appreciated how she worked and ran the ward. They made a good team, she thought.

Taking five minutes to soak up the spring sunshine in the courtyard after a hurried lunch, Rose bumped into Coral, who had clearly had the same idea. She thought the young woman still looked pale, but had not seen her since she'd passed on Effie's message, as she'd been asked.

'Have you heard from Effie at all?' she asked now, as there had been no word on her ward. Coral obligingly moved along the old wooden bench to make room.

She had let loose her bright hair, and it glinted in the sun's weak rays. 'Funny you should say that. I got a letter from her this morning,' she said, sounding almost like her old, lively self. 'She wanted me to tell you that she's feeling better, and I was going to come and find you later. She says she'll be back next week, she's missing work something awful.'

Rose smiled. 'That's good. We miss her as well.'

Coral turned her face up to the sun. 'It was horrid what happened to her, even though I'd warned her loads of times. But there's one good thing that's come of it.'

Rose was surprised. 'What can that be?'

Coral shut her eyes in the warmth, then opened them and met Rose's gaze. 'She's at home when her big brother's been on leave for a few days. She talks about him all the time and I know she hates it that he's away. Close as anything, they are. He's got to go again later today, but she's been able to spend lots of time with him. That has made her feel better, I bet.'

Rose remembered how Effie's tone of voice would alter when she spoke about her big brothers and she knew that Coral spoke the truth. Perhaps it had helped her recovery to have had him there, hearing all about his adventures. She didn't know if he was as hot-tempered as Percy, but perhaps, as the eldest, he was more responsible.

'Well, I'm glad to hear it. Anything to set her back on her feet again,' Rose replied, then caught sight of her watch. 'I'd best get back to the ward, but how lucky we both fancied soaking up the sunshine at the same time.' She looked carefully at the young nurse, trying to decide if she could notice any changes in her face or figure, but Coral moved to stand up, twisting her hair back and neatly covering it with her cap in a practised motion.

'Me too,' she said. 'My ward sister will have my guts for garters if I'm late. She's not bad, but it's not like working for you, Sister Harrison.'

Rose held on to that comment over the next few days, cherishing the idea that the young nurse from Wales liked working on her ward. Even though she often told herself that Matron would never have promoted her if she had not been good at her job, there were still times when her confidence wavered or she felt almost overwhelmed by the mountain of tasks, the sheer difficulty in tending so many patients when resources were so stretched.

The temporary member of the ward team was more experienced than Effie, but Rose began to realise that the trainee had often gone the extra mile, and those little touches were now lacking. If a patient was lucky enough to be given a bunch of flowers, Effie would often change the water without being asked. She remembered the names of the patients' children or grandchildren. She remembered people's birthdays, not because they were written on the medical notes but because she liked to wish them many happy returns. Little things – but they made a difference, and added to the atmosphere on the ward. The ward itself might be in need of a coat of paint, and the furniture was chipped, but those small acts brought life to the place.

It made Rose curse Mr Prendergast all the more.

Not until the beginning of the following week did he show his face at the hospital again, and Rose could immediately see why he had had to take leave of absence. That face was a mess. It was bruised and swollen, and one eye did not open properly. From the colour of the bruises she could make a good guess when he'd got them. A dark suspicion formed in her mind. Counting back, she worked out when Coral had said Effie's big brother had been home. Of course, there was no proof. Yet there was what Daisy had seen for herself: the middle brother's instinct for violence, stoked by his urge to protect a woman. If he was like that with a stranger, then how much worse would he be when it came to his sister, who had always stressed how protective he was.

Then again, there was a rough justice in it. There was no proof against Mr Prendergast for the assault, only Effie's word against his. That didn't alter what had taken place. Rose wondered what cover story he would come up with.

At the next ward meeting he took his seat, flinching as he lowered himself stiffly onto one of the hard chairs, but holding his head high. The sheer brass neck of the man, Rose thought angrily. He's going to pretend there's nothing wrong, that he's as innocent as the day. She had a good mind to tell everyone what she knew, but it would be pointless. If Matron had not managed to achieve anything behind the scenes, then Rose would only endanger her own career, not the slimy surgeon's.

'I had a bad fall. Treacherous, that's what those pavements are in the blackout,' he said to his immediate neighbour, but loud enough for everyone else to hear. He caught Rose's eye, as if daring her to say anything different.

Rose gripped her notebook as tightly as she could to stop herself lashing out at him. How dare he sit there, when he'd attacked a young woman who'd put her trust in him? Her thoughts began to race. What if he'd done it before? Who else had he picked upon and attacked under cover of being a friend? The blackout that he'd blamed for his supposed fall was actually a useful cover for all sorts of crime.

The chairwoman called the meeting to order and Rose hastily set aside such speculation. It solved nothing. One of the other doctors was welcoming Mr Prendergast back, remarking that it was good to see him again, and Rose struggled not to groan. She caught the expression on Matron's face: she too looked like thunder.

It was so unfair. He'd carry on as normal, basking in his male colleagues' approval, hiding his true nature. There was absolutely nothing to prevent him doing it again. It made Rose's blood boil, and no doubt he knew that too. He was probably enjoying it, the knowledge that he was safe and untouchable.

When she came to speak, she even thought he was preparing another one of his groundless attacks on her work, but he seemed to reconsider at the last minute. He opened his mouth but closed it again when Matron turned her formidable gaze on him. Instead, he looked down at his fountain pen and adjusted it slightly. Rose hoped he was feeling under scrutiny, but somehow she doubted it.

She tried not to grind her teeth in frustration when it came to the surgeon's turn. He made a fuss about aligning his pen perfectly with his notes, extending the moment so that everyone was made to wait for whatever he had to say. Sure of his audience, he cleared his throat.

'I'm delighted to be back among my colleagues,' he began, in his self-satisfied way. 'In fact, I was in my office yesterday afternoon, but I did not wish to trouble any of you. It was only so that I could prepare for this meeting.' Several of the others nodded in approval that he had made such an effort when so obviously in pain.

'Yes, I would hate to let any of you down,' he went on smoothly, making Rose want to scream even more. He continued with the list of statistics from his area of expertise, numbers of patients treated, successfully discharged, the cost of equipment – all necessary but, given what she knew, hardly the most important matter.

'So you see, the department was so well organised it could almost function on its own, without me!' he concluded, as if this was some kind of triumph. There were more approving nods around the room.

Mrs Gleeson, the chairwoman, flicked over a page. 'If that's the last report . . .'

Then Matron drew her chair closer to the big table and raised her hand slightly. 'If I may,' she interrupted, with a polite smile to the chairwoman.

'Of course.' Mrs Gleeson could hardly say no to the most senior member of nursing staff.

Matron's expression was carefully neutral now. 'I simply have a few questions about your report, Mr Prendergast.' Rose was instantly on the alert. What was Matron up to? 'No doubt you can clear these up without a problem. When you say the expenses reached a certain level, I can't quite see how this adds up . . .'

Rose didn't follow the details of the queries. She had not paid much attention to what the man had said. No, she was far more interested in the effect the challenge had on him. His eyes were furious, shooting deadly darts at Matron, but she carried on unperturbed. The more she asked, the angrier he clearly became.

Finally he broke in to her line of questioning. 'That's all very well,' he blustered, 'but you must understand that I have been on sick leave and therefore cannot be held responsible for this report. It would be unreasonable to do so.'

'Really?' Matron's tone was lethally mild. 'And yet you started by informing us that you had come in specially yesterday with the specific intention of preparing this. I cannot quite see how it can be both.' She raised her eyebrows. 'Can it?'

Rose wanted to clap her hands at Matron's reasoning. It was simple and made the surgeon's position a nonsense. How clever of her to turn the tables, realising that he was only too happy to nitpick other people's information with no cause, but deeply unhappy at being challenged himself.

Eventually the chairwoman put him out of his

misery. 'Matron has made a series of valid points,' she announced. 'Mr Prendergast, I strongly suggest you re-present the amended version next week. Now, ladies and gentlemen, our time is up.'

The surgeon rose from his chair a deflated man, his shoulders curled over, not in pain from the beating but in humiliation. Instead of chatting to his admirers and basking in their congratulation as he often did, he turned for the door.

The midwife also rose without delay. 'I wouldn't be surprised if there's a message waiting for me outside,' she said in an undertone to Rose. 'One of my ladies is in difficulty and I promised to get back to her the minute this was over.'

Rose followed her to the door, from where she could see the messenger – none other than Coral – standing with a piece of paper in her hand, clearly on the lookout for her boss. She waved at the pair of them, in the low hubbub of the room emptying out. 'Mrs Jessop's having twins, just like you thought, and here are the times of her contractions,' she muttered hurriedly. Then she did a double take.

'Oh, he's back, is he?'

Her voice carried and the remaining attendees drew to a standstill.

Rose held up her hand in caution, but Coral was having none of it. Perhaps she felt she had little to lose since, as Rose alone knew, she was going to be leaving soon to have her own baby. Turning on the spot to face the surgeon, but still speaking as if she was addressing Rose and the midwife, she plunged ahead.

'Didn't think he'd have the nerve. After what he did.'

The surgeon would have avoided her, but there were too many people in the way. 'And what's that,' he said gruffly.

As Rose hoped, Coral had too much sense to make the direct accusation. However, she gave a small smile with a hint of slyness. 'You made friends with Effie. Nurse Jenkins,' she said. 'Well, she's coming back to work this week too. She's told me everything. And,' she took a swift breath, 'she reckons you are a sad and pathetic old man. Such a pity she couldn't trust someone as old as you.'

He took a step back as if he'd been hit, as if her words were as painful as the beating he'd endured at the hands of the Jenkins brothers. She'd got him where he was most vulnerable – his self-image of the suave ladies' man. Now she'd labelled him old, over the hill. He looked around, unable to disguise his anger. 'I'll thank you to keep your interfering mouth shut,' he growled. 'Clear off and stay out of it. You know nothing.'

Mrs Gleeson had heard. So had Matron. Right beside her was the clutch of doctors who'd nodded approvingly at him at the start of the meeting. Now they were glaring at him in suspicion. He was letting the side down.

Rose decided that she could back Coral up. 'Yes,' she said clearly, but as if in conversation with the Welsh nurse, 'she said the same to me, on several occasions. So you're right, Nurse. And we'll be delighted to see her back where she belongs.' She stressed the last few words, to emphasise that the hospital was in need of the young trainee – and that the surgeon did not deserve his privileged place there.

'Come on, old chap, no need to worry,' one of the doctors said, trying to take the surgeon's arm, but he brushed him off, still furious.

Before he could say anything further, the chairwoman stepped in. 'If there is a problem then here is not the place to discuss it. I shall have to take this to the appropriate authority. Matron, a word.'

'I shall be with you shortly,' Matron assured her.

Then the moment was over, the chairwoman hurrying off to whatever business needed her next, and Coral was swept away by the midwife, to see to Mrs Jessop's twins. In the midst of this, Mr Prendergast vanished and Rose was left with Matron, wondering if all of it had really happened.

'How did you do that?' she breathed. 'Were there really so many mistakes in those figures? How did you read them all so fast and understand what was wrong? You really rattled him and then he began to show his true colours.'

Matron regarded her steadily. 'I didn't need to read them,' she replied, allowing herself a gleam of triumph. 'That is not what's important to a man like that. It's all about the outward show. You can query anything – well, you know that, he's done it to you. They may or may not add up. He clearly doesn't know; someone else will have done the sums behind the scenes. The very fact that his abilities have been cast into doubt will be mortifying for him. And then for young Nurse Davies to come out with that – well, it's a double humiliation, he was shaken up and let his guard down.'

'Good,' said Rose shortly.

Matron nodded briskly. 'I shall go and see Mrs Gleeson and now feel I can share our suspicions, as she'll have seen he's not all he makes himself out to be. Questions will have to be asked higher up. It's not proof, and nothing is certain, but let's just see if his position is as unassailable as we thought. Leave it with me, Sister Harrison.'

CHAPTER THIRTY-ONE

'Not long till Easter!' Patty always loved this time of year. Finally the winter was properly lifting, the daylight hours cheered the soul and she could get on with serious planting. She was pleased with her haul from the seed swap, and just as pleased to have met some like-minded keen gardeners, all trying to cope with little space and the problem that equipment was hard to come by. One or two had managed to get allotments, and so were at a great advantage.

Patty had thought about this before, but knew she was so busy she would not have sufficient time for one. There had been tentative suggestions of sharing one between the group at the seed swap, but Patty felt that she did not know the other people well enough, or not yet, as it was a big commitment. She also was aware that she was lucky working where she did, as she always knew when there was fresh produce available. Yet buying it did not match the joy of growing it herself.

Now she brought down her precious tin of sugar from the top shelf, passing it to Robbie, who stood waiting beside the wobbly chair she was balancing on. 'We can make hot cross buns, if I have enough dried fruit,' she said. 'You like them, Robbie.'

He nodded. 'Will there be any chocolate?' he asked.

'Will I get an egg?'

Patty pursed her lips. 'Now you know they're hard to get hold of at the moment, Robbie.' Her heart sank as she saw his disappointment, and even more as he quickly tried to hide it. He was still a little boy in many ways, even if he was nearly twelve. 'We'll just have to see. If I can find you one, you know I will.'

He nodded. 'I know.' He scuffed his foot along the kitchen floor. 'I hate this war, Ma.'

She could have cried to see him downcast, her baby who she had feared so many times would not make it to this age, with his frequent childhood illnesses and asthma. He should have a chocolate egg for Easter; he'd put up with so much and hardly ever complained. However, it was beyond her to magic one up if there were none to be had.

'I know,' she said, stepping down from the chair and ruffling his hair. For once he did not pull away. 'We all do.'

Daisy overheard the latter part of this conversation as she came into the hallway from the brisk spring breeze. She loitered by the stairs as she took off her coat, catching something in her little brother's voice. He would not want her to know he'd been so sad. She wondered if she could find somewhere to buy him an egg. Perhaps Mrs Nicholls and the WVS ladies would know how to do it. She would ask tomorrow.

'Anyone in?' she called, after silence fell. 'I'm back early – time off for good behaviour!'

Patty stuck her head round the doorframe. 'Nothing

wrong, is there?' She was wiping her hands on a tea towel.

Daisy shrugged out of her work jacket. 'No, no, the opposite. I've worked so many extra hours these past few weeks that Mr Rathbone said I should take advantage of the light evenings and come home before the shift strictly ended. Somebody from Wood Green has come in to do a few half-shifts, as they were on the Central line before and have only just been transferred. He's showing them the ropes.'

Patty nodded, satisfied that her daughter was safe and well. 'There's a letter come for you,' she told her. 'On the stairs behind you. I think I can guess the handwriting.'

Daisy grabbed it and ran up to her room, recognising Freddy's writing at once. It had been far too long since she'd heard from him – two whole weeks. She knew she should not worry unduly: that he could not always find the time to write or, even if he did manage to dash off a letter, it might be ages before he could send it.

All the same, the action was hotting up where he was. The German U-boats were stepping up their fight and Winston Churchill had recently called it the Battle of the Atlantic. For some reason that made her even more concerned; it sounded so huge and final. To see his handwriting on the envelope, her name with a special little squiggle after it, made her heart beat faster.

Throwing herself down on the bed, she tore open the letter. She loved to read what he wrote. He could make the most everyday activities sound interesting, find the drama no matter how repetitive his days might be. There was no shortage of real drama to report now, though. He had been involved in several close shaves – she drew in a sharp breath at the thought of him narrowly avoiding being injured. She knew some vessels had been sunk, the crews drowned. Now she smiled as he wrote that the biggest danger of all was the food on board. How she wished he was home, to share one of her mother's hot cross buns.

Rose had walked over from the hospital to clear her head. She had cut across the broad expanse of Hackney Downs, not really noticing the trees in bud, as her mind was whirling. Events had moved fast all around her and she was finding it hard to keep up.

First of all, Effie had returned, with a renewed sense of determination. Rose had taken her to one side to check that the trainee was sure she felt up to it, but the girl was adamant.

'He ain't stopping me finishing my training, Sister,' she'd said, as they stood in one corner of the canteen, quiet before the lunchtime crowds poured in. 'He won't try that again. I won't be so stupid, for starters. And then he was taught a lesson, wasn't he?'

Rose cocked her head. 'So I believe. I don't suppose you know who did that?'

Effie had stared out of the window as she answered. 'I shan't say. I don't want to get no one in trouble. But they did it good and proper, and I'm glad.'

Rose knew she should disapprove and yet she could not bring herself to do so. Effie was protecting her brothers, just like they protected her. It was the way,

317

where she was brought up: people were used to looking out for themselves. They did not expect the police or any authority to act, and in this case, they were right. In the absence of formal punishment, the family had stepped in.

The long-term patients were delighted to have Effie back on the ward and Rose was, too. The whole atmosphere changed – not in a big way but because of all those little touches that nobody else thought to bring to the work. The ward felt happier for having her there.

Then had come the unexpected bombshell. Mr Prendergast had resigned. Strictly speaking, he had put in for a transfer, effective immediately. But nobody was in any doubt: he would not be working at Hackney Hospital any longer.

To begin with Rose did not believe it. He was practically part of the furniture, after all. He had been there long before she herself had started training as a nurse and that felt like a lifetime ago. She had been sure he would try to ride out the trouble, perhaps keeping a low profile until it had all blown over.

But his momentary loss of control in front of everybody had had consequences after all. Matron had obviously told Mrs Gleeson everything, and between them they commanded a great deal of respect at the hospital. The powers that be must have decided that something had to be done. He was too experienced a surgeon to be sacked or struck off, but he was no longer welcome in Homerton.

Matron had indicated the course of events when

she had dropped by Rose's ward to discuss further improving burns treatments.

'I just can't take it in,' Rose had said. 'To think he was quite happy to return to work, knowing full well that you and I knew what he had done.'

Matron had given a terse laugh. 'He was prepared to front it out, but it was all built on sand. He showed himself up. He thought nothing of insulting a junior member of staff. That's a different matter when it's done in front of the other doctors and the chairwoman. It started a chain of questions and it turned out plenty of other people had had their concerns about him. So he's off.'

Rose had shaken her head. 'I can't believe we're rid of him.'

'Indeed.' Then Matron had faced her directly. 'And how are you keeping, in all of this, Sister Harrison?'

Rose was taken aback by the change of subject. 'I . . . well, all right, I suppose.'

Matron eyed her keenly. 'I do see the staff records, you know. No, no, nothing is amiss. The opposite, in fact. You have taken hardly any of your leave since way back in the early autumn. For nearly the entirety of the Blitz you have been on duty here, with no proper break. That's very commendable, but not always good for the health.'

Rose shrugged. 'I was needed here. And then with Katherine having to leave . . .'

Matron nodded. 'Exactly my point. You have in effect been doing the work of two. I'm very grateful. We've needed you, and I realise I am in part responsible,

319

asking you to step up, but with no experienced deputy to share the burden.'

Rose was puzzled. 'But we all do it, it's nothing . . .'

Matron held up her hand. 'It is not nothing. It is working flat out, on little sleep, for months on end. And look what you've had to contend with – the bombs, certainly, but also this whole business with Prendergast. You've been watching out for Effie. Believe me, Sister Harrison, it is not nothing.'

Rose had blushed, knowing, on the one hand, that this was true. But it felt wrong all the same when, on the other hand, she was far from the only one in the same situation, and she said as much.

Matron was adamant. 'You need some time off, Sister. Easter is coming up. I dare say your family celebrate. Why not take a block of days together, and come back refreshed?'

Rose had not agreed at the time, but now as she strode across the Downs, her thoughts returned to Matron's idea. Why *not* do as she suggested? There were fewer raids now; the ward would be in good hands; Effie would be in no danger once the surgeon had left for good.

Then another idea came to her. Rounding the corner at the edge of the Downs to turn up towards Victory Walk, a plan began to form in her mind.

'Look, Rose, Ma found the currants!' Robbie greeted her as she stepped into the kitchen. He waved the jam jar in her face before she had a chance to take off her scarf or work out what was going on.

'That's nice,' she said. Of course: their mother was preparing another batch of seasonal baking. She sniffed and caught the scent of spices, as Patty brought another couple of jars across to the table.

'Rose! Just in time for a cup of tea,' she beamed. 'And to help with the hot cross buns, if you aren't too tired. We're looking forward to them, aren't we, Robbie?'

Robbie had gathered a handful of cabbage leaves, ready to take out to the rabbit, so he grinned from the back kitchen door. 'I would really like a chocolate egg as well,' he said cheerfully, his good spirits restored.

'I bet you would.' Rose hung up her scarf on the back of the door and went after him to the sink, to wash her hands.

Daisy came rushing into the room, waving Freddy's letter. 'He's safe!' she cried. 'He sends his love.'

Rose smiled, but answered soberly. 'He'll be right in the middle of the Battle of the Atlantic, won't he? And that will mean Clover is busier than ever. Ah, sorry, Ma.' She caught her mother's sharp intake of breath. 'She knows what she's doing. She'll be all right.'

Patty bustled around a dining chair to reach the cupboard where the flour was kept. 'Well, yes, I dare say,' she replied, in a tone that clearly conveyed that she did not want to think of her middle daughter in danger, all over again.

Rose turned to her sister. 'Don't suppose Freddy has any more leave coming up?'

Daisy pulled a face. 'Don't think so. He hasn't said, but it's so soon since he last came home – I won't get my hopes up for ages yet.'

321

Rose drummed her fingers on the table, wondering whether to share her idea with her family yet. She had not quite thought it through. Then again, voicing it might help.

'Matron told me I should take some leave,' she began.

Patty brightened at once. 'That's a very sensible suggestion. I like the sound of your matron.'

Rose laughed. 'Yes, you'd get along very well. I should introduce you two one day. But I don't know what's best.'

Daisy gave her a straight look. 'Wait a minute, if you haven't even had to ask for leave but your boss has told you to take it . . . you aren't seriously intending to turn it down?'

Patty took out her old set of kitchen scales, which had once belonged to her mother. The weighing pan was cream enamel, but its grass-green edge was chipped. The weights were shiny grey, kept carefully clean so that they would be as accurate as possible. 'Here's your granny's scales,' she said, just as she did every time she got them out.

Rose did not comment. She was still forming her thoughts. While Daisy moved to bring across the sugar tin, she frowned and bit her lip. 'No, not turn it down,' she said eventually. 'It's true, I am owed time off. It's just what's best to do with it. And, well, I had a letter today too, from Philip.'

Daisy glanced at her sister with interest. 'How is he? And where is he – can he say?'

They all knew Philip had been based in Kent when

he'd had his accident, a plane crash at the height of the Battle of Britain. Since Christmas he had dropped heavy hints that he'd been moved several times, as the enemy's methods of attack had changed. Now, though, Rose nodded. 'He's back where he was, at least for a few months, as far as he knows. So, I was thinking . . .'

'Go on,' said Daisy.

'I haven't asked him, it's only just occurred to me,' Rose continued, her face growing pink at the daring of what she was about to say. 'If he can arrange leave at the same time as me, maybe we can meet near his airbase, or halfway between, or something like that. Perhaps for a few days, even.'

Patty immediately looked up from where she was preparing a baking tray. 'In a hotel?'

Rose bit her lip before explaining further. 'Well, we could afford two rooms at a small hotel or country inn or something like that. I don't even know what there might be, or if he can take leave. Perhaps over Easter . . .'

Patty's face fell. 'But you always come to us if you aren't working over the holidays.'

Rose pressed her hands together. 'It's not that I don't love coming home for Easter. Of course I do. I just thought there might be a better chance of him taking leave then. I don't even know if that's true. They can't give everyone a long weekend all at the same time – that wouldn't make sense. So I'll maybe ask him when would be best. I expect Matron will allow me to take my leave whenever I ask, after the last few weeks.' She hoped that this would make her mother feel better, but she wasn't sure.

Patty sighed, but then brightened again. 'I understand,' she said. 'You have to fit in with when it is convenient for him, I realise that. And I trust you to be sensible. He's a real gentleman, I know that much.'

Rose felt a wave of relief. 'Yes, he is,' she said with certainty. 'I trust him, Ma. And – and I so want to see him again.'

Patty poured out the flour into the enamel pan and a puff of white powder floated upwards. 'I know you do. Well, you'll just have to let us know when you find out. Then you could join us for all or part of Easter, depending on what Philip can do.'

CHAPTER THIRTY-TWO

'Might as well take her back to the depot,' said Jimmy, patting the dashboard of the battered old ambulance. 'That's our time up, and this old warhorse could do with a bit of an overhaul. She was tricky when you came to change that tyre, wasn't she? But you managed it all right.'

Hope swung the steering wheel around, and the vehicle juddered as it hit a loose brick lying in the middle of the road. 'Yes, everything had stuck. Looked like rust had got in. Anyway, it worked in the end.'

Jimmy nodded, pleased. 'Looks as if those lessons have had an effect, even if you've moaned about them.'

Hope pulled down the tattered visor. 'Sun's in my eyes – not that I'm complaining,' she added hastily. The promise of springtime warmth was welcome. 'All right, I admit that Mr Macleod has done his job. I am now safe to maintain an ambulance while out on duty, or at least for everyday breakdowns. I'm not overhauling her, though. That's beyond me.'

Jimmy coughed into his creased handkerchief. 'Early hay fever,' he said shortly. 'Happens every year. And what with all the dust we got nowadays – it's no wonder people cough.'

'If you say so.' Hope swerved to avoid a football that

flew into their path, as a group of young children ran out of a bombsite between two rows of houses. 'Little perishers,' she remarked.

Jimmy was more forgiving. 'Well, they got to play somewhere. Half the parks are getting dug up to grow veg – where are they to go? My sister's nippers are on at me all the time – come and play football, Uncle Jimmy.' He coughed again at the thought of it. 'I tell them, not at my age. You'll run rings around me.'

'Perhaps that's their idea,' Hope suggested as the depot gates appeared at the end of the street. 'Are they any closer to finding a house?'

Jimmy gave a gruff laugh. 'Not on your nelly. There's fat chance of that at the moment. Anyhow, I don't mind them, apart from the football. I like it really. As I say, keeps me young.'

Hope changed down into first gear and the clutch creaked. 'Come on, come on,' she encouraged it. 'Almost back now.'

Jimmy shot her a glance. 'Don't let Macleod hear you talking to the engine. He'll tell you it's not rational.'

'Don't care,' Hope replied, swinging the vehicle round into the depot yard and pulling up next to an equally battered one. 'This old girl likes it. As for kids keeping you young, I swear I've aged half a lifetime since Christmas.'

Jimmy made a wry face. 'And how is the little lad?'

Hope checked that the handbrake was fully on. 'Oh, he's coming on nicely,' she groaned. 'Just started to roll over, so you can't be sure he'll be where you left him.

Worse, he can push himself up a bit when he's on his tummy so that means crawling isn't far off. He's grand. It's all the adults around him that are suffering.' She got out of the driver's door as Jimmy did the same from the passenger side.

'Now you don't mean that,' he said gently as they headed in for a well-deserved cup of tea.

Hope groaned. 'I suppose you're right. Or at least partly. I only say it to you because I can't really do so at home. Mother would have my guts for garters.'

Jimmy nodded in sympathy. 'Of course it's not easy, but think of all the fun you'll have when he's a bit bigger. When he can say his favourite auntie's name.'

Hope joined the tea queue. 'Maybe,' she said, not really convinced.

The train platform was surprisingly empty considering it was Maundy Thursday. Before the war, workers would have been taking advantage of the forthcoming long weekend, trying to get away early to family and friends. Rose gazed around, holding tightly on to the handle of her small suitcase, taking in the unfamiliar station. She had hardly ever been on holiday, just a few day trips, and had forgotten what it was like to arrive somewhere new.

Very few people were coming through the barrier ready to get on the up train back to London. Everyone knew the capital had taken a pounding over the past six months or so, and Rose could well understand that if you lived in a place such as Canterbury, then you would want to stay there. It was comparatively untouched by the war, certainly compared to the devastation in the East End and docklands.

There were small groups of service personnel, some with big kitbags over their shoulders, others with smaller bags or satchels. Their uniforms were distinctive: khaki or navy- or air-force blue. She kept her eyes on the lookout for one very special figure in air-force uniform, as she was guessing he would not have bothered going back to his barracks to change. It was mid-afternoon; the train had of course been delayed, and now the April sunshine was warm, almost too warm for a coat. Rose had come in civilian clothes for once. It felt strange not to have on at least some articles of nursing uniform. She held on to her new confidence now she had been successfully working as a sister, reminding herself that it didn't matter what Mrs Sutherland thought. She wasn't here to meet that woman – she was here for her son.

She'd kept her watch with her, though, even if it was now in her skirt pocket and not pinned to her apron. She took it out and checked it. Five to three; he'd be here by quarter past, he had written in his most recent letter. God and RAF command willing, of course.

Her heart was hammering in her chest as she took in the sight of a WVS stand, almost identical to the one she'd passed to catch the train down. A few soldiers were making the most of it, a chance to set down their duffel bags, sling their heavy greatcoats over their shoulders and grab a drink. Their voices rose in the warm air of the station, floating towards the high roof. Canterbury station was not as grand as the London terminus, but that would make it easier for her to see Philip, she decided.

So she jumped in shock and nearly dropped her case when a voice spoke from just behind her. 'Fancy seeing you here.'

She turned and fell into his arms, which wrapped her tightly to him. For a moment she couldn't speak, simply stood there, hugging him back, knowing that this was where she belonged. No matter where they stood, she was at home in his embrace. She didn't care if the soldiers were watching, or anyone else. The only person that mattered was right there before her, his arms strong and safe. He was there, in the flesh, and not in her imagination.

Then he released her and laughed into her smiling face. 'See? I'm early. One of the chaps got me space on a requisitioned lorry heading this way. Messed up my best trousers a bit but I told him you wouldn't mind.'

Rose grinned even more broadly. 'As if I'd care. As long as you're here.'

'I'm here.' His deep eyes assured her it was true. Then he bent down to pick up her case. She noticed he had a similar one, a dark grey grip, by his feet. 'Come on, it's not far. I hope you like it.'

Rose thought she didn't mind if they ended up in a garden shed as long as they were together. So much had happened since she'd last seen him, even though it was only a few months ago. The terrible raids in January, her sudden promotion, the horror of Effie's assault and Prendergast's humiliation – that alone was enough drama for a lifetime. Then again, as she walked along the Canterbury pavements, her arm tucked through his, it was as if they'd always been together and Christmas was only a blink of the eye ago. Time was playing tricks in her mind, but she didn't care. Nothing mattered, except she was here with Philip.

'This is it.' They had come to a halt outside a pretty inn on a side street, very old, but spick and span from its outside appearance – so unlike the pubs Rose passed day to day, none of which had fully escaped the bomb damage. A window box of early flowers stood by the old front door, slightly ajar, on which the brassware was polished to a bright sheen. It was welcoming without being showy. Rose loved it immediately.

'I do hope you like it.'

She suddenly realised he was nervous – at their being together after such a break, at being on unfamiliar territory. She hastened to reassure him. 'It's perfect. Let's go inside.'

In the dimness of the little vestibule he squeezed her hand and breathed into her ear, 'I'm glad. I want it to be perfect. You deserve the best, Rose – and it's our first time away together, properly on our own.' He squeezed her hand again. 'But not the last.'

The inn was just as welcoming as it first seemed, and Rose twirled around to look at her little room with pleasure. It was comfortable and full of old-fashioned furnishings, tapestry cushions and views of the cathedral painted in oils. For a moment it was as if there was no war going on. This room most likely had not changed for many years, except there were fresh flowers in a vase, and the bed linen was neatly pressed and smelled of lemony soap.

She wandered with Philip through the historic streets, with the beamed buildings overhanging the pavements, and small shops bravely displaying whatever they had available to buy. It was a world away from London, the constant fear of attack, the rubble, the dust, the sense of having to allow extra time for everything because of so many delays, while being short of time all the while. She had not realised the strain she had been living under. Now she took a deep breath and held on to Philip's elbow. He turned to look down at her and gave his wide smile.

'Penny for them,' he teased.

Rose gazed up at him and then threw her head back and laughed. 'It's nothing. Really. Just that this feels so different, and yet it's normal. No rushing, no sirens, no sense of having to run for cover at any moment.'

He nodded in instant understanding. 'This is what life should be like,' he said. 'And it will be again, Rose. We have to believe that. Hang on to that hope.'

She leant her cheek against his shoulder as they walked on. 'Yes, you're right,' she agreed. 'It's what we are fighting for. A future like this, where we don't have to worry, don't have to live looking over our shoulders all the time.'

Then she stopped, wondering if she had overstepped the mark by mentioning the future. If it sounded as if she was presuming their future would be together. Which, she realised, she was.

Philip had not noticed her hesitation and was still

331

smiling at her when she glanced up again. 'I've taken the liberty of booking us somewhere nice to eat,' he told her. 'Nothing fancy, but one of my crew recommended it. Not sure that there will be a big choice on the menu, but I wanted to treat you.'

Rose gasped a little. She was not used to eating out, other than the tea shop with Robbie or any of the cafés near the market. The place she ate at mostly was the staff canteen, where the food was always filling but there was not much else you could say to recommend it. She recognised that Philip came from a family where eating out was the norm, that he'd be accustomed to foreign-sounding dishes, whereas she would not even know what they were. Then again, she trusted him. He knew what she was like, what her family was like.

'Sounds lovely,' she said gamely.

It turned out that she was right to have faith in him, because it was not a grand room of the best hotel he'd chosen, but a modest restaurant on a corner, with small windowpanes framing the picturesque narrow street. Philip had a quiet word with the waiter, who showed them to a table by the window for the best view, laid with a pristine white tablecloth and polished old cutlery. Rose approved.

'I'll have to ask who does their laundry,' she commented, 'as this is better than the pillowcases on the ward.' She was tempted to chatter on to hide her nervousness, but Philip gave another one of his wonderful smiles and she relaxed.

He was right; there was not a big choice, but it was a step above the canteen, although not, Rose thought loyally, in any way close to her mother's home cooking. They had roast chicken with vegetables and a delicious gravy, which Philp explained had been made with wine. 'Would you like a glass to drink with it?' he asked, but Rose told him she'd prefer lemonade. She didn't want any alcohol to cloud her brain; she wanted to remember every magical moment of this marvellous evening.

Then there was a fruit mousse, something Rose had not tasted in a very long time. 'I suppose they have a way of buying extra eggs, as they're close to farms,' she said, spooning the delicious dessert into her mouth. Philip watched her with pleasure.

'I don't know and I shan't ask. I'll just be grateful that they have,' he replied, tucking into his own. 'They don't feed us like this at the airfield, I can tell you.'

The dusk was deepening and the waiter came over to pull the crimson velvet curtains across the quaint old window, observing the blackout even here, far away from London. Rose gazed at Philip in the soft light from the wall lamps and the candle on their table. He was more handsome than ever, she decided, his face unmarked by his terrible crash, his eyes now fully alert. How close he had come to death. Maybe he did not realise, but she, who had sat there day after day while he lay in his coma, had known it all too well. It was a miracle he was here.

He held out his hand and took hold of hers. 'I'm so glad you suggested that we do this,' he said warmly. 'I had thought of it, I must confess, but I was afraid you'd take it the wrong way, or wouldn't want to come or . . . or think it's too soon.'

She stroked his hand a little. 'I almost didn't dare. Then I thought, after all that's gone on, why shouldn't we seize the day? I don't mean to rush things – it's not so much that – it's just I really, really wanted to see you. And to have the chance to spend some proper time with you, not rushing off to get back to the hospital . . .'

'Or having to meet my family,' he added, naming the problem that she was avoiding. 'Like I said before, it's all right, I know what they are like. Or rather, what my mother can be like. She can't help it. It's the way she was brought up.'

Rose nodded, not trusting herself to comment.

'You're so lucky, with your family,' he went on. 'I keep thinking about the way they welcomed me at Christmas. I know it must have been hard for them – the son of your father's boss coming round, with hardly any notice. In some ways I wish that it wasn't the case – that they didn't know of me before. But that's impossible, and my father has often said how much he values yours.'

Rose acknowledged this. 'And Pa always says the same. How much he regards your father as a boss.'

Philip shifted in his chair. 'We can't help who our parents are. It's who we are that matters,' he stated, and Rose agreed.

'They've helped to shape us. But it's what we do with that upbringing that counts.' She ate the final spoonful of mousse. 'They must be proud of you, Philip.' She blushed a little. 'I know I am.'

He ran his hand through his short hair. 'Well, I don't know about that. But I have to tell you just how proud of you I am.' He leant forward and took her hand again. 'Even since I've known you, you've taken on such responsibility at the hospital, you've had to contend with a senior colleague trying to bring you down, you've helped that young nurse – and all on no sleep! You're one in a million, Rose.'

Rose was about to protest that he was exaggerating, but his attention was distracted by the waiter wondering if they wanted anything else.

'No, let's just walk back,' she suggested. She was loath to leave the lovely restaurant but they had tomorrow and Saturday to look forward to, and it had been an early start. Besides, she longed to walk along the streets in the night-time air, being held close by Philip.

It was cooler as they stepped out onto the pavement once again, and sure enough he pulled her towards him, resting his arm across her shoulder. She snuggled in to him, feeling very daring for putting her arm along the back of his waist. She would not have walked like this back home in Hackney in case anyone saw, but here nobody would know them. It felt brazen and yet exactly right, as she was so certain they belonged together.

Back at the inn, they made their way upstairs and instinctively both came to a halt on the landing, lit by one small lamp with a pretty shade.

'We'd better go to our rooms,' she breathed. Then, honestly, 'I don't want to. I want to stay here with you. But it's best . . .'

'Shh.' He leant down so that his warm lips met hers and kissed her at first softly and then more passionately,

335

until her knees almost gave way. 'Sorry,' he murmured, 'but I've been waiting all day to do that.'

She looked up at him through half-closed eyes. 'So have I,' she admitted.

'I wish we could . . . no, I'll never do anything to put you under pressure.' He suddenly sounded more formal and she recognised that he was steeling himself to break away for the night. He didn't want to separate, any more than she did.

'Good night, then,' she whispered. 'I'll see you in the morning. Sleep well.'

He reluctantly let her go. 'The same to you. I'll be thinking of you all night long.'

On Good Friday the streets were buzzing, with families gathering together for the beginning of Easter. All eyes turned to the magnificent ancient cathedral, which stood tall above all the other buildings, and it was the obvious place for Rose and Philip to head for, after a delicious cooked breakfast with the freshest eggs that they could imagine. 'We'll try to time it when there isn't a service going on and then we can look around,' he said. 'Have you ever been in? It's like a big slice of history, full of beautiful carvings and stonework, but it's been years since I went inside. There I am, stationed not very far away really, but I might as well be at the other end of the country.'

Rose swung along the street, full of energy on this bright morning, in her best spring frock of delicately patterned cotton and a light jacket. 'I do know what you mean. It's like us being a bus ride away from St Paul's cathedral, but we never go. Because it's so close, you think it will always be there, and so don't make the time. Although I did consider it, after it was so nearly destroyed in the raids.'

'Exactly.' He grinned, happy that she understood him.

People were filing out of the impressive main doors as they approached, dressed in their best for the solemn service. Rose could see that many of the women had made an effort to mark the occasion, subtle lipsticks, colourful yet not gaudy scarves. Children were running around, happy to be away from the severity of the church atmosphere and having to sit quietly with their elders. She remembered having to do the same in their far smaller church back home, always being the one to attempt to keep her siblings in order, but that had often been an impossible task.

'Come on, let's see if we can get in through a side door.' She was happy for Philip to lead the way, as he knew the place far better than she did. The grand building cast the surrounding narrow streets into deep shadow, and she shivered in the sudden chill, which gave him another excuse to hold her hand.

Rose was not given to visiting historic buildings, but once inside the cathedral she began to see why it was so important. The very air seemed different – timeless, somehow. Dust motes floated in the air, as the sound of the organ drifted across to where they stood in the ancient nave. As she took it all in, she was speechless. People had stood here for many centuries, bringing their deepest hopes and fears, whether they were important members of the clergy or famous figures, now commemorated in stone, or the inhabitants of the old city. She felt at once insignificant in the presence of such history and yet vital, more alive somehow.

'It's . . . wonderful,' she breathed at last.

'Isn't it? I'm so glad you feel like that. It's full of echoes of the past and yet you sense it will be here for the future too.'

There it was again – that mention of the future. She shivered, at the coolness of the still air lit by the age-old stained-glass windows, and at the thought of what might happen in the weeks, months, years to come.

Philip drew her towards the solidity of the stone walls. He too seemed at a loss for words for a moment.

She leant into him, not to be as bold as to put her arms around him in such a place, but to sense his closeness nonetheless.

'I don't want to speak out of turn,' he said at last. 'I realise we haven't known each other very long really. And out of that time we haven't been together face to face for much of it.'

'That's true,' she agreed, wondering where this was leading.

'But do you feel as I do – that we've known each other for much longer somehow?' His expression was intent.

'Yes. Yes, I do.' There was no doubt that this was exactly how she felt as well.

'I can't promise you anything. We none of us know what the future has in store, especially the way things stand at the moment. I'm not one to rush into anything and I sense you aren't either. But if – no, *when* – we get through all this . . . Rose, can we be together? It's not how I wanted to say this and I haven't planned it properly . . . but we will be, won't we?'

He suddenly sounded so different, not the daring heroic pilot, but unsure, hesitant.

She turned to face him. There was no doubt in her mind. It was not a standard proposal but she knew precisely what he meant and it echoed how she felt in her heart. 'Of course,' she said. 'Of course. It's what I want more than anything.'

CHAPTER THIRTY-THREE

The moment had come. Coral could no longer hide the growing bump straining the seams of her uniform. Rose realised she would have to act before somebody higher up got wind of the situation. If anyone was going to break the news to Matron, it had better be her.

'Today's the day,' Rose told Coral as they began their shift. The Welsh nurse was back on the men's general ward, lively as ever, but most definitely spinning around slightly differently to account for the weight out in front. Most of the patients wouldn't know what to look for, but some might. The risk was too great.

Coral stood for a moment, hands on her hips. Then she nodded. 'I knew it had to come some time soon, Sister,' she said. 'I just wanted this to last as long as possible. I love nursing, I do. Being in a big hospital like this, I learn so much. I got to keep going if I can – well, like the other sister did.'

'I understand.' Rose could well imagine the young woman's dilemma. It was so unfair that she would have to give up the work she loved. 'But if I've noticed, others will too. Will you be all right? You'll have to go home, won't you?'

Coral stood up straighter and pushed back her cap. 'Don't you worry about me, Sister. I wrote to Jonnie ages ago and he's happy as can be. We'll get married soon as I'm back, like we was going to anyway, just a bit sooner. It don't matter. Then his brother's got a little house – real tiny, it is – but he's joined the army and it'll need looking after.'

Rose smiled wryly. Coral had been organising everything behind the scenes.

'Mam will be thrilled. Loves babies, she does. Then we got Jonnie's mam in the next village. She'll help out too. No, we're all set, except I don't want to stop nursing.' For the first time Coral's smile slipped. 'I can't tell you how much I enjoy working here, Sister. So my idea is, soon as the baby's big enough to leave, I'll join one of the big hospitals down there, if they'll have me. I'll fit in some shifts somehow. Now I've found something I love and I'm good at, I don't want to stop it for ever.'

Rose was pleased. 'Well, they'll be lucky to have you. You're right, it would be a crying shame to waste your training so far.' She checked her watch. 'So now, I'm going to speak to Matron today. She'll have ten minutes before her next meeting. Do you want to come along?'

Coral's reply was instant. 'No, Sister, you do it. She scares me, does Matron. She might take against me falling for a baby when I'm not yet wed.'

Rose shrugged. 'I know she can seem like that, but I don't think she'll judge you. And like you say, you'll be getting married soon anyway. She'll more likely be sorry to lose a promising young nurse.'

That did it. Coral gulped to hide her tears. 'Do you think I am, Sister? Promising, I mean? Really?'

Rose did not hesitate but nodded vigorously. 'Really, Coral. Look how you've come on. Like I say, any hospital will be lucky to have you. Now, I must go.'

It turned out that Rose's prediction was right. Matron had scarcely raised an eyebrow. 'She's not the first and she won't be the last,' she sighed. 'You'll be sorry to lose her, won't you? We shall have to find you a new trainee. I can write to an old colleague who now works at one of the big Cardiff hospitals, if you like. My main concern is for that other young nurse of yours. Doesn't she rely on her friend? After all that's happened, I should like to be reassured she will be able to cope on her own, as it were.'

Rose had been worried about Effie too, but once again it turned out the fear was groundless.

'Course I knew she'd have to stop soon,' Effie said later that day. 'She's struggling to bend over to make the beds but she won't say so. I'll miss her,' she went on, answering Rose's unspoken question. 'We can write and all that, but once she's got a nipper she'll be too busy, I bet. Never mind, she's been the best friend I could have asked for. She's taught me heaps, Sister, like how I should believe in myself more. I ain't afraid of anything now.'

Rose had been immensely relieved. Even with Mr Prendergast out of the picture – rumour had it that he'd relocated to Newcastle – she had been concerned for Effie, as she always seemed so fragile. Perhaps her friendship with Coral had helped her find an inner core of steel.

Rose had been tempted to join the two young

nurses as they sat together for their evening meal, but then decided they should make the most of their time together while they still could. She ate at a corner table, reading the latest edition of *Nursing Times*, but could not concentrate. She weighed up her options. She could read on, but she could always look at it tomorrow. She could go up to her room and read a book, or Philip's latest letter. But she had already read it so often it was practically falling apart. She treasured the words of love he'd sent her. And he'd been happy to hear how Robbie had enjoyed the chocolate egg that he'd managed to find for him, somewhere in Canterbury's web of shops.

Then again, she could go back home for the night. She glanced towards the window. It was May and the dusk had not yet fallen. It would be full moon, and so plenty light enough anyway. There had been raids the week after Easter, but not much since then. She would be as safe as she was ever likely to be. She'd take the chance and go.

'You should have come sooner! I'd have saved you some dinner,' Patty exclaimed when her eldest child arrived, just as the daylight had left the dark skies. 'Look at you, coming over in the dark. It's a wonder you haven't twisted your ankle.'

'Not in these old shoes,' Rose laughed, pointing her toes to show how little life the sensible lace-ups had left in them. 'Sorry, Ma, it was a bit of a spur-of-the-moment decision. Where is everyone?'

Patty automatically turned to put the kettle on.

'Your pa is due back at any moment – he had to go back to the factory to sort out some problem with the fire-watching rota. I told him not to volunteer himself – he's done it far too often recently. Robbie's just gone upstairs. He says to finish his homework but I bet it's to read his comic. Daisy's just getting changed – that's her now, coming back down.'

Rose stepped away from the hallway door as her sister came through it, knitting in hand.

'Look, Rose, I'm practising!' she announced, holding up a needle from which hung a triangle of knitted wool in a mixture of colours.

'What is it going to be?'

'A scarf, of course.' Daisy said it as if it was evident, which it wasn't.

Patty poured the tea. 'Practice makes perfect, and you can't expect to be good at it immediately,' she said steadily. 'You just need a bit of patience.'

Rose laughed out loud. 'Yes, that's always been your middle name, Daisy.'

Daisy stuck out her tongue but was not really offended. 'All right, I can see I'm not quite there yet,' she conceded. 'Have you had a bad day, Rose? Have you come home to recover?'

Rose sat down, stretched out her legs in their old shoes and began her story, of Coral's unconcealable pregnancy and the lack of shock when it was all out in the open. 'Just think about that,' she finished. 'Before the war there would have been a scandal. Now hardly anyone cares, or not who matters. The main thing is we'll be a nurse down on the ward.'

Daisy and Patty commiserated, and Rose once again felt the balm of relief at being back in her true home and able to say just about anything. The slam of the front door heralded her father's return and she knew that all was well in her world.

Rose had taken Clover's bed, deciding that there was no need to risk walking back to the hospital now it had grown late, and she was not on shift until the late morning. She had sat up chatting to Daisy, enjoying the rare chance to be with her sister on her own. Before the war they had been realms apart: Daisy, the spoilt youngest until Robbie had come along so many years later, had been more of a child when the fighting had broken out. Rose was a nurse who'd already completed her training. Daisy had had to grow up fast. Rose knew it had been hard for her in many ways but now they could talk together on much more equal terms, and she liked it.

Daisy had begun to snore very softly, but it was so dark that Rose could not tell if she was lying on her back or not. Perhaps she should prod her gently to see if she would turn over. Cautiously Rose pulled the blackout blind away from the window to see if the anti-aircraft beams would provide a sliver of light.

Then the siren started, the all-too-familiar wail of the air-raid warning. Rose groaned. She had allowed herself to believe that for once they would be safe. She'd taken other colleagues to task for this very belief not so long ago and now she had fallen into the trap of wishful thinking.

345

Daisy stopped snoring and sat up, her outline just visible against the old wallpaper. 'Not again,' she groaned, hoisting her legs to the floor, shuffling around for her shoes. 'I was just having a lovely dream . . .'

Rose could well imagine what, or rather who, it would be about. How unfair, to be pulled abruptly out of it and into the real world.

She began to grope blindly along the floor until she found her own shoes and the pile of discarded clothes. Hastily she pulled them back on, as Daisy did the same.

'Have you got enough warm stuff? Here, it's Clover's big cardigan.' Daisy reached across and Rose took the bundle with gratitude, as it could get very cold out in the shelter. The pair of them turned on their torches and went out to the landing, checking that their parents and little brother were awake and ready to go downstairs. Then they fell into the usual routine, Patty gathering together the flask of tea she always made before going to bed just in case, the emergency tin of biscuits and bread and butter, and her big coat, while Bert saw to it that the gas was turned off. 'All set,' he said briefly, and then they trod the short, familiar path to the shelter.

Daisy shivered and drew her old scarf around her face. During the daytime she no longer needed to wear it, as the days of spring grew warmer. In the Anderson shelter it was still necessary, and she thought about how hot it would be on the tube platforms now. Some of the WVS team would be there, with the transport workers, checking that all was well. This led her thoughts to turn once more to the night she had spent down there with Freddy. How she longed to be held by him now, or even simply to know that he was safe.

She could make out the shapes of her family from the strobing lights outside filtering through the gaps in the corrugated roof. Robbie was lying across her mother's lap. Patty's head rested against Bert's shoulders. Rose huddled in a corner, with the rabbit at her feet. They were all asleep.

Daisy knew that rationally she had cause to be afraid, as the rumble of aircraft engines sounded overhead, but in truth she was too tired. She desperately wanted to stay alive, to be with Freddy again, to meet the future with open arms. She had to trust in that future, that it would happen. Too weary to worry any further, she fell back asleep.

Hope had been about to clock off from her shift on the ambulances. She was glad of the longer hours of daylight because at least she managed to spot most of the potholes and avoid them, giving her patients and colleagues a smoother ride. She'd worked past dusk, Jimmy in the passenger seat, as calls came in from young families with children they could not transport to hospital or, in one case, an old lady who had had a fall.

'Wasn't she sweet?' Hope said after they had driven her to safety. 'She was ever so grateful. She was like the grandmother you'd love to have.' She crunched the gearstick into second.

'I don't remember my grannies,' Jimmy said, staring straight ahead.

Hope puckered her lips in thought. 'Nor do I, or not well. Mother's mother was around when I was younger but somehow I can't think what she looked like. All the pictures we have of her show her wearing a hat that shades her face. As for my father's mother, she got the flu after the Great War. Wasn't that awful? People lived through all of that and then got wiped out by flu.'

Jimmy gave a short cough. 'It did for lots of my uncles and aunties too. Went over like ninepins, so they said.' He coughed again and tried to stifle it. 'Anyhow, let's not talk about such things. Let's concentrate on staying alive long enough to have a last cup of tea at the depot. Mind that corner, young Hope.'

Hope always liked to go slightly too fast at the end of the street before the depot, and Jimmy said the same thing every time. For some reason she was certain it brought them good luck. It did nothing for the tyres, though, and she'd been warned once already. Reluctantly she took it carefully, not wanting her friend to get hurt, least of all through her own actions.

No sooner had they parked their vehicle than the air-raid warning went off.

'Damn and blast,' muttered Jimmy, somewhat to Daisy's surprise. Usually he took the alarms in his stride. Perhaps he was more exhausted than he'd let on during the busy shift.

'Come on, a quick cuppa and then no doubt we'll have to go back out again.' Hope tried to sound encouraging, though she had been looking forward to finishing work. Then again, with the siren blaring, back home the baby would have been woken up and no doubt joining in with his own wail. She might as well stay on where she was needed.

They managed their well-deserved tea and then what had been a busy night descended into pandemonium. This was by far the worst raid for a long time, and they barely had time to think, let alone feel tired. Hope could feel her eyes were scratchy but, knowing she could do little to improve things, she just tried to ignore the urge to rub them. Fires had taken hold, painting the skies a livid orange. It was like the Bank station disaster all over again, except now it was closer to home.

She couldn't allow herself to think like that, couldn't start imagining what was happening at her family's house or at Victory Walk. There were shelters at both and she had to have faith that they would do their job. Her parents would guess that she was still on duty; it had happened before. Tomorrow her mother would give her an earful, but Hope knew deep down it was only because she was worried for her. Meanwhile she had to keep a clear head.

It was harder to hang on to that when she had to deliver two patients to the hospital at Homerton. The nearby Chatsworth Road had been hit, and several of the residential streets further along had been caught too. It was all far too close to where Rose worked, for Hope's liking, but again there was nothing to be done. Besides, she didn't know if Rose was on shift or not. She just had to hang on to the knowledge that the hospital had a tried-and-tested evacuation plan, and could keep taking patients there as long as they had room. Otherwise she would have to make the much longer journey down to the Royal London at Whitechapel.

Now, though, it was a matter of going wherever the ARP wardens directed her, and she found herself edging along the bomb-hit streets so close to her home and all the landmarks of her childhood – her schools, her best friend's house from when she was seven, the shop that used to sell sweets and let her fill a paper bag to share with Joy. Now its windows were gone. She could almost taste the sherbet lemons they had loved, but there was little chance of finding any to buy these days.

Two more trips to the Homerton hospital left her hands blistered from gripping the wheel and her legs aching from braking hard to avoid falling debris. She was glad of a few minutes' respite at the depot, although there was no time to wait for the water to heat up to make tea. The big urn had run dry and would take too long to be ready. She filled a flask with cold water from the brass tap, gulping it thirstily, soothing her throat. She had had to shout on the latest jobs, to be heard above the noise of the fires and aircraft engines.

Macleod joined her at the tap. 'Good idea,' he said gruffly, and she realised his voice had taken a pounding too. 'I'll just fill this glass.' He downed it in one.

'Didn't know you were rostered for this evening,' Hope commented, refilling her flask so it would be topped up to the brim for her next outing.

'Nor did I. Someone rang the factory, asked if I could

350

come in. I was on lates there so they aren't expecting me at home,' he went on, unusually communicative.

Hope nodded. 'Lucky they could reach you.' She held her hands under the tap to cool them. 'Won't your wife be worried?'

He stared at her. 'I've no wife.'

Hope was puzzled. Maybe the heat of the last journey had confused her brain. 'But didn't you say you had children? At primary school?'

He set down his cup. 'Well, yes. Fancy you remembering.' He paused. 'I do have small children. The thing is, their mother died before the war started. TB, it was, and very cruel. So nowadays, my sister helps out. She takes them when I'm on duty or at work.'

'I see.' Hope didn't know what to say. Her thoughts were very confused now. So he had been married, but was not any longer. But he had the children. Poor things, she thought, losing their mother when so little. Her hands shook. She must have held them in the cold water for too long.

'I . . . er, who are you rostered with?' She hoped she didn't sound too shaken.

He didn't have to answer as Geraldine came across the room at a run. 'Sorry to interrupt, but we're needed urgently.' Then she turned to Hope. 'You will be as well. Jimmy's waiting by the door. There's not a moment to lose.'

Macleod nodded, first at his fellow driver and then to Hope. 'Best get on with it,' he said. 'Keep on going until it's over. That's how I do it. One foot in front of the other, don't think about the rest of it.'

His words stayed with her as she went to join Jimmy, and the older man took her by the arm. 'You heard, then – we've been called out again.' He looked at her steadily with his eyes soft, the habitual good humour absent for once. 'Hope, you've got to be strong for this one. I said they should ask another crew but they're all out already.'

'Why? What?' Dread spread through her. Was it just exhaustion or was there something else? He'd never looked at her like this before.

Jimmy took a deep breath. 'I'm so sorry, Hope. It's your road.'

CHAPTER THIRTY-FOUR

The scene that met them was worse than anything she could have imagined.

Hope thought she had witnessed the worst that the raids could bring: death, destruction, anger and acute sorrow. Yet when it came to finding her own street ablaze, she realised there were far, far worse things to endure. So many houses, all bright with huge flames, and no way of knowing who was safe and who was not.

'All right?' asked Jimmy.

'Not really,' Hope muttered, but he had already jumped from the front seat, out to meet the approaching ARP warden to receive their immediate instructions.

She could hardly bear to look towards the end of the street, the corner house her mother had been so proud of. When she forced herself to check, she could see little of it anyway. Its top half was engulfed in flames, the roof above where her room had been totally gone, the chimney at an odd and dangerous angle. Her house. Her home, gone. Where were her family?

But the warden told her to go to another house where the flames were still at the back. On the front step sat two elderly people, neighbours that she knew slightly. They'd moved in just before the war. 'Smoke inhalation,' said the warden, and moved off to where Macleod and Geraldine had just arrived.

Through the smoke and swirling sooty debris, Hope carefully made her way up the short garden path. The couple were too shocked to speak but they nodded in recognition, either at her face or, more likely, her uniform. Everyone had got used to the waterproof coats her service often wore.

They were able to walk and so she stood between them, offering one elbow to each, and escorted them back down the path to where the ARP man waited. 'Walking wounded?' He immediately assessed the severity of their injuries. 'Very good, over there then. There's first-aiders on hand. Miss, we need you for the more severe cases. Over here.'

Hope handed over her elderly neighbours to a competent-looking middle-aged woman, who instantly began to chat to make them feel comfortable. Hope could do no more and turned away, following the warden.

The heat was unbearable and the smell from the fires made her gag. Jimmy was standing at the kerbside, his hanky held over his mouth. 'Over here,' he said, his words muffled, but she could guess what he was saying. 'Follow me.' She did as he asked, holding on blindly to the certainty he'd seen all this before and would know what to do now.

Fire-fighters had arrived from the opposite direction and they were training their hoses on her end of the street. They waved her over, and Jimmy led the way. Hope felt her throat constrict and it was not only the smell of burning buildings that was to blame. She couldn't breathe. She didn't want to see, didn't want to know. Everything that was dear to her was going up in flames. The fire-fighters didn't know this, though. They just saw an ambulance worker, ready to deal with any casualties. She had to go forward. This was her job.

Her legs as heavy as lead, she came to the corner where Jimmy was looking up. 'Who's likely to be there?' he asked sombrely.

'They'd be in the shelter round the side. My parents, my two sisters, and the baby.' Hope crossed her fingers that she'd spoken aloud, and not simply screamed, as she was desperate to do.

Jimmy stepped across to repeat this to the lead fire-fighter. The man said something back and it seemed as if he was checking what Jimmy had said. Then he shook his head, and bent to shout in Jimmy's ear. Jimmy stood totally still and then pulled back his shoulders. Then he turned back to Hope.

As he did so a figure approached and it took Hope a couple of seconds to recognise who it was. She'd never seen Faith like this, not even on the night she had given birth. Her hair was wild, her clothes a strange mix of pyjama bottoms and overcoat, and her feet were bare. 'I've lost him!' she shouted, her arms waving in a frenzy. 'He's not with Ma or Pa or Joy. We don't know what happened – what if he's still inside?'

'What?' Hope couldn't believe what she was hearing. 'Do you mean Artie? Artie is in there somewhere?'

Faith could hardly speak. 'I don't know! I don't know! I think so! Find him, Hope!'

Hope turned in shock to Jimmy, who was instantly resolute. 'Right. Come with me as far as the garden wall. I'm going in.'

Hope watched him as he disappeared into the smoke billowing around the side of what had been her home, obliterating the sight of the garden where she had played, the box hedge her father trimmed so neatly. This was no good. She could not wait here, doing nothing. She would be called to another house nearby, most likely, but now she had to know, had to find out what had gone on in that burning house in front of her. What had the fire-fighter said? She turned to look for him but he had gone, summoned to a blaze across the street. How could Artie have become separated from the rest of them? Had Faith got it wrong somehow? It was getting hotter and hotter.

She pulled at the collar of her coat, hesitating for just a second, and then plunged after Jimmy, or where he had been when she'd last seen him. She knew the terrain here without having to see, the paved path that led to the back door, the newer, rougher one that had been hastily laid down, which took her to the shelter. She reached for the metal roof to steady herself and then withdrew her hand at the last moment. She'd been seconds away from a terrible burn.

'Jimmy!' she cried. 'Jimmy! Where did you go?' And then, 'Artie, can you hear me? It's me!'

There was no answer. Scrabbling around at her feet she felt rather than saw a long piece of wood, and jammed it against where she knew the shelter door to be. The wind blew the smoke away for a few moments as she levered open the door, revealing the interior.

It was empty. That much was clear. On the floor lay some upturned cups and scattered cutlery, so they had been in here tonight; her mother would never have left the place like that after the previous raid. So they'd got out somehow, but the baby had not been left in here. Then where was he? Did another warden or fire-fighter have him? She should check, back on the road. First, though, she would try to find Jimmy. Where had he gone?

She called for him as she scrambled across shattered roof tiles now covering what had been the back garden. It was becoming harder to navigate by feel alone, it was all so different. 'Jimmy! Jimmy!' she shouted. The journey from the shelter to what had been their back door seemed to last for hours, though it could only have been half a minute at most.

Her heart was hammering in her chest. She had to find him. He'd put himself in danger for her, for her family, she just knew it. He always left this kind of search to the fire-fighters or ARP, but now he'd disappeared into the smoke behind her house, or what was left of it. She could not let him sacrifice himself for her, not when he'd been so kind to her for all her months of training and uncertainty. He had been her rock. She simply had to get him out, wherever he was. But she had to know if Artie was in there, if Jimmy had found him.

'Jimmy! Jimmy!' she shouted, her throat now aching and raw.

Then there was a movement, not even where the

doorway should have been, but to the side, where she could just about see part of the kitchen wall had given way. There was Jimmy, coming through the unnatural gap, illuminated from behind by flames, the walls all jagged. He was carrying something.

'I've got him!' he shouted at her, as from above came the ominous sounds of crashes, roof beams falling inward. 'He's here! Take him, Hope! Run!'

'What?' It took her a moment to realise what he meant. She didn't dare to hope. But it was true. He had Artie in his arms, baby Artie, who had somehow become separated from the others. She could see little movements, his little arms waving, but the noise all around was drowning out his cries.

'Take him and run, Hope!' Jimmy yelled. 'Run!' He'd reached the edge of the house and she could just about get close.

'What about you?'

'Doesn't matter. For the love of God, just *run*!'

She took in what was happening. She had no choice. Jimmy would have to save himself – but Artie could not do that. She had to save him. With the last of her breath, she dashed forward into the smoke, grasped the small bundle and ran. Behind her came an even louder crash. She did not look back.

The street was even more chaotic as she rounded the front wall of her old garden. More fire-fighters had come on the scene, pale curves of water arcing into the sky as they aimed their hoses at the blazing roofs. More ambulances lined up at the end of the street.

She looked around, now at a loss, wondering which way to turn.

'Hope. Over here.' A voice she knew, but not with its usual dour tone. Macleod raced over from where he and Geraldine were conferring with a warden, his face streaked with soot and perspiration. She realised that she must look the same.

'My nephew,' she gasped. 'He was in there. Jimmy got him out. I don't know where the others are. Faith was here, but now she's gone too. They must be here somewhere. I need to find them.'

'Right, well, the warden might know. Have you checked the baby? What am I saying, you're too close to him. Better pass him here, let me.'

Her arms trembling now, Hope passed Artie to Macleod, and she nearly gasped at the way he held him, gently but firmly. Of course he had held babies before. He'd had two of his own. He'd know what to do – a father and a trained first-aider. She didn't have the energy to be offended at the idea she wouldn't be able to do it. He was right. She couldn't think straight; this was her nephew.

Her nephew, who'd she'd done nothing but complain about ever since he was born, or even before that. She felt sick. He had to be all right. She could not bear for anything to be wrong with him. Now all her petty frustrations and annoyances had been swept away she could face the truth: she loved this baby, always had done.

'He seems to be fine.' Macleod looked up and gave a rare smile. Then he was businesslike again. 'Take him, go to the warden. Now where's Jimmy?'

Hope held tightly to the baby as she indicated with a nod of her head. 'He's still around the back. It's not safe. The house was falling down around us.'

'I'll go and see.' Macleod abruptly turned before she could say more, disappearing into the swirling smoke.

Hope stood for a moment, surveying the ruins of her street. There would be little left. So many of the houses were on fire, and those that weren't would have cracked windows from the heat and smoke damage to their contents. She felt a pang of sadness at the loss of all her belongings, her clothes, her books, the few furnishings she'd chosen herself. But it didn't matter. It was a shame, but she could replace them. Compared to the thought of what had so nearly happened – Artie somehow being trapped in the burning kitchen – it didn't matter at all.

Then Geraldine was waving at her to come over. 'Off we go, Artie,' she murmured, hurrying to the tall driver.

'Got some people here for you,' Geraldine said without preamble. 'Round the corner.' Then she was away, summoned by a shout from a warden halfway along the street, leaving Hope to turn in the direction the woman had indicated.

A huddle of people sat on the low wall of a house from the next street, visible only in silhouette, but instantly recognisable. Her parents and youngest sister, Joy. They were scarcely moving, pressed close together as if for comfort against the total destruction playing out before them. Hope squeezed her eyes briefly shut to make sure she had not imagined them. If they were sitting up then they must be all right, or near enough. She could at least set aside a thought that had been lurking at the back of her mind, of having to bring them on stretchers to the hospital.

Then there was Faith, half running, half staggering up to them, and her screams carried even above the cacophony of the fires. She must have been around the block, searching in her desperation. 'Where is he?' she wailed. 'Where did he go? What have you done with my baby? Where's he gone?'

Hope stared as another realisation struck her. She had wondered if her sister even noticed that she had a baby some of the time, with all the requests for help and attempts to get everyone to take him off her. Now she saw that Faith loved her baby more than anything. There was no doubt.

Hope stepped forward, holding out the little bundle. 'Faith,' she said when she was close enough to be heard, 'Faith. It's all right. I've got him.'

Again, time seemed to play tricks on her, as Hope found everything after the tearful reunion was a blur. There would be recriminations about how such a terrible thing had happened, the baby becoming lost in the panic, but they could wait. Artie was well, and held close by his mother as his grandmother looked on, weeping.

Hope had done one aspect of her job. Now she must return to the fray. No sooner had she approached the corner than Geraldine grabbed her. 'Macleod's still busy. Take the other end of my stretcher, would you?' Hope bent to pick it up by the handles and set to rescuing more neighbours, people too injured to walk to the first-aiders, and loaded them into yet another ambulance.

It was some while before she could go back to the end of the street where she'd last seen her colleagues, scanning ahead for the shapes of the Scotsman and Jimmy. While she'd been so busy she had convinced herself that somehow all would be well, that she'd get to her old front wall and find them both brushing down their coats, sharing a joke, ready to go on. To manage to do her own job she had shut out the knowledge that was hovering in the back of her mind. That crash, just as she'd taken Artie.

Her heart pounded harder yet again as she came closer to her old house and made out a tall shape, one that turned towards her as she hesitantly approached. She wanted to rush forward but something in his demeanour stopped her. Her mouth went dry.

'Hope. Over here. Best you sit down.' Brief and to the point as ever, Macleod led her to a sheltered spot behind what had once been a stone wall supporting a neighbour's shed. There were piles of brick against it, perhaps carefully stored to build an outhouse. 'Sit. It's best you sit.'

She knew, then, but could not say anything.

Silently she sank down onto the neat stack of bricks, settling herself carefully so that she could be steady, to take in what was to come. Macleod sat beside her and looked straight ahead, his profile lit by the still-blazing fires.

'I'm sorry, Hope. Jimmy is dead.'

It was like being hit hard in the stomach. She pitched forward, gasping. Then another thought struck her. 'It's my fault. He went in there for me, didn't he?'

A sob burst out but she bit back the rest that wanted so urgently to follow. She must not cry. She must hang on to her pride.

'No, it's not your fault.' He did not look at her, as if sensing she wanted to control her emotions. 'He was ill, Hope. Now that he's dead I can tell you. He made me promise not to before.'

'What – what do you mean?' Hope was horrified – she had been with Jimmy day in, day out. How could she not have known?

'He had a lung disease, Hope. You know he coughed now and again. Always tried to hide it or make an excuse. I challenged him, as I knew what my wife had sounded like when she got too bad to be helped. He didn't have TB, but his lungs were gone. He knew he didn't have much time left.' He glanced sideways at her, to check that she was listening, not falling apart.

'He would never have wanted to die in a hospital, or be a burden on his family. To die in the cause of duty – I know it's terrible but it's what he would have wanted. So, yes, he knew that that house belonged to your family, but he went in there because it was his job. He would have done it anyway. Of course he wanted to find the baby, but it is not your fault. Do you understand? It was not. He dreaded having to give up working on the ambulances, it was everything to him. Believe me. Honestly.'

'Really?' Hope asked shakily.

'He loved this job, you know that.'

'He did, it's true.' She felt a very little better.

'And, if it's any comfort, these last months, you've been the joy of his life. He told me it's been what's kept him going, seeing you start your training and then blossom the way you have. It's brought him such happiness, working alongside you. He thought the world of you, Hope.'

He turned to her and she could see the depth of his gaze from his dark blue eyes.

'As . . . as do I.'

Hope stared, unable to take in the words.

'But I thought . . . you hated me. And then, that you were married.'

'No, I never hated you. I hated the world, for a while. Then I couldn't stand the thought of becoming close to anyone, ever again. All my trust had gone and I know I put up a wall. It's how I coped. But then you were so funny and you loved life . . .'

She blinked, wondering if it could be true. Then she sank forward into his arms, her sobs finally breaking free, and he held her tight, as the fires blazed all around them.

CHAPTER THIRTY-FIVE

The all-clear did not sound until five thirty in the morning.

By then the sky was beginning to show the first streaks of dawn, although the sunrise was still some way off. The clocks had recently changed again, to give an extra hour of daylight in the evenings, but the mornings were darker for longer. The raiding aircraft had pushed their advantage and gone on bombing in wave after wave through the night.

Daisy woke with a start, freezing cold and with pins and needles in her feet. Patty was already moving around the shelter, collecting bits and pieces, keen to go back to the house. 'Come on,' she said cheerily. 'We have to get the gas back on and then we can have something warm to drink. I reckon we deserve cocoa with proper sugar after a night like that.'

Her words roused a sleepy Robbie, and Rose and Bert sat up straight, rubbing their eyes and taking in the realisation that this was one of the longest raids. Daisy dreaded what they would find as her mother pushed open the shelter door.

The house was still standing, though the tape had not held the back kitchen window together. Its glass lay shattered beside the pots clustered around the doorstep.

'Look at that, Bert. We'll have to get some of that waxed cotton to put over the gap until you find us some glass,' Patty said. 'I can't do the washing-up in the dark.'

Daisy thought that if this was the only damage the house had suffered then they had got off lightly. It turned out to be true. While her mother made the cocoa and Bert swept up the shards of glass, Daisy and Rose did a swift inspection of every room, but all was well. There were no more broken windows and not even a cup fallen from a shelf. They had been lucky.

'Let's go out the front and see if we can spot any damage to the roof,' she suggested, and so she and Rose went back downstairs and out of the main door.

Out in the pre-dawn street, they could just about make out the state of the roof and yet again luck was on their side. 'Thank God for that,' Rose sighed. 'I hate to think of Pa up a ladder trying to mend the ridge tiles. I've seen the results of too many falls from that sort of thing.'

Daisy's eyes followed her sister's gaze up to the ridge. Then in the growing daylight she pointed.

'That's a lot of smoke, and it's not far away. Oh no, it can't be . . .'

Rose caught her meaning. 'It could be. It's the exact direction of Aunt Vera's street.'

'We'd better go and find out,' Daisy said, but Rose stood firm.

'Cocoa first. Then we'll be better set up if anything has happened.'

* * *

In the end they all decided to go. Bert knew he could be useful if any practical repairs were needed. Rose, of course, could help with any medical issues, Daisy was prepared to run errands to wherever might be necessary, and Robbie was too young to leave on his own. Patty simply wanted to see her sister and her family, to know that they were safe.

Even though they had all, even Robbie, seen streets destroyed, nothing had prepared them for the scene that met their eyes. A street where you knew so many people – where Rose, Daisy and Robbie had all gone as children to stay with their cousins, to play with them when they were all small. Daisy felt a pang of guilt; even though she had often taken the mickey out of her aunt and uncle, and been downright rude about Faith, she would not have wished this on anyone. Their house, Vera's pride and joy, was gone, or at least the entire top half of it. The remaining bricks and mortar could not be called a house. What was left of the walls was all blackened and the windows were mere shells.

Patty looked around frantically, trying to find her sister. It was rare to see their mother upset. Daisy struggled to remember a time when she'd seen her like this. Now she herself was older she understood that her mother must hide her sadness and worry, like the time when Peter had gone missing after Dunkirk. But here it was, raw despair. Daisy wondered what she would feel like if Rose or Clover had suddenly vanished, and then retreated from the idea. It was simply too painful to bear.

Then they heard a shout from around the corner.

'Over here, we're over here.' It was Hope, waving from where a group of people were sitting on a low wall. In the light of full dawn, she could clearly make out the whole family, along with someone she didn't know but in one of those ugly ambulance service coats. She waved back, and sprinted across, but Patty, for once, was faster.

'Oh, Vera.' It was all Patty could say. 'Your lovely house. But you're all here, all safe. Is anyone hurt? How's Artie?'

Faith was cuddling him tightly to her. 'He's all right – well, he is now. And thanks to Hope and her colleague,' she said, nodding to the tall man in the ambulance service coat, perched on the wall at the far end.

Vera's face was ashen, and Uncle Arthur was for once without his smug superiority. They simply stared at the Harrisons. Then Vera got up, stuttered out, 'Patty' and cried in her sister's arms. Patty stroked her back, as if her big sister was just a child, comforting her without the need for words.

Daisy noticed that, even in a catastrophe, Vera had saved her favourite purple coat.

Her father went over to Uncle Arthur and began to talk in an undertone, deep and reassuring, although Arthur seemed too dazed to take it in. Joy was slouched over, half asleep. Daisy made a beeline for Hope and her colleague.

'You really are all fine?' She couldn't quite believe they had all escaped the conflagration. 'Nobody hurt? Rose is here,' as Rose came up beside her, 'so just say if not.'

368

Hope smiled weakly. 'They were all in the shelter when it happened. There was a terrible mix-up when Mother and Faith went back inside the kitchen to fetch biscuits or something, about who had Artie. But we got him out. Well, Ian here, and our . . . our colleague, Jimmy. But anyway, Artie is all right, breathing properly, although Faith would probably like it if you checked, Rose.' Rose nodded and immediately went across to her eldest cousin.

Daisy stared at the shelter, its roof buckled but not destroyed, and shut her eyes at the vision of being stuck in there for hours without knowing what exactly what had happened outside, with the heat from the fires increasing. It was pure hell. No wonder that they were all sitting shellshocked on a wall, their few belongings around their feet.

'What are you going to do?' she asked, trying to comprehend the enormity of the disaster.

Patty overheard and turned to face them all. 'You'll come to us, of course.'

Vera began to cry again, and Daisy felt a rising panic. Of course they must be welcomed; but where on earth would they all go? Victory Walk had been bursting at the seams before Clover and Peter had been posted away. But she knew it was mean to think this.

Bert cleared his throat and Arthur stood, shakily but determined. 'I . . . I have use of a small flat, over the business premises. But it is just one bedroom. Some of us can go there . . .'

Faith interrupted. 'Martin's family have always said I could take Artie and stay with them. They'd like that, I know, so you don't have to worry about me.'

Typical of Faith to fall on her feet, Daisy thought, knowing she was being unkind.

'Joy can sleep on the sofa in the flat,' Arthur went on.

Patty folded her arms. 'Then Hope will live with us. Don't even consider saying no. We've got Peter's room. He's hardly ever home, so now it can be yours. We'd love to have you. It will be even closer to your depot, Hope, so that's settled.'

Daisy looked at her cousin. Hope had instantly darted a glance at her colleague, who was plainly a man of few words, but something was going on there. There was a definite atmosphere between the two of them, and on another day, Daisy would have been in there at once, demanding to know exactly what was what. Today, though, she held her tongue.

Hope also stood and went over to her aunt and hugged her tightly. 'I'd love that,' she said. 'Thank you, Auntie Patty. That would mean the world to me.'

The tall colleague nodded and smiled slightly, as if happy for her.

Patty surveyed the ruins of the house, the garden, the remains of the shelter – which had at least done what it had been built for. Without it, the entire family could have been killed. She shuddered. Yes, her big sister, Vera, annoyed her often, and she was sure the feeling was mutual. But compared to losing her, and all of her family – no, that was unbearable. She realised just how close to it they had come only a few hours ago. Life without Vera – no, that simply did not make sense.

There was no question that she would do whatever she could to help, and to think that she could take care of her niece filled her heart with warmth. Vera would do the same for any of her, Patty's, children had the positions been reversed. To have Hope under her roof would be a privilege.

Sighing in the cold morning air, she turned to her husband, her daughters, her sister, her nieces. 'Then that's what we'll do,' she said, pausing a little, as if to absorb the changes that were to come, the vast unknown future that awaited them all. She took a deep breath and spoke the simple truth. 'That's what families are for.'

ACKNOWLEDGEMENTS

Many thanks are due to the library staff of the London Transport Museum, especially Caroline Warhurst. Their archives depicting life sheltering in the tube stations during the war are both terrifying and fascinating. Any errors are all the fault of the author, not the historical records.

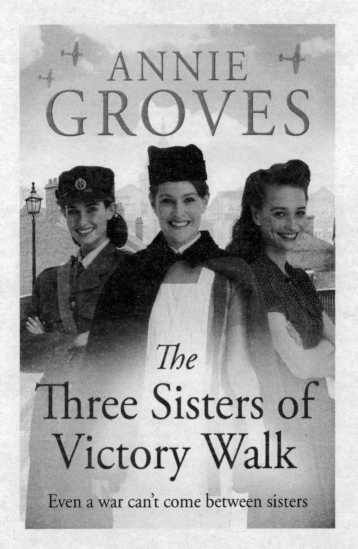

Why not dive into **more** of Annie Groves' engrossing stories?

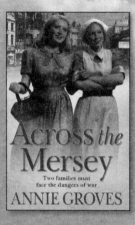

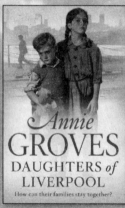

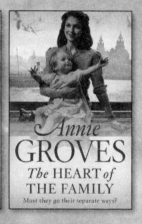

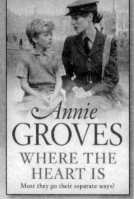

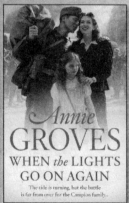